Trevorode the Defender

Holly Bebernitz

For Ashley
Holly Bebernitz
Is. 12.5

Quinn Rose
PRESS

Trevorode the Defender is a work of fiction. Names, characters, places, and incidents are the products of the author's imagination and are used fictitiously. Any resemblance to actual events, locales, or persons, living or dead, is entirely coincidental.

Published in the United States by QuinnRose Press

ISBN: 978-0-9891721-0-3

Cover design: Michael Regina
Cover photograph: Dan Thompson

Heck-Andrews House, located in Raleigh, North Carolina, image used by permission of State of North Carolina, N.C. Department of Administration.

Printed in the United States of America

www.Trevorode.com

Acknowledgments

I first acknowledge my debt to the host of teachers who taught me the mechanics of writing. Beyond that, I thank those who inspired and equipped me to realize this lifelong dream.

"The Proclaimers" (a drama/music team): restored my confidence in my abilities when I was disheartened and disillusioned.

University of North Florida professors: Dr. Dan Schafer, Dr. Elizabeth Furdell, and Dr. Theo Prousis, broadened my horizons, challenged me to excel, and inspired me with the idea my full potential was something I had not yet attained.

My "Forum Friends" (aka "48ers"): not only afforded me a venue to revitalize my writing skills, but also patiently and expertly guided me into the wider world of acumen with the computer.

DD Bolan: informed me of the 2010 UNF Writers' Conference and paid my way. Without her urging, I wouldn't have attended and this book wouldn't have been started, much less finished.

Vic DiGenti and Sharon Cobb: professional authors who welcomed me as a "friend" rather than an "upstart" novice. Without their assuring me I could succeed, I wouldn't have continued.

Linda Foley, Kathy Combass, Topher Sanders and Larry Brasington: my critique group, who gave honest praise and asked hard questions, were crucial throughout this entire process.

Rachael Stringer: not only for her interest and encouragement, but also for her critiquing and formatting of the manuscript. Her attention to detail and peerless computer expertise I could not do without.

Todd and Lisa Eppard: for their enthusiasm and support. Their attachment to my characters warmed my heart and kept my imagination simmering.

Jim Hamlett: for his advice about structure and syntax and also for recommending my protagonist and narrator should be a female.

Joe Kotvas: website designer, who captured my vision after only a few conferences.

Jonathan Cordell: videographer, who exceeded my expectations.

Anna Adams: who provided answers for all the legal issues involved in the ownership and inheritance of the Magnolia Arms.

Becca Parrish: whose drawing is featured in the video previews.

Michael Regina: cover artist.

Dan Thompson: photographer of Heck-Andrews House featured on the cover.

Beth Mansbridge: my editor.

John Simmons: formatted the book for e-publication.

Dr. Brooks Landon: whose course "Building Great Sentences" bolstered my confidence and inspired me with the joy of cumulative syntax.

Dr. Timothy Spurgin: whose course, "The Art of Reading," reminded me what my readers would expect and enjoy.

My children and grandchildren: in all ways, in all times, my joy.

Dedicated to my parents, Carl (in memory) and Virginia Arends,
who taught me early to love good stories.

Chapter 1

A Novel Beginning

The gray walls of the lecture hall throbbed with subdued panic as frightened students skidded into their seats and rummaged through their notes. Prof. Garmon Harwood's English 101 final exam, rumored to be the undoing of countless Stanton-Giles University freshmen, was only minutes away. In my assigned seat in the back of the musty room, I shut out frantic whispers about tenses and participles and brushed my fingers along the edges of the spiral notebook which held the rough draft of my novel. I closed my eyes and pictured my valiant heroine in a large circle of tall black trees.

Gathering up the hem of her cloak, Lyda Rose tried to run, but her shoes sank in the half-frozen mud and hindered her escape. The pounding of her pursuers' feet was maddening. Why had she ignored Grimwulf's warning to start home before dark? She reached the cliff's edge. Intending to leap to the lake below, swim to shore, and hide till morning, she removed her cloak and shoes. As she poised on the edge of the precipice, a strong hand grasped her shoulder from behind. She whirled around and stumbled into the arms of Redthorn the Avenger. He spoke:

"So do you have the notes for the exam? I lost mine."

The floor of the ancient forest crumbled away and Redthorn slid into the chasm. Lyda Rose faded into the mist. The bandits halted in their tracks and the dark woods fell silent.

I scribbled out *"The lake is frozen, My Lady. You'd be leaping to your death"* and closed the notebook. I reached under my chair for my English 101 notes and handed them to Trevor Rhodes, as I had every class period since September. He leaned over the armrest that separated our lecture hall seats until his strong arm pressed against mine.

"Thanks, Agnes. You're the best."

Get a grip, Agnes, I thought. He doesn't mean it.

He leaned in closer. He smelled of peppermint and unrealized dreams.

"So, Agnes, can you help me out? What should I study first?"

I was glad to have an excuse to gaze into his eyes. He looked so much like I'd pictured Redthorn the Avenger, I sometimes wondered if I'd coaxed a real person from my imagination.

My stomach fluttered. "Well, do you remember what an objective complement is?"

He gaped at my notes like a starving man at a sandwich. "Isn't that when you're saying something nice to someone without getting all emotional about it?"

"Uh, no. That's different. A complement is—"

"Miss Quinn." From the front of the lecture hall Dr. Harwood growled.

I looked up. "Sir?"

"If you're finished talking to—" he lowered his head to examine the seating chart on the lectern—"Mr. Rhodes—perhaps you'll notice my assistant is passing out the exam."

"I ... didn't see you come in."

He pushed his reading glasses down on his nose and scowled over them. "If you were a little less interested in your neighbor," he said, "you might have."

Suppressed laughter rippled across the sea of chairs.

For the briefest moment I hoped Trevor would rise to my defense, but he remained absorbed in his studying. When the assistant arrived at our row in the back of the room, Trevor returned my notes and pulled out the pen I'd loaned him on Wednesday. He passed the exams to me. His hand lingered on mine for a moment. He winked. My heart melted. My pulse raced as I tried to concentrate on the exam.

Once again I was muddled in another ill-fated, one-sided romance—mired in misery I had not invited and did not welcome. My only comfort was I hadn't brought this sorry state of affairs on myself—fate had thrown Trevor in my path the first day I stepped on campus. I'd replayed the scene in my mind a thousand times, alternately savoring and regretting it. I dropped my new books. Trevor stopped to help. We stooped down, grabbed for papers scooting away in the wind. Our eyes met. I fell in love. Trevor did not.

From the very beginning, I told myself he could never think of me in a romantic way.

Tall, broad-shouldered, with dark wavy hair, deep brooding eyes, and perfectly formed lips, he resembled a Greek god lately arrived from Olympus. I, tall, asthmatic, freckled, with thick, curly hair and a practical wardrobe, was the sort of awkward girl Charlotte Brontë described as *unprepossessing*. In spite of the fact I'd gotten the braces off my teeth before I came to college, I still couldn't possibly compete with the horde of petite blondes who prowled the campus to snare men like Trevor.

I might have recovered from our first meeting and even managed to forget Trevor if we hadn't ended up in the same English class. Old Dr. Harwood was notorious for adhering to the ancient practice of an alphabetized seating chart. On the first day of class the other students grumbled as they separated from their friends to locate their assigned seats. I rejoiced. This sensible system placed me as a "Q" on Trevor "R's" left for an entire semester of blissful proximity. On the first day of class my heart pounded as I sat down next to him.

"Hello again," I said, almost breathless.

"Do I know you?" he said.

We fell into a curious rhythm as the semester wore away. Every day I headed to class early so I wouldn't miss a single minute with him. Every day he arrived with a different girl in tow. To them he said, "See you after class." To me he said, "Got a pen I can borrow?" Every night as I drifted off to sleep I resolved to be more sensible, but every day I headed to class early. And so it went. In spite of all the stern lectures I gave myself, I never lost hope that one day Trevor would see we were made for each other.

Eventually, fate again took a hand—once our grades began to accumulate. When the midterm exam was returned, Trevor had made yet another D. He wadded up his paper, tossed it on the floor, and then tapped his finger on the A written on mine.

"How do you know so much about this stuff?"

It was the first time he'd asked me a question about myself.

"I've ... always been good at English."

"So you think you could help me out? I've got to make a C to stay eligible."

Our routine changed—well, Trevor's did. Now *he* was arriving early so I could coach him enough to scrape by on tests. When the girls called to him as they walked past us on their way to their seats, Trevor gave them a casual wave and then turned his attention back to me. Those were golden hours when the stale air of the lecture hall seemed filled with spices.

One day I was bold enough to move our relationship to the next level.

"If you want, I could meet you in the library for a longer tutoring session."

He looked up from my notes, shook his head, and said, "I don't think so."

His snub of my offer puzzled me, but failed to dampen my devotion. As long as he didn't know a predicate from a preposition, he'd still need me till the semester was over. Test by test, paper by paper, I transported him safely to the final exam, like a soldier bearing a wounded comrade across a minefield.

And now the final exam was in our hands. I could have answered the questions in a few minutes, but since this was the last time I'd see Trevor till January, I dawdled over the pages, pretending to think. When I finished, I turned back to the first page to "review my answers." Then I gathered up my notes and my novel and peeked at Trevor from the corner of my eye. He was bent over his test, rubbing his forehead and biting his lip. His beautiful black hair had drooped down over one eye.

Without thinking, I reached over and brushed his hair back from his face.

His hand jerked up and knocked mine away. "What are you doing?"

"Nothing. There was a ..."

"Miss Quinn." Professor Harwood's voice thundered through the silence. "Is there a problem?"

I broke out in a cold sweat. "No. No, sir."

"Finished with your exam?"

"Yes, sir."

"Then turn it in and excuse yourself."

Trevor was still scratching out answers when I left. At semester's end, he squeaked by with a C- and rewarded my efforts by inviting Wendy Mayfield home for the holidays.

As I drove home alone, my own Ghost of Christmas Present revealed scenes of Trevor and Wendy celebrating. I hovered above, watching them breakfast with Trevor's family, shop for matching sweaters, pose for photos with a department store Santa, cuddle on Trevor's living room sofa, drink hot chocolate, and gaze out at falling snow. Mile after weary mile, their love story played out in my mind. Unlike the reformed and jubilant Ebenezer Scrooge, however, I was deflated by my visions.

My mother, her "Happy Holly Days" apron tied around her red plaid flannel pajamas, had waited up past midnight for me. Her tear-soaked face left a damp stain on my shoulder when she hugged me. The living room pulsated with holiday cheer: the Christmas tree blinked, a warm fire crackled, apple-scented candles glowed. Mom dabbed at her eyes with a candy cane printed napkin and pointed toward the kitchen.

"I have fruitcake—Aunt Minnie sent it."

"I'm sorry, Mom. I need to go to bed. I have a headache."

I might as well have knocked over the tree and doused the fire.

"Oh. Well, I understand. You've had a long trip." She took a plastic sandwich bag from the kitchen drawer and tucked the slice of fruitcake inside. "Tomorrow's another day. We're having pancakes for breakfast."

Exhausted, I fell into bed and vowed to be more cheerful for my mother's sake.

I came down to breakfast the next morning and found my father cutting his pancakes into perfect square bites. I put my arm around his shoulders, kissed him on the cheek, and sat down in my usual place at the table.

He winked at me. "How are ya, kiddo?"

My mother interrupted. "Aggie's a little tired, Stu." She slid four steaming pancakes onto a plate and set it in front of me.

Dad passed the syrup. "Grades gonna be okay?"

"Oh, you know, the usual for me. Doing great in English, barely scraping by in biology." And then without thinking, I blurted out, "I don't know why I have to take biology anyway. It's not like it's going to help me become a better writer."

Dad looked up at me, his knife and fork hovering in midair. "I thought we settled this last summer before we took you to school. Don't you remember what I said?"

Mom grabbed the coffeepot and rushed to the table. "Now, Stuart, we can talk about that later. I have leftover meatloaf. Would you like that in a sandwich for your lunch?"

He fixed his eyes on mine. "Just a minute, Betty. I thought I made it clear I'm not paying good money for tuition so my daughter can pursue her hobby."

Still reeling from Trevor's rejection, I bristled at my father's demeaning my chosen profession. I laid down my fork and propped my elbows on the table.

"Hobby?"

My mother, with four more pancakes rising to golden-brown perfection on the griddle behind her, stared open-mouthed at us, tears glistening and ready to gush.

I remembered my resolve and smiled at her. "Do we have boysenberry syrup?"

She opened the pantry and brought a bottle, still sealed, to the table.

I handed it to my father. "Could you open this for me, Dad?"

He understood my call for a truce. We finished breakfast in silence. When he left for work, he whispered in my mom's ear before he kissed her goodbye. I put my plate in the sink and retreated to my room to unpack. I lifted out my folded clothes, laid them on the dresser, and retrieved *Redthorn the Avenger* from the bottom of my suitcase. I sat down on my bed and thumbed through the pages.

Hobby—if only writing were as simple as that. Anyone who has never felt compelled to apply words to paper, never been induced to find a quiet place to sweat out the fever of an ailing plot thread, cannot know what it is to be afflicted with the writing virus. The art is malarial in its tenacity, infectious in its essence. Though my parents and teachers warned me of its contagion, once I saw my first paragraph on the page, I became powerless to stop. I'd drunk from the enchanted chalice of *Writing* and would be forever under its spell.

Mom knocked on my door. "Agnes? Want to do a little Christmas shopping? Emerson's is having a sale on thermoses."

I closed the notebook. "Sure. I'll be ready in a few minutes."

As we strolled through the stores, Mom peppered me with questions about my teachers and new college friends. When she asked if I had any romantic prospects, I said no.

"Now, don't worry. Remember, Toby didn't meet Janette till his senior year and now look how happy they are."

My brother, Toby, was the quintessential firstborn son. Serious, focused, successful, accomplished, he was everything I was not. Eight years old when I was born, he'd chosen the role of third parent rather than lovable big brother, and tolerated me with bemused benevolence. He was the serious scholar in the family, orator of two valedictorian addresses, and now a tenured high school math teacher in a progressive school district. His wife, Janette, a surgical nurse, had given birth to two sons, the apples of my mother's eye and the heirs apparent to the Quinn family name.

Toby and his family arrived three days before Christmas. Two-year-old William and baby Lewis were precisely what we all needed. While my parents doted on them, they focused less on me, and I was able to slip away to my room to write. Besides that, I wanted to avoid the inevitable family discussion of "how school was going" and had no intention of allowing Toby to interrogate me. He was more prone to lecture than my father was.

When Toby offered to take the family to dinner, I insisted on staying home with the boys. After Lewis went to sleep, William and I had a quiet dinner of macaroni and cheese and nibbled on Christmas cookies. I read "Twas the Night before Christmas" to him, tucked him in bed, and spent the rest of the evening writing. The relentless longing for Trevor had brought out the best in me. I crafted brilliant, complex scenes of the struggle for human existence and the inevitable disappointments of love. Redthorn grew more like Trevor; Lyda Rose, nobler and lovelier.

When I heard the car in the driveway, I turned out my light and hopped into bed. I lay there listening till my family was quiet, wondering if Trevor and Wendy had gotten on each other's nerves by now and thinking of my next chapter title. When I thought everyone had gone to sleep, I tiptoed to the kitchen, made a cup of tea, and sat down by the Christmas tree.

Toby came downstairs. When he saw me, he paused on his way to the kitchen. "Can I get you anything?"

I held up my cup. "No, thanks. This is fine."

I hoped he'd go back upstairs to bed, but coffee mug in one hand and fruitcake in the other, he stood in the kitchen doorway.

"We haven't had much of a chance to catch up, Aggie. How's college?"

I stared at the seven stockings hung on the mantle. "Fine."

"Enjoying your classes?"

"Not yet."

His Puritan forefather tone emerged. "Plan to enjoy them anytime soon?"

"Once I get my requirements out of the way and start taking my writing courses."

He paused for effect. "You haven't given up on that yet?"

I turned to him. "No, I haven't given up on that yet. That's why I went to Stanton-Giles—to study under Robinson Trask."

"Who?"

"Robinson Trask, the famous novelist. You've never heard of him?"

"No, I guess I don't read the kinds of books he writes." He sat down in my dad's recliner, put his coffee mug on the end table, and picked pineapple out of his fruitcake as he expounded.

"Look, Aggie. I've always thought it was really cute that you want to write. It's your dream, I get that. But college is the time to start making decisions and figuring things out."

My voice quivered. "Did you come all this way just to make fun of me?"

"Of course not. We came for Christmas."

He laughed. I didn't.

I put my cup on the floor and stood up. "Well, then, Merry Christmas."

I headed for the stairs. He started after me and grabbed my elbow.

"Wait a minute, Aggie. Let me explain."

I looked up at him. He wiped my tears with his crumpled napkin. Aunt Minnie's rum-flavored crumbs stuck to my face.

"Look, I didn't mean to upset you. You're my little sister and I love you—you know that. That's why I'm trying to keep you from making a mistake you'll always regret. Understand?"

I wanted him to leave me alone, so I nodded.

"Besides that, you're worrying Mom and Dad, and you don't want to do that. Now let's get some sleep. My little guys will be awake before the sun's up."

On Christmas Day I played on the floor with William, snuggled with Lewis, thanked my parents for my new coat, ate turkey, green bean casserole, and pecan pie, hoped Trevor hated what Wendy had bought him for Christmas, avoided the subject of college at the dinner table, and spent the afternoon in my room with Redthorn. Toby and his family left the next day. When he hugged me goodbye, he whispered, "Remember what I said."

On New Year's Eve, I sat upstairs and listened to my parents and their friends sing "Auld Lang Syne" and marked December 31 off my calendar. I took out my new calendar and gazed at the pristine white numbered squares. So much possibility and potential lay ahead in 1972. This is the year I'll turn the corner, I thought. I'll finish my required courses and start working on my major. And who knows? Maybe this is the year Trevor will come to his senses and kick Wendy Mayfield to the curb.

On the first day of Dr. Harwood's class, I checked the seating chart posted on the back wall. I nearly broke out in hives when I saw Trevor and I were still assigned to the same seats.

I'd been in my chair for ten minutes when Trevor came in with Wendy hanging on his arm. They stood in the aisle and talked till Dr. Harwood entered. Then Wendy headed to her chair, and Trevor slid in next to me. He didn't even say hello. When class was finished, he waited for Wendy in the aisle. She looked at me and whispered to him. He laughed, and they left the room.

I waited through January, February, and March for him to ask for a pen. But he never once asked what chapter the quiz was on, or to borrow my notes, and never touched my hand when he passed papers to me. His grades continued to improve. It didn't take a rocket scientist to figure out Wendy, snobby but smart, was helping him.

After spring break of our freshman year, the news was heralded: Trevor was engaged. Like so many other melancholy authors, I found solace in my work and poured all my grief, angst, and frustration into my writing. In honor of unrealized love, I changed the name of my Saxon hero from Redthorn the Avenger to Trevorode the Defender. The lovely Lyda Rose, a loftier version of me, still appeared as heroine. This wholly irrational obsession comforted me and gave new focus and impetus to my writing.

Trevorode the Defender was my Sistine Chapel ceiling.

The following autumn I secured a spot in Dr. Robinson Trask's Fiction Writing class. I deemed this happy circumstance as a course correction of my universe. Though I'd failed at romance, I'd completed two successful semesters of required courses. I entered Dr. Trask's classroom with the same clear conscience and awestruck silence as a mother superior at vespers. I was going to place myself squarely under the tutelage of the man I most admired and wanted to emulate.

That semester, I wrote as if I had an irrevocable bond to a muse. I fulfilled every assignment with aplomb. I was always included among those who were asked to read their work aloud. It appeared the old days were gone. I, Agnes Quinn, was growing confident, self-assured, and optimistic. When, one day, I read Dr. Trask's comments at the end of an assignment and saw "Brilliant" inscribed in red with the bold stroke of his pen, my heart nearly stopped. But the next sentence—could it be?—was even better: "Please see me in my office tomorrow at 9:30."

I passed a sleepless night in which I played out a variety of scenarios, all starring me in some invaluable role in Robinson Trask's life. I arrived at his office at 9:00. He arrived at 9:29, gave me a quick glance, motioned me toward his door, and offered a perfunctory "Good morning." Seated in his office, he leaned back in his chair, placed the fingertips of both hands together, and glanced briefly at the ceiling.

"I have a great opportunity for you, Miss Quinn. You've heard of Stockton-Trask Publishing?" He asked this as if everyone had naturally done so.

I had not, but dared not appear ill-informed.

"Of course," I said. "I seem to remember the name."

"My brother Ferguson is the 'Trask' of that partnership. He's … tried his hand at many enterprises and has … shall we say, *impacted* many of them."

I wondered why my mentor, famous for his syntax, hesitated over his words.

"Mr. Stockton, my brother's partner, has demanded—rather, assigned—my brother to develop a new money-making idea. Since I have … connections, Ferguson turned to me."

"I … see," I said, though I didn't.

"Your … style is what Ferguson is looking for. Is it possible you have a longer, more developed story than those you've submitted in class … some idea Ferguson could use?"

I hesitated. Was I ready to allow someone else to enter the sacred world of Trevorode? Was I prepared to hand off my Holy Grail to another's keeping? Was it time for *that*?

"As a matter of fact," I said, "I've been working on a project for quite a while."

He brightened.

"It's about a warrior, a Saxon hero, who—"

He bolted upright in his chair and looked at me with the same hope as a shipwrecked sailor views an approaching sail.

"Excellent! Could it be made into a co … a continuing story? Something with a sequel? A whole series of stories?"

Sequel? I thought. Series? He has a higher opinion of me than I imagined.

"Yes, I suppose that would be possible. But there's one thing. I work at Norman's Grocery Store to help pay my tuition. I don't think I'll have time to—"

With a wave of his hand, he dismissed my objections. "No problem. Ferguson wants to offer you a job in his publishing company. When can you meet with him?"

I suggested Monday.

"Good idea," he said. "Leave a copy of your manuscript with my secretary tomorrow. Once Ferguson reads it, you can meet with him for further instructions."

When he picked up his phone and began to dial, I realized our interview was concluded.

"Dr. Trask, I want to tell you how much I appreciate this oppor—"

But he didn't hear a word I said. He spoke into his phone.

"Crawford? Robinson. Tell Ferguson to be in his office on time Monday morning. Call my mother and tell her I took care of everything and she won't be able to reach me for a while."

I don't think he noticed when I left.

The next morning I left the manuscript with his secretary and wrote my two-week notice to the grocery store manager. That weekend, anticipating my new position, I packed a few supplies and mementoes in a box so I'd be ready to move into my new office.

I arrived at Ferguson Trask's office on time.

"Have a seat," he said.

My manuscript, the title page stained where a cup of coffee had sat and spilled, was on his green desk pad.

"I read your piece about Troubadour," he said.

"Trevorode?"

"Whatever—you know, Miss Quan,"—he glanced at the title page—"I really like this 'Destroyer' of yours—"

"Defender."

"Whatever—I've been trying to get ahead in the publishing business for a while now, and it looks like your character—"

"Trevorode."

"Whatever—may be precisely what I'm looking for. I took it home. My son read it—loved when the invader guy got stabbed in the neck. Do you know what he said?"

Afraid to ask, I raised my eyebrows and shook my head.

"He *said* he wished he could get a lunch box with that on it."

Lunch box? What was next?

"Do you have any experience with panels? Robbie didn't say."

"Panels?"

"Yes, and if not, do you have an artist in mind or do we need to find one for you?"

My mind was spinning. What did he mean by "panels"?

"I hadn't thought about illustrations yet," I said. "I assumed a publisher would take care of that. Don't you have an illustrator on staff?"

"No, not yet. This is an entirely new venture for Stockton-Trask. But what with the market being the way it is and the surge in superhero TV shows—"

The interview at last was taking a more predictable turn.

"I see," I said. "Yes, I've often thought Trevorode was similar to *Beowulf.*"

"Beowart? Who's that?"

"Beowulf. The Anglo-Saxon epic. Trevorode has many of the same traits."

"Have they ever made *that* into a comic book?"

We both sank deeper into our morass of miscommunication.

"I don't know," I said. "I'm not much of a fan of comic books."

He squared his shoulders. "Then how, young woman, do you propose to write one?"

"I don't intend to write one," I said, and wondered for the first time if Ferguson Trask had been recently released from a mental hospital.

He stood. His bald head reddened.

"I thought Robbie explained. This project is to be the *protobyte* of the new division of Stockton-Trask Publishing."

"You mean prototype?"

He didn't hear me. "When it succeeds, I'm going to start my own company, Trask Comics. And you, Miss Quill, are going to be on the cutting edge of that project with me."

Stunned, I retrieved my sullied manuscript from Ferguson Trask's cluttered desk.

"The name is *Quinn*, and I wouldn't let you or your brother near my story if you offered me an office *and* a partnership. Comic book? Are you kidding me?"

He snorted. "Office? Is that what you thought? You were going to work in the copy room and make coffee."

The last words I heard as I slammed the door behind me were, "I'm telling Robbie!"

That night I tore up the letter to my store manager and unpacked my office supplies.

The next assignment I submitted to Robinson Trask received a B and no comments.

At semester's end, I packed *Trevorode* away, leaving my Sistine Chapel ceiling unfinished and my dignity intact.

Chapter 2

A Kind Stranger

Trembling, Lyda Rose crossed the threshold of the Great Hall, where Trevorode the Defender held court from a high-backed oaken chair. His scarred, sinewy hands gripped the chair's arms with fearful strength as he leaned forward, looming over the scrawny Sir Traskalot cowering at his feet.

"You've been summoned," Trevorode said, "to answer for your crimes against the fair Lady Lyda Rose of Grimsdale Manor."

The accused could only whimper.

Trevorode's voice thundered: "Speak up. If you fail to explain yourself, you'll be judged unworthy to rule your—"Quinn"*—and thus, your—*"Quinn"*—will be taken from you and—"*

"Quinn."

I snapped out of my story and turned to my best friend Xander Plumley, who, unlike me, was a serious scholar and never allowed his mind to wander even during lunch. We'd reached final exam week of our sophomore year, and as usual, Xander was worried I wasn't prepared. While we were freshmen, he'd put up with my daydreaming, but he'd grown less tolerant as our junior year approached. He knew the blank look on my face meant I had withdrawn from the racket of the dining common to ponder my plotline, and he'd called me back.

"Sorry," I said. "As much as I hate to admit it, Ferguson Trask gave me the best idea for my next chapter."

Xander took the pencil from behind his ear and tapped it on the table.

"And have you had the 'best idea' for how you're going to pass your biology exam?"

"I have my book with me," I said.

I unzipped my book bag and displayed the heavy volume. My biology final, less than twenty-four hours away, would conclude my second attempt to pass the course.

"And did you see the registrar about changing your major?" Xander asked.

"Yes. I'll spend all summer compiling bulletin board ideas and reviewing grammar."

"And counting down the days till Trevor's wedding?"

"I'm not sure when it is," I lied.

"Oh, come on—"

He stopped mid-sentence when Jonquil Putnam bumped into the back of my chair. She crooned over my shoulder as condensation from her glass, well-aimed, dripped down my neck.

"Hello, Xander. Ready for exams?" she asked.

"Not yet," Xander said.

"I finished my exams early so I could leave for Europe with my parents," she said. "Would you like to have dinner with us? I'm sure you'd enjoy talking to my stepfather. He's—"

"No, thanks," he said, "I need to study."

"All right," Jonquil said, deflated. "Have a good summer. See you next year."

And with a final drip from her glass and no farewell for me, she was gone. Jonquil Putnam was the great-granddaughter of *the* Putnams of old Carolina antebellum stock. Her family, well-known and "veh-eh-rih" well-respected, had been floating on an ocean of money for decades. She wasn't working *her* way through college by organizing vegetables at the grocery store. But neither, like Xander, was she resting on a stack of academic scholarships. I'd always suspected she'd been admitted to the university through some kind of connection. She was not the brightest star in the academic sky. Pampered and prissy, she'd considered me a boll weevil in her cotton field since the moment we met.

As my being a "Q" had destined Trevor to sit on my left in English 101, Jonquil as a "P-u," was perpetually on my right. Xander, assigned to sit on *her* right, always leaned over her to talk to me. Unaccustomed to being overlooked, Jonquil nurtured a deep and abiding resentment of me. One day she asked me to stay after class.

"This can't go on," she said. "I won't allow it."

"What?" I asked.

"You—coming between me and Xander."

"I can't help where I sit," I said. "Talk to Dr. Harwood."

She shook her finger in my face. "You leave him alone. I mean it."

"I'd never bother Dr. Harwood," I said. "I'm scared of him."

"Not Dr. Harwood. Xander."

"I don't bother Xander," I said. "We're friends."

"It's more than that," she said. "You're interested in him. Don't try to deny it."

Of course, I was "interested" in Xander. He was the most fascinating person I'd ever known. His father, Dr. Rufus Plumley, lectured at scholarly conferences and had two books published by Harvard. Xander's mother, Clementine, hosted formal teas. Beyond that, Xander was the eldest of triplets, born while their father was completing his doctoral dissertation on John Adams' presidency. The XYZ Affair of 1798 was the chapter underway when Dr. Plumley had been summoned to the hospital for the birth of his children. Inspired, he'd urged his wife to commemorate the occasion by naming the children Xander, Yolanda, and Zane.

Who wouldn't be interested in a family like his?

But no matter how much I admired the Plumleys, I could've never seen Xander in a romantic light. Devoted to scientific endeavors, he often stayed up all night studying chemistry and went to class the next morning wearing the same rumpled clothes he'd worn the day before.

After Jonquil's exit, I caught Xander staring at me.

"Seriously, Quinn, don't you feel better now that Trevor is finally a dead end and you can start focusing on your own goals?"

With a sigh, I shoved the tray aside and leaned back in the green vinyl chair.

"My goals—let's see. I wanted to write. Now I'm going to teach. I wanted to marry Trevor. He's going to marry Wendy. I wanted to work with Robinson Trask. He wanted to steal my idea for his idiot brother. Yeah, I feel great."

He stood and gathered his books. "First," he said, "Trevor was never going to marry you. Surely you realize that."

"He might have, if I—"

"Second, Trask hasn't written a good book in years."

"You don't know anything about fiction," I said. "All you read is—"

"Third, *your* novel is years away from publication."

"You think I don't know that?" I said. "I don't have time to work on—"

He slammed his philosophy book closed and shoved it inside his backpack. "Can't you see you're better off today than you were a year ago?" he asked.

"And how is that?"

"Because now you can stop acting out this absurd romantic comedy and decide what to do with *your* life—the life of Agnes Quinn, who's pretty amazing exactly as she is."

He slung his heavy book bag over his shoulder with such force he knocked himself off balance and stumbled into the table.

I was speechless. Xander had never talked this way to me before.

He regained his balance. "Instead of obsessing about what's wrong, you should think of all you've got going for you and concentrate on that."

He started toward the door. I shoved back from the table and grabbed my book bag, but before I could follow him, a hair-netted employee yelled at me from the end of our table.

"Hey, you," she said. "Clean up your mess."

By the time I got outside, there was no sign of Xander. I loped toward the science building. Never a graceful runner, I caught my toe in a crack on the sidewalk and splattered on the ground. I scrambled up and hobbled on, relieved to find Xander had slowed to maneuver through the throng of commencement visitors bustling around the bookstore.

"Xander, stop," I said.

He turned around. "I have to go, Agnes. I'm late for my lab."

Agnes? When was the last time he'd called me that?

I pushed my way through the crowd and grabbed his sleeve.

"Xander, what's wrong? I've never seen you like this."

"Can you honestly tell me—*you*, who cannot get through a single day without talking about how in love you are—you have no idea what's wrong with *me*?"

I let go of his arm. "I don't know what to say. I had no idea—"

"Of course not. You *talk* about love all the time, but you've been looking it right in the face for two years and haven't recognized it. I have to go. I'm late."

I watched Xander walk away, visible for a long time, then growing impossibly distant across a thousand miles of tulip-bordered sidewalk.

A familiar voice called my name.

"Agnes."

I ignored it.

The voice called again.

Dazed by Xander's confession, I couldn't make myself look back.

The voice persisted. "Agnes, no."

I sat down on a concrete bench and stared at a gum wrapper on the sidewalk.

The voice squealed. "Agnes, come back here."

A warm sprinkle on my left ankle stirred me from my stupor. The relentless honey-sweet whining was the voice of Jonquil Putnam. Her manicured hand scooped up a downy mound of white fur squatting at my feet.

She cooed to the bundle. "Naughty, naughty, to run away."

"Jonquil, darling." Her mother, with a bulging shopping bag, emerged from the bookstore. "Papa will be waiting."

I looked up at Jonquil. "What did you want?"

"What do you mean?" she asked.

"You were calling me."

"I wasn't calling you. I was calling my new puppy." She angled the pink-collared poodle to face me. "When Mother asked what we should name her, I naturally thought of 'Agnes.' It's a perfect name for a dog."

And with that final volley, she cruised away in her mother's wake.

Bewildered, I studied the stain on my shoe. How had this day gone so wrong? Only a few hours ago, noble and self-sacrificing, I'd entered the registrar's office to change my major, daring to think everyone would finally be happy with me. Yet here I sat—blighted and unblessed, and all because I'd failed to say "yes" when Xander asked if I felt better.

Yes, I do feel better and, by the way, thank you for being the best friend I've ever had.

But even that would have been wrong, because Xander did not want to be my friend. He was in love with me, and I hadn't seen it.

"Is this seat taken?"

A distinguished elderly gentleman was standing next to me. He wore a yellow sweater over a starched blue-checked shirt. The cuffs of his dark-blue trousers brushed the tops of pristine black wing-tip shoes. He leaned on a dark wood derby cane. Though he was older than my father, I couldn't help thinking he was the handsomest man I'd ever seen.

I blinked up at him. "Sir?"

"May I sit for a while?"

I edged over. He gripped the top of his cane with both hands and began lowering himself to the bench. Perspiration beaded on his forehead beneath the brim of a tweed newsboy cap.

When he winced, I reached for his arm. "Need some help?"

"No, I'm all right."

I ignored his refusal and put my hand under his elbow.

"Very kind of you. The bench was lower than I thought. Do you know if they sell the *Wall Street Journal* in the bookstore?"

"No, but I think they have it in the library."

"Is that far from here?"

I pointed down the sidewalk. "The fourth building on the left."

He looked in the direction I'd indicated. "If it's that far, I'd better catch my breath first." He patted the bench. "I hope you weren't saving this spot for anyone."

"No, I was just sitting here trying to decide what to do next."

He laid his hat next to him. "How admirable."

"Sir?"

"Not many people have the sense to stop and think before they act. If I'd done that when I was your age, I'd have saved myself a lot of heartache."

Embarrassed by his openness, I tried to change the subject.

"Are you here for commencement?" I asked.

"No, I've brought my wife to pick up her daughter, or rather *she's* brought *me*." A hint of bitterness tinged his voice. "I haven't introduced myself. Jameson Bridger."

"Agnes Quinn."

"My apologies for intruding on your thoughts, Agnes. You probably don't get much time alone."

"Oh, I'll have plenty of time alone after the mess I've made of things." Without warning, tears sprang to my eyes.

Mr. Bridger offered his handkerchief, crisp and white with *JB* monogrammed in navy blue on one corner. "What do you mean?"

I sniffled and wiped my nose. "I've just found out I've spent the last two years of my life being a complete moron, that's all."

"And who told you that?"

"My best friend ... only he wanted me for more than a friend and I didn't see it. I've wasted a lot of time loving the wrong person and trying to write a book. I haven't studied for my biology exam. I'm probably going to fail and then I'll have to take the class *again* in the fall."

I was near wailing by the time I rambled to a halt.

Mr. Bridger put on his hat and spoke as if conducting a board meeting.

"I was supposed to meet my wife here, but it looks like she's running late. Do you have time for a walk? I promised the doctor I'd keep up with my exercise on this trip. Hold this?"

He handed me his cane.

I stuffed his handkerchief in the pocket of my book bag. While he placed his hands on the bench and pushed himself up, I turned the cane over and ran my fingers along the smooth finish. The gold band beneath the handle was scratched and dull, but I could still read the inscription.

"*I'm a part of all I've met*. That's a nice thought," I said.

He took the cane and rubbed his thumb over the band. "Tennyson—my father's favorite. This is the only keepsake I have of his. Leo didn't manage to rob me of everything."

His voice was hollow, as if he were stranded in a desert, inhaling hot, dry air.

"Who's Leo?" I asked.

He looked as if he'd forgotten I was there. The pallor of grief faded from his face as suddenly as it had appeared. He turned toward the library. For a while we strolled along without talking. Then, in the same distant tone, he spoke again.

"My father died when I was very young. One of his business associates, Leo McBain, pursued my mother and manipulated her into marrying him."

"Why?"

"He was after my father's family inheritance—a piece of property Leo could get his hands on only if he married my mother."

"Your mother didn't realize what he was doing?"

"She was too pure of heart," he said, "always believed the best about people."

Mr. Bridger paused. Leaning on his cane, he labored to breathe.

"Maybe we should go back to the bookstore," I said.

He held up his hand. "I only need a moment."

I sensed his embarrassment and tried to fill the awkward silence. "Your mother sounds like a wonderful woman," I said.

"She was. That's why she was no match for a man like Leo."

"Did she love him?"

He looked up. "I'll never know, but I think she married him only because he played on her sympathies."

"You mean she felt sorry for him?"

He nodded. "He'd lost his wife and was trying to raise a son and a daughter on his own. He told her if she'd be a mother to his children—"

"He could be a father to you," I said.

"But he didn't mean a word of it. He treated me so badly I ran away, but I couldn't bear to think of my mother being alone, so I came back. That's when she told me."

"What?"

"About my father's property—mine someday, if I could just be patient. Leo never stopped badgering her about making him joint owner, but she always resisted."

He began to cough violently. He reached into his pants pocket, brought out a small bottle, and held it out to me. I twisted off the cap. He sipped and then bowed his head till the coughing subsided. His eyes red and watering, he looked up.

"Thank you, Agnes. My stepdaughter walks away when I start hacking and spewing."

I replaced the cap. "I'll hang on to this till we get to the library, in case you need it again." I pointed to the doorway of a nearby building. "Want to rest a few minutes?"

We stepped into the lobby, found some comfortable chairs, and sat down.

"Would you like me to call your wife, so she can pick you up?" I asked.

"No," he said. "You're the first person I've enjoyed talking to since I've been here."

"If you're sure you're okay," I said, "I'd love to hear the rest of your story."

He leaned back. "The day after I graduated from high school, I moved away and worked all summer to save enough money to start school in the fall."

"I guess you were glad to get away from Leo."

"I was, but I hated leaving my mother there with him. My absence took a toll on her—that, plus the constant pressure from Leo."

"What happened?"

"I'd only been gone a few weeks when I received word she was in the hospital. I rushed back to see her. Leo came into her hospital room and asked to speak to me in the hall."

"What did he want?"

"He said it was time I grew up and learned the ways of the world. He asked me to 'talk some sense into my mother while there was still time.'"

"Standing right outside his wife's hospital room? That's what he said?" I asked.

He nodded. "When I asked him what it was about, he said, 'That property, of course. I've never been able to make her see reason. If she doesn't make me joint owner before she dies ...'"

Mr. Bridger's face flamed red.

"What did *you* say?" I asked.

"I didn't say anything. I punched him—knocked him right on the floor."

"Good for you," I said. "What happened?"

"Hospital security kicked me out. Leo told them I wasn't allowed back in. After I left, he wrote to tell me I wasn't welcome in his home."

"You never went back?"

He closed his eyes and shook his head. "Let's go," he said.

He held out his hand. I helped him up.

When we stepped inside the library, Mr. Bridger took off his hat and leaned over the water fountain for a long drink. I retrieved the daily copy of the *Wall Street Journal* and the *New York Times* and guided him to a table by the window. He sank onto a chair.

He whispered. "I'll be all right now, Agnes. Thank you."

I set his medicine on the table and whispered back, "I'm going to study for my exam. I have to go upstairs to find a journal article I still haven't read, but it shouldn't take long. Then I'll walk back with you when you're ready."

I turned to go, but came back and sat down next to him. "I'm sorry. I know it's painful for you to talk about your mother, but I have to know. Did you ever get to talk to explain to her what happened?"

"No. She never left the hospital. She passed away within a few weeks," he said.

"What did you do after that? Start college?"

"No, I kept working. Turned out I had a knack for making money. I became what you might call a 'self-made man,' though I don't care for the title."

"Did you ever hear from Leo again?"

"Oh, yes. He wrote to tell me my mother was so upset with the way I'd treated him, she signed over the property to him before she died."

"Did you believe him?"

"No, but I was just a kid and didn't have the resources or know-how to go after him."

"You must've been heartbroken," I said.

He patted my hand. "It didn't matter. My mother and I were both free of him. Before long, I had more money and property than I knew what to do with. I didn't need more."

I stood. "I'll let you read now. I'll check back in awhile to see if you're ready to go."

He called to me as I walked away. I sat down again.

"You're a good girl, Agnes, and I'm sure you have great things ahead of you."

"Not many people share that opinion," I said.

"It doesn't matter," he said. "I know quality when I see it. You remember I said so."

"Thank you, Mr. Bridger," I said.

"One more thing."

"Yes?"

"I don't know what happened between you and your friend. You may not be able to fix your disagreement, but remember this: Nothing is as important as the people you love. Nothing."

I started up the stairs. My day gone wrong had righted itself thanks to Jameson Bridger. True, I'd relinquished Trevor, resigned *Trevorode*, and renounced Trask. But none of those things was as important as my friendship with Xander. The one tangible thing I could do to prove I was serious about being a better person and worthy of his love was to pass my biology exam. If I could pull that off, I might yet win back his heart.

I walked upstairs, located my article, and sat down to study the biology notes I'd scrawled during lectures I'd barely understood. Totally absorbed, I only gradually began to realize the library was buzzing with whispered conversation. Visitors on tour, I thought, and kept reading. I didn't look up till a library assistant tapped me on the shoulder.

"You see some old guy around here anywhere? They're tearing up the campus looking for him. He has a heart problem, and they're afraid he's dead under a bush somewhere."

My heart stopped. I crammed my book and notes into my bag and rushed back to where I'd left Mr. Bridger. Gathered around his table was a throng of people—uniformed security personnel, the head librarian, a dozen curious students and—of all people—the president of the university. The nearer I got, the sicker I felt.

"Move back. Give him some air."

"Papa. Papa, are you all right?"

"If anything has happened to my husband, you'll have a lawsuit you'll never be able to settle. I'll own this school."

I pushed my way through the crowd and saw Jameson Bridger slumped over the table, where I'd left him. On top of the scattered newspapers, his gray head face down, rested on his folded arms. A paramedic was feeling his pulse. As I moved closer, my breathing grew shallow. Crumpled at the feet of Jameson Bridger, squalling, "Papa, Papa," was Jonquil Putnam. Xander was kneeling beside her.

I stood soundless, like an escaped prisoner in the woods. Would I be arrested? Sued? Charged with kidnapping? Jonquil's mother would have no limit to legal resources. If her husband died, because I'd let him walk too far and then left him alone, would I be an accessory to murder? Was I guilty of manslaughter?

Thoughts of genes, cells, DNA, and amino acids shot right out of my mind. I was looking straight in the face of a disaster for which I might be blamed. And yet a new scene seeped into my mind like water trickling through cracks in a dam.

A deathly stillness had descended on the manor. The clang of kettles, prattle of maids, barking of dogs, neighing of horses all ceased, every creature silenced with grief.

The king was dead.

Lyda Rose stood still, the great sword, Bronsling, gripped in her pale white fingers.

Princess Hyacinth shrieked. "You did this. There you stand with the king's sword dripping with his own blood. There's but one recourse—death by hanging."

The queen motioned for a palace guard. "Take her away to await execution."

"Stop!"

The queen shrieked, "Who said 'stop'?"

The king lifted his head. "I did."

Jameson Bridger's voice cracked like a rifle shot. He pulled his arm from the paramedic's hand and pushed himself back from the table to face the frenzied crowd.

"Do stop it, Cornelia. I fell asleep—nothing more. This was the first peaceful moment I've had on this trip, and I took advantage of it." He looked at the university president. "Dr. Whitmire, please accept my apologies." He addressed the librarian. "I'm sorry I've disrupted your workplace. It was not my intention. And as for you, Jonquil, do get up and stop that noise."

As he caught sight of me at the edge of the crowd, our eyes met for a splendid second. He picked up his hat. "I was tired, that's all. I'm sorry I caused all this trouble." He turned to Xander. "Young man, if you'll be so kind as to help me to our car, I'd appreciate it."

As the four of them, still trailed by the university entourage, moved toward the door, I heard Mrs. Bridger say to her husband, "If only you'd told us where you were going, we wouldn't have worried. How did you get all the way over here, anyway?"

"The kindness of a stranger," Mr. Bridger said.

As they passed by, he didn't look my way and neither did Xander.

Chapter 3

A Tale of Two Letters

As the crowd dispersed, I crept upstairs to a window on the third floor and watched Jameson Bridger climb into the backseat of his Lincoln Town Car. Having concluded he was neither dying nor impaired, I started back to my dorm. So, I thought, Xander would have dinner with Jonquil after all. Over steak in some ritzy restaurant, Jonquil's mother would quiz Xander about his family. Then over coffee and cheesecake, Mr. Bridger and Xander would discuss the stock market while Mrs. Bridger winked at Jonquil and squeezed her hand under the linen tablecloth. The thought was nauseating.

I was so miserable I might've walked off the campus, never to be heard of again, if it hadn't been for Chester Cranston and a stray cat.

As I passed by a thick clump of holly bushes, I saw Chester, our resident environmental zealot, flat on his stomach, his head and shoulders hidden under the hedge. A paper bag and large cardboard box with holes in the lid sat next to his sparse frame and shoeless feet. Inch by painful inch, he edged forward, coaxing his prey.

"Here, kitty. Ow. Here, kitty. Ow."

"Chester. It's me, Agnes. Do you need some help?"

His voice muffled by the undergrowth, he said, "Agnes, I'm glad it's you. I've been trying for two weeks to catch this cat. Some lowlife has put a cardboard ring around his neck."

"Ring?" I asked.

"Yeah. Ow. You know—like from a roll of duct tape. Must've been on him since he was a kitten. Now it's choking him. If he'd stop biting me, I could pull him out."

I knelt down beside him. "Ever think of using a trap?"

"Trap? That would fly in the face of everything I believe in."

"But if it's this hard to grab him, he must not be too bad off," I said.

"Don't be absurd. He's scared. Ow. Of course he's resisting. If you could come around to the other side and head him off, maybe we could catch him."

The cat and I both needed distraction. Maybe I could do *one* thing right today. Always at my finest when undertaking a noble cause, I stepped off the sidewalk and circled to the other side of the shrubs. I could dimly make out the white tip of a grey-striped tail, whipping wildly. I knelt down and positioned myself to block the poor beast's escape. When the victim heard my approach, he lunged toward Chester. Careless of his own welfare, Chester captured the creature in a flurry of gray fur and flailing legs and secured him in the cardboard box.

We carried the cat to my car and arrived at a veterinarian's within a few minutes. The vet quickly determined the terrified animal would have to be sedated in order to have the cardboard ring removed. Chester spoke up at once.

"Go ahead and neuter him while he's asleep." Chester turned to me. "Can you split the cost of this with me, Agnes?"

Because Chester had rescued so many animals he'd qualified for the "multiple pet discount," the vet assured me it was affordable. After the successful surgery, we left our patient to recover overnight and returned to the car.

"Want to stop and eat on the way back?" Chester asked.

"Sure," I said. "I could use a good meal."

I'd always liked Chester. He was a physics major, so he was in Xander's circle of friends.

"So, Agnes," he said, his mouth full of salad, "what will you do this summer?"

His tone implied he possessed inside information, but I couldn't make sense of his grin.

"I'm going home and get a job and take a few summer classes—try to make up some of the credits I'm missing."

"Missing credits?"

"Yeah, I changed my major to education and now I'm a little behind."

"That's great," he said. "I've always thought you were a born teacher."

I looked up from my lettuce. "Why would you say that?"

"Ever since you did that speech on Harry Truman last year—I remember thinking you'd make a good teacher. I read a whole book about Truman on account of you."

I'd never once imagined myself as a teacher.

"So when are you going to Xander's house?" he asked.

"Xander's house? What are you talking about?"

"Oh, come on. You don't have to play dumb. He told me once you finally wised up about Trevor, he was going to tell you he loved you and invite you to meet his family."

If I hadn't been sitting down, I'd have fainted.

"You knew?" I asked.

"Everybody in the science building knew. He was going to tell you today. Did he?"

"Not exactly," I said. "Something came up."

"Oh. I hope I didn't spoil the surprise. He's been planning it a long time."

"No worries," I said. "I'll act surprised when the time comes."

"That's a relief." He paused. "Could I ask you a favor?"

"Sure," I said.

"It's about Saturn."

"Saturn?"

"The cat. I thought I'd name him Saturn on account of the ring around his neck."

"Saturn. Clever," I said.

"I can't take him home. I'm spending the summer in the Amazon rainforest."

"You were going to keep him?" I thought the cat's next move would be to a shelter.

"No one's going to adopt a cat that age," he said. "One of us has to keep him."

"You don't think—no—I told you I'll be working this summer and going to school. I don't have time for a cat."

"Couldn't your mom take care of him? I thought you said she loved animals."

"She does, but the last time she brought home a mangy dog, my dad put his foot down."

"But this is a cat, and he's perfectly healthy. Come on. What could I do to make this an offer you can't refuse?"

My good deed had nudged fate in my direction.

"How much do you remember about Biology 101?" I asked.

"Everything," he said.

"Could you help me study tonight?"

"I don't know. My quantum mechanics final is tomorrow and—"

"Those are the terms. Help me pass that exam, and Saturn will be settled in a new home within seventy-two hours."

With Chester's expert tutoring I managed to pull off a healthy 78 on my biology exam. Not only did I avoid repeating the course, but I was confident my resourcefulness and initiative would turn Xander's heart back toward mine.

I called to tell my mother the story of Saturn's rescue and got the expected reaction.

She sniffled. "The poor thing. Who would do such a thing? Is he going to be all right?"

"Yes, Mom, he's fine. We even had him neutered while he was asleep."

"Where is he now?"

"Still at the vet's," I said. "That's why I'm calling. May I bring him home with me?"

Since she hadn't had a pet in years, she agreed. I'd let her worry about Dad's reaction.

I'd covered all the bases. Saturn was recovering. I'd passed biology. Chester, though disappointed with a 98 on his own exam, deemed his sacrifice noble. Fired with new optimism, I began packing to go home. Every time I left the dorm, I carried my biology exam with me. How was I to know when I might bump into Xander again? Maybe the encounter with Jonquil's family had not gone well after all. Maybe he found her mother irritating. Maybe Jonquil was getting on his nerves.

But Xander was nowhere to be found, and I heard nothing from him.

On commencement day my hopes revived. He wouldn't miss celebrating with his graduating chemistry buddies. As I stood at the edge of the crowd, I felt a tap on my shoulder.

"You're Agnes Quinn, aren't you?" asked one of the graduates.

"Yes."

"Xander Plumley asked me to give this to you. He said I'd find you here."

I took the letter. "Thanks. Is he all right? He's not sick or anything?"

"No. He's gone."

I hurried to the first solitary place I could find and tore open the envelope. Inside was a single page of yellow legal paper scrawled over with Xander's half-printed, half-cursive script.

Dear Agnes,

Sorry I didn't say goodbye. Mr. Bridger said he could tell I'm the sort of man he's been looking for and he offered me a job after I graduate. He recommended I finish my studies in Scotland. I went straight home after exams to get ready. This is the chance I've been hoping for, Quinn. I didn't know it would come this soon. Maybe you were right all along—it's better to dream big.

Your friend,
Xander

I sat there reading and rereading the letter that explained everything and yet said nothing. Didn't have time to say goodbye? Scotland? How can you make a decision like that in a few days? Would he work for Mr. Bridger? Was that one of the perks of being his … son-in-law? Big chance? Dream big? Who wrote this letter, anyway? Not the guy who told me I needed to *stop* dreaming.

Only my promise to pick up Saturn before the vet's office closed stirred me from my stupor and sent me on my way. When I arrived, the assistant lifted Saturn from his cage and handed him across the counter. The cat nestled his head in my arm and purred. I tucked him into a carrier in the backseat and headed out of town.

"Well, Saturn, it looks like it's me and you against the world. Our pal Chester's off to save the rainforest, and Xander is off to—"

I couldn't bring myself to say more, not even to a cat.

When we arrived at home, my tireless mother hugged me and scooped up Saturn. After she pointed out the litter box in the laundry room, she carted Saturn upstairs to my room, where his new bed, treats, toys, and scratching post awaited his arrival. Exhausted from the drive, the day, the week, the year, my life, I didn't feel like talking or unpacking. The one thing I did before I fell into bed was to take Xander's letter from my purse, read it once more, and place it, unfolded, face up on the corner of my desk.

The next morning I stunned my father by coming downstairs before sunrise to have breakfast with him. When I asked if there were any summer jobs available at his company, he almost choked on his coffee.

"I'll see what I can do, if that's what you want," he said. "The last time I offered you a job, you said you wouldn't do 'menial' labor."

"That was the old Agnes, Dad."

He filled his travel mug with the last of the coffee from the pot.

"I'll talk to the boss and call you at noon," he said.

"Won't be here—I'm enrolling in some summer classes and buying my books today."

Lunchbox in hand, he opened the back door. "More writing?"

"Nope—all done with that. I'm going to be a teacher."

I'd never seen my father at a loss for words. After a couple moments he said, "That's good news. I'll call you later."

Mom kissed me on the cheek after he left. "You've made your father very happy."

Under the table Saturn lay on my foot and purred.

At last, all was right in the world of Agnes Quinn.

Dad got me a job as a courier. I'd lived in the same town my whole life, so I never lost my way and had no trouble completing my assignments. I began evening classes at the community college and found the education track wasn't as bad as I'd imagined. One course, "Drama in Literature," required me to participate in a production of *Cyrano de Bergerac.* Though I auditioned well, the director explained I was too tall for the romantic female lead. He offered me the role of Mother Superior in the final act and made me his assistant.

True to form, I developed a terrific crush on the lead actor, a gorgeous, curly-haired, deep-voiced guy named Thomas Fox. But every night, when I got home from rehearsal, the sight of Xander's letter would remind me to live a serious and purposeful life. I was neither disillusioned nor broken-hearted when Thomas fell for the girl who played Roxanne.

The director's praise for me was never-ending. He appreciated my help with line rehearsals and the actors' interpretation of their characters. On closing night as the cast bowed to a standing ovation, the director summoned me to the stage and presented me with a dozen red roses. He spoke above the applause: "After you graduate, you'll have a job here if you want one." The cast members gave me an autographed copy of the program. When I arrived at home, still glowing with memories of the evening, I placed the program on top of Xander's letter.

I was making progress.

For my class on "Teaching Poetry," I constructed a unit on William Blake. During the required oral presentation, I quoted "The Tyger" and "The Lamb" with such passion I received not only an A, but applause from the class. I took the comment sheet home and placed it on top of the autographed copy of the program on top of Xander's letter. Other commendations followed, including a job offer from my dad's boss for the next summer and a Good Citizen citation from the city fire department for my heroism in helping the victims of a traffic accident.

I didn't add a single word to *Trevorode the Defender.*

At summer's end I left Saturn with my doting mother and returned to school for my junior year. Nothing, including me, was the same. Trevor was married, gaining weight, and working at an auto parts store. Dr. Trask was on sabbatical. I was glad I'd never run into him, even by accident. Jonquil was also absent. Having located a suitable candidate for marriage, I assumed she no longer found a university career necessary and was probably preparing for her wedding. Even Chester had written to say he'd secured a grant to stay in the rainforest until December.

For the first half of the semester I tried to find out where Xander was. Because he had a short friends list, and they all judged me to be the cause of his leaving, they wouldn't answer my questions. Left to my own devices, I scanned science journals, checked chemistry conference listings, and even glanced at society columns to see if Jonquil's wedding had been announced, all to no avail. After awhile, looking for Xander took more time than I cared to spend. He hadn't bothered to contact me. Why should I pursue a friendship he wanted no part of?

Only two reminders of the previous year remained—Xander's letter and *Trevorode the Defender.* With a mortician's grim respect, I secured the manuscript in a blue three-ring binder, taped a note card with the title on the front cover, and buried the project in a drawer. Convinced Xander's letter had inspired my success, I was less willing to squirrel it away. The page, however—unfolded, refolded—needed preserving. So, handling the yellow paper like a delicate blossom, I sealed the letter in an envelope and pressed it between the pages of *Classics of Western Literature.*

With only my textbooks and my resolve to keep me company, I became a scholar.

Two years later I graduated with honors.

I took Xander's letter with me to commencement. Walking down the aisle to "Pomp and Circumstance," I remembered the graduation ceremony years before when a stranger had handed me this letter—this letter which had jolted me into reality and set me on a sane and responsible course. Moments before I turned into my assigned row, I spotted Trevor Rhodes, dressed in dark-blue pants and a white uniform shirt. "T. Rhodes" was inscribed on a patch over his pocket. Next to him, Mrs. Wendy Rhodes, cute and petite no longer, was in the full bloom of expectant motherhood.

Things had ended well.

After the ceremony, my parents hosted a graduation dinner in my honor. Mr. and Mrs. Norman, my longtime employers, joined us. As he was leaving, Mr. Norman said, "I hate to lose you, Agnes. If I let you hang your diploma on the storeroom wall, would you stay here and work for us a little longer?"

"I'd like that," I said.

"What do you mean, Aggie?" my father asked. "Aren't you coming home?"

"Only for the summer," I said. "I've been accepted into graduate school."

Even my brother Toby was stunned into silence.

I bowed out of summer theatre in favor of devoting time to my master's thesis—*Unlikely Heroines: A Critical Comparison of Lizzie Hexam and Molly Gibson*. The next spring, after I submitted my thesis, I was completing my application to Brighton Park Community College when I looked up and saw *Classics of Western Literature* on my shelf. I opened the book and pulled out Xander's letter.

What would he think of me now?

With M.A. after my name, I resigned from my job at Norman's grocery store and journeyed home for my final summer as a courier. I declined a job offer from both my father's boss and my former director, assuaging the latter's disappointment by agreeing to play Henry Higgins' mother in the summer production of *Pygmalion*. By the end of August, I was out of school, out of debt, single-minded, successful, packed up, and prepared to make my way in the world. Three weeks before the fall term I left home with my parents' blessing and moved to Plainview, North Carolina.

When I arrived at my new apartment, a cozy one-bedroom nook on the first floor of a dingy white Spanish stucco building, I put out a welcome mat and placed Xander's letter ceremonially on the corner of my new desk.

"Welcome home, Agnes," I said.

On Monday afternoon, the first day of new teacher orientation, my mother called for an update. Before she hung up, she said, "There's a letter here for you, forwarded from Stanton-Giles. Do you want me to open it, in case it's important?"

I poured food into Saturn's dish. "Is there a return address?" I asked.

"Someone named Plumley. Was that one of your professors?"

Saturn ran from the shower of cat food as his dish clattered to the floor.

I could hardly breathe. "Plumley?"

"Dr. and Mrs. Rufus Plumley," she said.

Xander's parents. I knew at once something was wrong.

My mother promised to forward the letter the next day. Convinced the approaching letter brought bad news, I thought of nothing else. The training sessions to which I'd given such careful attention now seemed endless and unnecessary. My passion for my new job evaporated.

The letter arrived on Friday afternoon.

Dear Miss Quinn,

Please excuse my writing without a proper introduction, but Xander has spoken of you so often, I feel I know you.

I don't know if you've heard, but Xander has been in trouble because of that Putnam girl. He's left his work at the university and has all but disappeared. We know he backpacked across Europe for a while, but the last postcard we had was from Australia.

You can imagine how glad I was when he asked me to contact you. If anyone can talk him into coming home, you can.

Please call me at your earliest convenience, so when we hear from him again, I can tell him I found you and you still think of him ... if you do.

With kind regards,
Clementine Plumley

The next morning I dialed the unlisted number she'd included at the end of her letter.

"Plumley residence."

"Hello," I said. "My name is Agnes Quinn. Mrs. Plum—"

"One moment, please. She's been expecting your call."

A receiver clicked. Had she taken the call in the library?

"Agnes?" Her voice was trembling and breathless.

"Yes. Is this Mrs. Plumley?"

"Oh, Agnes ..." she sobbed, "I'm glad it's you."

The last time I'd heard those words was when Chester needed my help with a rescue.

Chapter 4

A Brief Encounter

"I'll help if I can," I said. "Why don't you start at the beginning and tell me—"

Mrs. Plumley raised her voice. "I'll have to check my list and get back to you later."

"Your list?"

"Who is that?" a voice in the background said.

"The caterer," Mrs. Plumley said.

"I'll ask you again," the voice said. "To whom are you speaking?"

Mrs. Plumley wilted. "One of Xander's friends."

"We agreed not to discuss this with anyone," the voice said.

"I only thought—" Mrs. Plumley said.

He snatched the phone. "Who is this?" he said to me.

"Agnes Quinn. Is this Dr. Plumley?"

"It is. This is a not a convenient time for you to call. My wife is not herself."

"She asked me to call," I said, irritated by his tone. "Is Xander all right?"

"No, I'm afraid he is not, and it's been very difficult on all of us. I'll say goodbye now."

"Is there a more convenient time when—?"

The receiver clicked in my ear.

Dumbfounded, I stared at the receiver. I'd been mistaken about the Plumleys. They were not remarkable at all. Mrs. Plumley was as pitiful as any other worried mother, and Dr. Plumley was just plain rude.

"And don't even get me started on Xander," I said to Saturn, who, impatient for dinner, brushed against my leg. I grabbed two cans from the cabinet—one of chicken soup and one of cat food. I filled Saturn's dish and then complained to him as I swirled the noodles in a pan.

"For years," I said, "I haven't taken a step without wondering what Xander would think of me, and now he's off touring the world while I'm stuck in a community college."

Occupied with his tuna, Saturn ignored me.

When I sat down to supper, someone knocked at the door.

I stood at the door and called out. "Who is it?"

"Your neighbor," a man said. "Warner Bingham."

I remembered his name from the mailboxes.

Brought up to be a good neighbor, I opened the door.

Warner scraped his thick-soled black boots on my welcome mat. Saturn, fearing the intruder, skittered behind the sofa where I wished I could follow. Outfitted in black jeans and a black leather jacket, Warner did nothing to put me at ease.

He held out a blue plastic measuring cup. "Honey."

I stepped back. "I'm sorry … what?"

"I need honey."

"I have apricot preserves," I said. "That's about it."

His face turned as red as the bandana on his head. "Not for toast—for a cough."

"I see. I have cough syrup."

He narrowed his eyes. "It will have to do. Go get it."

I was afraid to turn my back to Warner, but more afraid to refuse him. I rifled through the kitchen cabinet and produced a half-empty bottle of cherry-flavored cough syrup my mother had insisted I bring.

He held the bottle up to the light. "I hope it's enough, or she'll keep me awake all night."

"Your wife?" I asked, hoping he was not in charge of a sick child.

"No, my mother."

He left without saying thank you or goodbye. I made sure the door was locked, and returned to my lukewarm soup.

Exhausted, I went to bed early, but couldn't fall asleep. Every time I drifted off, images of the sinister Warner or weeping Mrs. Plumley jolted me awake. The next day I tried several times to call Mrs. Plumley, but could never get past the maid. I tried to keep busy by reviewing my lectures for the first day of class, but couldn't concentrate. When I learned from the evening news that a thunderstorm was approaching, I went to bed in a worse state of mind than the evening before. A clap of thunder rattled my building around midnight.

When I opened the door for a closer look at the storm, Saturn bolted out into the pouring rain. Since the day Chester and I had rescued him, I'd never let Saturn outside.

How would he find his way home?

Hoping for some sound from Saturn, I lay awake most of the night. He didn't reappear. On Monday morning, still worn out, I dressed, packed my lunch, and organized my book bag. Out of habit, I reached for Xander's letter, which I'd always taken with me on the first day of any new undertaking. I held the envelope for a moment, then opened the desk drawer, threw it in on top of *Trevorode the Defender*, and slammed the drawer shut.

Instead I took Mrs. Plumley's letter with me.

I called for Saturn as I opened my car door and looked in the rearview mirror one last time as I drove toward the Drifters' Rest. Housed on the first floor of a restored brown-brick, two-story house, the restaurant, owned by Muriel Porter, was well-known for serving the "best coffee in town."

"Good morning," Muriel said. "Have a seat. You look all done in. Coffee?"

"Yes, and keep it coming. This is a beautiful place. How long have you been here?"

She laughed. "Almost as long as the house itself. I inherited it from my great-grandmother, Emmaline. That's her over there on the wall."

I glanced at the portrait smiling down on all who entered.

"The city council wanted to turn the place into a museum," she said, "but I couldn't bear the thought of dirt and smudges everywhere, so I opened this place and moved in upstairs."

"I'm glad you did," I said. "This really is the best coffee I've ever had."

Shored up by caffeine, I summoned my will and drove to Brighton Park Community College. On the way, I urged myself to stop worrying about Xander and my cat and to focus on the job I'd been hired to do. I commended myself for how hard I'd worked to get to where I was. I reminded myself I'd signed a contract and had an obligation to fulfill. By the time I drove into the parking lot, my rhetoric had convinced me. My common sense had calmed me. I was ready to meet any challenge.

And my good intentions might have actually paid off—if only faculty orientation had not left out one unwritten rule: *No one ever parks in Jonas Grinstead's spot.* Had it not been for this fateful omission in my training, I might never have intersected with the reclusive Dr. Grinstead, who had mastered the art of being virtually invisible among the other eighty-seven professors. Out of dozens of empty spaces, I somehow managed to pull into the place where he had parked every day for thirty years.

Predictability and destiny seldom walk hand-in-hand.

When the rusty white pickup pulled in next to me, I assumed it was part of the maintenance fleet. No one but a first-year teacher or a janitor, I reasoned, would be so zealous about putting the best foot forward. Occupied with my books and file folders, I didn't look up till I heard a tap at my car window. Dr. Grinstead's frayed khaki pants and white shirt, perfectly starched and creased, did little to alert me to his true identity. A good wife ironed those clothes, I thought as I rolled down the window.

"Good morning," I said.

"You're new here, aren't you?" he asked.

His face was as unreadable as the fading logo on his truck door.

"Yes. First day."

"That explains it. Look, Miss, it will take awhile before you become acquainted with our patterns around here, and you're not to be faulted if you didn't realize …"

"Oh, I see. Have I blocked you from making a delivery?"

"In a manner of speaking. I'm here to deliver knowledge to the unlearned."

I chuckled. "I don't think it's quite that simple."

"Young woman, I know they don't cover anything useful in faculty orientation, but everyone knows this is my parking place."

"I didn't know reserved parking was available," I said.

I reached into the backseat for my umbrella. Though the sun had risen, dark clouds, lingering from the night before, hung low in the sky.

"It's not, but I'm used to having things a certain way."

"Your way, you mean?" My conscience cringed about my poor manners. I ignored it.

"No, I wouldn't put it that way," he said. "But I've been here a long time, and I have no intention of altering my habits for a newcomer."

"Look, Mr.—"

"Grinstead and it's 'Dr.'"

"Look, Dr. Grinstead, you may not have asked yourself why I'm here at this ridiculous hour, so I'll explain." A convenient clap of thunder punctuated my outburst. "I got some bad news on Friday." I glanced at the letter which lay on the seat beside me. "I didn't sleep well last night, so I stopped on my way here for coffee." I held up the cup labeled Drifters' Rest. "I was feeling better when I pulled into this parking lot—" I looked at my watch—"twelve short minutes ago. But you, sir, have undone all my efforts to regroup."

I threw my car into reverse, backed up a few feet, and angled into the spot next to the one I was vacating. I slammed the car into park and turned off the engine.

"Better?" I asked.

Jonas met my tirade with unexpected composure, rendering my childish triumph hollow. He bowed his head and exhaled, his silence stunning me. Large, languid raindrops descended, awaking in me the settled conviction that he was in reality a kindly wizard, deploying a seldom summoned power.

After a moment, he lifted his eyes to meet mine. "You must excuse me," he said in a low voice. "I've never been good at first impressions."

"I liked you better when I thought you were the janitor," I said.

"He has much better manners than I."

Jonas took an old black umbrella from his truck.

"Manners can be learned," I said.

"Yes, they can," he said.

He shouldered an olive green backpack, tattered perhaps by many a hike through the woods, and walked away without looking back.

Still, soft, silent, the rain fell as I watched Jonas, otherworldly, pace off purposeful steps, still visible far away, behind a silver silk curtain of tumbling water flowing and spilling over red brick walls, coarse gray pavement, and golden-yellow trees, on his way to—what had he said?—deliver knowledge to the unlearned.

I stared vacantly at the water cascading over my windshield. My attempt at an impressive first day at my new job had been thoroughly upended.

"Your first class is still ninety minutes away—review your lectures," my father would sermonize.

"Don't get your new shoes wet," my mother would admonish.

"Snap out of it, Aggie," my brother Toby would chide. "The old guy didn't make it rain. Don't be silly."

And so, bowing to the voices of reason in my mind, I sat.

I retrieved the bagel I'd intended as a midmorning snack and surveyed my surroundings. As I sipped coffee, I took note of a lone weed growing through a crack in the sidewalk. Then I looked at the offensive vehicle parked two spaces away. What was the big deal about that place? Maybe Dr. Grinstead was obsessive, afraid of germs and scratches. No. The truck was decades old, dented, and weathered. He couldn't be worried about the paint. I looked closer. That door had been through its fair share of—and then I took a second look at the logo.

Through the dense rain, I could make out pale gray lines, which skipped and blanked out like a connect-the-dots puzzle in a coloring book. The drawing was so eroded it took several minutes to conclude these traces had once been the picture of a tree. As the rain dwindled into a shower, I noticed faint flecks of green and yellow speckling the imperceptible branches. Flowers, I supposed. I had the strangest notion if Jonas could drive this truck out of the parking lot and into the past, these remnants of color would swirl, surge, and shape themselves into blooms again.

Waiting for the storm to subside, I reached several conclusions. First, there was some reason Jonas Grinstead was so rigid and controlled. Second, I'd been rude and thoughtless to a man whose age and experience warranted my respect. Third, I knew how school life played out. I was not going to be known as "the new teacher who yelled at Dr. Grinstead." I emerged from my car a much wiser woman and determined that the day, begun badly, had to be redeemed. A standard letter of apology was my first attempt at reconciliation.

Between morning classes, I scribbled out a note:

Dear Dr. Grinstead,

Please accept my apology for my rude behavior this morning. As I mentioned, I was very nervous about my first day on the job, and my frustrations got the best of me. Ordinarily, I'm easy to get along with or so I've been told. I was wondering if maybe we could start over.

Sincerely,
Agnes Quinn

I quizzed each of my classes about who might be going in the direction of Dr. Grinstead's classroom and found a student willing to deliver my message. Satisfied, I settled down at my desk to eat lunch and read. Within minutes a different student returned with my note. At the bottom in a small, scrawled script were the words: *Good fences make good neighbors. JG*

Furious, I wadded up the paper and tossed it in the trashcan. Unbidden scenes of revenge played out in my mind. I'd report him to an administrator. No, I'd write the college accrediting agency. No, I'd write a letter to the United States Department of Education. Who did he think he was—refusing the courteous request of a colleague? As the afternoon dragged on, I alternated from feeling like a naughty schoolchild, to a victim, to an avenging angel.

Determined to have the final word with Jonas, I stayed after my last class. On the back of the crumpled paper I'd retrieved from the trash, I wrote: *To err is human; to forgive divine.* I headed to the parking lot, pleased to find Jonas' truck still there and untended. I looked over my shoulder to be sure I was unobserved and approached the truck. Like an assassin drawing a silenced gun, I pulled the note from my pocket and lifted the windshield wiper to secure the message. There on the front seat was a bag from the Drifters' Rest.

Maybe bribery was a better option. I holstered my note and drove home.

Saturn was waiting for me in the driveway. There he sat, meowing as if he'd never been away. He pawed at the door while I fumbled with the lock. Tired from an honest day's work and eager to wake early for my visit to the coffee shop, I sank into a dreamless sleep with Saturn, cleaned, brushed, and fed, snuggled up and purring by my side.

When I arrived at the Drifters' Rest, Muriel set a cup of coffee on the counter before I could sit down. She slid a cinnamon-raisin bagel toward me.

"How was the first day of school?"

"Not bad. I got along great with the students, but I got off on the wrong foot with one of the teachers. In fact, I thought I might pick up a little something extra as a peace offering."

"What happened?"

"You won't believe it. I drove into the wrong parking place."

"Let me guess—Dr. Grinstead's?"

I spluttered, spraying crumbs. "How did you know?"

"Jonas has come by here every day since I opened this place." She took a French onion bagel from a basket on the shelf behind her. "In fact, if you wait another twenty minutes, he'll walk right through that door." She handed me the bag she'd filled. "Or you can hurry and get to school before he does. Make him a present of this, and he'll be your friend forever."

"Onion? You can't be serious. No one eats onion bagels for breakfast."

"No. He brings his own pastrami from home and makes the same sandwich every day. Insists on freshness—buys only one." She pointed to a shelf lined with small jars. "Take a little of that hot mustard to go with it. You'll win him over on the spot." She laughed. "I'll tell him I ran out of onion. Then you can step in and be the heroine."

I imagined the scene and broke out in a cold sweat. "He'll think I bought the last one," I said.

"Then tell him the truth," she said.

"I tried that yesterday."

"Try again. He's not at all what he seems."

Who was I to argue with Muriel Porter?

I scooped up my own breakfast along with the makings of Jonas' lunch and was out the door and on the campus before he arrived. We both left the distasteful parking place empty between us as we had the day before. Before he had time to turn off his engine, I was out of my car. Offering in hand, I approached.

"Dr. Grinstead."

By the time I reached him, his door was open. He had one foot on the pavement. "Yes?"

"I stopped by Drifters' Rest on the way. Everything looked so good I got a little carried away. I have this extra bagel. I wonder if you'd like to have it."

He appeared to ignore me as he exited his truck and stepped onto the sidewalk. But as I held out the bag to him, he paused, like a deer sensing a hunter in the woods.

"I don't think I'd be interested," he said. "I like only one flavor, and she was out of it this morning." Faint recognition flickered in his eyes.

"If you're not hungry now," I said, "you could always save it for lunch."

He took the bag and looked inside.

"Mustard, too. It seems I'm the victim of a conspiracy."

"Muriel said it would work," I said. "Do you really want to go back there tomorrow and tell her she was wrong?"

"No. Muriel believes herself to be the sum of all wisdom. Thank you—"

"Agnes."

"Thank you, Agnes." He turned to go.

Without thinking, I blurted out, "Jonas."

He stopped and looked back.

"The logo on your truck—what does it mean?"

"It's the place I built," he said, "and abandoned."

And with that impromptu confession, he walked away.

I was all but whistling a happy tune when I wandered into the English Department office later that morning to check my mailbox. I felt a sharp rap on my shoulder and turned to find a brittle-faced woman, primly dressed in a floral skirt and pearl-buttoned, peach-colored sweater, dyed-to-match peach-colored shoes, sprayed-stiff short blonde hair, and red-framed glasses.

"Excuse me," she said.

"Yes?"

"We haven't met. I'm Beatrix Thorpe."

"Agnes Quinn." I extended my hand, which she ignored. "Beatrice ..."

"No," she said. "Trix. Trix."

"Like the cereal?"

"No. Like the author. Beatrix Potter."

"Oh, Peter Rabbit."

She bristled. "Among others."

I had no idea how I'd gotten off on the wrong foot with this woman, but had no intention of allowing her to dampen my happy mood.

"I noticed," she said, "you stopped to talk to Jonas—Dr. Grinstead—this morning."

"Yes." I thumbed through my mail and hoped she would go away.

"And you gave him a gift of some sort?"

I felt as if I'd been called in from recess for throwing a rock at a classmate.

"You were watching?" I asked.

She reddened. "I was getting out of my car and happened to be looking that way."

"Yes?" I matched her tone icicle for icicle.

"I think you should be informed that Dr. Grinstead and I have an arrangement."

"Arrangement?"

Her friend, who had been looking on from a nearby table, stood and walked toward me.

"Let me help, Trixie," she said. "Young lady—"

I looked down on a short, lanky, gray-haired woman who seemed to be all elbows and knees. Her nose, beak-like, straddled pale, thin lips. Dressed in jeans shortened and hemmed by hand, and a royal blue jacket, she stared up at me like a fierce old bird of prey. I could have knocked her from her perch with one well-placed shove to her bony shoulder.

"You are?" I asked.

"Mavis Applewhite. Miss Quinn, I don't know how the faculty at your other school treated each other, but here at B-P-C-C, we—"

"Have a certain pecking order," I said.

"Have a certain code of conduct."

"Like chivalry?" I asked.

"That's for men," she said.

"The women don't have a code of conduct?" I asked.

"We—" With a sweep of her hand she indicated Beatrix, herself, and their silent partner at the table, "—have an established way of doing things. Certain situations are taken for granted and one of those is that Jonas Grinstead and Mrs. Thorpe are … I think your generation would call it 'an item.' So we'll thank you to keep your feminine wiles in check when you have contact with him."

This scene was too luscious to be believed. After all my years of being too tall, too plain, too loud, too silly to be considered dating material for desirable eligible men, at last—without even meaning to—I had become The Other Woman. Now I had two transgressions to my credit: I'd violated a sacred parking place *and* flirted with the off-limits man. I restrained the urge to laugh and squared my shoulders as I addressed my accusers.

"In the first place," I said, "if she's 'Mrs.' Thorpe, why is she pursuing Dr. Grinstead, who is, by the way, old enough to be my father? In the second place, the last time I checked, I believe the Constitution guarantees freedom of speech—even here. In the third place, you can put your spying skills to better use than watching me. I live a thoroughly pedestrian life. In the fourth place, I have far worse problems than concerning myself with what you and your tribe consider aggressive behavior. Now, if you'll excuse me, I have a class to teach."

I marched from the room. What had come over me? My whole life I'd bowed to the voices of authority, and now I was behaving like a raving lunatic. Poor Jonas, I thought, no wonder he's so guarded. If he's been dodging this bunch all these years, what a wretched life he must lead. Now I knew I'd been mistaken in at least one notion about Jonas Grinstead. His creases and starches were not evidence of a loving wife.

I was only a few steps down the hall when the office door swung open and another voice, almost whispering, called my name. I turned to find Mavis' and Trixie's silent friend tiptoeing after me. Her forehead wrinkled, her eyes darting, she urged my silence by holding her finger to pursed lips.

"Miss Quinn," she said in a low voice, as if warning a murderer was lurking around the next corner, "please excuse my friends. They tend to be a little … territorial."

"Territorial—that puts a nice spin on it."

"May I walk with you?" She looked over her shoulder.

Her gentle nature calmed me. "Yes, of course. I behaved badly. I shouldn't have—"

She shook her head. "You're not entirely to blame. For all their flaws, Trixie and Mavis are longtime friends, and I don't want you to get the wrong idea about them."

"And you are …"

"Elinor Parfrey. Librarian."

I wondered why such a mild-mannered person surrounded herself with spiteful friends.

"You mustn't think ill of Trixie," she said.

"As in Potter."

She smiled. "Yes, not 'as in cereal.' I did enjoy that. At any rate, I've long since given up trying to reason with those two. They should've retired years ago, but teaching is all they know."

"That and Dr. Grinstead."

She nodded. "Trixie went through a nasty divorce last year, and Jonas is the only eligible man in her age bracket. She fixated on him as her best option."

"Is he aware of her interest?" I asked.

"I couldn't say. He's always behaved as the sole resident of his own world."

We arrived at my classroom. "Why does Trixie keep waiting?" I asked.

"Dreams die hard. Anyway, I'm sorry you received such a poor welcome."

As Elinor and I stood at my door, I noticed a man in a wrinkled blue suit staring at us from the end of the hall. I thought at first he might be another teacher, waiting to talk to Elinor, but when she walked past him on her way to the library, he only nodded. I realized he was staring at *me*. I shut the door and began my class. All during my lecture I half-expected him to interrupt. I couldn't shake the persistent feeling of dread that he'd be waiting for me when the hour was over.

There was no sign of him when I left the room or for the rest of the day. But I still ended my last class five minutes early so I could pack my books and lose myself in the horde of retreating students. Keys in hand, I hurried to my car, telling myself I was being ridiculous, but I was glad to see my car's white vinyl top come into view and rushed over to put the key in the door.

Someone stepped beside me.

"Excuse me."

Terrified, I turned to face the mysterious man.

"May I help you?" I looked at him and pretended confidence.

"Name's Brooker. I'd like to ask you a few questions."

I stepped back and prepared to run. "May I see some identification?"

"Sure." He held out a business card.

I took it. "What's this about?"

"That."

With his left thumb he pointed over his shoulder at Jonas Grinstead's truck.

Chapter 5

A Crippled Rider

I read Mr. Brooker's card aloud: "Brooker's Blades: We Sharpen and Repair Chainsaws."

Brooker grabbed the card from my hand.

"Sorry. That's my brother, Castor. I try to help him when I can, so I carry his card, too." He retrieved his own card from the inside pocket of his soiled suit coat and held it out.

I suspended the wrinkled card by the corner. "Wilkie Brooker Investigations," I said.

"So?" he said. "What about the guy who owns that truck?"

I returned his card. "I only started working here yesterday," I said. "I hardly know him."

"Don't play games with me," he said. "I saw you talking to him this morning."

"Even if you did, I still wouldn't discuss his business with you—not without asking him."

Brooker stood his ground. "Grinstead is part-owner of some property. The other owner died. The family wants to find out if your boy will sell his share. That's all."

"My boy?"

"Don't get bent out of shape. It's only an expression. Will you ask Grinstead to call me?" He held out his card on his open palm.

Once again, I lifted the card by the corner, then tossed it onto the floorboard of my car.

"All right," I said. "Now, if you're not out of here in five minutes, I'll call the police."

"You watch too many movies," he said.

No prisoner who'd had his life sentence commuted could have been as relieved as I was to drive away from Brighton Park that afternoon. None of my college courses had groomed me for what I'd faced on the job. No one had mentioned the lists of unwritten rules you must figure out as you go along. No one had warned me about the variety of soap opera plots which play out every day in offices, hallways, and classrooms. In short, I was woefully unprepared for daily life in this twilight zone of a community college.

What had I gotten myself into? And how could I get out of it?

As I was unlocking my apartment door, the phone rang. Brooker, I thought. I picked up the receiver. "Yes?"

"Agnes?" my mother said. "What's wrong? You don't sound like yourself."

I put down the groceries I'd brought in. "Sorry. I thought it might be someone else."

"Someone you're mad at?"

"Yeah, a private investigator stopped me as I was leaving school today to ask me about another teacher."

I knew it was a mistake as soon as I'd said the words. In my mother's mind, serial killers lurked around every corner. She'd be horrified a strange man had approached me.

"Stu! Stu!" she called. "Come to the phone."

"Please don't tell—" I said.

"What is it?" my father asked her.

"Some stranger bothered Agnes after school. Here—talk to her."

"Agnes?" he said. "Do I need to come up there?"

"No, Dad. It's nothing." I filled Saturn's empty bowl.

"Tell me what happened."

"A man stopped me after school. He asked me about another teacher, who owns some property or something. I didn't talk to him."

"Good. You should report him to the administration in the morning."

"Okay, Dad." I intended to tell no one except Jonas.

"So, how were the first two days?"

"I didn't get off to a good start. I'm not sure this is the right place for me."

"You can't judge a place after two days," he said. "If I'd quit every job I didn't like, you and your brother wouldn't have had a roof over your heads."

"I know." I opened a can of tomato soup. "I'm simply saying I don't feel like I belong here. Haven't you ever had a bad feeling about a place?"

"Nope. And even if I did, I'd keep it to myself. You can't live your life on feelings. Give yourself some time. You'll start to fit in."

Fit in? With Trixie and Mavis? I pictured myself decades from now, scolding some wide-eyed teacher as I glared over my bifocals. *Young woman, we have a certain way of doing things around here.* Nothing—not Ferguson Trask, not Rufus Plumley, not Wilkie Brooker—ever paralyzed me to the core like that vision.

There had to be other perfectly ordinary teachers I hadn't met yet. Why hadn't I run into one of *them* on the first day of school?

Why had I parked in Jonas Grinstead's place?

If I hadn't parked there, I wouldn't have bought him a bagel.

If I hadn't bought the bagel, Trixie Thorpe wouldn't have seen me talking to him. I might have become her protégé rather than a rival.

If I hadn't bought the bagel, Wilkie Brooker wouldn't be stalking me.

For the third night in a row, I lay awake till almost dawn. When at three forty-five I decided I'd stared enough at the ceiling, I sat up and leaned against the pillows. I might as well get dressed and go to the Drifters' Rest on the way to school, I thought. Muriel had told me what to do about Jonas. It stood to reason she could advise me about Brooker. If I arrived when she opened, I'd have a few minutes with her before the other customers started showing up.

The next thing I remember was blinking at the clock after dawn. I threw on some clothes, sped to the Drifters' Rest, and rushed into the shop. Behind the counter Muriel was polishing coffee mugs with a clean white cloth. I climbed up on a stool.

"Don't tell me you were awake again last night," she said. "You've got to relax."

I accepted the bagel she slid toward me.

"It's not the teachers I'm worried about now," I said. "I'm being followed."

She poured steaming coffee into a white ceramic mug.

"Followed? That's not likely, is it?"

"It's because of Jonas."

"Morning, Jim," she called to a tall young man in sweatpants and a t-shirt. "Have a nice run? No cherry turnovers today—only apple." She turned back to me. "Jonas again? What now? Did you tussle with some of his lady friends?"

"Yeah. Trixie Thorpe. But that's not why I'm here."

"Oh, no wonder you're rattled. Beatrice Thorpe is a tiger."

I stirred half-and-half into my coffee. "Trix—Beatrix—like the author."

Muriel exploded with laughter. "Yeah, I know. She gave me the same lecture when I first met her. Don't worry about her. Morning, Colonel," she called to a square-shouldered man with a cane.

Curious at Muriel's greeting, I turned to look. Middle-aged, with ramrod posture and a stiff crew cut, the colonel appeared rugged and fit except for a pronounced limp. Over his left eye a jagged scar coursed down his cheek and looped under his jaw. On his right eye was a black patch. He saluted.

"Colonel?" I asked.

She lowered her voice. "Retired military." She took a cup from the shelf behind her. "His rank means a lot to him. He was in bad shape when he came back from Korea. Wife left him—took the kids. His worst scars are on the inside. How many eggs today, Colonel?" she called.

He held up two fingers as he walked toward the table in the farthest corner of the room. He placed the handle of his cane over the back of the chair beside him and eased himself into a seat. He ducked his head, glanced from side to side, and then leaned back, folded his hands in his lap, and looked over at his hostess.

Muriel pushed open the swinging door that led to the kitchen and called to the cook. "Annabelle, two eggs over easy for the colonel, and don't burn the toast."

She winked and nodded at the colonel. He removed the napkin wrapped around his silverware and placed the knife and spoon on his right and the fork on his left, leaving room for the expected plate. Then he shoved the glass bud vase holding three white daisies to the corner of the table and slid the salt and pepper shakers to the center.

Muriel whispered. "She's never once burned the toast, but if I don't say that before I bring his coffee to the table, he'll ask me to tell her. It saves a step."

Muriel delivered the colonel's coffee, made one more circuit of the room, and returned to the counter. "Now, where were we?"

"You were going to tell me what to do about Brooker."

"Who?"

"Brooker. The private investigator asking about Jonas."

"That doesn't sound good."

I raised my voice. "I know. That's what I've been trying to tell you."

My few hours of sleep had done nothing to improve my state of mind.

From the corner of my eye, I saw the colonel push back from the table and angle his chair in our direction.

Muriel wiped the counter. "Okay, start from the beginning. Who's Brooker?"

"Yesterday afternoon," I said, "I was standing in the hallway talking to Elinor when—"

"Wait a minute, dear." She leaned her head to one side so she could see around me. "Good morning, Mrs. Hart. Table's all set up. Other ladies aren't here yet. I'll bring your tea."

She turned back to me. "Now, you were asking about Trixie, and I told you not to worry."

"No, I wasn't. We were past that. I was asking about Brooker."

"The private eye," she said.

"Yes, I saw him when I was standing in the hallway and then he followed me to—"

She held up her hand. "Wait a second. Morning, Joe." She greeted the mailman, who had entered with his Drifters' Rest thermal mug in hand. "Making another pot of dark roast. Sorry you'll have to wait. Have a donut on the house."

I looked at my watch as Muriel refilled my cup.

"Sorry, where were we?" she asked.

"After school yesterday, Brooker followed me to my car and—"

A teacher I recognized from school slid onto the stool beside me and bumped my elbow, sloshing coffee on the counter. He grabbed Muriel's arm.

"Muriel, please, *please* tell me you found a folder. If it's not here, I—"

The colonel reached for his cane.

Muriel pulled a folder from beneath the counter and handed it to the frantic professor. "Waffles this morning, or want to try the special?"

"Just coffee. Thanks, Muriel. You're a lifesaver." He hurried to a table.

The colonel approached the counter. "Muriel, was that man bothering you?"

"No, not at all. He left something here last night and was worried he'd lost it."

He indicated me with his thumb. "And her? It seems she's taking a lot of your time."

The heat rose in my face as I whirled to face him. "Excuse me?"

Muriel laid her hand on mine. "It's all right, Agnes. Everything's fine, Colonel. She needs some information, and I'm too busy to help at the moment."

He turned to me. "Come earlier, before Muriel's so busy."

"I tried to come earlier," I said.

He ignored me and peered at Muriel. "If you need anything, you know where I am."

"Yes, I do," Muriel said. "You'd better sit down. Your order's almost ready."

"He acts like he owns the place," I said after he returned to his chair.

"It's not that," Muriel said. "I was there when he needed a friend, and he feels he owes me. Now, where were we? Trixie Thorpe. Take my word for it. She has no chance with Jonas. There will never be but one woman for him."

"I didn't come here to talk about Trixie. I wanted to ask—wait … what woman?"

"That's too long a story to tell right now. You should have come earlier—"

"I know … before you got busy. I tried, but I haven't slept in several days and I—"

"Excuse me, Agnes." She looked past me again. "I'll take this tray to Mrs. Hart and then I can give you five minutes. But the colonel's right. If you need to talk, you'll have to come back early tomorrow or late this afternoon." She laid four spoons on the serving tray and nodded toward the elderly Mrs. Hart. "She and her friends play bridge here every Wednesday. They bring a tablecloth with them. Isn't that sweet?"

I had no choice but to wait. After all the trouble I'd gone to, I wasn't going away empty-handed. I sneaked another look at the colonel and tried to imagine him young and happy, with a family around him. I studied the professor poring over the contents of the indispensable folder. I saw the mailman tighten the cap on his mug and shoulder his bag of letters. I tried to see in them what Muriel saw—people who needed more from her than simply a cup of coffee and a muffin.

She stepped back behind the counter. "You're smiling," she said.

"I feel safe here."

"Precisely the atmosphere I try to create. Now, about this Brooker fellow?"

I looked at my watch. "I have to go. I'll come back tomorrow."

I laid five dollars on the counter and started for the door.

Muriel stepped from behind the counter and called to me. "Could you come back later this afternoon?"

My hand on the doorknob, I shook my head and gave a hasty wave in reply.

A husky voice shouted from across the room, "The lady asked you a question!"

An object whooshed past my head. I dodged it, but stumbled over an umbrella stand and slammed head first into the door. The last thing I remember was a scream from Mrs. Hart's bridge table and Muriel shouting, "Colonel. Sit down."

I woke up in a pale-green room. Afternoon sunlight filtered through white venetian blinds. On a gray metal table next to my bed, a yellow plastic pitcher, water drops dripping down its sides, sat next to a black phone and a box of tissues. A nurse in a stiff white cap and starched white dress squeezed my wrist in her hand.

"You hit your head pretty hard," she said. "You were unconscious long enough that the doctor wants to keep you overnight for observation."

I grasped very little of what she said, but had enough presence of mind to realize I was seeing her out of only one eye. Alarmed, I reached up to find the left side of my face enclosed in a thick bandage.

I gasped. "My eye."

"Your eye was not hurt. We made sure. Now get some rest."

Thanks to painkillers and exhaustion, I sank into a deep, satisfying nap. A nurse, who introduced herself as Dolley, woke me. Without asking, she raised the head of my bed.

"Time for dinner."

"I can't eat. I'm too dizzy. I'm going to throw up."

"That's because you've had a lot of medication and no food. Come on now. Sit up."

She gave me no choice. She put one arm behind my shoulders, the other under my elbow, and tugged till I yielded.

The room spun out of control. I gripped the sheets. "I'm going to fall off the bed."

"No, you're not. Close your eyes for a minute. You'll adjust."

"I only have one eye to close."

She patted my shoulder. "Then close that one and relax. Here's your dinner."

An orderly placed a tray of food in front of me and turned to Dolley. "Should I leave a tray for the new patient? Judy's bringing her down the hall now."

"No, she won't be able to eat for a while."

Dolley held open the door as the orderly left. Another appeared, backing into the room, guiding a heavy gurney with painstaking slowness. Halfway through the door, the patient wailed.

"Stop. Stop. My leg. Don't hit my leg."

A firm voice spoke from the hallway. "It's all right, Mrs. Gilbey. Relax. There's plenty of room on both sides. You won't hit your leg."

The orderly cleared the door and turned left toward the empty bed. Mrs. Gilbey's long silver hair draped across the pillow and spilled over her sturdy shoulders. She held a swollen hand to the side of her bruised face.

"Can somebody please get the sawdust out of my eye?"

The nurse entered. "There's no sawdust in your eye. It only feels that way. Can you give us some help, Dolley?"

The retinue halted in front of me as the nurse named Judy prepared Mrs. Gilbey's bed. I pretended to examine the green beans on my tray while I peeked at my roommate. On top of her ample stomach rested a yellow cowboy hat. *Geneva* was stamped in bold ornate letters on a broad brown leather band at the base of the brim.

When all was ready, the orderlies steered Mrs. Gilbey alongside her bed.

Judy addressed her squadron. "All right—on three. One. Two. Three."

The assistants heaved. The gurney squeaked. The patient groaned. We were all relieved when Geneva Gilbey came to rest on the creaking bed.

"My leg."

Out of breath, Dolley patted a perspiring orderly on the back as they left the room.

Judy followed and called over her shoulder, "All right, Mrs. Gilbey, rest easy. I'll get you something for the pain."

I was left alone with Mrs. Gilbey. While I ate chocolate pudding, she began to sing.

"As I walked out in the streets of Laredo—"

Her voice was a rich, lilting melancholy alto so sweet it almost brought me to tears.

"Come sit down beside me and hear my sad story—"

Judy returned. "Okay, here you go." She filled a glass with water and lifted her patient's head. "Two of these and you'll be feeling better in no time."

Mrs. Gilbey lay back again.

The nurse reached for the cowboy hat, saying, "Why don't you let me hang this up for you?"

Mrs. Gilbey released her grip on the hat and brushed tears from her face. "Is my nephew still out there?" she asked.

"No. He said he'd see you in the morning."

"I wanted to ask him about Buttercup."

"Buttercup?"

"My horse. She didn't mean to throw me. She must have stumbled over something. Can you find out if she's all right? I won't be able to sleep till I know."

Judy drew the curtain between our beds.

"Don't worry about that, dear. You'll be asleep in no time. Take my word for it."

Judy stopped by my bed to pick up the dinner tray. She pointed in the direction of Geneva's bed, put her hands together, and laid her face on them to pantomime sleeping. Then she turned out the overhead light and closed the door.

Geneva sang: "Go fetch me some water—a cool cup of water."

I lay back on the flimsy pillow and reflected on my predicament. I wasn't supposed to be in the hospital. One week ago today, I had been taking notes as administrators lectured me on policies and procedures. I had smiled and nodded as they lauded the nobility of my vocation. I had been poised on the precipice of a successful career. But instead of leaping into the white rapids of higher education, I had nose-dived into a bucket of water and ended up in a hospital room with a woman singing cowboy songs.

Mrs. Gilbey's voice softened. Maybe the nurse was right—she'd soon be asleep, and I could get some rest, too. It had been days since I'd slept more than a few hours at a time. But now I was in a hospital, a place of healing, a place to improve and get well. Medical professionals were right outside my door. Best of all, security guards were stationed in the parking lot and lobby. I was safe at last from Wilkie Brooker and the colonel.

"For I'm a young cowboy and I know I've done wrong."

I closed my eye and imagined Geneva and me sitting around a campfire with the other cowpokes, eating beans from a cast-iron kettle and drinking coffee from a dented tin pot.

"You look mighty rough there, little lady," Slim the cook would say.

"I ain't no lady," I'd reply. "I'll have you know I survived a cattle stampede today."

I hadn't been asleep long before Geneva started snoring. Once I was awake, there was no ignoring her. She made enough racket to loosen the light bulbs from their sockets. I thought of calling the nurse, but what would I say? The poor woman wasn't keeping me awake on purpose. I couldn't ask to be moved. I didn't know how I was going to pay for all this in the first place, much less upgrade to a private room.

Maybe I could ask them to knock me out, too. The pills had worked wonders for Geneva. I was struggling up on one elbow to reach the call button, when the door opened.

"I was about to call you," I said. "I was wondering if—"

Even in the dim light and with only one good eye, I could tell it wasn't the nurse.

The colonel held a finger to his lips, urging me to be quiet. He didn't need to bother. I was speechless.

He closed the door. "Don't be afraid. I'm not going to hurt you."

I eased my hand toward the bedside table to reach for anything I might throw at him. "How did you get in here?" I asked.

"A buddy of mine works security—he let me in. I told him I had to talk to you."

"I have nothing to say." I was terrified I'd upset him again.

He walked toward my bed as he spoke. "I wanted to tell you I'm sorry and—"

I closed my fingers around the handle of the water pitcher. It wasn't very heavy, but maybe I could surprise him.

"You're sorry. Okay."

"No, you don't understand. The police will be here tomorrow. I'm sure of it. The last time this happened, they said they'd give me one more chance and—"

I lifted the pitcher.

"—they'd send me back to the VA hospital. I can't go there. I have to stay here. If my wife comes back, she won't know where to find me."

He was standing at the foot of my bed.

"Oh. My leg. My leg."

Geneva Gilbey was awake. The colonel bolted for the door.

Dolley was in my room in an instant. She made sure I wasn't hurt and then apologized again and again. "I don't know how he managed to get in here."

"A buddy of his works security," I said.

Dolley charged out the door. I had a feeling the colonel's accomplice would be out of a job by the end of the day.

Geneva groaned. "Nurse … nurse."

I sat up. "She's gone. Want me to call her for you?"

"Yes, please. My leg hurts."

I pressed the call button. A nurse returned with Geneva's pills.

After the light was out and the door closed, I once again lay awake with little hope I'd sleep the rest of the night.

Geneva whispered. "Excuse me."

"Yes."

"I wondered if you were still awake."

"Yes. Is there something you need?"

She hesitated. "I was hoping we could pull back this curtain between us. I don't want to bother you, but I'd feel less alone—if you wouldn't mind."

"Not at all."

Since Geneva had spared me another incident with the colonel, I felt I owed her.

I dangled my legs off the bed, slid my feet to the floor, and leaned against the side till the dizziness passed. Then I shuffled over to the chair by Geneva's bed and sat down.

She reached out her swollen hand and laid it in mine. The palm of her hand was as rough as my father's.

"I'm Geneva Gilbey."

"Agnes Quinn."

"Why are you in here?" she asked.

"I made someone mad."

She winced with pain. "I can't imagine that. You seem like such a nice person."

"I was in the wrong place at the wrong time. You broke your leg in a riding accident?"

"Afraid so. I still can't believe I did it. I used to fall all the time, but lately the saddle felt more natural to me than sitting in a chair."

"When did you learn to ride?"

"Four years ago."

She must be getting drowsy, I thought. She meant forty.

"When?" I asked.

"Four years ago."

"But you must have been—"

"Fifty-six."

"You took up horseback riding at fifty-six? Why?"

Geneva told me her story. She had grown up in Chicago, a city kid, the third child of six. Her parents supported their brood by running a neighborhood store.

"We had all we needed," she said, "but there was never anything to spare. I always wanted a pony. Papa said to get a good education and a job, and I could buy my own. I never forgot that. I met my husband in college. After we graduated and got married, I taught high school history, and he became an accountant. We didn't work as hard as my parents had to, but we poured all our money into our family, just like they did. After our last child got married, I wanted to retire and buy some land."

"My mother wants to travel after my father retires," I said.

"So did my husband. After all those years behind a desk, he was ready for some adventure and a change of scenery. He didn't want to buy land, let alone a horse."

"You'd asked him before?"

"Many times. He insisted we go on cruises instead. But when he died, I took his life insurance money and bought Buttercup and a big red stable for her to live in."

She laughed hard enough to jostle her bed. The pain shot through her leg again.

"Ow. I just hope she's okay."

"I'm sure she is, if she's as tough as her owner." I pointed to the clock. "It's almost morning. You'll be able to call and find out."

"Thank you, Agnes. I think I'll get a little sleep now."

She closed her eyes. I went back to bed.

I was about to doze off when she said, "I guess I must seem pretty silly."

"Actually, I was thinking how much I admire you. Not everyone can keep believing in their dream when no one takes them seriously."

We both slept.

When I woke up hungry and sore, I looked over at Geneva's bed. She was gone.

Dolley bustled in.

"You're awake," she said. "How do you feel?"

"I've felt better," I said.

She handed me an envelope from her pocket. "Muriel asked me to give you this."

"Are you friends?" I asked

"No, she's my sister." She raised the bed and fluffed my pillows. "They'll be bringing your breakfast soon."

"Where's Geneva?"

"She went downstairs for X-rays."

"Will she be okay?"

Dolley stopped at the door. "You know I can't discuss another patient with you."

"Can you tell me if her horse is okay?"

She laughed. "If you're still here when her nephew visits, you can ask him."

Alone, I opened the envelope and unfolded the letter. A faded photograph of a husband, wife, and two children was inside. I stared at the picture a long time. Though the people were strangers to me, I couldn't help smiling when I looked at them. Whether the photographer had said something to make them laugh or they were simply happy to be together, their joy was infectious. They were seated on the steps of the Drifters' Rest. The father, holding a baby girl, sat between his wife and son.

The letter explained.

Dear Agnes,

I'm so sorry about your accident. Don't worry about your medical bills. I'll take care of everything.

I won't ask you to excuse the colonel, though in many ways he is not responsible for his actions. But before you talk to the police, take a close look at this photo. If you knew the man Ryder once was and tried to understand how much he's lost, perhaps you could find it in your heart to forgive him.

I'll do all I can to find out about this Brooker fellow, and I'll let Jonas know as well.

Muriel

I ate my oatmeal and hummed Geneva's song.

Chapter 6

A Meeting of Minds

Tote bag in hand and tears in her eyes, my mother surged into my hospital room as I was finishing breakfast.

"Oh, Agnes, it was that man, wasn't it, the strange man who was following you? He did this, didn't he? Have they found him yet? Have you pressed charges?"

"No, Mom. It wasn't him. It was someone else."

"Your father is so upset. He's coming up after work on Friday."

She lifted the lid on the water pitcher.

A doctor opened the door.

"Miss Quinn, is it? I'm Dr. Monroe." He flipped through my chart. "On a scale of one to ten, how much pain are you experiencing?"

"About a seven. I hurt everywhere, but I can't feel my eye. It's still under there, isn't it?"

"Yes, your eye is fine. You were very fortunate. If you'd fallen a few inches the other way, you'd be wearing a patch."

"I'm Mrs. Quinn. Is my daughter going to be all right?"

"Yes. She has a mild concussion, but the only treatment for that is rest." He pulled on latex gloves and undid the bandage. "The laceration required eight stitches, but you have no broken bones. Amazing—after such a fall."

"How long do I need to stay?" I asked.

"After the nurse applies a new bandage, you'll be free to go. I'll send you home with antibiotics and something for pain. The nurse will give you instructions for cleaning the wound. Call my office this afternoon to make an appointment to have the stitches removed."

My mother spoke up. "Will she have a scar?"

"Probably. It was a very irregular cut." He peered at my eye for a final time. "You're going to have a black eye for a while. I can refer you to a plastic surgeon to get rid of the scar."

When he left, my mother collapsed into the chair and sank her head into her hands.

"What's wrong, Mom? Are you all right?"

She sobbed. "I'm so relieved. When the police called and said you'd had an accident and were unconscious, we were so worried."

"How did you get here?"

"I rode the bus and then took a taxi at the station."

"You must be exhausted. Go have some breakfast. I'll get dressed, and we'll go home."

She brightened. "I'll get to see Saturn again. I hadn't thought of that."

"Saturn," I said. "I forgot all about him. He must wonder what happened to me."

"I'm sure he's all right. Cats are very resourceful. I'll get some coffee and be right back."

I waited till she closed the door before I sat up. My head was still cloudy, but I was determined to get back to my cat, now that I'd had enough presence of mind to think of him. At the moment I stood, Dolley strode into the room.

"Hold on a minute. You can't try that without help. Besides, I have to re-bandage that eye. Last thing I need to do before I go home."

She put her hand under my elbow and eased me onto the bed.

"I need to go home," I said. "I forgot about my cat. He must be starving by now."

"You have to wait for the police anyway. They came last night, but you weren't up to talking to them."

"Police? What for?"

"This isn't the first time Mr. Ellershaw has scared the daylights out of somebody. Muriel says he can't be blamed for his actions, but quite frankly, I wish they'd put him away."

"Mr. Who?" I winced as she pressed on the adhesive tape.

"Ryder Ellershaw. The man she calls Colonel. His wife's been gone for years—divorced him and remarried. Muriel's not helping him by buying into his delusions."

"I wish I knew what I did to upset him," I said.

"Muriel could explain. She knows what sets him off." She gave the bandage a final look. "Now don't get that wet for twenty-four hours. I'll bring the instructions for cleaning your wound, along with your discharge papers."

When Dolley opened the door, a stocky man in a dark-brown suit stood aside to let her leave. "Agnes Quinn?" he asked. "Lieutenant Watson. Are you up for a few questions?"

He took notes as I described the events of the previous morning.

"So Mr. Ellershaw didn't threaten or warn you. The object he threw did not hit you, but when you dodged it, you tripped and fell, and that's what caused your injury."

"That's correct."

"This is good news for the assailant, but you won't have your day in court."

"I don't want a day in court. He may be a basket case, but he's Muriel's friend. I don't care about seeing him in jail."

By the time my mother came back, I was ready to go. I hated to leave without saying goodbye to Geneva or knowing how she was, but I had no choice. Armed with two prescriptions, I yielded to Dolley's order to sit in the wheelchair. As she pushed me toward the exit she reached in her pocket and held a card over my shoulder.

"If you need anything, call me at this number. I may not be able to get back to you right away, but I will return your call."

I blinked my good eye at her card.

"Does this say 'Dolley Madison, R.N.'?" I asked.

"Yes, that's my name. The 'Dolley' is for my great-grandmother. I married into the 'Madison.' I did give that some thought before I agreed. Here's your ride."

A rusty white pickup pulled next to the curb. Jonas Grinstead got out of the truck and approached my mother.

"Mrs. Quinn, it's a pleasure to meet you. My name is Jonas Grinstead. I teach with your daughter. Morning, Dolley."

"Jonas," Dolley said, "why in the world are you in that truck? I thought Muriel was going to loan you her van."

"She offered, but I refused." He took my hand to help me from the wheelchair. "There is no smoother riding vehicle in this town. Dual air shocks."

I climbed in to sit on the seat beside him. He was right—no limousine could've provided a smoother ride.

When we reached my apartment, Jonas told my mother to wait so he could open her door. She giggled like a teenager.

"Do you have your key, Agnes?" Mom asked.

"It's in my purse." I leaned forward to reach it.

"No need," Jonas said.

He nodded toward my front door. There stood Muriel with Saturn in her arms.

She waved. "Welcome home."

As my mother hurried toward Saturn, Jonas helped me out of the truck.

"There you go," he said. "Are you okay?"

"I think so—a little rough around the edges."

He lowered his voice. "I want to thank you, Agnes, for your act of kindness."

"What do you mean?"

"Muriel told me about Brooker and how you refused to talk to him. If he'd asked anyone else, I'm sure they'd have been happy to provide all the details of my life."

"Does anyone know the details of your life?" I asked.

"They think they do." He winked at me. This was the real Jonas Grinstead—not the irritable man I'd mistaken for a janitor, not the elusive bachelor Trixie was trying to snag, and not the mysterious real estate partner Brooker was trying to locate.

We walked toward the front door.

"Muriel said you came to the shop to ask her advice and that's when Ryder got out of hand. If you hadn't been there on my account, this never would've happened," he said.

"Don't worry about it. I have a feeling this is going to end up being one of the best things that ever happened to me."

Muriel welcomed us. My apartment was spotless. The table, which I'd never actually set with plates and serving dishes, was adorned from end to end with steaming bowls and luscious colors. Jonas guided me toward a chair. Muriel swept her hand through the air like a magician.

"We have Swiss steak, mashed potatoes, gravy, a lovely squash casserole, homemade rolls, and, in honor of the occasion, cherry pie for dessert."

Jonas sat across the table from my mother. "How does cherry pie honor the occasion?"

"Don't be silly. Cherry pie is as American as George Washington and always suitable."

"I think that's 'as American as apple pie,'" my mother said.

"Either way, it's better than the twenty-four cans of soup in the pantry."

I reached for the potatoes. "There was a two-for-one sale. How did you pull this off, Muriel? I mean, how did you get in?"

"Your landlord is a long-time customer, so there was no problem getting a key."

"You shouldn't have gone to all this trouble," I said.

"It's the least I could do after I nearly got you killed," Muriel said.

"You didn't almost get me killed. It was my own fault. I never should have bothered you when I knew you were busy."

"Thank you for not making a scene with Lieutenant Watson," Muriel said. "The police have lost their patience with Ryder. They'd love to have an excuse to commit him."

I started to say "I know," but decided to wait till my mother went home before I mentioned Ryder's midnight visit.

My mother spooned gravy over her potatoes. "I think he *should* be committed," she said. "People who don't know how to behave in polite society don't need to be running loose. You'll forgive me for saying so."

"It was all a misunderstanding," Muriel said. "More squash, Jonas? Ryder thought Agnes was insulting me when she left like that—"

"Like what?" I said. "All I did was walk out the door."

"Unfortunately, that's how his wife said goodbye—turned her back on him and waved over her shoulder while he was begging her to stay."

"You need to stop humoring him," Jonas said.

"I know. But I've listened to you plenty of times when you poured out your heart—"

Jonas glared at Muriel as if she were revealing state secrets. Quick and effective, the silent exchange was lost on my mother, but not on me.

Muriel changed course. "Coffee, anyone?"

As I sat there savoring delectable food and pleasant company, I realized I'd been living the self-imposed life of a hermit for too long. I looked around at my apartment—bare walls, simple furnishings, half-empty bookshelves. If Ryder Ellershaw had hit his intended target or if I'd fallen through the window, my life would have been over. What would I have to show for it? A couple of diplomas and a stack of ungraded vocabulary quizzes.

"Agnes. Agnes," my mother said.

"What? Sorry—I was someplace else."

"Muriel asked if we'd like to sleep at her house tonight, since she has plenty of rooms and you have only one bed."

"Thanks, but I want to stay here," I said. "I don't want to leave Saturn."

"I'm not going to leave you here alone," my mother said. "I'll be fine on the couch."

Muriel refilled Jonas' coffee cup. "All right. I'll finish cleaning up and then we'll leave you two to catch up on family news."

"What about you, Jonas?" my mother said. "Don't you need to get back to school?"

"I took the day off," he said. He stood and stepped behind my chair. "Come along now, Agnes. You need to rest. Sofa okay?"

"Wait a minute," Muriel said. "She needs to take her pills."

"I'll get them," my mother said.

An insistent pounding on my front door startled us. My mother moved toward the door. She'd barely opened it when I heard a voice I thought I recognized.

"Is this the residence of Agnes Quinn?"

"Yes," my mother said.

"I need to speak to her," the visitor said.

Jonas walked to my mother and pulled the door open. "We've just brought her home from the hospital. She's not up to visitors. May I ask your name and give her a message?"

"Yes, you can. Tell her Zane Plumley is here and wants to know why she ruined my brother's life."

Chapter 7

A Fork in the Road

I pictured Zane Plumley bursting into song. As his hand pressed against the half-open door, the afternoon sun, like a spotlight, framed his silhouette. Scowling, he resembled a lead tenor in opera, preparing to sing an aria which would modulate our happy scene into a minor key. Jonas, Muriel, Mother, and I, like a well-rehearsed quartet, mingled our voices in a libretto to rival *The Magic Flute*.

"What have you done?" my mother asked.

"Nothing," I said. "It wasn't my fault."

"Who is your brother?" she asked Zane.

"Stay where you are," Jonas said, his foot wedged at the base of the door.

"Xander," Zane said. "We have a sister, too."

"Is your sister with you?" Mother asked.

"No, she's home planning her wedding."

Muriel came from the kitchen. "Do you know this man?"

"I've heard of him," I said, "and seen his picture, but never met him till today."

She dried her hands with a towel. "Then how can he say you've hurt his brother?"

"It wasn't my fault," I said.

"He's gone to Australia because of her."

Zane edged in; Jonas stayed by the door.

"Let him in," I said. "It's Xander's brother. They look exactly alike."

"*Everyone* has a twin," my mother said. "I read it somewhere."

"Not twins—triplets—their sister's Yolanda. Let him in. He's tired. Xander looked just like that when he stayed up all night."

My mother turned pale. "And when were you up all night with Andrew?"

"Not Andrew—Xander. I wasn't up all night with him. We met for lunch every day. Let him in, so we can get this settled."

Jonas stepped aside and Zane slipped in.

Dizzy again, I leaned back against the pillows. Seeing "Xander" when it wasn't Xander was more than I could handle. I closed my eye.

Jonas brought a chair from the kitchen. "Would you like to sit down?"

"Thank you," Zane said. "I've been on the road since yesterday."

My mother sat on the sofa next to me. "All right, Agnes, who is Xander?" she asked.

"A friend of mine in college," I said.

Zane jumped up, saying, "He was in love with her, and she broke his heart. Now he's in the Australian outback, most likely with a ring in his nose and having babies with an aboriginal wife."

"I don't think they do that in Australia," my mother said. "Put rings in their noses, I mean, not 'have children,' because of course anyone anywhere can have children."

I opened my eye but found nothing changed. There sat Zane glaring at me, my mother smiling at him, Jonas with one eyebrow raised, and Muriel with a dish towel over her shoulder.

"Would you like something to eat?" Muriel asked Zane. "We have leftovers."

"I … haven't eaten since breakfast," he said.

I called down silent blessings on Muriel, who always knew what to do. Without a single blow, she'd knocked him off balance.

Mother took her cue from Muriel.

"We've gotten off to a bad start, Mr.—what was your name again?"

"Plumley," he said.

"Plum-ley." She made a mental note. "We don't mean to be rude. We're still a little on edge about the violent crime committed against my daughter yesterday."

"It wasn't a violent crime," I said. "It was an accident."

Zane's voice softened. "What happened?"

"You had to be there," I said.

"She's right," my mother said. "I've heard the story twice and it still makes no sense."

"You look pretty rough," Zane said. "Do you have other injuries?"

"I didn't break anything except my pride … what little I have left."

"She has *eight* stitches," my mother said, "and an awful black eye."

"This does complicate matters," Zane said. He rubbed his forehead.

"Need some aspirin?" I asked. "We have plenty."

Despite his abrupt entrance, he was so like Xander I had to fight the compulsion to rush into his arms.

He nodded. "I have a terrible headache—drove too long, nothing to eat. I thought I'd feel better once I told you off, but now that I've seen you, I can't say what I planned."

"That's very thoughtful of you," my mother said.

"*Thoughtful* isn't the word I'd use," Jonas said. "Chances are he would've said precisely what he wanted if he'd found Agnes alone."

"I'm not that kind of man," Zane said.

"Then what *did* you hope to accomplish?" Jonas asked.

Zane took the plate Muriel gave him. "I'm not sure. My sister's getting married in a few months and wants Xander at her wedding. She thought Agnes might—"

"Coffee, anyone?" Muriel said.

"You can't reach him in Australia?" Jonas asked.

"No. For the last year he's only communicated with his roommate, who's kind enough to forward his messages to my mother."

"That doesn't sound like Xander," I said. "He talked about your family all the time."

"He's staying away because of my father," Zane said. "He's never tolerated failure from us, much less a scandal. I couldn't face him either, if I'd been through what Xander has."

Muriel laid a napkin on Zane's knee. "Have you thought of hiring a private investigator?"

"My mother wanted to," Zane said, "but my father said he wouldn't waste good money to have Xander chased all over the planet."

Muriel smiled. "Agnes knows one you could hire."

"Not funny," I said.

"But it would solve everyone's problem," Muriel said. "Brooker would be out of our hair, and who knows? He might find Zane's brother."

"Who's Brooker?" my mother asked.

"I'll tell you later," Muriel said and returned to the kitchen.

"But why would you think I could help you find Xander?" I asked.

"Because of the package we got in the mail," Zane said.

"From Xander?"

"No, his roommate—Rupert Hornby. He's graduating, so he had to clean everything out of their apartment."

"What was in the package?" I asked.

"Research notes, letters, photos, the police report, and Xander's journal. When my mother read what Xander wrote about you, she decided to look for you."

"What did he say?" I asked.

Zane glanced at my mother. "You'd probably rather read that for yourself."

"Do you have it with you?" I asked.

He nodded.

"But does he say it was Agnes who ruined his life?" my mother asked.

"He didn't say that in the letter he wrote to me," I said.

Zane leaned forward. "When was that?"

"Graduation—at the end of our sophomore year."

"That was years ago," Zane said.

"May of '73," I said, surprising all of us when tears spilled onto my cheeks. "And since then, not a day has gone by I haven't thought of Xander. I owe him so much. It was because of him I got serious about my education. I gave up writing my book and became a teacher. I took this job because ...." I couldn't go on.

Four startled faces stared at me.

Plate in hand, Zane stood. "I'm still hungry. May I have seconds?"

Muriel took Zane's plate. "Good idea. We have pie."

"I thought you did all those things to please your father," my mother said.

Only Jonas remained silent, his pale-blue eyes locked onto mine as if he'd always known.

Thus does pain recognize itself in the eyes of another.

Muriel rejoined us. "Betty," she said, "how about a tour of the Drifters' Rest? Annabelle will be making scones and fresh coffee. You could relax awhile."

"I appreciate the offer," my mother said, "but Agnes might need—"

"I'll be all right," I said. "I'm going to answer Zane's questions and then take a nap. Go with Muriel. I'll be fine."

"All right, but call if you need anything." Mom reached for her purse.

Jonas stood. "I'll be going, too. You can stay at my place tonight, Mr. Plumley, if you have no other plans."

"Thank you," Zane said. "I'll take you up on that."

"My number's by the phone," Jonas said. "Call when Mr. Plumley's ready to leave."

"Thank you, Jonas," I said, "for everything."

Muriel opened the door for my mother. Jonas followed them out.

Left alone, Zane and I stared at the floor till he said, "I never should've come here."

"I'm glad you did," I said. "You've provided a way for me to have contact with your mother. Does she know you've come?"

"No, Yolanda didn't want to get her hopes up."

"And your father?"

"He's at a conference in Seattle—won't be home till the end of next week. Do you want some help with that?"

I'd been rubbing my sore eye as Zane talked. The gush of tears had soaked the bandage and I was struggling to remove it.

"I wasn't supposed to get these stitches wet for twenty-four hours," I said. "You don't think I broke them loose, do you?"

"Want me to take a look at it? I have experience with treating injuries."

"Xander said you were majoring in modern languages. Did you switch to pre-med?"

"No," Zane said. "I spent a semester working at a refugee camp in Africa—got some medical training before I went. I'll wash my hands."

When he returned, he moved his chair next to the sofa and removed the bandage.

"There—is that better?" he asked.

"Thank you. It's not bleeding, is it?"

"No, but that's quite a shiner you've got. Look, Agnes, I need to apologize. I don't usually behave like an idiot when I meet someone."

"Don't give it a thought. I've always wanted to meet you. You comb your hair."

"What?"

"You comb your hair. I always wondered what Xander would look like if he'd only comb his hair, and now I know."

"I've always thought I was better looking than Xander," he said.

I did, too, but didn't say so.

"All right," I said. "I've been waiting a long time to find out about Xander. Start talking."

He sighed. "You know Xander left for Scotland three years ago."

"I do," I said. "I could never find out anything after that."

"The first year was fine, but at the start of the next year, that Putnam girl showed up."

"Jonquil? How did she manage? Her grades were nowhere near good enough."

"She wasn't a student," Zane said. "Her stepfather got her a job as a nanny. The father of the family she worked for was heading up an overseas branch for Bridger's business."

I shuddered. "Nanny? No one in his right mind would trust Jonquil with children."

"When Jameson Bridger recommended her, that was enough," Zane said. "How do you refuse a reference from your boss?"

"Good point."

"Every weekend Jonquil took a train to Glasgow to visit Xander. He was nice to her out of respect for her stepfather, but she started demanding his time. His work suffered."

"He never liked his schedule interrupted," I said.

"After two months of it, he finally had enough. He told her she couldn't visit every weekend. He stopped taking her calls. She still came. One weekend he left early on Friday—"

"Xander left the lab early? He must've really been rattled."

Zane nodded. "—and took a train to Edinburgh to avoid her. He came back Sunday night and found a note on his door. She said she'd be back and if he didn't see her, he'd be sorry."

"What happened?"

"The next Friday she stormed into his lab dragging a screaming child behind her."

"She went to his lab?"

"Pitched a fit—scraped equipment onto the floor and flew into Xander with all fours. Before he could calm her down, somebody called the police."

"Please tell me they arrested her," I said.

"The police took her and Xander and the little boy. When they got to the station, they discovered the parents had reported their son missing."

"They didn't know Jonquil had him with her?"

"No. When the police questioned her, she claimed it was Xander's idea, so they detained both of them till the parents arrived."

"Xander must have been mortified."

"The next day the story was in the paper. When Xander came to the lab that morning, his supervisor said the dean wanted to see him. Xander never showed up in the dean's office."

"So … if you know this whole story and Jonquil is obviously to blame, why do think I'm the one who ruined Xander's life?"

He slumped down in his chair. "I guess it's because we want to blame someone, and there's no way to get to Jonquil."

"To be honest," I said, "I've never stopped blaming *myself* for losing Xander."

"That's the idea we got from some of the things he wrote—that somehow his change of direction all began when he lost you."

"He didn't *lose* me. He *left* me."

Zane stood. "Maybe it'd be better if you read his notes for yourself. I'll be right back."

"Did you bring a bag, too," I asked, "or leave home in such a fury you forgot?"

He laughed. "Yes, I brought a toothbrush and a change of clothes."

"Then take a shower if you want. After that, you can take a nap on my bed while I read. When you wake up, we'll try to piece the story together."

He came in from his car and handed me the journal.

"I'd like to take a look at Xander's letter to you," he said, "if you still have it."

He was startled when I laughed. "Oh, I still have it. It's in the bottom drawer of the desk over there. Help yourself."

He opened the drawer and lifted out the letter. "Is this it?"

"That's it."

He looked down again. "And is this the book you mentioned?"

"Book?"

"When you were crying, you said you 'gave up writing your book.' May I read it?"

He held up the blue binder, the index card bearing the title still taped to the cover.

"Be my guest," I said.

When Zane left the room, I took a deep breath and opened the journal.

I was surprised Xander had begun his entries our freshman year. Though he'd penned poisonous insults about Trevor, he hardly mentioned Jonquil, whom I'd considered a pervasive presence in our lives. His opinions of me varied from affection to amusement to despair. He wrote at length about my obsession with Robinson Trask and cited newspaper accounts about the Trask family's crooked business practices. He wrote pages and pages about his classes, his grades, his projects, and his experiments. Then there was Xander's infamous meeting with Jameson Bridger, which he described as being "in the right place at the right time."

After ninety minutes I was worn out, not only because my one good eye was overworked, but also because Xander's praise for his own "sense of purpose" and his impatience with my "skewed sense of reality" annoyed me. Though his writing revealed he'd been as idealistic about his future as I'd been about mine, he'd rated his objectives "substantial" and mine "flimsy." But when I read, *maybe if I'd stayed at Stanton-Giles, Agnes and I could've straightened things out and started over. I could've helped her through college ...* I'd had enough of his sermonizing.

I pitched the book over my shoulder so hard it bounced off the wall and hit the floor.

The noise brought Zane into the living room. He had my manuscript in his hand.

"What happened?" he asked.

"I ... dropped Xander's journal on the floor."

He walked to the front of the sofa. "Where is it?"

"Back there," I said, pointing behind me.

He looked where I'd indicated. "Dropped it? Looks more like you threw it."

"I did throw it," I said. "Xander said he would've 'helped me' through college? I got through college just fine without him. Tell me—has he bothered to graduate yet?"

"Whoa, hold on," Zane said. He handed me my manuscript and walked across the room to retrieve the battered volume. "You should've kept reading."

"I can't right now. My eye hurts."

"Allow me." He flipped through the pages and read: "*I can't help loving Agnes even when she's confused, which is most of the time. I used to wish she'd stop daydreaming ...*"

"Right," I said. "I wouldn't have wanted to miss hearing that—"

Zane read louder, silencing me. " … *but now I know that's what I loved most about her—her insistence on dreaming big.*"

"Too late for that now, isn't it?" I said.

Zane turned the page. "*If only I'd told her I loved her, instead of lecturing her, maybe she could've loved me, too. How could I know I'd never be the same without Agnes?*"

I sank back into the sofa. "Why didn't he tell me sooner? I guess I didn't make it easy for him. When I think how I went on and on about Trevor and the whole time Xander was—"

Zane sat next to me. "Want to tell me about it?"

I began with our freshman year and the fateful line-up—Plumley, Putnam, Quinn, and Rhodes—in Professor Harwood's class. I tried to paint myself in the best possible light, justifying my obsession with Trevor and making light of my ambition to write. I ended with my unfortunate discussion with Ferguson Trask, my subsequent disillusionment with my mentor, Robinson Trask, and my resolve to prove myself worthy of Xander's love.

"So," Zane said, "you gave up writing because the Trask brothers wanted to turn your story into a comic book, and you thought your sacrifice would please Xander?"

"I never thought of it in exactly that way, but yes, that's about the size of it."

He took my manuscript. "You'll forgive me, Agnes, but those are poor reasons."

"What?"

He thumbed through my pages. "Your story is far from finished and needs some tightening in places, but your idea is workable and your style is engaging."

"You mean that?"

"I do. I'll admit I find Trevorode tiresome, but Lyda Rose is fully fleshed out. She practically jumps off the page."

"Really?"

"Yes, really. You need to stop making excuses and get back to work."

"I won't have much time now that I'm teaching."

"We make time for what we want time for," he said. "You know that."

The phone rang. It was my mother. "Jonas came by and said he hadn't heard from Mr. Plumley yet. It's almost dinnertime. Are you two finished talking?"

"Yes. Tell Jonas he can pick up Zane when it's convenient."

"No need for that," Zane said. "I'll drive my car if he'll give me directions."

I relayed the message to my mother, who told Jonas. I hung up the phone.

"Jonas is bringing my mother home. You can follow him to his place. Will you leave in the morning or stay another day?"

"No need to stay longer. I want to spend some time with my mother. She'll want to hear every detail. I'd better get my things together before Jonas gets here."

He walked into my bedroom. There was a knock at the door.

Before I could walk the few steps to the door, the knocking grew louder and faster. If I'd been thinking clearly, I would've realized there was no way Jonas and my mother could have arrived so soon. When I opened the door, I found my father, a suitcase in one hand and a sleeping bag in the other.

"Dad? What are you doing here?"

"Can't a father visit his only daughter when she's been hurt?"

"Of course. I didn't think you'd come till—"

He pushed into the room and set his bags down by the door. "This is a nice little place you have here." He put his arms around me.

At that moment Zane came out of my bedroom with his suitcase in hand.

Dad released his grip on me. "And who, may I ask, are you?"

Zane held out his hand. "Zane Plumley. I'm a friend of Agnes."

Dad stared at Zane's suitcase. "And what sort of *friend* are you, exactly?"

"No, Dad, it's not like that," I said. "Zane came a long way … on business and—"

"What kind of business are you in?"

"I'm working on my doctorate in—"

Dad turned to me. "And where is your mother?"

"She's visiting a friend of mine."

"I thought she came up here to take care of you."

"She did, but after we had lunch, Muriel—"

"Who's Muriel?"

"She's the friend."

"If you'll excuse me," Zane said, "I'll put this in my car and wait outside for Jonas."

Dad's face reddened. "Who's Jonas?"

"A teacher at my school—the one I told you about," I said.

Dad turned to Zane. "And how do *you* know him?"

"We met earlier. He offered me a place to stay. I'll let myself out. Goodbye, Agnes."

When Zane opened the door, there stood my mother, laughing. Either she had tripped on the step or Zane startled her when he opened the door as she was about to knock. Jonas, apparently to keep her from falling, had her by the arm. She was blushing and giddy. Zane backed into the room to let them in.

"Mom, look who's here," I said.

"Stuart," she said, "I thought you weren't coming till tomorrow."

"When I told the boss Agnes was in the hospital, he said I could leave right away." He pointed to Jonas. "And who is this?"

Jonas held out his hand. "Jonas Grinstead. I teach with your daughter."

Mother interrupted. "Jonas offered to give me a ride after I spent the afternoon with Muriel. He came back here so Mr. Plumley could follow him to his house."

Zane seized the moment. "Ready if you are, Jonas." Again he tried to escape through the open door and again, instead of leaving, he stepped backwards into the room. "Excuse me," Zane said to the new visitor, "may I help you?"

"I'm looking for Agnes Quinn."

"Is she expecting you?" Zane asked.

"Maybe."

"And you are ..."

"Name's Brooker. It's not really her I need to see. My business is with Mr. Grinstead, and don't bother telling me he's not here. That's his truck in the driveway. I followed him."

"Look here," Dad said to Brooker, "I don't know who you think you are, but—"

"Jonas," Mother said, "what's this about?"

"Why are you asking *him*?" Dad said. "What's going on between you two?"

My mother turned red from her top button up to the gray roots of her brown bangs.

"Nothing," Mother said. "Agnes, is this the man who knocked you out?"

Before I could say no, my father thundered, "*What*?" and lunged for Brooker, grabbed him by his dingy shirt, and pulled him into the room. "I was hoping I'd get to meet you while I was here." Dad pinned Brooker to the wall.

Jonas stepped forward. "Wait, Mr. Quinn, this is not the man you want."

"And how would *you* know?" Dad said.

"Because I know the man who hurt Agnes and this isn't him."

Dad released Brooker.

"I have no business with you," Brooker said to my father. "I'm here because this guy's truck is out front. I want to settle with him so I can go home and collect for my services."

"Let's step outside," Jonas said, "and leave these people out of this."

Brooker straightened his rumpled clothes. "That's more like it. If this girl had answered my questions two days ago, none of this would've happened."

"I told her not to," Dad said. "Real men don't ask girls to do their dirty work for them."

"I'm not a girl, Dad," I said as Brooker followed Jonas out the door.

"My father feels the same way about my sister," Zane said.

Dad waited till Zane closed the door. "Now, would one of you tell me what's going on?"

"It's all right, Stu. Come in here and let me fix you some dinner."

"I think I'll take a bath," I said.

I went into my bedroom, closed the door, left the light off, tiptoed to the window, pulled back the curtain, and peeked out. Brooker, Jonas, and Zane were still in the driveway. Brooker leaned against his gray sedan. He had a stack of papers in his hand and was punctuating his sentences by shaking them in Jonas' face. Zane stood motionless beside Jonas.

My mother tapped on the door. "Agnes, are you all right?"

"I'm getting my pajamas." I stepped away from the window and turned on the light. As I rummaged through my dresser drawer, Saturn crept out from under the bed.

"Smart cat," I said.

After a long bath, I returned to my room and looked out again. The driveway was empty.

I noticed Xander's journal on my nightstand. Glad Zane had left it behind, I opened my dresser drawer and hid the brown leather volume under my sweaters. Then I put on the pink seersucker robe my mother had given me the previous Christmas and rejoined my parents.

"How nice," Mom said. "That robe has really held up to washing. It looks almost new."

"Yes, it's very nice." I wore it only when I was around my mother.

"Now, Agnes," Dad said, "can you start from the beginning and tell me what happened?"

I complied, though I felt too tired to go through the story yet again. I painted Brighton Park in the worst possible light and stressed Trixie's and Mavis' distaste for me.

"See what I meant when I told you I don't belong here?" I asked.

"Like I told you on the phone, Aggie, if I'd left a job every time I didn't get along with my coworkers, you wouldn't be sitting here today, healthy, well-educated, and employed."

"And with straight teeth," Mom said.

I pointed to my black eye and scar. "Do you call this *healthy*?"

"Freak accident," Dad said. "Could've happened anywhere. There are all kinds of troubled people in this world, and you happened to run into one of them."

Mom spoke up. "I don't think it will happen again. He promised me."

"He promised you?" I said.

"What are you talking about, Betty?" Dad set his coffee cup on the end table.

Mom lowered her eyes. "I met him today."

"Where?" Dad placed his elbows on his knees and leaned forward—never a good sign.

"At Muriel's restaurant. I introduced myself and after we talked awhile, I asked him what Agnes did to make him so angry."

"How many men have you met, anyway?" Dad asked. "First, you're driving all over town with this Jonas guy and now you're cozying up to the man who assaulted our daughter?"

"I didn't cozy up to him," Mom said.

I walked to the front door.

"And where do you think you're going?" Dad asked.

"I'm going to sit on the porch. I've been cooped up for two days."

"Should you be out there alone?" Mom asked.

"I'll be all right. You can have my bed, Mom. There's plenty of room on the floor for Dad's sleeping bag. I'll take the sofa."

I closed the door behind me and stepped out into the warm night air. Suspended low, the moon shone full and wondrous between the branches of the live oaks. I wished Zane were standing beside me. He would've quoted Yeats—"The Silver Apples of the Moon." Xander would've mumbled something about the moon "being in its perigee." Why had I met the wrong Plumley man first? Zane was perfect for me. And he liked my book.

My mother opened the front door. "Dad and I are going to turn in. Lock the door before you go to sleep."

I took one last look at the moon, went inside, picked up my unfinished novel, lay down on the sofa, and fell asleep reading the first page, written in those far-off foolish years when I still believed in my silly dream and the boundless possibilities ahead.

When I woke I found my father reading the newspaper.

"Morning," he said. "Your friend called."

I sat up. "Who?"

"Your friend. Said he forgot something. Needs to stop by on his way out of town."

I tried to smooth my hair as I sprinted toward the bathroom, but I was too late. When my father heard Zane knock on the door, he let him in before I could object.

"Good morning," Zane said. "I forgot the journal. I can't go home without it."

I brought the journal from my bedroom and gave it to him.

"Thank you," I said. "No matter what I said yesterday, it really did help to read this."

He leaned in, kissed me on the cheek, and then whispered in my ear, "Finish your book."

Chapter 8

A Promising Future

The second time a Plumley man left me was no easier than the first.

I longed to linger in the open door till Zane drove out of sight, but not wanting to appear wistful I gave a sprightly wave and stepped back inside. Grateful my father was hidden behind his morning paper, I sank onto the sofa, leaned my head back, and gazed at the ceiling.

This wasn't the first time I'd fallen in love in less than twenty-four hours.

My mother came out of the bedroom. "What's wrong, honey? Dizzy again?"

I sat up. "No. I was … thinking about how embarrassing it will be when I go back to work. Everyone's going to stare."

Not what I was pondering, but plausible enough.

"I'm sure word has gotten around by now," she said. "Everyone will be glad you're all right, no matter how you look."

"I hate starting my career looking like a kid who fell off her bike." I paused, and then took the plunge. "This week has been like some sort of omen."

My father bent down a corner of his paper, peered at me, and went back to reading.

Mom sat down and patted me on the shoulder. "Don't worry. Daddy and I are going to help you get on your feet and ready to go back to work."

Dad folded his paper. "How about breakfast?"

"There's nothing here to eat," I said. "Maybe half a box of cereal. No milk."

He laid the paper on the table. "I spotted a Bob's Pancake World on my way into town. I could do with some good coffee and a couple of eggs, couldn't you, Betty?"

"Oh, Stu, what a good idea. Wouldn't that be nice, Agnes? Remember how we used to *love* to go to breakfast together?"

Not exactly. Once I was old enough to stay home alone, I declined my parents' weekly invitation to Bob's. I hated the smell of frying pork and the servers' wearing grits-spattered aprons and calling everyone "Sugar." But how could I say no to my parents' offer? They'd travelled a long way. My dad was missing work. And I had to appear in public sooner or later. Bob's, frequented for the most part by truck drivers and construction workers, would be the perfect place for me to slip in unnoticed. Besides that, people-watching at Bob's would keep my mind off Zane.

Riding in the backseat of the family car, I felt like a nine-year-old on my way to Grandma's house. I nodded as my mother complimented the "tidy" streets of my town and remarked how near I lived to a grocery store and the post office. Mom reached her hand over the seat to pat my knee. "You'll come home for Thanksgiving this year, won't you? I have a new recipe for corn casserole. Toby and Janette will be there with the boys."

My brother and his wife had added a third son, Alfred David, to their family. William, excelling in first grade, and Lewis, already reading at the age of four, offered further evidence my parents' capable rearing of their son was being propagated to another generation of Quinns. Every nickel they'd invested in Toby's life—every loaf of bread for his lunches, every spiral notebook for his homework, every pair of shoes for track season, and every dollar squirreled away for his college tuition—had been well spent. He was everything they could have hoped for.

They'd never worried about Toby the way they'd worried about me. I stared at my dad's profile and noticed his thinning hair and weathered face. It made me sad to think I might yet disappoint him. At the moment, my parents were proud of me and had peace of mind about my future. They were happy to have me in the backseat of their car. They were happy I'd agreed to have breakfast at a place they knew I didn't like. They were happy I had two degrees and a promising career as an English professor in a community college.

If they'd only known I'd already vowed to leave Brighton Park as soon as possible, they'd have driven straight past Bob's Pancake World to their house so they could keep an eye on me till I came to my senses.

Part of the ritual of eating at Bob's Pancake World was the challenge of actually locating one. Though billboards welcomed travelers and directed them to the proper exit, the restaurant was almost impossible to find. Not to be thwarted, my dad guided our tank-sized Buick past a gas station on the corner, left at a traffic light, and into the entry for Hilda's Motor Inn. There beyond a weed-covered vacant lot were the parking spaces for Bob's. Threading our way among station wagons, rusting panel vans, dented pickup trucks, and towering semis, we came at last to an empty spot.

Though none of the working folks who'd arrived in *these* vehicles would expect their fellow patrons to be well-groomed, I still held my hand to the side of my face as we entered the building. A waitress with a pencil behind her ear greeted us.

"Welcome to Bob's. My name's Flo, and I'll be serving you today. Can I get coffee for everyone?" My parents agreed. "Coffee for you, too, hon?" she asked me.

When I turned to reply, she gasped. "What in the world happened to you, sweetie?"

"Accident," I said.

"Bless your heart. My boyfriend—not the one I have now—gave me a black eye. It took forever to go away. I got good tips that week. People feel sorry for you when you get beat up."

"I didn't get beat up—"

She continued without pausing to breathe. "The Grampa Joe is the special today. Three eggs any way you want, two waffles, bacon or sausage, biscuits and gravy. Buy one, get one free. I'll get your coffee and be right back."

Dad ordered the Grampa Joe special and asked for an extra plate. Sharing a meal among two or more was standard practice in our family.

After our coffee was served, our conversation turned to ordinary things. Mom reflected on Toby's completing his first week as the newly appointed chairman of the Math Department. Dad caught me up on the goings-on at work and shared greetings and get-well wishes from the people I'd worked with during my summer employment.

"And," Dad said, "the boss said to tell you if this town is too dangerous, you're still welcome back at your old job."

Mom laughed. "Isn't that a thought—Agnes' spending all that time getting *two* degrees only to walk away from her job?"

"Excuse me. Miss Quinn?"

One of my students stood at the end of our table. Though I couldn't have recalled most of the faces I'd seen on my first day in the classroom, I remembered this young man. He was exceptional in every way—well-mannered, polite, and with an unforgettable name.

"I'm sorry to bother you," he said. "When I saw you come in, I pointed you out to my grandmother. She's asked for a larger table so you can join us, if you'd like."

"Thanks just the same," my father said, "but—"

Coffee mug in hand, my mother stood. "How nice," she said. "Thank you."

"These are my parents," I said. "Stuart and Betty Quinn."

My student extended his hand to my father. "I'm—"

"Exton Wrayburn the 4th," I said.

Exton grinned. "Wow! How did you remember after only one class period?"

The truth was I thought his name sounded like a character in a novel, but I only said, "Your name is so distinctive—it's hard to forget."

"My grandmother will be pleased to hear you say that," he said. "She's right over here."

Exton led us to his table and introduced his grandmother, Charlotte Wrayburn. Silver-haired, dressed in a long-sleeved navy-blue dress with pearl buttons, an exquisite diamond on her left hand, Charlotte seemed out of place in the plain, homespun setting.

She gestured to three chairs opposite her. "I'm so glad you could join us."

Exton pulled out my chair. My mother waited for my father to do the same for her.

When we were all seated, Exton asked my father what line of work he was in.

While the men talked business, Charlotte addressed me and my mother. "I was deeply sorry to hear about your accident, Miss Quinn."

"Please call me Agnes," I said.

"And call me Betty," my mother said.

"I heard about your kindness to Mr. Ellershaw, Agnes," Charlotte said. "I commend you for not pressing charges."

"You know him?" I asked.

"He and my husband were great friends. Ryder was a local hero when he first came home. Sadly, after his trouble with his wife, he became better known for being irascible."

"But how did you find out I—?"

"I'm on the board of trustees of your school. It's my duty to check on our teachers."

"The doctor said she was lucky to be alive," my mother said.

Charlotte glanced at my eye. "I'm sure that's true," she said.

Breakfast arrived. Though I was mortified when my parents parceled out their food onto the extra plate and handed it to me, Charlotte gave no indication she noticed this frugality. She asked the server for more coffee and proceeded to cut her waffles into delicate bites and dip them into a pool of syrup on her plate.

"Ex rarely mentions his teachers anymore," Charlotte said, "but he couldn't wait to tell me his English professor had read the first chapter of *Great Expectations* to his class."

"Agnes has always loved to read," my mother said.

Charlotte looked at me. "He said you made the convict come alive."

"I wanted to get my class interested from the beginning, so I wouldn't need to persuade them to keep reading."

"Following in the Dickensian tradition," Charlotte said.

"The what?" my father asked.

"Dickens gave public readings of his works," I said.

"Would you be interested in doing the same?" Charlotte asked.

"Agnes did some acting when she was in college," my mother said.

"Not public readings, exactly," Charlotte said. "Private readings for me."

"In your home?" my mother asked, her eyes wide.

"I've always loved to read," Charlotte said, "but my eyesight is poor. When Ex told me how much he'd enjoyed your class, I thought you might not mind reading to me."

"I'd love to," I said.

"Friday evenings?" she asked.

"Perfect," I said. "When do you want to start?"

"This week," she said, "if that will fit your schedule."

The five of us had more coffee and parted as mutual admirers.

That afternoon while I rested, my father washed my car. Then he and my mother bought enough groceries to keep me in food for two weeks. After a home-cooked meal that night, Mom and I cleaned the kitchen while my father watched the evening news.

Dad called from the living room: "Better hurry. *Singin' in the Rain* is coming on."

Mom reached for the dish towel. "How nice. We can watch it together on our last night here." She dried the last plate, and we joined my dad on the sofa.

Before long, Dad dozed off. I couldn't blame him. We'd seen the film dozens of times. But my mother always gazed, starry-eyed, as if viewing each scene for the first time. For as long as I could remember, when she heard Gene Kelly sing, "You Were Meant for Me," she'd turn to me and say, "I wish that was me dancing with him." Tonight she was silent. I looked to see if she'd gone to sleep too, and found her staring at the television as if the screen had gone blank. Then she said something I never imagined I'd hear.

"I wish I hadn't stopped dancing," she said.

"You what?"

"I started lessons when I was six. When I got to be a teenager, I put on weight and my face broke out. I couldn't bear the thought of a recital, so I quit. I've regretted it my whole life."

I didn't know what to say. My mother in a pink tutu? Pirouetting? Or had she tapped?

"Why have you never told me this?" I asked.

She kept her eyes on the movie. "I don't know. When I look back on those days, I can hardly believe I used to be graceful and poised—not at all like I am now."

I sat on the edge of the sofa and faced her. "There are all kinds of places you and Dad could go to dance."

"I wanted to dance at our wedding reception," she said, "but your dad said it was silly. He refused to learn how and that was the end of that."

"But it's not too late," I said, and told her the story of Geneva Gilbey.

She was unmoved. "My point exactly."

"What do you mean?"

"Think, Agnes. Where is that poor woman at this moment?"

"In the hospital," I said.

"Not exactly a happy ending, is it?"

"So she's had a setback. She'll ride again someday. I'm sure of it."

Mom shook her head. "Do you know how hard it is for someone her age to recover from a broken bone? If she's as overweight as you say, healing will take even longer."

"That may be true, but dancing isn't as risky as horseback riding."

She looked at my father and then at me. "It might as well be. Let's not waste our last night together arguing about something that's never going to happen."

We watched the rest of the movie in silence. Mom woke Dad so they could go to bed. I lay awake on the sofa and imagined my mother in an emerald-green sequined gown, gliding over a gleaming floor. As I fell asleep, her image faded into Geneva Gilbey in blue jeans, a red-checked shirt, and a yellow cowboy hat. When the music ended, Geneva tipped her hat and sashayed through the doors of the ballroom, her boots leaving a trail of scuff marks on the floor.

I woke the next morning in a melancholy mood. I couldn't decide what made me sadder—Geneva with her broken leg or my mother with her broken dream. The morning passed quietly by. Dad checked under the hood of my car.

Mom prepared her peerless macaroni and cheese and divided it into six servings. She placed five in the freezer and instructed me to eat the other one for dinner that night. We ate sandwiches for lunch and hugged each other goodbye.

I wasn't prepared for how alone I'd feel. After constant companionship for the last few days, the solitude was oppressive. I sat next to Saturn on the sofa and scratched his head.

"Even when I was in the hospital, I had Geneva to keep me company," I said, and thought of her lying there alone. Would her new roommate pull back the curtain between the beds?

"Don't take this personally," I said to Saturn, "but I have to get out of here for a while."

I made myself as presentable as possible and grabbed my car keys.

As I left my apartment, I heard a voice call, "Hey, you."

I turned to find Warner Bingham. Still dressed in black jeans and jacket, he had added aviator glasses to his attire and was holding a rake.

"Hello," I said. "Warner, isn't it?"

"You have a cat?" he asked.

"Yes."

He stood between me and my car. "Inside or outside?"

"What do you mean?"

He slid his glasses to the edge of his nose and glared over them.

"It's a simple question. Is your cat an inside cat or an outside cat?"

"Inside."

I edged backward toward my apartment. One black eye was enough.

He tapped his rake on the pavement. "What color is your cat?"

"Gray."

"So, if your cat is an *inside* cat," he said, like a lawyer questioning a perjured witness, "why did I see it in my mother's flower bed on Sunday night?"

I took another step backward and forced a timid laugh. "Oh, that." I explained Saturn's escape during the storm. "You haven't seen him in your flower bed since Sunday, have you?"

I walked around him, opened my car door, and stood behind it. "Are those your begonias?" I pointed toward the only flower bed in bloom.

"Yes."

"And is that your motorcycle?"

"Yeah. What about it?"

"Nothing. I—never knew bikers enjoyed gardening."

"I told you they're my mother's flowers."

"I'd like to meet her sometime," I said, "but I have to go. I'm on my way to the hospital."

He shouldered his rake like a rifle and swaggered back to the blossoms.

Shaking off images of Mrs. Bingham locked in a closet, I drove away.

I entered the hospital and walked toward the information desk, where I saw a burly man in jeans and a white, long-sleeved cowboy shirt with snaps on the pockets and cuffs. The silver buckle on his belt, straining against his considerable stomach, tapped on the front of the counter as he leaned in and addressed the receptionist.

"Since you're a lady," he said, "I'm gonna give you one more chance to tell me where my aunt Geneva is. Then I'm gonna yank them papers out of your hands and see for myself."

When I heard "Geneva," I stopped.

"I told you," the receptionist said, "her son authorized a transfer to another hospital."

He banged his hand on the counter. "I know that. What I'm askin' is *where.*"

"Her son specified no information about her whereabouts was to be given to anyone."

He hit the counter again. "I ain't 'anyone.' I'm her flesh and blood."

The receptionist picked up the phone. "Security," she said.

"This ain't over," he said. "Not by a long shot."

He walked to a chair in the lobby, sat down, and buried his face in his hands.

I approached the receptionist. "Did I hear you say Mrs. Gilbey has been moved?"

"Yes, she's been moved," the receptionist said, "and no, I can't tell you where."

"I didn't ask," I said.

I approached Geneva's nephew and sat next to him.

"Excuse me," I said, "were you looking for Geneva Gilbey?"

He looked up, his brown eyes full of tears. "You a friend of hers?"

"We met a few nights ago. We were in the same hospital room." I pointed to my eye.

His face broke into a broad smile. "You're Agnes. You sure have saved me a lot of trouble, little lady."

"Me? How?"

"Aunt Genny told me to find you. She told me how nice you was to her that night in the hospital." He held out his hand. "I'm Buck Sloan. Would you like to get some coffee?"

"I'd love some."

"I know just the place," he said. "Have you ever been to Bob's Pancake World?"

"It's a family favorite," I said.

I followed Buck in my car and then joined him at a table by a window. He must have been a regular. The server, Barb, touched his shoulder. "Hey there, Buck. You want your usual?"

"Nah. I ate a big lunch. Just bring me a glass of milk and some cornbread."

"Whole or low fat?"

"Better bring the hard stuff today and two glasses of water. What'll you have, Agnes?"

"Cousin Linda's Homemade Peach Cobbler."

Barb scowled at me and snatched my menu. Apparently, she entertained romantic notions about Buck and misinterpreted my presence at his table.

Buck stretched out his right arm across the back of the chair next to him. His face, bronzed by many hot summers, was smooth except for deep lines etched at the corners of his eyes. His dark hair was creased above his ears. He'd left a cowboy hat, no doubt, in his truck.

"Aunt Genny didn't tell me what happened to you," he said.

"It's a long story," I said. "I'd rather talk about Geneva."

Barb returned with two glasses of water, two glasses of milk, and six pieces of golden brown cornbread. The crust of my cobbler was burned around the edges.

"I heard your aunt took a fall, Buck. Was she hurt bad?" Barb asked.

He crumbled cornbread into his glass. "I'll tell you the truth. Since my dad put me on a horse forty years ago, when I was only three, I ain't never seen a rider hit the ground so hard."

"Is she doing better?" Barb asked. She angled her body so her back was to me.

"I don't know," Buck said. "Her son moved her to another hospital and didn't tell me."

"I'm sorry," she said, her hand on his shoulder again. "Maybe he'll call when he knows something. I'll be back later with more milk."

She did not inquire about a refill for me.

"I have to know," I said. "Is Buttercup all right?"

He smiled. "She's fine. Vet said she's got a bad sprain and won't win any races, but that's not why we bought her anyway."

"So Geneva will be able to ride her again after she recovers?"

He leaned on the table. "Mark my word. As long as there is one breath left in Geneva Gilbey's body, she'll come home to Sloan's Canyon."

"There are canyons around here?" I asked.

He laughed. "No. She wanted a Western-sounding name for her property and insisted on naming it after me."

"She told me how you offered to help her when she told you what she wanted to do."

He wiped his mouth. "My wife had just died. I needed to start a new life. Genny's son was ten kinds of put out with me, but then he's always hated me, even when we was kids."

I nibbled at a bit of lukewarm peach. "I guess her son was angry about the accident."

He slammed his spoon on the table. "You know what he said when I told him? He said, 'I knew this would happen. I hope you're satisfied.' Can you believe that?"

"I'm sorry," I said.

"In the years she's lived here, do you know how many times he's come to see her?" He held up his index finger. "Once." He took a blue bandana from his pocket and blew his nose.

Barb returned. When she laid the check by Buck's plate, I noticed she'd drawn a heart beneath her name. She reached for Buck's empty milk glass and pointed to my uneaten cobbler.

"You done with that?" she asked.

I met her gaze. "Yes. I'm done."

Buck peered around Barb as she cleared the table. "Aunt Genny said when I found you I should invite you to meet Buttercup. Would you like to—?"

With a quick flick of her wrist, Barb tipped over the water glass into my lap. She grabbed a cloth from her tray and dabbed at the spill.

"I'm so sorry," she said.

I stood and peeled the wet napkin from my leg.

"I guess I'll be going now," I said. "It was nice meeting you, Buck."

Buck handed Barb a twenty-dollar bill, told her to keep the change and followed me to the parking lot. When we got to my car, he reached in his shirt pocket, pulled out a business card, and handed it to me.

"Here's the number of the ranch," he said. "Buttercup will be expecting your call."

Chapter 9

A Loose Thread

When I arrived at home, Warner Bingham, polishing his motorcycle in the parking lot, ignored me when I waved. I hurried past him to my door. The phone was ringing.

"Hello, Agnes, we're home."

"Glad to hear it," I said. "Did you have a nice trip?"

"Yes, we made good time. Did you have dinner yet?"

"No, I went for a long drive and just got back." I decided not to mention Geneva or Buck.

"Good. Now remember—you promised to go to church in the morning and see Sharon."

While my parents had been visiting, my father and I had done our best to divert our conversations from the subject of Sharon Merriman-Cheswick. But here was her name again—like a popcorn kernel wedged between two molars.

This wasn't going to go away—it was time to put this task behind me and begin the second week of my last year at Brighton Park Community College with a clear conscience.

I sighed for effect. "What's the name of the church again?" I hadn't forgotten.

"First Episcopal of Maplewood."

"You know that's forty-five miles from here?"

"You don't have to go every Sunday—just tomorrow. Can't you do this for me?"

"O-oh-ka-ay." I sounded like a four-year-old even to myself.

"Thank you. I'd hate to tell Jewel we came all that way and didn't try to see her daughter. She'd be so disappointed, especially since she just got back from visiting Roger in prison."

"I know, Mom. I'll take care of it."

"But you've been saying that ever since you moved to Plainview."

I kept my voice even. "I've been kind of busy—moving and getting ready for school and then there was *that trip to the hospital.*"

My sarcasm was lost on her. "I tried not to mention Sharon while you were recovering, but you're better now. Besides, going to church will be a good way to start your week."

I couldn't imagine a worse way to begin the week than a reunion with Sharon Merriman.

"Oh, and Agnes—one more thing," my mother said. "When you see Sharon, don't mention Roger. She doesn't want the church members to know her brother is in prison."

I left early as I had promised. I was surprised how beautiful the highway to Maplewood was. Lofty oaks lined both sides of the road and formed a lush green canopy, already dappled red, promising the brisker air of autumn. My spirits would have lifted if I hadn't been engaged on such a grim errand. Even worse, the long drive to Maplewood allowed plenty of time to review my longtime feud with Sharon.

I was barely five years old when I first became conscious of Sharon's overarching presence in my life. She was eleven then and already dazzling everyone she knew. I still remember coming in from the backyard to find Sharon sitting at our kitchen table while our mothers talked.

"You're getting prettier every day," my mother said to Sharon—an observation I could not remember her saying to me.

Jewel smoothed Sharon's long blonde hair. "She's so much like her father."

I couldn't see the resemblance at all. Doc Merriman was a wiry, bald-headed man with a long nose and thick glasses.

My brother and I never liked Sharon and liked her brother Roger even less. Nevertheless, my mother's friendship with Jewel jumbled our families together in an uneasy pile for many years. Polite attendance by both families was expected at Toby's annual science fair, my yearly piano recital, and the one football game Roger played in before he got kicked off the team.

This display of good manners seemed reasonable to my young mind for a while. But when Sharon's dance recitals, voice recitals, and cheerleading competitions occurred with tedious and grating repetition, we all began to complain. Eventually my father and brother were spared. But my mother assumed I, as a girl, would profit from observing Sharon's feminine mystique on display. I had precious little myself.

I might have tolerated all this misery if only Sharon had been worth the trouble. But she was quite simply the meanest person I ever knew. She never missed an opportunity to make fun of my freckles, height, weight, or curly hair. When I appealed to my mother, she admonished me to "be nice to Sharon for Jewel's sake." So I kept my mouth shut, especially when Doc Merriman broke Jewel's heart by shipping Roger off to military school.

As our families sat through Sharon's high school valedictorian speech, I was delighted she was going to college in another state. When she became Mrs. Merriman-Cheswick, I was even happier she and her husband were moving to California so he could go to seminary.

It wasn't until after I'd been hired at Brighton Park that my mother informed me Sharon's husband had been appointed rector of the Episcopal church in Maplewood, the town nearest to Plainview. When Mom came to visit and found herself a "mere forty-five miles" from her best friend's daughter, she couldn't rest till she'd seen her.

Mom was breathless when her first call connected her to Sharon's maid. She gave her name and then put her hand over the receiver. "Imagine that—a maid." Mrs. Merriman-Cheswick was out. The call was not returned.

The second call was a repeat of the first.

The third call was to the church. Mom was breathless when the secretary answered. She gave her name and then put her hand over the receiver. "The secretary's putting me through." But when the secretary returned to the phone, she explained the reverend's wife had been called out of town unexpectedly and wouldn't return until late Saturday evening.

There would be no visit with Sharon. My father and I sneaked a smile at each other.

But here I was in the parking lot of the church, moments away from a reunion with the person who had less use for me than Jonquil Putnam did.

In spite of myself, I liked the church at once. A stone-paved walkway cut a winding path through a thick green lawn. The quaint old building was pristine white with arched stained-glass windows, a tall steeple, and an iron bell. A sign by the front steps read: *First Episcopal Church, Maplewood. Dr. Sherman Cheswick, Rector.*

The usher at the door greeted me, glanced at my eye, and offered me the weekly bulletin. "Welcome. If you're new to our church, you might also want one of these." He reached for a brochure from a wooden rack on the wall. "This gives the details about our stained-glass windows. People come from all over to see them." I thanked him and walked halfway down the middle aisle which separated the two sections of pews. From a central location, I reasoned, I could locate Sharon quickly, hurry to her after the service, say a quick hello, and leave.

I chose a seat on the right and sat down near the end of the row. The morning sun gleamed through the colored glass, filling the quiet room with rich reds, restful blues, and luscious greens. I opened the brochure and read:

On the eastern wall, the lives of King David and his son Solomon are presented in eight separate scenes. Beginning with David as a shepherd tending his flock, the viewer can follow David's life through his slaying of Goliath, his flight from King Saul, and his reign over Israel.

I leaned forward to study the panes. The usher was right—these were inspiring works of art, well worth the drive to Maplewood.

There was David with a lamb in his arms, resting by a blue stream. Next was David, the young warrior, standing over the giant's severed head, the blood, ruby red, coursing across the sand. As I turned to look over my shoulder at the next scene, the organist began a Bach prelude. The melody resonated through the building, echoed from the cedar-timbered ceiling, and swept me up a calming embrace. I hadn't expected such joy—not here. Maybe this *would* be a good way to start the week. I relaxed against the royal-blue seat cushions and closed my eyes.

And then—the most astonishing thing happened.

For the first time since the day I thought I killed Jameson Bridger in the library, Lyda Rose, long banished from my thoughts, appeared, unsummoned, in my mind. A scene played out before me, effortlessly, spilling from my imagination as if I were watching a play. I grabbed a pen from my purse and began writing in the edges of the brochure.

Lyda Rose knelt in the cathedral and stared up at the great window. She'd come there to rest—to remember the courage of the warrior kings who had come before her. Ever since King Jardon's untimely death, she'd been running for her life.

"Excuse me."

Everyone in the realm, noble and commoner alike, knew she was the rightful heir to the throne. But Romar, the king's minister, was plotting …

"Excuse me."

... to place his weak-willed nephew on the throne.

Someone behind me tapped my shoulder. I stopped writing and turned around. He pointed to a woman in a gray dress standing at the end of my row. A large red silk rose adorned her shoulder.

I turned to her. "Me?"

She scowled. "Yes. You're in my seat."

"Oh. I didn't know there was reserved seating in churches."

She pointed to the gold-plated tag bolted to the arm of the pew. "See here? My family bought this pew ninety years ago."

"You own this pew?"

"Yes—and that window." She pointed to young David with dead Goliath.

In former days, before Ferguson Trask, Rufus Plumley, and Ryder Ellershaw, I would've deferred to my social superior, muttered apologies, and stumbled over my own feet as I retreated.

But not today.

Still weary, on edge, dreading my prospects, and impatient to get back to my story, I remained where I was. The prelude surged toward a crescendo. I squinted at the window for several moments and then turned back to the Lady in Gray.

"Which window is yours?" I asked.

My feigned stupidity achieved the desired effect.

She pursed her lips and stabbed the air with such vigor the red rose fluttered on her shoulder. "*That* one," she said, "at the end of *this* row. See the family name in the inscription?"

Again I perused the window and turned back to her. "I'm sorry," I said, "but the sun is so bright, I couldn't quite make out the words. Your name is Goliath?"

Her eyes flamed. Her nostrils flared as she drew in a lungful of air. She squared her shoulders and marched up the aisle to the lobby to fetch an usher, I supposed, or maybe a policeman. I stepped over the people next to me and sauntered down the middle aisle to an empty spot several rows ahead on the opposite side of the room.

I slipped into place as the song leader announced the first hymn, "Rescue the Perishing." An elderly gentleman offered me his hymnal. I accepted his kindness, but did not sing. Instead I scanned the room for Sharon. There she was in the front row. She was wearing a long-sleeved pale-turquoise dress, her blonde hair pulled back in a French twist. When the song ended, she turned to whisper to the woman next to her.

I nearly dropped the hymnbook. It was Trixie Thorpe.

Half sick, I sat down. The Lady in Gray was still fuming behind me, and my two worst enemies were conspiring in front of me. The rector stepped to the pulpit and asked visitors to raise their hands and be recognized. I did not comply. I clutched my papers and pen in my hand, hugged my purse, and remained seated as the congregation stood to greet each other.

"Hello, Agnes."

A strange little woman, standing in the aisle, held out her hand to me. Her silver hair, piled on her head in a mass of tangles and loose ends, was held in place by a bright pink hat. Round, gold-rimmed glasses perched on the end of her nose. Dressed in black, she'd draped a crocheted shawl, made of variegated red, blue, green, and yellow yarn, around her pudgy shoulders and fastened the ends in place with a large dragonfly brooch. Her apparel and impish grin were unsettling enough, but what she said next downright alarmed me.

"Could you wait for me after church, dear? I need a ride home."

Without saying more, she patted my arm and hurried away. I watched her shuffle across the aisle and scoot in a few rows ahead of me. Dr. Cheswick stepped to the pulpit and began his sermon. Though I had every intention of disliking him—he was, after all, Sharon's husband—I was grateful to have someplace to fix my gaze so I could avoid making eye contact with the Woman in Black who turned around every few minutes to look at me.

Wilkie Brooker wasn't so distant a memory that I could cope with another mysterious stranger in my life.

As if on cue, clouds obscured the sun, shadowed the room, and dimmed the windows' luster. The organ was silent. Only Sherman Cheswick's pompous tone shattered the stillness, firing like a cannon from the pulpit, searing the air as it exploded up the aisle and ricocheted off the front door to shower embers on our heads. And all the while, the Woman in Black turned and stared, nodding at me. I bowed my head and placed my hand over my eyes as if in contrition. Maybe if she thought I was praying, she'd leave me alone.

I peeked at her through the space between my fingers. Her back was to me now, and she was rummaging through something in her lap. When she turned around again and found me still "in prayer," she tried another approach.

"Pssst."

I didn't respond.

"PS—SS—SS—TT."

The elderly gentleman nudged me. I looked up. The Woman in Black had positioned a photo on her shoulder. She pointed first to the image and then to herself and mouthed words I could not possibly interpret.

Dr. Cheswick concluded his sermon. When he said, "Let us pray," I thought of making a run for the parking lot. But the threat of having to return next Sunday kept me in place through the final "Amen." The organist began the postlude; the Woman in Black, still smiling, motioned for me to wait. She shoved past everyone in her path, jostling them in her effort to reach the middle aisle and cross over to me. I ignored her, pushed toward the side aisle, and hurried toward the front. A quick hello, and I would be out of there.

I reached the first row of the church where Sharon was holding court with the church members. I stood quietly until she turned around.

She extended her hand. "Aa-aa-gnes. Mother told me you might be visiting. I think you know Mrs. Thorpe."

"Oh, dear," Trixie said. "You look worse than I imagined. How dreadful. You're surely not coming back to school tomorrow. You'll frighten your students to death."

"As a matter of fact I am coming back," I said. I felt my face growing hot as the two vixens stared at me.

"I was so surprised when my mother told me you were teaching at Brighton Park," Sharon said. "I still remember how amazed I was when I found out you'd gone to college."

"How ironic," I said. "I remember how pleased I was when *you* went to college."

Trixie chimed in. "And to think—now you'll be teaching in the same school."

My jaw dropped. "What?"

Trixie looked at Sharon and then at me. "The home economics teacher is on maternity leave. Mrs. Merriman-Cheswick is going to fill in for her this term."

"There you are, Agnes. I thought you'd left." The Woman in Black had found me. She forced her way between Sharon and Trixie, snagging the fringe of her shawl on the pearl buttons of Sharon's sleeve.

Sharon grimaced and yanked back her arm as if fending off contamination. The dragonfly brooch unhinged. The shawl slipped from the woman's shoulders and scraped along the floor as Sharon tried to shake loose. Trixie stepped in, snatched the shawl, and swung her arm in a wide arc like a matador taunting a bull. A long strand of green yarn, looped around the button, unraveled as Trixie pulled.

"Careful." The Woman in Black had tears in her eyes. "I just finished that yesterday. It's the first time I've worn it."

Without thinking, I grabbed Trixie's arm. "Stop," I said. "You're getting all worked up over nothing. Be still, Sharon."

Everyone halted. I held Sharon's wrist in one hand and carefully untwisted the yarn from the button. I returned the shawl to its owner, who thanked me and tried to poke the loose thread back through the weaving.

The four of us might have parted without further incident if only Reverend Cheswick hadn't descended on us in a fury, his burgundy robe flapping behind him as he approached.

The Woman in Black turned to face him, the green thread dangling from her hand.

Sharon, nervous, spoke first. "Sherman, you know Mrs. Thorpe, and this is—"

He held up his hand and addressed the Woman in Black. "Flossie, I've *told* you not to interrupt my sermons. I will *not* tolerate this behavior any longer. *Every* Sunday you make some kind of commotion and distract the members."

Flossie's tears flowed faster. "I was just trying to get Agnes' attention."

Sharon interrupted. "How do you know Agnes?"

Flossie pushed her glasses up on her nose. "She and my son are friends."

"Agnes? And *your* son?" Sharon said. She was pleased, but I didn't know why.

I turned to Flossie. "You must have me confused with someone else. We've never met, and I have no idea who your son is."

Flossie brushed away her tears with her fingertips and tilted her head back to look at me through her glasses. "That's right. We've never met, but you know my son, Warner. He said you admired my flowers." She turned back to the rector. "I thought Agnes might give me a ride home so I wouldn't have to take the bus. That's why I was trying to get her attention."

Sherman was unmoved. "You could have done that *after* the service. I could hear your hissing all the way to the pulpit."

Flossie kept fumbling with her repairs. "But she didn't know who I was and had no reason to wait. That's why I was trying to show her Warner's picture, but she wouldn't look up."

"You're Warner's mother?" I said.

She smiled. "I am. And I was so glad when he told me you two were friends. I've wished for the longest time that he could find a nice girl like you to marry."

Sharon beamed. "Oh, how nice. Does your mother know, Agnes?"

Trixie joined in. "Wait till I tell Mavis you have a boyfriend. Does Jonas know?"

"Jonas?" Sharon said.

"A coworker of ours," Trixie said. "He and Agnes have been getting to know each other."

Sharon laid her hand on my arm. "Oh, how nice. I remember your mother's being frantic you'd never find a husband. And now *two* men are pursuing you. This is good news."

Sherman was not to be ignored. "This is all very interesting, Flossie, but—"

"Reverend. Reverend." The Lady in Gray had swept in from the rear. She pointed at me, her long fingernails swiping the air like a dragon's claws. "This person was in my seat this morning and refused to move, though I asked her very nicely. If she's a friend of yours, I'm going to have to ask that—"

Sherman turned white to the lips. "No, Mrs. Wimpley. I've never seen her till now."

Sharon and Trixie exchanged smiles.

"I apologize," I said, "but you can surely appreciate that it's impossible for a newcomer to be aware of your unwritten protocol. Perhaps you could post a list of rules in the foyer." I took Flossie's shawl, placed it back on her shoulders, and looked the rector square in the eye. "Be sure to add 'love thy neighbor' to the list."

Had she been armed with a sharp instrument, Mrs. Wimpley would have skewered me on the spot.

"See what I mean?" she said. "We don't need people like her in this church."

Sherman, hoarse with fear, barely whispered. "It won't happen again, Mrs. Wimpley."

"No, it won't," I said, "because I won't be back. I came only as a favor to my mother. She regretted not seeing Sharon when she was visiting while I was in the hospital."

"Oh, well," Sharon said, "I had too much to do to fit your mother into my schedule."

"Schedule?" I said. "Your husband's secretary said you were out of town."

She laughed. "Well, I was. I was in Plainview meeting with Mrs. Thorpe."

My head was throbbing. "My mother tried for days to call you."

"I know," Sharon said, "but once she starts talking, she doesn't know when to stop. You, of all people, should know how she is."

I was quivering with rage. My throat went dry and beads of sweat seeped out on my forehead. My knees wobbled. I was raising my arm to slap the smug expression off Sharon's beautiful face, when I felt Flossie's soft hand clasping mine.

And then my course of action appeared to me like a vision.

I turned to Trixie. "Mrs. Thorpe, I'll be too busy to see you tomorrow, but I hope you'll give Mavis my regards."

I tugged on the sleeve of the rector's robe. "Don't worry, Sherm. I know you're afraid Mrs. Goliath here is going to take her donations somewhere else if you don't keep toeing the line. But she won't. She loves being a big fish in this little pond."

And then I locked my eyes on Sharon's. "I'll tell my mother I saw you today, Sharon, and that you haven't changed a bit. Come on, Flossie. I'll treat you to lunch on the way home. I know just the place."

We started toward the door. When we were halfway up the aisle, I stopped, turned around, and called out in the loudest voice I could manage, "Oh, Mrs. Merriman-Cheswick—"

The chatter ceased as everyone still mingling in the sanctuary looked in my direction.

I enunciated slowly and distinctly, savoring my words. "One more thing. I forgot to tell you. Your mother just got home from visiting your brother in prison. He's fine, by the way. Sends you his love."

And with that parting shot, Flossie and I strolled from the room.

Chapter 10

A Knock at the Door

From across our table at Bob's Pancake World, I studied Flossie Bingham as she gobbled down the last of her roast beef and mashed potatoes. She had a chaotic beauty all her own—like an overgrown, ramshackle yard where roses peek through a white picket fence in front, sunflowers climb up a tool shed in back, and morning glories droop from wire strung between aluminum poles on either side.

She slid a biscuit around her plate to soak up the last of the gravy and peeked over her glasses. "Thank you," she said.

"You're welcome. It's been a long time since I ate a real Sunday dinner."

She snagged the last green bean with her fingers and popped it in her mouth. "I don't mean just the dinner—I mean 'thank you' for standing up for me with those ladies."

"You're welcome, but I wouldn't call them ladies."

Our server returned. "Dessert today?"

Flossie's eyes twinkled.

I ordered cobbler and coffee for both of us. Flossie took her mirror from her purse and rubbed her finger over her front teeth. "I shouldn't eat corn on the cob." She tugged at a piece of corn silk till she pulled it loose.

"Tell me, Flossie, why do you ride a bus so far to church—especially that one?"

"We used to live in Maplewood, and it was the closest church to our house. I don't make friends very easy, so I hate to change churches this late in the game."

When the cobbler arrived, she lifted the dish to her face and inhaled deeply. A tiny drop of glaze stuck to the tip of her nose and remained. We welcomed the soft peaches to our taste buds, let the warm crust linger in our mouths, and eased into that comfortable kind of stupor that follows a busy morning and a midday meal. I was glad to delay the call I expected from my mother when I got home.

Flossie tilted her head back and slurped the final drop from her coffee cup. She smacked her lips and then set the mug in the dessert bowl. She leaned back in her chair, folded her hands across her stomach, ducked her chin, and peeked over her glasses at me.

"How long have you known the reverend's wife?"

"My whole life," I said. "They lived in the house across the street from us."

She tilted her head to one side and furrowed her brow. "Then, why would she treat your mother that way?"

"Because that's what Sharon does."

Flossie leaned across the table and laid her hand on mine. "You must never tell your mother what Sharon said about her. You know that, don't you?"

"I think she deserves to know—"

"No, you don't. You think it'll make you feel better to get back at Sharon."

"Yes. It would."

She shook her head. "It won't. It will only hurt your mother and cause a rift between her and her best friend. Is that what you want?"

Dear, gentle Flossie, I thought, you're a lady from the top of your pink hat to the bottom of your thrift store shoes—shoes Sharon Merriman-Cheswick isn't fit to shine.

Flossie dozed on the way home. I nudged her gently when we pulled up to her apartment. Before she got out of the car, she squeezed my hand.

"Would you like to have an afghan for your sofa? I got the nicest magenta yarn on sale."

I did not want an afghan, much less one woven from magenta yarn, but I knew this was her way of thanking me.

"I'd love to have one," I said, "but there's no rush."

When she reached her front door, she turned around and gave me a thumbs up. I had a feeling this signal meant she was headed straight for her knitting basket.

As I entered my apartment, the phone rang. I braced myself and picked up the receiver. "Hello?"

"Where have you been?"

I hadn't heard that edge in my mother's voice since I threw a rock through the bathroom window of the high school gym.

"I went to church like you told me to."

She was hoarse with rage. "Church was over a long time ago. I've been trying to call for hours. Do you know what you've done?"

"A good deed."

"What do you mean—good deed?"

"I ran into one of my neighbors at church. She asked me for a ride because she didn't have enough money for bus fare. So I brought her home. We stopped and had lunch."

"And you think that somehow *atones* for what you did to Sharon?"

"Do I need atonement?" I asked.

"Don't play dumb with me, Agnes. How could you do something so despicable—blurting out in front of the *entire church* about Roger? I *told* you not to bring it up."

"It wasn't in front of the entire church. The place was practically empty. There couldn't have been more than thirty people left."

She held her ground. "Jewel said you were standing in the lobby and yelled all the way to the front of the building."

Saturn pawed at my shoe. I reached down to scratch his head.

"Not true. I was only halfway to the door when I remembered what I wanted to say."

And then my mild-mannered, soft-hearted mother came the nearest to screaming at me I'd ever remembered.

"Sharon told Jewel their phone's been ringing ever since they got home. They finally had to take it off the hook."

"That's nothing new," I said. "They don't answer their phone anyway, as you'll recall. Besides that, the maid can get it."

"The maid doesn't work on Sundays."

"How unfortunate," I said. "Sharon might actually have to get up off her—"

"Now you listen to me, Agnes. You're going to call Sharon and apologize, and I mean it."

"I am not."

"Don't use that tone with me."

"If you knew what she said, Mom, you'd understand."

"Understand what?"

Flossie's gentle warning still fresh in my mind, I paused. "Understand … what she did to Flossie."

"Who's Flossie?" she asked.

"My neighbor. When she came to find me, Sharon and Trixie—"

"Who's Trixie?" My mother was near hysteria.

"She's a teacher at my school. She and Sharon—"

"Never mind. When we hang up this phone, you call Sharon and tell her you're sorry. You can *never* make up for what you did, but at least I can tell Jewel you tried."

And then—my own mother hung up on me.

I walked to the kitchen, filled Saturn's dish with food, and then sank down on the sofa. If every week turned out like this one, it was going to be a long, brutal year.

Saturn finished lunch and hopped on my lap. We curled up on the sofa and drifted off into a well-deserved nap. I dreamed of Lyda Rose. I woke with a start, hurried to my desk, and began to type.

Lyda Rose beckoned Grimwulf to approach. He bowed.

"Queen Bittershaft is moving her forces across our western border, My Lady," he said. "Someone must ride by night to bring Trevorode to our aid, or all will be lost."

I typed for two glorious hours before the phone rang.

"Did you call Sharon yet?"

Lost in the woods bordering Grimsdale Manor, I couldn't quite make sense of what my mother was saying. "No, I've been working on … schoolwork all afternoon."

"I told you to call her."

"I know, but I'm busy and I'm sure the last person on the planet she wants to hear from this afternoon is me. I'll see her at school in the morning and tell her then."

"I don't know why this is such an issue, Agnes."

"I don't either."

She hung up again.

I went back to work.

Exhausted from her journey, Lyda Rose reached the edge of the forest. The dark moor stretched out before her. She sat down to rest by the ancient Stone of Wulfgar and ate bread and cheese. A dragon of fearsome portent appeared out of the fog. He reared his head and sniffed the air. Moonlight glistened on his gray scales, and scarlet blood dripped from a gaping wound on his shoulder. Lyda Rose stood and drew her sword.

The dragon approached. He called out, "Excuse me. You're in my seat."

I leaned back in my chair, read the sentence aloud, and laughed so hard I had to wipe tears off my chin.

The day had ended well.

I took a long bath and went to bed.

As I had the week before, I woke early on Monday morning and left in plenty of time to stop by the Drifters' Rest. But when I pulled into the parking lot and saw Ryder Ellershaw through the window, I didn't get out of my car.

When I arrived at Brighton Park just after dawn, I was glad to find Jonas already there, parked in his usual place and still sitting in his truck. I pulled into the same space I'd used the week before, got out of my car, and walked around to the driver's side of his truck. He was leafing through a pile of papers propped on the steering wheel.

He rolled down his window. "Good morning. Feeling better?"

"I think so."

"Get in. You can wait with me."

Before I opened his passenger door, I reached down and ran my fingertips over the logo again and wondered if the tiny bits of paint, still tangible, might reveal some secret.

I climbed into the passenger seat.

He didn't look up from his reading. "Ready to try again?"

I laughed. "Yeah. Over the weekend I took some time to think."

He kept reading. "Thinking is always good. It's a shame people don't try it more often. Come to any conclusions?"

I nodded my head. "First of all, I'm going to—"

He looked out his windshield. "You'll have to hold that thought, Agnes. There's something I need to take care of." He pointed to a man coming toward us, then straightened the pages and placed them in a large manila envelope. When he turned it over, I read the return address: *Camden, Lockwood, Osgood, & Tuttle, Attorneys at Law.*

I pointed to the envelope. "Are you in some kind of trouble?"

"I've been in some kind of trouble a long time." He opened his door. "Care to join me?"

I got out of the truck and stepped onto the sidewalk as Wilkie Brooker reached us. He was wearing the same clothes he'd worn to my apartment.

Brooker smacked his hand on the hood of Jonas' truck. "When are you gonna get rid of this old clunker, anyway?"

Silent and stoic, Jonas held out the envelope.

Brooker laid it on the hood of the truck, removed the contents, and shuffled through them. "Signed, sealed, and delivered?"

"No. Tell Mrs. Pillburn I'm not ready to make a decision."

"She's not going to like that."

"I stopped caring about *that* a long time ago."

Brooker smirked. "Mind if I quote you?"

"Tell her anything you like."

Brooker didn't seem to notice Jonas was quivering with suppressed rage.

Brooker stacked the document on top of the envelope and tucked the whole pile under his arm. "Okay, but you probably haven't heard the last of her … or of me."

And then like a sleek cat pouncing on a rat, Jonas grabbed Brooker by his wrinkled lapels and shoved him into the truck. He tilted Brooker backward until his greasy head lay flat on the hood and his scuffed shoes lifted off the sidewalk. The papers slipped out of his grasp and scattered.

Jonas, nose to nose with him, clenched his jaw and spoke in a low tone. "Now you listen to me. I've had enough of you and your second-rate tactics and bullying. You go back to Olympia Pillburn and tell her if I were starving in the street, I would die in the gutter before I sell my interest in that property."

Jonas pulled Brooker upright and stepped back. Brooker, wide-eyed and sweating, made a feeble effort at reclaiming his dignity.

"I don't know what the fuss is over that old rattle-trap house anyway. Doesn't look to me like it's worth the powder it would take to blow it up."

"That could be said about a lot of us," Jonas said. "And now, if you'll excuse me, I have a class to teach."

After Jonas left, Brooker knelt on the pavement to reach for the papers that had fluttered under the truck. I scooped up the stray papers near me and resisted the urge to slip away to a secluded place to read them. Brooker lumbered up from the ground. I held the pages out to him.

He took his dingy handkerchief from his pocket. "Thanks. Could you hold on to those for just a second?"

I was watching Brooker wipe sweat from his face and feeling a twinge of pity for him, when out of the corner of my eye I saw a small square of white by my left front tire. I picked it up. The moment my fingers felt the smooth finish on the other side, I knew it was a photograph. I glanced at the inscription on the back, written with a woman's delicate handwriting: *Magnolia Arms*. Before I had time to turn it over, Brooker called to me.

"Is that mine?"

I dropped my hand to my side and eased it behind my back. "No, I dropped this when I got out of my car. Parking ticket." I unlocked my car and laid the photo face down on the seat.

Brooker approached. "Look, Miss—"

"Quinn." I closed my door.

"Yeah. Look—try to talk some sense into your friend, would you?"

"Mr. Brooker, of all the people I've ever met, Jonas Grinstead is by far the most sensible of all of them."

"Whatever you say. I just hope I never see this miserable campus again."

"That makes two of us." I opened my car door and slid the photo, face down, into my British literature book and then turned to face Brooker.

"Sure you have everything?" I asked.

He wiped his face again. "I think so."

"Then do us all a favor and go home."

Books in hand, I rambled through the vacant halls, piecing together the fragments of the story. But, like a jigsaw puzzle too long in a musty attic, the pieces did not fit easily into place. *Rattle-trap house*—Brooker must've meant the Magnolia Arms. This was the property Jonas refused to sell. When I'd asked Jonas about the logo on his truck, he'd said it was the *place he'd built.* The drawing on his truck must've been a magnolia tree. But why had Jonas left? Was that where he'd met the "only woman" he'd ever loved—the one Muriel had mentioned?

And *who* was Olympia Pillburn?

Worried Brooker might reappear, I locked the door of my classroom behind me and sat down at my desk. I took out the photo and turned it over.

And there was the house Jonas Grinstead had built.

A high-pitched gray shingled roof topped three stories of pale yellow walls. Tall, full-paned windows framed with gleaming white casements lined the lower two floors. Smaller gabled windows circled the third. A widow's walk sat atop a splendid cupola adorned with an arched stained-glass window. Four wide steps led up to a spacious columned porch which ran the length of the house—a house so beautiful a thousand lifetimes lived within its walls would be too few.

One look—and I was convinced if I could walk through that front door, I'd feel like I'd come home, back to the place I belonged. I'd greet people I'd never met, but they would not object when I climbed the stairs to claim the room with the stained-glass window under the topmost gable. I'd join those people at the long table in the high-ceilinged dining room. We'd linger over a sumptuous meal and listen to each other's petty concerns. The kitchen would smell of apples and vanilla, and there would always be a pot of fresh-brewed tea and clean china cups.

There would be an old upright piano in the sitting room and sometimes someone would play it and someone else would sing and ladies who walked with canes would get up and dance in a makeshift chorus line and say they hoped no one was looking through the window. And then they'd all laugh so hard they'd fall down on the faded blue-striped sofa and say, "Agnes, are there any teacakes left?" And I would wander off to the kitchen and bring them back a plateful, but they'd already be dozing, worn out from their dancing.

An insistent knocking tumbled me back into the hostile world of Brighton Park. I stashed the photo in my book and made a lunge for the door, colliding with the corner of my desk in the process. Limping, I called to the students stranded in the hallway. "Sorry, I guess I forgot—"

Still bent over, rubbing my aching knee, I fumbled with the lock and opened the door.

There stood Beatrix Thorpe, her face compressed with contempt.

I stared at her bony legs sticking out below the pleats of her red skirt. I looked up at her white cashmere sweater and double string of pearls. Her recently dyed red hair and red-framed glasses completed the look of a skinny old hen preening in the barnyard, so I wasn't all that surprised when she pulled back her shoulders, stuck out her chin, and began to squawk.

"Do you realize you're *stealing*?"

She must have spotted me with Brooker and followed me as I crept down the hall like a common thief.

"What's that supposed to mean?" I asked.

Her jaw clenched and lips pursed, she pointed to the clock on the wall and enunciated as if practicing a diction exercise. "*Eight. Oh. Two.* You've kept your students standing out here in the hall for *two* minutes of time their tuition dollars have already paid for."

She pressed against the door; I resisted.

"I'm sorry. This is my first day back after my accident—"

Her thin fingers turned white as she pushed harder. "I'm getting a little *tired* of your talking about your *accident*. You appeared to be in *perfect* health when I saw you *yesterday*." She glanced over her shoulder at someone in the hall and softened her tone to a semblance of civility. "Now let's keep our doors unlocked, shall we, so our students can get full value for their dollar." She stepped back. "Besides that—it's against the fire code." She smiled and swished away, her red high heels clicking on the terrazzo floor.

When I pulled the door open, Exton Wrayburn stepped in.

"Sorry, Miss Quinn. That was for my benefit. Mrs. Thorpe seems to think I report to my grandmother every night."

The students filed in as I hobbled to my desk. "Well, that explains her—" I took a deep breath. "Never mind."

Exton sat down near the front and took out his books. "Everybody knows how she is. I signed up for one of her classes once, but dropped it after two weeks. Are you feeling better?"

I brought my notes to the lectern. "Yes, I think so. At least I did when I got here."

For the next three hours, students swept in and flowed out like a recurring tide. Whether or not my bruised eye earned their polite attention, I couldn't guess. But even those who had appeared skeptical the week before, when I'd introduced Saxon village life, listened with genuine interest as I read aloud Beowulf's battle with Grendel. There's something about sinews snapping and bones breaking that sways any audience.

A boy nicknamed "Big Tony" stopped by my desk on his way out. "I like that story."

I looked up at him. "Have you read a classic before?"

"No. I never saw much point in reading made-up stories, but I like this one." He tapped on his temple. "I could see the whole thing in my head while you were reading."

I peeked in the front my book to make sure the photo was still there, closed my book bag, and picked up my keys off the desk. "I've got good news for you. There are two monsters left, and they're worse than Grendel. One of them breathes fire."

I ventured out to find Sharon. Though I could've easily asked Trixie where to find her, I headed toward the administration building instead where I found a perky blonde stationed at the information desk. She directed me to Building E. I located Sharon's classroom and stood outside the open door the few remaining minutes of her class. If I hadn't known her, I would have been impressed. There was no denying she was beautiful and accomplished. I ambled in after the students filed out.

"Hello, Sharon."

She glanced over at me and returned to her work. "Agnes."

I stepped closer. "Look, Sharon, I got a little out of hand yesterday, and I'm sorry."

"Is that all you have to say?"

"I think so," I said. "I hope I didn't cause too much trouble with your church members."

Her voice was glacial. "No, you didn't cause any trouble. I explained to them what a miserable person you've always been."

With memories of Beowulf still clanging through my mind, I opened my mouth to slay Sharon verbally, but stopped. I had loftier goals to pursue. I wasn't going to distract myself by prolonging an endless cycle of Sharon's tattling to her mother and my mother's badgering me over the phone.

When I reached the door, I turned to face her. "Well then, I guess we'll have to leave the great mystery unsolved."

"What's that?"

"Which of us loathes the other more."

My next class wasn't until four. My own office, a musty, windowless room in a portable building, was ridiculously far removed from the central core of the campus. I'd already determined to spend as little time there as possible. I made my way to the library and stopped by Elinor's office to say hello. She seemed bewildered to see me.

"Agnes, what are you doing here? Is the luncheon over already?" She rummaged through papers on her desk. "I thought it would last at least an hour and a half—maybe longer."

"Luncheon?"

"The English Department luncheon, the first of the school year. That British poet, Glynis Sudbury, was scheduled to speak. I thought you told me she was one of your favorites."

She scanned the room and then moved to the file cabinet, where she attacked another pile of papers sitting on top.

I pulled out my planner and flipped through the pages.

"No. That meeting is scheduled for a week from today."

She didn't look up. "It was *originally* scheduled a week from today, but Sudbury's mother is ill. Her publicist asked to move things up a week so she could go home early. Trixie notified everyone of the change. Didn't you get the memo?"

"No, I didn't get the memo. I was in the hospital."

"Yes, I know, but Trixie should've called you."

In a moment all the pieces fell into place. I settled in a chair across from Elinor's desk. "I've gone and done it now," I said.

"What's that, dear?"

Elinor, distracted, spoke more into the air than to me. She grabbed a cardboard box, dumped its contents on the floor, and plunked it down next to the filing cabinet. One by one, she picked up a folder from the pile she was working on, gave it a quick once-over, and tossed it into the waiting box.

I stared at a photo of Robert Scott on the wall. "Maybe Trixie *would* have told me about the luncheon yesterday if I hadn't insulted Sharon."

Elinor opened the bottom drawer of the filing cabinet and dropped in a folder. "Sharon?"

"Trixie's friend." The latest evidence of Trixie's malice woke the dormant resentments I'd been nursing. "I mean … I *expected* to have a crummy schedule. First-year teachers are always at the bottom of the food chain. Three classes early in the morning and the next one not till four … and don't even get me *started* on my Tuesday/Thursday schedule."

"It can't be replaced," Elinor said as papers fluttered to the floor.

"—and okay, so maybe I don't deserve an office bigger than a closet, but couldn't I at least have a window? I feel like I'm in a cell."

Elinor kicked the bottom file drawer closed. "On interlibrary loan and from my own alma mater—what could be worse?"

"But to deprive me of a professional opportunity—is that even ethical?"

Elinor hurried toward her bookcase and lifted a heap of magazines from the bottom shelf. "How can I possibly explain?"

"I don't think rudeness like Trixie's *can* be explained," I said.

The magazines fell from Elinor's hands. She leaned her head against the bookcase and began to sob. "I'll be ruined. I can't file another report saying I've lost something else."

For the first time since our pinball conversation began, I intersected with Elinor. I took her by the elbow and guided her to her desk. She slumped into her chair. Her face was pale, eyes vacant. I handed her a tissue from the box on the corner of the desk and then knelt down to gather the magazines scattered on the floor.

"What do you mean … you've lost something else?" I asked.

She dabbed at her eyes and wiped her nose. "I keep misplacing things. Something goes missing almost every day. It's one thing if it's a pen or a pair of scissors, but now …."

I walked back to my chair and sat down to face her. "Now what?"

"The History Department chair wanted a manuscript from the University of Florida, a Civil War diary. It arrived yesterday, but now I can't find it anywhere."

I handed her another tissue. "It has to be here somewhere. I have a long time till my next class. I'll stay and help you look."

She shook her head. "You don't understand. It isn't the first time this has happened. I'm afraid I'm losing my mind. What good is a librarian who can't keep track of books?"

I stood. "Now, you get that thought right out of your head. You have a lot of responsibility and not enough help. Let's start looking."

We scoured the library for the missing diary. Elinor was even more upset when we failed.

After my last class in remedial grammar and composition, I drove to the Drifters' Rest.

Muriel set a menu in front of me. "I'd say 'you look like something the cat dragged in,' but I don't think that's what you need to hear."

I handed the menu back to her. "Bring me the soup of the day and a glass of tea."

"Leave everything to me," she said. "I know exactly what you need."

Muriel returned with a steaming bowl of creamy potato soup garnished with grated cheese and crumbled bacon, a chicken salad sandwich, and a fruit plate with honeydew melon, mandarin oranges, and cherries.

She stood back and crossed her arms as she admired the meal.

"I always serve something colorful with potato soup. It's nutritious, but lackluster."

I dipped my spoon in the bowl and closed my eyes as I breathed in the wonderful smell. Then I ate a spoonful of what could only be described as *Heaven in Your Mouth.*

The concerns of the day faded. "It's delicious," I said.

"My mother's recipe," Muriel said.

I lingered, requested extra cheese, and found my iced tea glass was never empty. Too full for dessert, I asked for the check.

"No charge," Muriel said.

I leaned back in my chair. "Look, I appreciate your taking care of me when I came home from the hospital, but you're running a business here. I can't take free food forever."

"Your dinner has already been paid for from the account opened in your name. Your credit should last through, oh … I guess about May … if you keep eating sensibly."

"Credit? You're making that up."

Muriel cleared the table. "No. It's the truth."

I laid a twenty-dollar bill on the table. "Who would do such a thing? You and Jonas are my only friends, and neither of you has money to spare."

She picked up the twenty and returned it. "For your information, it wasn't Jonas or me."

I followed her toward the kitchen. "Then who?"

"I'm not supposed to tell." The kitchen door closed behind her.

I waited by the counter till she returned. "You have to tell me. I won't be able to sleep."

She stepped behind the counter. "Coffee to go?"

I nodded. She filled the cup.

"He was grateful you didn't file charges," Muriel said.

Ryder Ellershaw.

It was after seven by the time I arrived at home. Saturn, miffed at being left alone for twelve hours, remained by the pantry till I retrieved the cat food.

My mother called at seven thirty. I squeaked out a weak hello.

Her voice exploded through the receiver. "*Which of us loathes the other more*? You call *that* an apology?"

"She called me a 'miserable person.' I lost what little patience I had left."

She was unsympathetic. "Now you listen to me. You're going back to that school tomorrow and you're going to find Sharon and—"

A knock at the door spared me.

"I have to go. Someone's at the door. Don't worry, I won't insult Sharon again. She'll finish her substitute teaching and go home to her husband, and that will be the end of it."

"I'm not through talking about this, Agnes."

"Okay, Mom. I gotta go. Bye."

I opened the door to find Flossie, afghan in hand, beaming at me.

"Hello, Agnes. I'm almost finished, but I wanted to try it on the back of your sofa first."

"Maybe another time," I said. "I have a lot of grading—"

Before I could close the door, she stepped inside. "Oh, how cozy. I wish Warner would let me put pictures on our walls, but he doesn't want to mess up the paint."

Flossie draped the afghan over the sofa, tugged, smoothed, pulled, and straightened the edges, and then stood back, like Michelangelo, to survey the effect. Without her pink Sunday hat, her hair fluffed out in all directions.

I stood in the doorway of the kitchen. "Looks like that's about right," I said, "but you didn't need to go to all that trouble."

She walked around the sofa, sat down, and eased her shoulders into the magenta folds. "Don't you just love the feel of knitted yarn?"

"I've never given it much thought." I appreciated Flossie's sparing me from a painful conversation with my mother, but I was too tired to entertain her. "If you'll excuse me, I'll make my lunch for tomorrow. I never have time in the morning."

I thought she might get the hint, but she stayed where she was.

"That's fine, dear. You go right ahead."

I took the loaf of bread from the pantry and called to Flossie from the kitchen as I worked. "That was my mother on the phone. I took your advice and didn't tell her what Sharon said about her. Of course, now she's mad at me instead of being mad at Sharon, but at least her feelings aren't hurt." I put my lunch in the refrigerator. "I guess you were right—" I added as I stepped to the kitchen door, but my remarks had gone unheeded.

Flossie Bingham was snoring.

Chapter 11

A Tangled Web

I let Flossie sleep while I graded essays. I tried to convince myself this gesture was motivated by kindness, but in reality, I wanted to avoid a lengthy chat. When it was too late for her to do anything but go home and go to bed, I tapped her on the shoulder. Her eyes popped open; she was disoriented and panicked.

"It's dark. Warner will be furious I'm out so late. Where are my glasses?"

I lifted her glasses off the top of her head. She jiggled them onto her nose, stood, and smoothed her dress. I folded the afghan and handed it to her.

"Don't worry," I said. "I'll walk home with you and explain everything."

When we reached her apartment, she thanked me for a nice evening—a jab my conscience could have done without. She unlocked the door and pushed it open. Warner was asleep in the sagging recliner. She pressed her finger to her lips, then stepped inside and pushed the door closed without a sound.

I resolved never again to be unkind to Flossie.

The next morning I arrived at Brighton Park an hour before my first class. My first stop would be the English Department office where I'd demonstrate to Trixie I was "on time." In the future, I'd skip this step, but today I had to begin charting where she was at any given hour.

As I hurried past Jonas' truck, I brushed my fingers along the hood. This very truck, I thought, was once parked in the driveway of the Magnolia Arms.

When I entered the office, Trixie and Mavis stopped talking.

I chirped as I breezed by them. "Hello, ladies. Chilly this morning, isn't it?"

Trixie looked at her planner, opened on the table.

"I need to speak to you, Agnes," she said. "When can you come to my office?"

I checked my watch. "I have time now."

She licked her spoon. "I'd rather not discuss this in front of another teacher."

"But if we talk now," I said, as I put my lunch in the refrigerator, "you'll be saved the trouble of repeating the story." I winked at Mavis.

Trixie's face turned as red as her glasses. "Have it your way. I noticed you dismissed your last class five minutes early yesterday."

"Is that all? I thought you were going to apologize for not telling me about the luncheon."

As if reciting a sacred creed, Mavis intoned a passage from the faculty handbook. "Each teacher is responsible to check the calendar of events. Mrs. Thorpe isn't to blame if—"

Trixie rallied. "Actually, the reason I came to your classroom yesterday was to tell you the luncheon had been rescheduled. When I found your door locked, I lost my train of thought."

I turned toward my mailbox, though I knew nothing was there.

"Perfectly understandable," I said.

"Don't use that tone with me, young woman." Trixie stood and tapped the table with her manicured nails. "I answer to the board of trustees. Why did you release your—?"

I picked up my book bag. "Charlotte Wrayburn is on the board, isn't she?"

"Yes, but how ..."

"Then that solves everything. I'm having dinner with her on Friday. I'll give her a full account of my week then."

I pushed open the door and left the room.

Only fifteen minutes into Tuesday, and I'd scored a decisive victory.

One day closer to leaving for the Magnolia Arms, I imagined myself strolling toward the stately yellow house. The dingy hall gave way to a tree-lined street where pink azaleas drooped over fences and Confederate jasmine clung to trellises. Someday, I thought, I won't have to dodge trashcans piled with leftovers from yesterday's lunches. Someday I'll wake up to mockingbirds and honeysuckle. Someday I'll walk down this hall and out of Brighton Park for the last time. I quickened my pace.

"What's your hurry?"

For a moment I thought a fictional neighbor had called to me. I turned to find Jonas Grinstead.

"Hello," I said. "I'm not in a hurry—just happy."

He held out a piece of paper. "Then you may not need Muriel's assistance after all."

I stopped and unfolded the note.

Dear Agnes, Meet Jonas for lunch in the Math Dept. at 11:00. If Trixie finds out, tell her you're having a conference. Muriel

I could hear Muriel laughing as she signed the note.

Jonas held up a large bag from the Drifters' Rest.

"You'll join me, won't you?" he asked. "This is too much for me to eat by myself."

I tucked the note in my book bag. "How can I refuse?"

"Walk with me," he said, "and I'll show you where the math building is. Any particular reason you're so happy?"

"I got the upper hand with Trixie."

"That's quite an accomplishment for a novice. Can you give me a few pointers at lunch?"

I shook my head. "I'd much rather talk about the Magnolia Arms."

He stopped and turned to me, his friendly tone altered to cool civility.

"Where did you hear about that?" he asked.

"I … when … Brooker said …"

He relaxed. "I'm sorry. I forgot. You stayed with Brooker after I stormed off yesterday."

I was still shaken. "I … helped him pick up the papers he dropped."

"How much did he tell you?" Jonas asked.

"Not much. He was in a hurry." This statement, at least, was true.

I stopped talking. When we reached the corner, Jonas pointed to a building on his right.

"The Math Department office is in there—on the second floor," he said.

I nodded and turned to walk away.

"Agnes," Jonas said, "I'm sorry if I seem a little … abrupt. My worlds have never intersected till now. It's going to take some getting used to—someone knowing about my past."

"It's all right, Jonas," I said. "We all have secrets to keep."

His face relaxed into a trace of a smile. "See you at eleven." He pointed at the gathering clouds. "Bring an umbrella."

The rain poured all through my grammar and composition class, making the painful ninety-minute session seem unending. When I freed my students, I headed toward the library to check on Elinor. Her desk and bookshelves were scraped clean. Empty filing cabinet drawers gaped open. Elinor's hair, usually parted on the side and layered in neat rows of tight springy curls, drooped over her face. Her eyes were ringed with dark circles.

"Any success?" I asked.

She didn't look up. Instead she pulled a black plastic bag from a box labeled *Acme Lawn and Leaf Bags*, snapped it open, and thrust it toward me. "Hold this for me, would you?"

I complied. She lifted a large pile of papers from the floor and dropped them in. Then she picked up a wilted plant from her desk and threw it in on top.

"I never liked that plant."

I twisted the bag closed and set it by the door.

"Why don't you rest awhile and let me take a turn?" I asked.

She sat on the edge of a chair in the corner and stared at the floor.

"This is all I have, Agnes," she said. This is who I am. I take care of books and help people find what they need. If I can't do *that*, what *good* am I?"

I knelt in front of her. "Listen to me, Elinor. You're an amazing woman—lovely, intelligent, and accomplished. There's more to you than a pile of dusty old books."

She did not reply.

I carried four black bags to the workroom and instructed Elinor's assistant, Grace Bonner, to open them and make sure nothing valuable had been discarded. Then I searched the workroom, perused the shelves under the checkout desk, and sorted through a pile of mail. The journal was nowhere to be found. Ten minutes before my lunch with Jonas, I returned to Elinor's office.

I laid my hand on her arm. "I have to go, but I'll be back after lunch. My next class isn't until three. Could I leave my books here, so I don't have to carry them in the rain?"

"If you're not afraid I'll lose them while you're gone," she said.

In the Math Department office, Jonas had laid out the feast Muriel had prepared. At my place was a sandwich wrapped in paper. On his plate was a portion of pastrami and an onion bagel. A small bowl of potato salad served as a centerpiece. A plastic container of tea waited to be poured over ice in two plastic cups.

Jonas pulled out my chair. "We have forty-five minutes."

"Understood." I took my turkey sandwich from its wrapper.

He dipped potato salad onto his plate. "Enjoying your classes?"

"I am. There's a lot to be said for investing your life in a worthy occupation."

He leaned back his head and laughed. "You sound like me thirty years ago."

I seized the opportunity. "Teaching wasn't your first choice either?"

He opened the jar of mustard. "I had to get away from where I was. I wanted to make a new start, find a piece of property I could afford, and—"

"Build another house?"

He spread mustard on the bagel. "Brooker told you that too, did he?"

"You did. When I asked about the logo on the truck, you said it was the place you built."

He studied his sandwich, rested the knife in the middle, and cut it into precise halves.

"I guess I did. Yes, I thought I might build another house, but that never happened."

I wanted to press him further, but opted to play it safe. I wanted this meal to be the first of many lunches together—not the last. For a while we ate in silence. Then I ventured a question.

"May I ask you something—as a new teacher, to someone with years of experience?"

"Sure."

"Do you regret not building another house?"

He refilled his half-empty cup. "That's not exactly a question about teaching, is it?"

"No … but I need to know if you look back and wish—"

"I could have never built another house like that one."

"It was that extravagant?"

"No. I mean I was a different person back then—young and idealistic and full of hope. That house was my dream. It was supposed to be the beginning, not the end."

His voice trailed off as he sank deeper into his memories. I sat motionless, listening to the clock on the wall tick off the seconds.

"The end of what?"

He stood, walked to the counter where he'd left the bag from the Drifters' Rest, and lifted out a small white box.

"Almond cookies. A new recipe. Muriel wants us to be her taste testers."

A delicate scent drifted up as I opened the box. I lifted out a perfectly round cookie, golden brown at the edges, and bit into it. The inside was soft, airy, melting on my tongue before I could chew. Muriel had outdone herself. I licked powdered sugar from my fingertips and reached in the box for two more.

"Thank goodness Muriel found her true calling, even if we didn't," I said.

Jonas sat down again. "Family business. She came by her gift honestly."

"And you? Was your father a builder?"

"No, he loved dirt—not wood."

"Dirt?"

"Cotton farmer—worked his whole life to own a piece of land he could hand down to his son. Nearly lost hope when he had four daughters before I came along. Coffee?"

I analyzed the stained coffeepot sitting by the paper cutter.

"No, thanks," I said. "You have *four* sisters?"

He smiled. "All named after flowers, in honor of my grandmother Magnolia."

"Magnolia? You named your house after your grandmother? That's nice."

"You overestimate me," he said. "It wasn't homage to my grandmother. It was a peace offering to my father."

"Was he pleased?"

Jonas stared into his coffee cup and shook his head. "No, nothing I could do could atone for leaving the farm. Dad thought I loved the land because I worked with him. But I did it because I loved *him*, not because I loved soil."

"Then how did you get interested in building?"

He reached in his back pocket for his wallet, opened it, and gently removed a faded photograph from its yellowed plastic casing. I held it close to my face. Looking out from a fenced yard was a woman in a flowered housedress. Her hair, neatly brushed, framed a pleasant face; her work-worn hands cradled a wooden birdhouse.

"I made that for my mother's birthday when I was twelve. Once I got the feel of wood in my hands, I was never the same. I saved my allowance for months to buy my own set of tools."

I took the last sip of tea. "People underestimate the power of a childhood dream."

He reached for my empty plate as he stood. "What about you? Did your parents encourage your writing?"

"They used to think my stories were cute, but insisted I give up 'my hobby' when I started college."

"And did you?" he asked.

"Not at first. It took me two years to wise up enough to toss my dream in a drawer."

"When you lost Xander?"

"Who told you that?"

He smiled. "You did—well, you told Zane Plumley. You said when Xander left, you gave up writing. Was that when you decided to *invest your life in a worthy occupation*?"

His tone annoyed me. "I'd think you'd be the last person in the world to joke about that."

"I'm sorry, Agnes," he said. "You mustn't take it that way. It's just that I see myself in you. I was so foolish to think I could run away from …"

"From what?"

The phone rang. Jonas answered. "Math Department. Who? Slow down. When? Okay, I'm on my way." He grabbed his jacket. "Could you clean up, Agnes? I have to go."

I dropped my napkin in the trashcan as I rushed after him. "What's wrong?"

"It's the librarian."

"Elinor? What happened?"

"There's been an accident. She's been hit by a car."

Jonas slowed as we neared the parking lot. When we reached the edge of the crowd, he took my hand and pushed through the swarm of students and teachers. A policeman knelt on the pavement next to Elinor, who lay face down, barely breathing. Blood oozed from a gash on her forehead. Her arm, purple and swollen to twice its size, lay twisted at an odd angle beside her.

Jonas knelt and put his hand on her shoulder. "Elinor, it's Jonas. Can you hear me?"

The sight of Elinor's broken arm made me nauseated. I stood, brushed the gravel from my knees, and began backing away. Near the curb another policeman was filling out a report as a hysterical young woman, waving her arms, said, "She walked right out in front of me. It's like she didn't even see me. There was no way I could stop in time."

Rain began to fall as I jostled through the crowd on my way back to the math office. Why hadn't I stayed with Elinor or at least offered to drive her home?

"Here, Agnes. Share my umbrella." Mavis Applewhite had stepped beside me and shoved her umbrella up over my head. She was trembling. "Did you find out how Elinor is?"

"She's unconscious. Her arm is definitely broken. I couldn't stand to look at it, so I left. Jonas is with her."

Mavis squeezed my hand. "Did you pick up her purse?"

"No. I don't remember seeing it."

She gripped my hand tighter as I tried to pull away from her clammy fingers.

"I think you should find it," she said. "A woman needs her purse."

"You've been her friend longer than I have, Mavis. Why don't you go?"

"I can't. I … can't stand the sight of blood."

"We'll ask Jonas later," I said. "I'm not going back in the rain."

"Take my umbrella. Please, Agnes, go back and look. I'll wait in my office. Bring her purse to me, and I'll keep it for her. It's the least we can do."

Her concern—the only glimmer of human kindness I'd observed in her—touched my heart. I turned back, hopped over puddles, dodged water pouring from drain spouts, and arrived at the parking lot in a few minutes. The crowd scattered as the ambulance turned onto the road. Jonas was gone. I approached the only police officer still on the scene.

"Excuse me," I said.

He didn't look up from his report. "Yes?" he said, still writing.

"The victim … the woman who was hurt … is a friend of mine. I was wondering if I could take her personal belongings with me. I'm sure she'd want someone to look after them."

He scanned his report. "All she had with her was a handbag. Personal belongings always stay with the patient so the hospital will have proper identification."

I walked back to the Math Department office and cleaned the table. Then I dropped by Mavis' office, but she wasn't there. I scribbled a note saying Elinor's purse had gone with her to the hospital, and then I returned to the library to pick up my books. When I entered, Grace Bonner waved me over to the checkout desk.

"How is Miss Parfrey?" she asked.

I shared the information I knew. "I'm going straight to the hospital after my last class."

"What time is that?" she asked.

When I told her, she motioned for me to follow her. Once we were inside Elinor's office, Grace closed the door and lowered her voice.

"Remember how you told me to check the garbage bags for anything valuable? When I opened the last bag, I found this on top. I didn't know if I should read it."

She handed me a wrinkled envelope with Elinor's name typed on the front.

"Close the door as you leave," I said. "If someone asks later, you can honestly say you didn't read this and have no idea what it says. There's no need in both of us getting in trouble."

She thanked me and left me alone in the office. I studied the envelope. Elinor had used a letter opener. Had she been so upset by this note she stumbled out of her office and into the path of a car? I paused, considered the consequences of snooping, and then took the crumpled letter from the envelope and read:

Dear Elinor, I noticed you've been distracted lately, so I asked Trixie about it. She says you've been misplacing things and thinks maybe you're working too hard. I have a longtime friend, also a librarian, who needs to move to a milder climate, but he's been unable to find a job. Perhaps if you need help, he might come here and work with you. I only want to help. Mavis

The whole sordid story fell into place. Mavis' feigned concern for Elinor's purse was because she thought *this* letter was in it. Knowing Elinor was in a fragile state of mind, Mavis had to assume this "helpful" letter had precipitated the accident. Elinor was neither losing nor misplacing anything. Mavis had been pilfering. A teacher and "the librarian's friend," she could frequent Elinor's office without attracting attention. She must have been sneaking around the library for weeks, discrediting Elinor so her own "longtime friend" could step into her job.

I read the letter again: "*he's* been unable to find a job." A man. An old college friend Mavis had "loved and lost"? Did she entertain the same delusions for her "librarian friend" as Trixie did for Jonas? Had she dropped by to "visit" Elinor, asked her for a cup of tea, and then dropped the journal in her purse while Elinor was out of her office?

After my last class I drove to the hospital and entered Elinor's room. Her arm, wrapped in an elastic bandage, was supported by a sling, her hand still swollen, her face scraped and bruised. I was glad to find her asleep. First, the worried expression she'd worn so many days was gone, and second, I could continue my detective work.

A vase of pink roses sat on her bedside table. I read the accompanying card, not at all surprised at the signature:

Trixie and I stopped by to see you. We're so sorry about your accident. Please call as soon as you're awake, and let me know if there's any way I can help. Mavis

Yeah, right, I thought. You'd like to help Elinor right over a cliff.

On the floor in front of the closet was a large clear plastic bag which contained Elinor's clothes and purse. I wondered if Trixie had kept watch at the door while Mavis plundered through to search for the condemning note. I opened the plastic bag and took out Elinor's white sweater, the sleeve ripped and stained from her fall. Then I lifted out her purse. I was about to open it when I heard a voice from the doorway.

"Looking for something?" Jonas asked.

"Not really," I said. "I'm just trying to confirm my theory."

He walked toward the bed. "She looks much better now, doesn't she?"

I rifled through Elinor's purse, empty except for her wallet, two pens, and a receipt.

"Has the doctor said anything?" I asked.

"They're going to keep her overnight. Muriel will pick her up when she's released and let her stay upstairs at the Drifters' Rest till she's better."

"I should have known you two would already have a plan," I said.

He smiled and squeezed Elinor's uninjured hand. "Now," he said, looking across the bed at me, "I'll walk you to your car, and you can explain yourself."

Outside the hospital, I told him the story of Elinor's growing panic and Mavis' note. "Don't you think it's likely Mavis is behind all this?" I said as I opened my car door.

"That's quite a leap, Agnes, but if it is true, you'd better be careful about making accusations. Mavis is an institution at Brighton Park, and she and Trixie are thick as—"

"Thieves?"

He laughed. "I'm not saying it's impossible. I've never known Elinor to be less than perfect at her job. But I repeat: be careful. You think you know Trixie and Mavis, but you don't."

Jonas closed my door and walked across the parking lot to his truck. I was backing out my car when I heard a tap on my window. I turned to find Dolley Madison smiling at me.

I rolled down my window.

"Did you miss us so much you came back for a visit?" she asked.

"No, I was visiting a friend."

"Elinor Parfrey?" she asked. "Muriel's already asked me to keep an eye on her."

"Do you think she'll be all right?"

"You know very well I can't—"

"I know," I said. "You can't discuss another patient with me."

"You should be glad we have that rule," she said.

"What do you mean?"

"Because someone came here asking about you, and I told him the same thing."

"Him?" I asked.

"Don't worry. He's a good man, but I still didn't give him your phone number."

I put the car in park. "Who?"

"Buck Sloan," she said. "You've made quite an impression on him."

"Oh, no," I said. "That's the last thing I need."

"I wouldn't be too hasty, Agnes. He's a nice man."

"He's old enough to be my father."

"You're exaggerating," she said.

"What should I do?" I asked. "I don't want to hurt his feelings."

"Let him down easy, but you'd better hurry. He's smitten."

"Now you're exaggerating," I said.

"Just a little," she said. "Now go home and get some rest."

After Dolley left, I spotted Buck's card still lying on the seat. "Buttercup will be expecting your call," he'd said. Was this his subtle way of saying he hoped I'd call to schedule a visit? I drove toward home. Dolley was right. I had to make it clear to Buck I wasn't interested in him. But while he still grieved over Geneva, I couldn't hurt his feelings. I brooded over the problem all evening till an idea came to me. I could use Elinor's accident as an excuse and even appear self-sacrificing. I dialed his number.

He answered, "Sloan's Canyon."

"Hello, Mr. Sloan. This is Agnes Quinn."

"Agnes, I'm glad to hear from you. Please call me Buck."

"All right then, Buck. I called to say I won't be able to visit the ranch anytime soon. I have a friend who was in an accident and she's going to need my help for a while."

"You mean Elinor Parfrey?"

"Yes. How did you know?"

"It was on the evening news. She's a friend of yours?"

"Yes. I've only known her a short time, but we've become close."

He paused. "Let's say this: give me another call on Friday. If Elinor is better, bring her with you on Saturday. Folks say a ride around the ranch makes 'em feel better every time."

There was no way to refuse his offer. I agreed to call again on Friday. Maybe Elinor wouldn't be up to going.

The next day I began frequenting the English Department office, chatting with other teachers, asking questions about how long they'd been teaching and how well they knew Mavis and Trixie. I visited Mavis' office to update her about Elinor. I wanted her to think of my visits as friendly, so I could poke around without her becoming suspicious. If she were stealing from the library, I reasoned, she wouldn't take the items home. If she kept them in her office, she could say she borrowed them and forgot to return them. If I could find them there, I'd nail her.

The rest of the week passed without incident. Muriel retrieved Elinor from the hospital and took her to the Drifters' Rest. I waited till Thursday to visit and was pleased to find Elinor sitting at a table by the window. She smiled when she saw me and motioned for me to sit down.

Her injured arm lay in her lap. "I'm glad to see you, Agnes. I wanted to thank you."

"For what?" I asked.

Muriel approached with a mug of coffee and a spoon.

"For being there when I needed you," Elinor said.

"But I wasn't there when you needed me. I should've offered to take you home."

She patted my hand. "No, no. Things have worked out exactly as they should. I've been wondering for a long time when I should retire, and now that's been decided for me."

Muriel stepped behind Elinor, caught my eye, and shook her head. I understood her meaning. Elinor was trying to convince herself.

"Don't be silly," I said. "A broken arm won't stop you from doing your job."

"Oh, haven't you heard? I've been put on administrative leave. They're interviewing an interim librarian next week."

My heart fell into my shoes. "Next week? College librarians aren't that easy to find."

"Not usually. But it turns out Mavis has an old friend who's been looking for a job. The dean is going to interview him."

"How convenient," I said. "It's almost too perfect, isn't it?"

She sipped her tea. "Would you like something to eat?"

"No, thanks. I don't feel like eating."

"You mean you came just to see me?"

"Yes ... and to invite you on an outing, if you feel like it."

"Outing?"

I explained how I'd met Geneva Gilbey and Buck.

"He heard about your accident and thought you might enjoy a ride around the ranch."

"How nice," she said. "Sounds just like what I need. I've heard about that place. Everyone says it's breathtaking."

On Friday morning Exton delivered his grandmother's handwritten note with directions to her home and a promise of beef bourguignon and lemon mousse.

I was admitted to the Wrayburn home by an honest-to-goodness butler. As I surveyed the lofty foyer, I wished I'd worn last year's Easter dress for the occasion, but when Charlotte appeared, she was comfortably attired in a pair of black pants and a white lace-collared blouse with a cameo brooch. We sat down in a formal dining room at a table that seated twelve.

She took her place at the head of the table and directed me to the chair on her right. "Ordinarily," she said, "you'd sit opposite me, but I wanted to make it easier to chat."

I stood by my chair and gaped at the magnificent room. The furnishings, chandelier, paintings, and fresh flowers did not inspire me half so much as the wall of wood-framed windows which looked out onto a cobblestone-paved garden. From a white fountain in the center, water spurted up from a stone lily. At the end of the path, a white gazebo, lined with yellow and purple pansies in Oriental pots, beckoned.

I stood at the windows. "I feel like I'm in the house I dreamed about when I was a child."

"What a nice thing to say. My husband worked hard to make a home for our family. But first, you must tell me all about yourself. Come sit down."

I couldn't imagine the chronicle of my thoroughly ordinary existence would appeal to this cultured woman, but she seemed genuinely interested in my family and my brief, perplexing life. She was so gracious and charming that before I realized what was happening, I spilled out the entire story of my failed dreams, petty frustrations, and lost loves. She never once diverted her eyes from mine.

When I realized I was twisting my linen napkin in my fingers, I stopped.

"Please forgive me," I said. "You didn't invite me here to talk about myself."

She pushed back from the table. “Nonsense. I appreciate both your candor and your passion. Let’s walk in the garden and then you can read while we have coffee.”

As we strolled, Charlotte pointed out one plant and then another, sharing the story of where she’d bought this one, when she’d planted that one, and how this one survived a hard freeze and that one endured a hurricane.

We sat down in the gazebo and looked toward the house. “You must come back in the spring and see the azaleas in full bloom,” she said.

“Do you sit out here often?” I asked.

“No, too many memories of my husband.” She stood and ran her hand along the railing. “But this place will still be here when I’m ready to enjoy it again. Jonas built it to last.”

“Jonas?” I asked.

She stepped down. As we started back toward the house, she put her arm through mine.

“Dr. Jonas Grinstead, a math professor at your school. He’s a truly gifted man. I hope you can meet him someday, but it’s not likely. He keeps to himself.”

“As a matter of fact, we had lunch last Tuesday,” I said.

“How remarkable. He usually doesn’t talk to strangers.”

“How do you know him?” I asked.

“He worked for us the summer he moved here, before he began teaching. He lived in the apartment over our garage. I suppose you met him during faculty orientation?”

I repeated the story of my first encounter with Jonas and how Muriel had helped me earn a second chance with him. I thought Charlotte would find the story amusing, but I was wrong.

She didn’t speak again till we reached the house.

“Sad, isn’t it, that Jonas has spent his life grieving and worrying over petty things like parking places? He’d have been a different man if he’d married Margaret Hawthorne.”

Margaret Hawthorne—the only woman Jonas would ever love. Now I knew her name.

I followed Charlotte into the library. A leather-bound copy of *Great Expectations* was lying on the brocade sofa. She requested coffee to be served, and I began: *My father’s family name being Pirrip, and my Christian name Philip, my infant tongue could make of both names nothing longer or more explicit than Pip. So, I called myself Pip, and came to be called Pip.*

I read a full hour before I paused to look up. Charlotte had nestled her head in the corner of her wingback chair. In the glow of the tall lamp on the end table, her glistening silver hair and soft complexion made her appear angelic.

With her eyes still closed, she said, "You've quite transported me to another time and place."

"My pleasure," I said. "I've enjoyed the evening more than I can say."

She sat up. "What is the fee for your recitals?"

I closed the book. "I owe you for the pleasure of being in your beautiful home."

"Then we have an appointment again next Friday?"

"Absolutely."

When I reached the library door, I stopped and turned around. "Maybe next time you could tell me more about Jonas … and Margaret?"

"Jonas told me in confidence," she said.

"Can you at least tell me if Margaret lived at the Magnolia Arms?" I asked.

Her mouth dropped open. "You must have a rare gift, my dear, to have learned that from Jonas in such a short time. How did you manage?"

"I'm not sure, but I'm convinced our meeting was meant to happen, as if the Magnolia Arms is … my destiny."

I expected her to laugh, but she didn't. "You may be right," she said. "Good night."

When I got home, I called Buck and told him Elinor and I would arrive at nine.

"I'll have pancakes on the griddle and saddles on the horses," he said.

I could tell by his voice he was smiling.

Chapter 12

A Romantic Interlude

When I stepped out of my car at Sloan's Canyon, Buck welcomed me and then lumbered around to open Elinor's door and offer her his rough, strong hand. He treated her as if she were a rare blue orchid lately arrived from Brazil.

After serving us a breakfast of pancakes and berries, he guided us to the stable. The moment I entered I recognized Geneva's horse, more majestic than I'd imagined. The morning sun, streaming through the hayloft door, embraced Buttercup, infusing her golden coat and mane with a rosy color for which there is no name.

In spite of my polite resistance, Buck persuaded me to mount Buttercup for a walk around the pasture. I pointed to the fading bruise around my eye.

"See this? I don't want another one to match it."

"I'll lead her," he said. "There's nothing to worry about."

He escorted Elinor to a wooden swing beneath a massive oak. She laughed and applauded when I put my left foot in the stirrup, swung my right leg over, and settled in the saddle like a newly sworn member of a posse.

Buck mounted his own horse, Buster, and took Buttercup's reins in his hand. "Hold on to the saddle horn," he said, "and your knees snug into her sides. Keep your heels down."

We circled the pasture once and then he stopped and handed me the reins. After five minutes of instruction, I was on my own and doing remarkably well. I credited Buttercup with being a good horse, not any natural grace of my own. When I felt compelled to sing, I understood at once why Geneva had refused to give up riding.

When we rejoined Elinor, we found her crying. Buck was off his horse in seconds. He pulled a faded red bandana from his back pocket and handed it to Elinor as he knelt by the swing.

"What's wrong, little lady? Sad because you can't ride yet, when Agnes made it look so easy?"

She laid her hand on his. "No, I'm not sad. It's so beautiful here. I'm beginning to feel like myself again."

He put his hand beneath her elbow and helped her up. "Remember you're always welcome." He kissed her on the cheek and winked at me. The "you" was plural.

A funny thing happened when I got home from Sloan's Canyon.

I sat down and began to write.

When Saturn leaped up on the desk, I looked at the clock. I'd been at the typewriter for four hours. I hadn't written so effortlessly since I was a teenager. Though I'd forgotten dinner, Saturn had not. I lifted him off the table, onto my lap and scratched his head.

"All right," I said. "Let me proofread this last page, and I'll be right with you."

From the back of her golden stallion, Lyda Rose surveyed the valley, then slid from her horse's back and led him to the stream. Wincing from the pain in her shoulder, she knelt and scooped up a handful of water, scanning the horizon as she sipped from her palm.

Her servant, Brodgar, spread his cloak on the ground.

"Sleep, My Lady," he said. "When you wake, there'll be trout to eat and apples."

She sank onto Brodgar's cloak and let her tears flow unimpeded.

Why had she fought another battle alone? Why hadn't he arrived?

Where was Trevorode the Defender?

On Monday morning, I found a note from Jonas in my mailbox. The ceiling of the Math Department office was leaking, and the room was closed for repairs. Tomorrow I was to bring my lunch to his office instead. *P.S. We need to talk about Elinor.*

"A note from an admirer?"

Somewhere behind me, Trixie's gardenia-scented perfume blighted the air.

I half-crumpled the note and crammed it in my coat pocket. I remembered Muriel's advice. "No. A change of location for a conference I'd scheduled." Stone-faced, I turned to her. "I haven't had an admirer in years."

"That's not what I hear. Elinor told Mavis about your … soirée with Mr. Sloan. It's a charming concept, really—the schoolmarm and the cowhand. Did you teach him to read in exchange for calf roping lessons?"

I bit my lip to keep from smarting off. I had to stay on Trixie's good side from now on. If I lost my temper, I'd never be able to wheedle information from her about Mavis.

"No," I said. "On the contrary, Mr. Sloan has an extensive library. We spent most of the morning discussing Dostoevsky."

On Tuesday, impatient to learn more about Margaret Hawthorne, I entered Jonas' office. The stark room was a monument to inscrutability. His books, grouped according to subject, were lined up like piano keys. On his desk were a green banker's lamp, gray stapler, and pewter mug containing five sharpened pencils and two black pens. In a dark frame on the wall behind his desk, a clipper ship, poised on the crest of a white-capped wave, forever awaited its impending doom and the loss of all aboard. No personal photos, faces smiling at him from another time and place, were visible.

I sat down across from him and balanced my lunch in my lap. Somehow I knew not to touch anything on his desk.

"I made a spot for you," he said and pointed to the bare corner next to the mug.

"I'm fine," I said. "I'm a spiller. I wouldn't want to make a stain on this beautiful wood. I touched the smooth finish. "Did you build this?"

He nodded. "This was my prototype. The finished product is at home."

I washed down a mouthful of bologna sandwich with a swig of tea from my thermos. "I can't imagine this was your trial product. It looks perfect."

"That's the point of practice, isn't it?" he asked.

While he was at ease, I dipped my proverbial foot in the water. "You know, Jonas," I said, peeling my orange with feigned concentration, "something's been bothering me ever since we talked last Tuesday." I peeked up at him.

He stiffened and ran his finger along the wood grain of his desk. "Listen, Agnes, I need to make one thing clear … my past is—"

"What were your sisters' names? I've spent the last seven days thinking of flower names for girls, but all I came up with were Rose and Lily."

His mouth eased into a faint smile. "Dahlia, Camellia, Iris, and Poppy."

"Dahlia, Camellia, Iris, Poppy," I repeated. The names felt like music in my mouth. "Did your foot ever touch the floor before you were three, or did one of them always carry you?"

He folded his lunch bag and slipped it into the outer pocket of his backpack.

"Poppy was six when I was born," he said. "Dahlia was twelve. So yes, they were all old enough to mother me, but my dad eventually put a stop to it."

We were moving in the right direction. "Did you have a favorite?"

"No, but Camellia understood me best. When I began applying to architectural colleges, she let me use her house as my return address, so my parents wouldn't know my plans."

Two quick raps sounded on Jonas' door. Before he could say "Come in," the door swung open to reveal Trixie Thorpe. When she noticed me, her eyes blazed behind her red glasses. I couldn't tell if she was disillusioned, infuriated, or some combination of both.

"Oh," she said, "I didn't realize you were busy."

The room felt suddenly airless.

Jonas was unruffled. "Agnes and I were discussing ways to help Elinor."

Trixie hardened imperceptibly, incrementally, as if she'd stepped in wet cement and was quick-drying upward from her ankles. I barely breathed as she fixed her eyes on Jonas. And then a gentle sound broke the stillness of the room. *Swish. Swish.* Like a nervous eighth-grader fidgeting through an oral report on an unread book, Trixie was pinching a fold of her lime-green taffeta skirt between her thumb and finger.

"It's a pity," she said. "A town the size of ours has no psychiatrist. Elinor will have to go to Greenville to find one."

Jonas stood. "Elinor doesn't need a psychiatrist any more than I do."

She blushed and pivoted to me. "I'm glad to see you keep office hours in *someone's* office, Miss Quinn. You never spend any time in your own."

I summoned my resolve to stay in my opponent's good graces, such as they were.

"It's so far away," I said, managing a slight whine as I ducked my head. "I usually don't tell people, but I have claustrophobia. I get panicky in a room with no windows."

She let go of her skirt. "New teachers have to take what is available."

Jonas walked to the door. "Thanks for stopping by, Agnes. Please tell Elinor I'll see her later this week."

I understood his signal and stood to go. Trixie, satisfied I'd been dismissed, moved in closer to Jonas. I dawdled with my lunch things and book bag as long as I could.

"I don't know if you're aware," she told him, "the dean is interviewing the new librarian on Thursday."

Jonas sat down behind his desk. "I wasn't aware Elinor was being replaced."

Trixie stammered. "I mean the 'interim' librarian … while Elinor is on leave. He's an old friend of Mavis'. She's invited him to dinner on Friday. She thought we might join them."

By this time, I was behind Trixie with my hand on the doorknob. I looked over her shoulder at Jonas and mouthed, "I told you so."

After my classes on Wednesday morning, I visited Mavis' office and found her in a flurry of furniture spray, flitting around the room, wiping, polishing, buffing. I coughed and waved my hand to dispel the lemony-fresh fragrance.

"A little early for spring cleaning, isn't it?" I asked.

Sporting a white apron and brandishing a dustcloth, she resembled a well-dressed upstairs maid, preparing the guest quarters for a visiting baron. Her desk and shelves were scraped bare. Her books and belongings were stacked around the walls of her office. Before she could evict me, I pulled a few books off the nearest heap, sat down, and leafed through them.

She straightened her shoulders and tucked a loose strand of hair behind one ear.

"What are you doing here?" she asked.

"Giving you an update on Elinor."

She inched toward me and confiscated the books. We both pretended not to notice.

I stood and examined the picture of Edgar Allan Poe on her wall.

"I still remember," I said, "how concerned you were over Elinor's purse. And those lovely pink roses you brought to the hospital … so thoughtful."

Distracted, she peered at me as if she'd recently emerged from a coma.

"Elinor … yes, Trixie gave me a full report," she said. "Now, if you'll excuse me, I'm expecting a visitor tomorrow, and I really must—"

I rubbed a smudge off Poe's mustache. "Your librarian friend?"

She elbowed me aside and straightened Poe's frame.

"Where did you hear about him?" she asked.

"I was in Jonas' office yesterday when Trixie invited him to double-date with you and Mr.—" I raised my eyebrows.

"Loncraine. Asher Loncraine," she said.

The melancholy lilt of her voice and the distant look in her eye confirmed what I already knew. She was besotted.

I walked to her window and stuck my finger in the soil of her African violet. "This is a little dry, Mavis. Want me to water it?"

She whirled around. "What are you doing?"

"Admiring your plant. The blooms look healthy, but the soil's a little dry."

"You obviously know nothing about the care of African violets."

I fingered the leaves. "Could you advise me? A plant might cheer up my office."

She slid the plant toward the corner of the window, tossed her dustcloth on her desk, and picked up a stack of books. As she guided them onto a glossy shelf, one of the volumes slipped from her grasp. A single sheet of parchment paper escaped and fluttered, face down, to the floor. She dropped to her knees and slapped her hand firmly over one corner.

"Need some help?" I asked.

"No. Will you please go?" Her voice was hoarse with restraint and strangled tears. "I have to finish before I leave. I have an appointment."

"The dentist?" I picked up the dustcloth and returned to Poe's mustache.

On all fours, her hand still stuck to the paper, she frowned at me like a bad-tempered dachshund snarling over a steak bone. "No. I'm having my hair dyed—done."

"Of course. Asher Loncraine." I patted her on the shoulder as I passed by. "I'll let you finish. Elinor asked me to check her office to make sure she left nothing behind. We don't want clutter in Asher's new office, do we?"

That evening I stepped inside my apartment and leaned against the door. All afternoon I wondered if I'd been too hard on Mavis. After all, I'd once been as sappy about Trevor Rhodes as she appeared to be about Asher. Maybe Jonas was right. I'd made "quite a leap" with my theory that Mavis was trying to discredit Elinor so Asher could take her job. After dinner I sat down at the kitchen table with a pencil and yellow legal pad to analyze my hypothesis. I'd written only a few words when Flossie called.

"Hello, Agnes. May I come over? I made chicken pot pie."

I agreed. Flossie had visited every night since Warner left town with Daring Darla's Motorcycle Stunt Show.

Ten minutes later, she set the casserole dish on a white knitted pot holder in the middle of my table. Steam billowed up as she poked a serving spoon through the flaky crust. Saturn hopped off the couch and headed to the empty chair next to Flossie.

"You might need to blow on it," Flossie said.

She spooned a generous portion onto my plate.

Savoring the best of all comfort foods, we ate, she, taking pleasure in another evening with a neighbor who never snubbed her proffered gifts of food or yarn, and I, absorbed in the mental notes of my amateur investigation.

"You're very quiet tonight, Agnes," she said. "Still worried about your librarian friend?"

I had told Flossie about Elinor's accident as well as my suspicions about Mavis. I recounted my visit to Mavis' office.

"You should've seen how panicked she was when that paper fell," I said. "She dived onto it like—"

"Like a hawk on a corn snake," Flossie said as she ran her finger around the edge of her plate. Flossie's impromptu simile, eloquence from a poet in a baggy bargain-center dress, impressed me. Beneath her tousled hair and purple hat thrived a keen mind.

"Exactly. Very suspicious, if you ask me," I said.

Flossie licked her finger. "So far, *no one* is 'asking you,' but if they do, will you be prepared?" she asked.

"What do you mean?" I skewered a stray bit of carrot and finished it off.

She scraped the crust from the corner of the casserole dish. "Even if that paper had landed face up, could you have said—?"

Toppling her chair as she pushed back from the table, she stood, squared her shoulders, arched her back, lifted her chin, and slowly raising her pudgy arm, pointed to an imaginary parchment on the floor and exclaimed in a sonorous voice, "Ah-ha! Here is one of the missing documents. *J'accuse*!"

Flossie's flamboyance, not to mention her quoting Émile Zola, startled me, but I was most disturbed about the flaws in my plan. Journals, sketches, department meeting minutes, all irreplaceable, had been disappearing since July, long before I arrived at Brighton Park. Without detailed descriptions, I wouldn't recognize the stolen items if I tripped over them on the floor.

I called the Drifters' Rest and asked for Elinor.

"May I meet you for breakfast in the morning?" I asked. "We need to talk."

She hesitated. "I'm ... expecting another guest, but you're welcome to join us."

"How nice," I said. "Jonas told me he was going to check on you later this week."

"No ... not Jonas."

"Then—?"

"Come tomorrow," she said. "You'll see."

Early the next morning, I peeked through the window of the Drifters' Rest before I opened the door. Elinor was sitting alone at a table in the corner. Yellow legal pad in hand, I stepped inside and walked toward her. She waved and pointed to the chair opposite her.

"You look a little better every time I see you," I said.

"Thank you. I feel well enough to go home today."

"That's a good idea. You'll feel even better when—"

Without looking back, I knew her guest had arrived. Insensible to my voice, Elinor stared past me, her gaze fixed on the opening door. As a firm step and the tap of a cane on the wooden floor drew nearer, her lips parted, then pursed into a girlish smile. I watched the years fall away from her, as if the hand of an invisible sculptor were smoothing the creases and crinkles from her face. Luminous, the gentle eyes of the mystical girl inside the aging woman gleamed with a radiance no artist could have captured or poet described.

Before he sat down at our table, Ryder Ellershaw laid a red rose at Elinor's place.

Chapter 13

A Change of Heart

"So, how did you two meet?" I asked Elinor, as she gazed into the colonel's eyes.

"This past Monday," Elinor said, "I was sitting at this very table, and Ryder came over to ask if I needed more Earl Grey."

"It all started with a refill," Ryder said.

Muriel emerged from the kitchen. I glanced at her; she shrugged her shoulders.

"May I get you some coffee?" Ryder asked me.

I laid my pencil on top of the yellow legal pad and stood. "No, thanks. I need to ask Muriel about ... today's ... featured item. I'll be right back."

Muriel, wiping the counter, did not look up as I approached. "Now, be careful, Agnes," she said, "and keep your voice down. They're very happy, and I won't have you upsetting that."

So I whispered. "How in the world did this happen?"

She took a mug from the shelf behind her. "When the colonel came in Monday, he noticed Elinor crying over her oatmeal. Before I knew what was happening, he sat next to her. He's never done that with anyone else. It's a miracle. He hasn't bothered me all week."

"I don't know if I like it," I said.

"It doesn't matter whether you like it or not, does it? Here. Try the strudel. It's delicious."

Quieted with a pastry, I returned to the table.

"Now," Elinor said, "what was it you wanted to talk to me about?"

Ryder's presence during this interview was not a variable I'd considered. Dreamy over Elinor and persuaded Mavis was trying to steal Elinor's job, would he do something reckless?

Like a sailor in a leaky boat, I ventured out into deeper waters.

I doodled on my paper as I spoke.

"I haven't said anything yet, Elinor, because I'm not sure. But … in my opinion … you haven't been losing things. I think someone's stealing from the library."

She gasped. "Who in the world would do such a thing?"

I heard Ryder, jaw clenched, grind his teeth, but I didn't look up.

"I don't know," I said, still doodling, "not yet, but if I could locate the missing items, I could clear your name. You could get your job back."

"I'm not sure I want it back," Elinor said. "I like having time for other things."

I glanced up in time to watch Ryder take her hand. "But it would be nice for you to retire without this dark cloud over your head," he said. "Wouldn't it?"

She agreed.

Within a few minutes, I had a complete list of the missing items: Volume I of the first edition of *A Complete History of the Orkneys*, by Bartholomew Burkins; original drawings of the red-necked grebe, puffin, and waxwing from the sketchbook of the reclusive Irish bird artist, Fiona Mulcahy; the history faculty meeting minutes from March of the previous year (chronicling a crisis over the change of the chairmanship); Landon Brookshire's antique map of the Georgia Sea Islands; and the journal of Confederate soldier Tucker Wingait.

I wrapped my strudel in a napkin and accepted the to-go cup Muriel held out to me as I headed for the door.

After lecturing my class on pronoun-antecedent agreement, I passed out a quiz and sat behind my desk to review the notes I'd compiled. My first order of business was to size up Asher Loncraine. Was he oblivious to Mavis' obsession or, as Flossie had mumbled, eyes closed, before she fell asleep on my sofa, had he conned her into stealing for him? I considered this plausible. Vulnerable, insecure, the perpetual second fiddle to Trixie, Mavis could've easily fallen prey to an unprincipled man. In fact, I added, *Asher may have coached her on the kinds of things to take.*

After the last remaining student ambled up to my desk to deposit his quiz, I straightened the stack of papers, paper-clipped them together, and hurried out the door.

Eyeing her fake diamond watch, Trixie was lurking in the hall.

"There are fourteen minutes of your class time left, Miss Quinn."

I held up my evidence. "They finished their quiz early. I guess I did a good job teaching them." I squeaked out a fake giggle.

She scowled. "You could have introduced the next unit."

I ducked my head. "I'm sorry," I said. "I'll remember that next time."

My swift apology stymied her. She whooshed down the hall.

I headed for the library. When I entered, I spotted Grace Bonner at the checkout desk.

"Is he here yet?" I asked.

She tilted her head in the direction of Elinor's office. I walked around the corner for my first look at Asher Loncraine.

He was standing in front of Elinor's chair, his bony hands placed flat on her desk. He looked like a worn-out scarecrow, the loser in a fracas with bandit birds, sighing over a decimated crop. Tall, thin, angular, he had a long, square-tipped nose, sagging skin underneath obtrusive eyes, and a prominent magenta mole above the left corner of his mouth. With his right hand, he brushed away a fleck of dust and then retrieved a wooden desk nameplate from a box on the floor. He placed it front and center on Elinor's desk.

Asher Loncraine. Head Librarian.

"Moving in?" I asked from the open door.

Slowly he raised his head and peered at me. "And you are—?"

"Agnes Quinn. I teach English. Elinor is a friend of mine."

"Ah, Miss Quinn," he said, as if addressing a recently arrested fugitive. He sat down, placed his fingertips together, and leaned back in Elinor's chair. "Miss Applewhite and Mrs. Thorpe have told me all about you. They failed to mention how lovely you are."

This was no scarecrow. This was a dragon, who razed crops—birds, scarecrow, and all—with one well-aimed gust of fire.

If I'd been thinking the least bit logically, I would have said, "Welcome to Brighton Park" and escaped to my stuffy office where no one would look for me.

But there I stood, blinking like a wide-eyed doe at a rabid wolf, thinking of a new foe for my heroine to fight, sinking into my story.

Lyda Rose, bound by her oath to rescue Queen Lenore, stood motionless at the entrance to the dragon's den. She drew in her breath, growing faint at the noxious reek of the dragon, but stood her ground as he came slithering out. When his massive tail, itself the size of a tree trunk, cleared the opening, he drew himself up to his full height and spread his fearsome wings to their broadest span. Emerald green, amethyst purple, gold-flecked, he glistened in the midday sun. "Shield your eyes," Grimwulf had warned, "lest you fall under his spell."

"What is it you want, Miss Quinn?" Asher's voice stirred me from my daydream.

Lovely? Had he called me *lovely*?

"Excuse me." From behind me in the hallway, Mavis poked me on the shoulder.

Trixie, standing next to her, said, "So this is why you dismissed your class early." She pushed past me. "You know what they say about curiosity."

Mavis followed Trixie into the office and then stepped around her to be closer to Asher.

I moved farther in and edged back against the wall, still speechless, gaping. The two women glared at me. Jonas' words—*You think you know Trixie and Mavis, but you don't*—resonated through my mind.

"I seem to keep running into you in everyone's office but your own," Trixie said.

"This actually makes only two," I said, grinning.

"And they always seem to be older men's offices," she said.

"Actually, I was in Mavis' office just yesterday, wasn't I, Mavis?"

Mavis, toting a sizeable canna lily in a pot, was not amused.

Outnumbered, I retreated, defeated and deflated.

They'd won the first battle without firing a shot.

I left the library, started down the sidewalk, and sank, weak-kneed, onto the first bench I spotted. My career as a detective had begun badly. Face to face with my prime suspect and her likely accomplices, I'd recoiled from them like an alley cat shooed by a kitchen broom. I unstuck my yellow legal pad from my sweaty palm and appended my entries on Asher Loncraine, noting he appeared to have no attraction to Mavis, but exhibited keen interest in usurping Elinor. He must have been dozing during that segment of his interview, when the administration advised his appointment was "interim."

I stared stupidly at my notes, astonished my plans had disintegrated so abruptly, wondering why I had ensnared myself in yet another mess. So far I'd failed at sparing Jonas from Brooker, myself from Ryder, or Elinor from Mavis. In fact, I mused, from the moment I'd arrived at Brighton Park, I'd been in one sort of quagmire or another.

Why couldn't I simply devote myself to the job I was being paid to do?

Lecturing, grading papers, making lesson plans were such straightforward enterprises and seemed to be paying off. Just yesterday, Big Tony had stayed after class to ask me what he should read after he finished *Great Expectations*. Exton had asked me to write a reference letter to the university he was entering next fall. Priscilla had confided in me about her parents' divorce. Dane had asked me for advice about changing his major to music, and Will had told me I was "the best teacher he ever had."

Why couldn't I simply embrace the nobility of my profession?

It was high time I settled down to the business of being a teacher, focused my attention on the job I'd been hired to do, and stopped engaging in causes I'd never win.

I opened my bag and stuffed the yellow legal pad inside. For once I'd stopped myself before I made yet another stupid mistake. As I closed the bag, a shadow fell across my hand.

"You left this in my office," Asher Loncraine said. He held out a pen.

"Not mine," I said, though I knew it was.

He examined the pen. "My mistake. At any rate, this gave me an excuse to get away from the old hens."

Though I had no affection for Trixie or Mavis, this sentence froze my bones.

"I thought you were old friends," I said.

He shook his head. "I've been trying to avoid Mavis since college. I thought I'd seen the last of her once I got married, but she called five weeks after my wife died. Very undignified."

I stood. "Maybe she wanted to offer her sympathy."

"Maybe," he said, and held out the pen. "Take this. A teacher always needs another pen."

When I took it, his hand lingered on mine. "I hear you visit the library almost every day."

I pulled away. "I used to. Like I said, Elinor is my friend. I came to visit her."

"The door is still open," he said. "Don't forget."

After he left, I lifted my hand to eye level and inspected it, turning it over and back, expecting to find some sort of filmy residue. My hand close to my face, I got an unwanted whiff of Asher's expensive department store cologne. I cringed to think of his scent still seeping into my skin and rushed toward the nearest restroom, doused my hands in lime-green institutional soap, and scrubbed like a surgeon.

Eager to widen the distance between Asher and me, I hurried toward the portable building which housed my windowless office. Outfitted with an old desk, broken chair, and cheap pressboard bookshelves, the closet-sized room was a perfect replica of a medieval nun's cell. Standing in the door I'd propped open to let in the fresh air, I tilted my head and narrowed my eyes to picture my Charles Dickens print on the wall. If I stacked my poetry books on the desk and tacked a map of England to the back of the door, I might create a scholarly setting.

On Friday morning I ferried in my personal belongings and officially "moved in" to my office, something I should have done weeks before. Then I rushed to the opposite side of the campus for my first class. In spite of being out of breath, I approached my task with vigor, reading the death of *Beowulf* with such passion I was teary-eyed by the time I'd lit his funeral pyre. I graded essays during lunch, conducted a help class at day's end, and left the campus exhausted but self-satisfied.

"How was your week?" Charlotte asked as we sat down to dinner that evening.

I unfolded the linen napkin and placed it in my lap. "It got off to a rough start. In fact," I said, sliding a thick slice of meatloaf onto my plate, "since I've been here, *every* week has gotten off to a—I'm sorry, is this *meatloaf*?"

She smiled as she dipped ketchup from a silver bowl onto her plate. "I made it myself."

"I never pictured you eating something as ordinary as meatloaf."

She passed the asparagus. "Today is my husband's birthday. I always served meatloaf on this day. It was his favorite. Now, you were telling me about your week."

I began with Trixie's ridicule of Buck on Monday, moved to her dinner invitation to Jonas on Tuesday, glossed over my visit to Mavis on Wednesday, touched on Asher's stalking me on Thursday, and ended with my act of resolve on Friday.

Charlotte dabbed a delicate bite of meatloaf into the ketchup on her plate.

"You don't think Jonas went to dinner with those three, do you?" she asked. "I'd hate to see him in the clutches of another conniving woman."

"Like Olympia?" I asked.

My bold question achieved the desired effect. Charlotte laid down her fork and leaned into the table till her silk scarf draped over her rice pilaf.

"How do you know about Olympia?"

"I guess I haven't told you about Brooker yet," I said.

I related the encounter with Brooker, ending with Jonas' vow to "die in the gutter" before he would sell Olympia Pillburn his interest in the property.

Charlotte drew a lace handkerchief from her pocket and dabbed at her eyes. "That wretched woman. It's not enough she ruined his life. Now she wants his house."

"I'm sorry I upset you," I said. "I wouldn't have said anything if—"

"I still remember the night," Charlotte said. "Jonas sat in that very chair and poured out his heart to us." Her voice broke. "To think, Olympia is *still* after him."

"Still after him?" I asked.

"Olympia is the reason Jonas lost Margaret." She reached for a roll. "I didn't think I'd ever hear Olympia's name again. I always hoped she married some foreign aristocrat and—"

"Died in a peasant revolt?" I passed the butter.

Charlotte laughed. "I was going to say, 'immigrated to another continent.' It would be impolite to wish for anything worse."

After chocolate cake, we headed for the library. *Great Expectations* still lay on the table by the sofa. I opened the book to the place we'd left off the week before and began to read. "*She was dressed in rich materials—satins, and lace, and silks—all of white. Her shoes were white and she had a long white veil—*

Charlotte stopped me. "Ironic, isn't it, we'd be reading about Miss Havisham on the very night we were talking about Olympia?"

"Why?" I asked.

"They're exactly alike. I hope Olympia hasn't been rattling around the Magnolia Arms all these years. I'd hate to think of her desecrating the house Jonas built as a monument to love."

"For Margaret?"

"No, as homage to his father."

I closed the book. "He told me he named the house Magnolia after his father's mother."

"Yes, but his father never knew. He died while Jonas was away at Ridgeland."

"Ridgeland?"

"Ridgeland Architectural College," she said. "That's where he met Olympia. Her father was Jonas' professor."

"What was his name?"

Charlotte sighed. "I was afraid you'd ask. My memory isn't what it used to be. Seems like it was Irish or Scottish—something with 'O' or 'Mac' in front of it."

"You'll think of it later," I said. "Go on with your story."

"This professor was Jonas' mentor. Jonas became a regular guest at their home, which suited Olympia just fine. She'd been infatuated with Jonas from the moment she saw him."

Unwelcomed, Jonquil Putnam came to mind. "There may be nothing in the world more dangerous than a spoiled girl with a powerful father," I said.

Charlotte sipped her tea. "Certainly true in this case, but Jonas was willing to put up with Olympia for the privilege of learning from her father."

"I had a professor like that once, but things didn't work out like I hoped."

"Things didn't work out for Jonas either—not in the long run."

"What happened?" I asked, wondering if Jonas' professor was another "Robinson Trask."

"One reason the professor devoted so much time to Jonas was because his own son was such a disappointment."

"The 'black sheep of the family?'" I asked.

As though the room were full of people, Charlotte leaned closer and whispered: "A compulsive gambler—racked up a mountain of debt. When Benson—or was it Bentley?—first got in trouble, the professor paid the gambling debts, but eventually refused to help him."

"What did that have to do with Jonas?"

"Bentley was so desperate for money, he broke into a neighbor's house and was arrested. After the professor bailed him out of jail, he went straight to his lawyer's office, wrote his son out of his will, and handed over Bentley's portion of the family property to Jonas."

"And that was the property where he built the Magnolia Arms?"

She nodded. "Olympia was delighted. A legal partnership with her father drew Jonas closer into the family circle. The next logical step, so far as she was concerned—"

"Would be marrying the boss's daughter."

"So she thought."

"How did Jonas escape?" I asked.

"His only hope was that once he'd graduated and moved away to build his house, Olympia would find someone she liked better."

"But she didn't."

"No. She promised she'd wait for him and wrote him love letters every week."

"Poor Jonas," I said. "To have his dream within reach and the threat of Olympia hanging over his head with every nail he hammered."

"That's why he took longer to build the house than he needed to, but Olympia was only part of the reason. You can guess the other."

"Margaret?"

She nodded. "Yes."

"So he met Margaret while he was building the Magnolia Arms?"

"She ran the boarding house where he lived while he was working."

"A boarding house. How romantic."

"Right out of a novel," Charlotte said. "For Jonas it was love at first sight, but—"

"Hello?" The door to the library swung open to admit Exton.

Charlotte's face glowed. "Ex, darling. How nice to see you."

He kissed her on the forehead. "I got off work early and thought Miss Quinn might still be here. I hope you won't mind if I join you for a chapter or two."

I did mind, but couldn't say so.

"Of course not," Charlotte said. "Sit down. Have you had dinner?"

I opened the book. Margaret's story remained unfinished.

Pursued by the twin specters of Olympia and Jonquil, I drove home, haunted and pestered, as if fleeing an approaching storm.

I was still awake when Buck Sloan called shortly after midnight.

The moment he said his name I hurried to concoct reasons I couldn't return to the ranch in the morning, but I never got to use one.

"I'm leaving before dawn," he said, "and I didn't want you to hear the news from anyone else. Aunt Geneva died this afternoon."

"Oh, Buck, I'm so sorry. What happened?"

"A blood clot," he said, his voice choked with grief.

I grasped at something to say. "My sister-in-law is a nurse. I remember her saying blood clots are a common problem after a broken bone."

He sniffled. "Her doctor said the same thing. But I can't regret she went the way she did."

"What do you mean?"

"When she was well enough to be moved, those nasty kids of hers was going to put her in a nursing home."

"That would've killed her," I said.

He chuckled. "I think she knew what they was up to, but she got the last word. She put in her will she wanted to be buried in a cemetery here, so I'll get to bring her home after all. There'll be a graveside service on Wednesday. Would you be able to make it?"

"Of course," I said.

After we hung up, I lay half-awake, half-asleep for hours.

I pictured good, gentle Buck, his heart throbbing with dull pain as he drove on dark roads before sunrise, his face chiseled with forced politeness as he confronted Geneva's bitter children, his rough hands touching Geneva's lifeless face, his truck guiding the hearse on the long journey back to the burial place four miles from Sloan's Canyon.

I drifted off to sleep and dreamed of Jonas driving his truck, one strong hand on the steering wheel, the Magnolia Arms logo, green-leaved, white-flowered, restored to the door, windows down, Margaret next to him, his arm around her, her long, lavender-scented hair blown by a September breeze, a full moon suspended in the black sky.

I dreamed Xander came home and took a job teaching chemistry at Brighton Park.

Too early on Saturday morning, Flossie knocked on my door, a basket of blueberry muffins in her hands and her knitting bag slung over her shoulder.

"Warner came home last night," she said.

I took the muffins and let her in. "That's nice."

"No, it's not." She plopped down in a kitchen chair and rested her arm on the table. "He's gone and married that Darla woman—the one who runs the motorcycle show."

"Daring Darla?" I asked as I reached for the coffee canister.

"Yes."

"Is she nice?"

"No, she's not nice. Warner said Darla didn't think it was a good idea for me to live with them, and he said I'd have to find someplace else to stay."

"He kicked you out?"

"Can you imagine? Choosing a bleach-blonde bimbo in a blue leotard over your own mother?"

"I'm sure something can be worked out," I said.

And then Flossie stunned me. "Could I stay here till I find someplace to go?"

I couldn't say no.

Each lost in our own despair, we ate muffins and guzzled coffee. Then Flossie occupied herself with her knitting, pausing often to wipe her eyes. I cleaned the kitchen and graded papers. While we ate lunch I shared Geneva's story with Flossie, and then we went for a drive to locate the cemetery where Geneva would be buried.

"Could I come with you to the service?" Flossie asked. "To pay my respects?"

"I'll have to come straight from school," I said. "I won't be able to pick you up."

"I'll take the bus," she said, "and then ride home with you."

On Sunday night a fog rolled in.

On Monday morning I stopped by the Drifters' Rest for coffee.

"I'll take one to go, Muriel. I can't see a thing in this fog, and it will take me longer than usual to drive to school."

"How was your weekend?" she asked.

"Not one of the best, but I got a lot of work done."

"I was asking," she said, "because Friday night a man came here looking for you, and I wondered if he found you."

"What?"

"He said he knew you from school."

Because of my dream, for one sublime, ridiculous moment, I thought it must be Xander.

"What did he look like?" I asked.

Muriel wiped away the half-and-half I had sloshed onto the counter. "Tall, thinning gray hair, long nose, kind of sinister. I'd never seen him before, so I didn't tell him anything."

Asher Loncraine.

I sank onto a counter stool and held my cup in both hands. "What did he say?"

"He said he was new in town and wondered what we did for fun on Friday night. He said you'd given him your phone number, but he couldn't find it."

I tried to slow my breathing. "I didn't give him my number."

"I knew you hadn't," Muriel said. "Then he asked if I knew where you lived."

"What?"

"You'd better keep your distance from him, Agnes. I don't like him."

The dense morning fog crawled, hovered, lingered. I leaned into the steering wheel and squinted to see the street. Relieved when I reached Brighton Park, I pulled into my parking spot and looked over at Jonas' truck. Still haunted by my dream, I got out of my car and bent forward, rubbing my fingertips over the logo, disappointed to find it still eroded.

My hair was damp by the time I reached the English Department office.

I opened the door and found Mavis and Trixie huddled together at the table. Mavis, head bowed, quivered with silent sobs. Trixie, her red glasses lying on the table, had her arm around Mavis' shoulders.

"You mustn't keep on like this," Trixie said. "You have to pull yourself together."

Mavis gasped for air. "I'll … never … be … happy … not … now. He was my last chance … my last dream … of happiness."

"Get hold of yourself," Trixie said. "Jonas didn't come to dinner either, and you don't see me carrying on."

"Carrying on?" Mavis wailed. "Is that what you call it—carrying on? After all I've done to get Asher here, I have a right to carry on if I want to."

As a gesture of polite behavior, I tiptoed past them to my mailbox.

Without warning, Mavis sprang up and rushed toward me. She grabbed my shoulder, twirled me around, and shoved me into the rows of wooden mail slots. Her face soaked and splotched, she shrieked, "You. You ruined everything. You poisoned Asher against me."

"Me? What did I do?"

She leaned in. The smell of camphor drifted up from a nasty fever blister on her upper lip. "Asher never arrived at the restaurant Friday night."

"Neither did Jonas," Trixie said.

I bent my knees, eased down, and stepped away. Off balance, Mavis tilted forward, grabbed at the slots marked "Starkey" and "Wickfield," jammed her head against the edge of Mrs. Tuttle's *National Geographic*, and dissolved into tears again, dripping snot onto the large manila envelope sticking out of Dr. Zelnick's box.

I straightened my sweater and turned to Trixie.

"Would you mind telling me what's going on?" I asked.

She sat like a presiding judge. "I think you know what it's about."

"No," I said. "I don't."

"We know you were with Asher on Friday night."

"What?"

"Mavis and I arrived at the restaurant early. We had reservations for seven. We waited for an hour. When neither Jonas nor Asher arrived, we knew who was to blame."

"You can't be serious," I said.

She positioned her glasses on the end of her nose. "You may think you were subtle, dropping your pen in Asher's office, but we knew what you were up to."

"It wasn't my pen. I told him that."

Mavis lifted her head. "So you admit you had words with him."

"Had words with him? I was minding my own business when he came after me with that phony excuse. I haven't seen him since last Thursday."

Trixie tapped on the table. "Then where were you Friday night?"

"It's really none of your business," I said.

Mavis started toward me again. "We know you weren't at home."

Trixie intercepted her and guided her back to the table.

"When Asher didn't arrive," Trixie said, "we drove by your apartment."

"*No one* was there," Mavis said. "It was dark."

"You came to my apartment? How did you know where I live?"

"Your personnel file, of course," Trixie said.

With as much dignity as I could muster, I opened the door. "For your information," I said, "I was at Charlotte Wrayburn's house, like I was *last* Friday."

"Oh, come now," Trixie said, patting Mavis' back, "do you honestly expect us to believe that? A first-year teacher having dinner with the senior member of the board of trustees?"

"I don't care what you believe," I said. "This is absurd. Do you think I could ever be attracted to Asher Loncraine? He looks like a refugee from a grade B horror movie."

Mavis lunged at me again, but tripped over the table leg and stumbled into the filing cabinet. As Trixie rushed to her side, I left the room.

I walked toward my class, wondering if I would ever again drive into the parking lot of my apartment building without shuddering, thinking of those two peeping in my windows.

For the rest of the day I slinked around the campus like a wanted criminal, hoping I could elude the Deranged Duo till it was time to go home to more conversations with Flossie, who, except for the hours between dusk and dawn, chattered incessantly.

On Tuesday, hoping to find Jonas, I went to the Math Department office at lunchtime. He was there, spreading mustard on his onion bagel.

"I was hoping you'd remember," he said. "I didn't see you yesterday."

I was startled at how pale he was. "Do you feel all right?"

"I've been a little under the weather. Must be that flu going around."

I took out my sandwich. "So you didn't accept the dinner invitation from Trixie?"

He shook his head. "No, I couldn't have endured that even for Elinor's sake."

"Good decision," I said. "You'd have found yourself in a hornet's nest."

I reviewed the incident with Mavis and Trixie.

"I warned you, didn't I?" he said.

"Yes, and I'm glad I gave up the chase, even though I'm still convinced Mavis is guilty."

"Why?"

"What she said to Trixie—'After all she's gone through' to get Asher here. What else could that mean? She stole from the library to get rid of Elinor so Asher could have her job."

He rubbed his shoulder and sighed. "I get so tired of all the melodrama around this place. 'I am weary of words and people, sick of the city, wanting the sea.'"

"Wow," I said. "I didn't know math teachers talked like that."

He smiled. "We don't. It's a line of poetry from a book I gave to Margaret."

I stopped breathing. "Margaret?"

"Well played, Agnes. But there's no more need for pretense. As much time as you've spent with Muriel and Charlotte, I'm certain you know who Margaret is by now."

"Yes, but only because I wheedled it out of them."

He took his handkerchief from his pocket and wiped perspiration from his forehead.

"Relax, Agnes. I don't fault you for being curious. You're a writer. You've heard scattered bits of a story, and you want to know how the whole thing fits together. I get that."

"Plus I'm just plain nosy," I said.

He laughed. "That, too."

"So ... will you tell me about her?" I asked.

Sudden tears pooled in Jonas' eyes. "I haven't talked about Margaret in a long time. At least spare me the trouble of repeating what you already know."

I shared the facts I'd pieced together; his sandwich uneaten, he told me the rest.

"Margaret arrived in Dennisonville only a few months before I did. When the man she loved broke her heart, she quit college and—"

"Took a job running a boarding house," I said. "Maybe that's what I should've done."

He pushed his plate away, settled back in his chair, and closed his eyes. "It was the end of May when I came to town. I had a blueprint in my hand

and a dream in my heart, but not a nickel in my pocket. I'd spent everything on materials for my house, so I looked for the cheapest place in town to live."

His voice slowed, softened. "I was walking down the sidewalk, studying the house numbers, nearing the gate, when out … she … stepped. She wore a pale-green dress and had a bouquet of purple daylilies in her arms. She was the most beautiful woman I'd ever seen. 'May I speak to the owner?' I said. 'Yes,' she said, 'but you'll have to take off those muddy boots before you come in.' 'I'm a contractor,' I said. 'I've just come from my building site.' 'I'm the housekeeper,' she said. 'I've just come from my clean floors.'"

He opened his eyes. "I've relived that moment a thousand times."

"And she took you in," I said.

"I told the owner I was a carpenter, pointed out a few things in need of repair, and offered to fix up the place on weekends if I could get my rent cheap and my meals free."

"A sensible plan," I said.

"Even when Margaret only thought of me as a boarder, she got up before dawn to fix my breakfast and kept my dinner warm till I came home. After awhile, she joined me for meals and then for long walks in the park. One day we talked about spending the rest of our lives together."

"Sounds perfect," I said.

"It was … till Olympia showed up."

"Charlotte said she wrote to you every week."

"She did, but the letters came to a post office box, and I never told Margaret. That was the worst mistake I ever made."

"Why didn't you tell her?"

"I'd dodged Olympia for years. I wanted to forget her and make a fresh start. I'd take her letters out of the post office box, tear them up, and throw them away before I got home. Another very foolish mistake. My life would've been much different if only I'd read that last letter."

Jonas winced and drew in his breath sharply.

I stood. "Are you all right?"

He laid his hand on his chest. "Indigestion, that's all. After all this time, Olympia still makes me sick."

Worried, I suggested he should go home and rest.

"I think I will. Walk with me to my truck, and I'll finish the story on the way."

We cleared the table and left the office.

"Now, where were we?" Jonas asked as we walked.

"You were talking about Olympia's last letter."

"The one that would have warned me Olympia was coming to visit. If I'd known, I could've told Margaret, but it was too late."

"What happened?"

"One day when I got home from work, I found Olympia sitting on the porch. She rushed down the steps and threw her arms around me. I pushed her away and went in to find Margaret."

"What did she say?"

We'd reached the parking lot. Jonas leaned against his truck and stared down at the pavement.

"She was in the dining room setting the table. 'Your friend has told me everything,' she said. She wouldn't look at me, just kept walking around and around the table, folding napkins, straightening silverware.

"I told her I could explain. She said it was too late. She'd been through the same thing once before. 'I thought you were different,' she said, but ...'"

He bit his lip. I waited, watched his face twist with pain.

"It's all right, Jonas," I said. "You don't have to—"

" 'You're just like he was,' she said. 'This is the second time I've been lied to, but no more. You'll have to find someplace else to stay till you're ready to leave town.'"

"What did you do?"

"I went back to the porch, grabbed Olympia by the arm, dragged her out onto the sidewalk, and demanded she tell me what she'd said to Margaret. 'The truth,' she said, 'that we were only waiting to get married till you finished your house.' I told her I'd never marry her, no matter how much her father had done for me, and I left her standing there."

"Where did you go?"

"The Magnolia Arms was nearly finished, so I slept on the floor till the work was done. I wrote to Margaret and begged her forgiveness, but she never answered. I didn't give Olympia's father a chance to run me off the property. I left and came here. You know the rest."

"What have we here?"

Asher Loncraine had joined us on the sidewalk.

"And I thought the reason you haven't come to see me was because you don't like mature men," he said. "But I see I was wrong. Grinstead here beat me to the draw."

He slapped Jonas on the back.

"Dr. Grinstead isn't feeling well," I said.

Jonas did not respond. He got into his truck and drove away.

"Seriously, Agnes," Asher said, "I heard you used to come to the library all the time, but I haven't seen you since last week."

"I'm using the public library now," I said, and walked away.

I woke on Wednesday with Geneva's funeral on my mind. I arrived for work, pleased to find Jonas' truck was not there. A quiet day at home would do him good. I recited Shakespearean sonnets to my classes, ate lunch at my desk, gave a make-up test to Big Tony, and didn't go near the library or the English Department office all day. Relieved I'd gone through an entire day without incident and certain I had plenty of time to get to Geneva's service, I was walking toward the door when Asher Loncraine strolled into my room.

"I need that chart of the kings and queens of England you've had since the first week of school. Another teacher has requested it. May I have it back?"

"It's in my office," I said. "I'll bring it to the library in the morning."

"Could we walk over there now?" he asked.

"I have an appointment after school," I said.

"All right, then, I'll see you in the morning."

I waited for him to leave, so I could walk in the opposite direction. When he stepped out into the hall, I heard him say, "Hello, Beatrix. Is Mavis feeling better?"

"No, thanks to you," Trixie said from the hallway.

There was no way out but through the door. I shouldered my book bag, stepped into the hall, turned my back to the direction of Trixie's voice, locked the door, and headed in the opposite direction without looking behind me.

"Your name Quinn?"

When I heard a man's voice, I turned to find a campus policeman. I peeked around him to see Trixie prancing away.

"What do you need?" I asked.

"Could you come with me, please?"

"Whatever it is, can it wait? I'm going to a funeral and—"

"Sorry, Miss, I've been asked to escort you to your office."

To save time, I kept quiet and walked beside him. When we reached my office, Trixie and Dean Greeley were waiting.

"What's this about?" I asked.

"All will be clear in a moment," said Trixie as she turned the key in the lock. She motioned to the officer. "Over there," she said, "under the desk. The cleaning crew reported it."

The officer stooped and lifted up a stack of books and papers.

Trixie stepped to my desk. “Put them right here,” she said. “Dean, if you’ll be a witness, please.”

He joined her. She handed him a piece of paper and began sorting through the pile, reading titles as she went.

“Tucker Wingait’s journal, Landon Brookshire’s map, history faculty meeting minutes, Mulcahy’s drawings, and last but not least, Volume I of the first edition of *A Complete History of the Orkneys*, by Bartholomew Burkins.”

The dean turned to me. “As of now, Miss Quinn, you’ll be placed on administrative leave, pending further investigation into your involvement in this theft. We’ll contact you once a hearing has been scheduled.”

Confronted with the pilfered pile, I stood motionless, stranded in one of those moments when time scrapes to a halt. Then for lack of something better to do, I picked up my stapler and waved it like a loaded pistol as I spoke.

“I gotta hand it to you, Trixie,” I said. “I should’ve seen this coming.”

She glanced at the dean, a slight trace of fear fluttering in her eyes.

“I should’ve known Asher would be sent packing once he fell out of favor with Mavis.”

“Mavis?” Dean Greeley said.

I tucked the stapler under my arm, picked up the “evidence,” and held it out to him. “Don’t you see? Elinor will come back, Asher will be dismissed, and, as for me … well, who cares what happens to a first-year teacher?”

The officer stepped aside to let me through the door.

I drove to the cemetery in a daze and stepped beside Flossie moments before the service began. Standing at the foot of Geneva’s casket, Buck smiled at me and whispered, “Thank you.”

As the minister began reciting the Twenty-Third Psalm, Flossie tapped me on the arm.

“After this is over,” she whispered, “we have to go to the hospital. Your friend Jonas has had a heart attack.”

Chapter 14

A Noble Calling

Flossie and I rushed to my car after the final "amen." I slid behind the steering wheel and threw the car into reverse as she tumbled into her seat. When we lunged forward, she leaned toward me, pulling in her arm and leg as our momentum slammed her door shut.

"Closed?" I asked.

"I think so."

She tidied her hat, the blue one with forget-me-nots she wore only on formal occasions.

"I'd drive if I knew how," she said. "You've had a terrible shock."

Beneath the tires, gravel crunched and then flew up, spraying, as I roared onto the main road.

"I hated to leave without a word, but Buck was surrounded by so many people," I said.

"You can explain later," Flossie said. "I'm sure he'll understand."

In the center of town I stomped on the accelerator and zoomed through a yellow light.

Flossie stuck her right hand on the passenger window and her left on the roof of the car.

The needle on the gas gauge bounced on "E."

I urged the car forward. "Please don't run out gas. Please don't run out of gas."

"If you need money for gas," Flossie said, "I have my collection of two-dollar bills in the side pocket of my purse."

"No time," I said.

I swerved into the emergency room parking lot, ignored the speed limit sign, and smacked into a speed bump. Flossie lost her grip. Her hat launched onto the dashboard and her left shoe somehow ended up in her lap. I screeched beside the curb, yanked the keys out of the ignition, and loped toward the door, yelling to Flossie to wait for me in the lobby.

Breathless, I charged the information desk. "Jonas Grinstead. Can I see him?"

The receptionist scanned her list. "No."

Light-headed, I leaned on the counter. "Is he going to be all right?"

"Have a seat in the waiting room. We'll notify you when we have information. Family?"

"No, but I'm as close as he's got in this town. I have to see him."

"I'm sorry, Miss, if you'll sit down—"

"Agnes?"

Muriel laid her hand on my shoulder. I turned around, fell into her arms, and sobbed like a two-year-old.

"It's all my fault," I said. "I pestered him about Margaret. All those memories, dredged up … he was trying to forget … I broke his heart."

Muriel led me to a chair in the corner of the waiting room. I sank down and leaned my head against the wall.

Flossie, already busy with her knitting, handed me her purple-flowered handkerchief. "It's clean," she said.

Muriel reached in a canvas bag, pulled out a Drifters' Rest thermos, and poured coffee into Styrofoam cups.

"When the hospital called," she said, "I grabbed the nearest coffeepot and emptied it in here. I know you don't like dark roast, but I knew you'd need coffee."

She held out a small white box to Flossie. "You must be the lady I spoke to on the phone. Thank you for giving Agnes my message. Muffin?"

"Sorry," I said. "I should've introduced you. This is Flossie Bingham, my neighbor."

Flossie took the muffin. "Roommate," she said, as if the title were a badge of honor.

Muriel was puzzled, but didn't ask questions.

"When did this happen?" I asked.

"Dolley called. She said Jonas had called and said he wasn't feeling well. He described his symptoms to her; she told him to go to the hospital."

"Who's Dolley?" Flossie asked.

"My sister," Muriel said. "Dolley Madison. She's a nurse."

Flossie chuckled. "Dolley Madison. Good one."

"I knew Jonas was sick yesterday," I said. "Is there another muffin?"

"Blueberry or apple?"

"Both."

"Of course Dolley meant he should *find* someone to drive him," Muriel said. "But you know how stubborn he is. Apparently, he came in under his own power and collapsed when he walked through the door."

"Is he going to be all right?" I asked.

Muriel handed Flossie a napkin. "Dolley said she'd let us know. How was the funeral?"

"I don't remember much about it," I said. "I was kind of distracted."

"Worried about Jonas?" Muriel asked.

"Yes," I said, "but also because I just got fired."

"Fired? For what?"

"Remember the creepy guy who came looking for me?"

Muriel grimaced. "Who could forget *that* face?"

"It was because of him," I said.

I began with Mavis' meltdown and ended with Trixie's triumph.

Muriel shook her head. "I can't believe what those two get away with."

Smiling, Dolley emerged from behind the black double doors and sat down next to us.

"He's stable," she said. "He'll need to spend a few days in the hospital so they can run tests, but he should be all right."

"Can I see him?" I asked.

"Oh, no, sweetie, not till tomorrow," she said.

"Would you tell him something for me?" I asked.

Dolley patted my hand. "Sure, what is it?"

"Tell him I'm sorry."

"Sorry for what?" Muriel asked.

"For messing up his nice, quiet life," I said.

Muriel handed me the thermos. "Take this. Bring it back to the Drifters' Rest tomorrow. You won't be going to work anyway."

When we got in the car, Flossie handed me five two-dollar bills. "I'm sorry about your job," she said. "Let me buy the gas."

When we got home, Flossie changed into her nightgown while I opened a can of cat food. The phone rang.

"When were you going to call and tell us you got fired?" my mother asked.

"I ... tomorrow, I guess. I hadn't thought about it."

"You get fired from a perfectly good job, get branded as a thief, and you don't take time to call your parents?"

"I just walked in the door, Mom. I've buried one friend today and left another one in the hospital. My *job* is the last thing on my mind."

"It won't be the last thing on your mind when you have nothing to live on."

"I don't want to talk about this," I said. "How in the world did you find out, anyway?"

"Sharon called and told Jewel. You can imagine how I felt when my best friend called and told me my only daughter had been fired, and I didn't even know."

I laughed. "What was I thinking? Of course, Sharon would want to be in on the kill. She and Trixie are probably out celebrating."

"Who's Prissy?"

"Never mind. Tell Jewel it's all a mistake. I haven't been fired. I'm on administrative leave. Once they investigate, they'll clear my name, and I'll be back at work."

"Mistake?"

"Yes," I said, "I was framed."

"Framed? Who would want to do that?"

"You got me, Mom. Tell Jewel to ask Sharon, and then we'll all know."

"How would Sharon know?"

"The same way she knew I was fired—from Trixie."

"Who's Prissy? Oh, never mind. I'll ask Jewel. I promised to call back the minute I found out something."

She hung up.

Before I could walk to the kitchen sink, the phone rang again.

"What's the problem, Aggie?" my brother Toby asked.

"I'm fine. How are you?"

"Fine? How can you be fine when you've been accused of stealing?"

"I was set up," I said, "by two women who want to get rid of me."

"Spare me the theatrics. Mom and Dad are very upset. What happened?"

"It takes too long to explain—especially since this is the first time you've called since I've been here."

He was peeved. "At least contact your union. They probably have a lawyer on retainer."

"Okay," I said. I didn't tell him I hadn't joined the union.

When I plopped down on the couch, Flossie woke up.

"Could I ask you something?" she said.

"I didn't steal anything, if that's what you're wondering."

"I would never think that."

"Sorry, Flossie," I said. "I'm a little edgy."

She handed me the afghan. "You have every right to be."

I pulled my feet up and snuggled under the magenta folds. "What did you want to ask?"

"When you call Buck to tell him why we left early, would you ask if I could come to the ranch sometime? The way the minister described it made me want to see it."

On Thursday morning I called Buck.

He answered the phone with "Sloan's Canyon."

"Hello, Buck. This is Agnes."

"Mornin'. Sorry I didn't git to talk to you yesterday. So many old friends to see."

"Not your fault," I said. "I'd just gotten some bad news and had to leave in a hurry."

I started crying again as I told him about Jonas.

"Don't worry," he said. "Nowadays they can do so much for folks with bad hearts. I'm sure he'll be fine. Is there anything I can do?"

"Actually, there is," I said. "A friend came with me to the funeral yesterday."

He chuckled. "The little lady with the hat?"

"Yes. She wanted me to ask if I could bring her to the ranch sometime."

"How about Saturday?" he said.

"We'll be there. Thanks, Buck."

Flossie and I cleaned the apartment and drove to the Drifters' Rest for lunch.

Muriel took our orders. "Dolley called and said Jonas has been moved to a private room. You can talk to him for a few minutes later today."

When I started crying again, Flossie handed me a white hankie with a pink "F" embroidered on the corner.

We ate in silence, except for Flossie's slurping and smacking.

"This is way better than Bob's Pancake World," she said.

Muriel returned to our table. "Bread pudding for dessert? I'm testing a new recipe before the holidays."

She brought two servings to the table and refilled our coffee cups.

When Flossie tasted the bread pudding, she smiled up at Muriel. "You have magic in your fingers," she said. "Did your mother teach you?"

Muriel pointed to Emmaline's portrait on the opposite wall. "Like her mother taught her."

Flossie stood and leaned over the table for a closer look at the painting. The hem of her gray sweater dropped into her empty dessert dish. She lifted the hem to her lips and licked off the cinnamon-speckled glaze.

Muriel pretended not to notice. "Anything else?" she asked.

"No," I said. "I'd better get going."

"Agnes," Flossie said, "you go ahead to the hospital. I'll take the bus home."

"Nonsense," Muriel said. "You can wait here till Agnes gets back. I've been thinking of taking up knitting. I could use some pointers."

I knew this was not true.

Flossie's eyes sparkled.

"All right," she said. "I just happen to have my knitting bag in the car. I was thinking you could use a lovely blue afghan over that chair in the corner."

On my way to the hospital I steeled myself for what I'd face. Jonas would be lying on his back, a crisp white sheet folded back neatly across his chest, needles jabbed in his arms, wires and tubes attached to beeping machines, oxygen hissing from a gigantic green tank. I'd tap on the door, tiptoe across the quiet room, stand motionless by his bed, and whisper his name. His eyes would remain closed. I'd lay my hand on his and assure him I was there.

I reached Jonas' room, took Flossie's handkerchief from my pocket, and opened the door.

Through the open curtains, warm afternoon sun spilled amber light onto the floor. A clear blue vase of yellow roses sat on the bedside table. White-haired, white-gowned, white pillows propped up behind him, Jonas appeared luminous. Oxygen spurting into his nose, he was sitting up in bed, thumbing through *Architectural Digest,* tilting his head to one side and then the other as he rustled through the pages, smirking, smiling, mumbling approval or dismay.

His guarded pensive look was gone; his eyes glowed with quiet passion.

He looked up. "Come in," he said. "I'm ready for you."

He laid the magazine on his lap. I sat on the chair by the bed.

"Last night I dreamed about my father," he said.

This was what I'd expected—a near-death experience.

"I've heard of that," I said. "Was he in a white light at the end of a tunnel?"

"No, more like a memory. When I was nine, during a terrible drought, lightning struck our barn and started a fire. My father rushed in, drove out our tractor, and then fought the fire as the blaze surged toward our house."

"He sounds like a remarkable man," I said.

Lost in the past, he didn't respond except to say, "My mother stood there in her nightgown in the dark yard, her face pale, terror in her eyes as she watched the flames leap up around my father."

He lay back and stared at the ceiling a few moments. "When the fire was out, my sisters went back to bed. I stayed on the porch and watched my parents wrap their arms around each other and cry."

Jonas closed his eyes to savor the image. I waited.

At last he looked at me. Tears slipped onto his pillow.

"I once told you the difference between me and my father was that he loved dirt and I—"

"Loved wood," I said to spare him the effort of choking out the words.

"I was wrong," he said. "I realized that when I woke up. While he was battling that fire, he wasn't thinking of his livelihood. He was thinking of the people he loved."

Jonas reached for my hand.

"I have to save the Magnolia Arms, Agnes, because I built it—" His voice broke again.

"For the people you love," I said.

His chin quivered; his chest heaved.

Fearful, I glanced at the machines monitoring his heart.

"In the beginning," he said, "I *was* building as homage to my father."

"I remember," I said.

"But sometime between laying the cornerstone and putting the last brick in the chimney, I realized I was building the house as a home for Margaret."

The door swung open to admit a cheery nurse. "Good morning, Mr. Grindstone," she said.

"Grinstead," I said.

She looked down at the chart. "Oh, yes, Grinstead. And how are we this morning?"

He wiped his eyes with the edge of the sheet. "Better," he said.

"Let's check, shall we?" the nurse said. She turned to me. "Wait outside, please."

"Please don't leave, Agnes," he said. "I have to talk to you."

I squeezed his hand and stepped outside the door.

"What are *you* doing here?" Trixie Thorpe's voice echoed down the sterile hall.

"The nurse told me to wait out here."

"I mean," she said, pulling the long, thin strap of her neon-yellow purse up over her shoulder, "what are you doing visiting Jonas?"

"He asked me to come see him," I said.

"We'll see about that," she said and pushed open the door.

Only a few seconds later, Trixie reappeared. "The nurse is with him," she said.

"I know. That's why I'm out here."

"Will you be much longer?" she asked.

"Jonas asked me to stay. We're not finished talking."

"Very well, then, I'll come back tomorrow when *you're* not here."

She stormed away.

The nurse came out into the hall.

"Fifteen minutes," she said. "He needs to rest."

I agreed and slipped back into the room.

"Where were we?" Jonas asked.

"The Magnolia Arms," I said.

"You must wonder why I abandoned my dream. But once I lost Margaret, nothing else mattered. I couldn't have stayed in that town without her."

"You've never gone back?"

"I swore I never would. The memories are too painful."

"And Olympia's family never contacted you again?"

"Not till Brooker showed up."

"I don't understand why they never came after you. They don't seem to be the sort of people to take an insult lying down."

"I've never understood, either. If they'd wanted to renege on their contract with me, I wouldn't have stood a chance. They had an army of shifty lawyers."

"So do you stand a chance now?"

He smiled. "That's what I wanted to talk to you about."

Again the door burst open. Two women swept into the room. A sweet-faced, gray-haired lady in a blue skirt, white blouse, and maroon argyle sweater rushed toward Jonas' bed.

"Jonesie," she said. She leaned over and kissed him on the cheek. "What have you done to yourself? How often must we warn you about working so hard?"

She smoothed his hair away from his forehead as the other lady, taller, her dyed strawberry-blonde hair dramatically coiffed and sprayed, dressed in a pale-pink cashmere sweater and pink cashmere skirt took her place on the other side of the bed. Her long string of pearls draped over Jonas' chest as she embraced him.

"My darling boy," she said, kissing him on the forehead, "we haven't been so frightened since you fell into the stall with Zeke Spurgin's prize longhorn at the 4-H show."

Jonas acquiesced to their smothering.

"I'm all right," he said. "I told you not to come all this way."

The gray-haired lady removed her round wire-rimmed glasses and wiped her eyes with a tissue. "If you think for one minute wild horses could've kept us away—"

"Camellia wanted to come, but Fred's still nursing that broken hip," the blonde said.

"How did you get here?" Jonas asked, looking from one to the other.

"Charlotte's chauffeur picked us up at the airport and brought us," the blonde said.

The gray-haired lady spoke again. "Dahlia insisted we come, and, as you know, whatever Dahlia says …"

"I know," Jonas said. "Mother Hen."

I gasped. "You must be Jonas' sisters," I said.

The gray-haired lady turned to me, hugged me, and kissed me on the cheek.

"Oh, thank you," she said, "for coming to visit Jonesie. He's told us about his wonderful friends. Which one are you?"

Jonas spoke up. "This is Agnes Quinn. Agnes, these are my sisters." He pointed to the gray-haired lady. "Poppy Hornbeam …"

The blonde extended her hand over Jonas' bed. "And I'm Iris Rutherford."

"Jonesie?" I said.

"Nickname," Jonas said. "A baby brother thing I've never been allowed to outgrow."

Poppy picked up Jonas' water pitcher. "Empty. Which way is the nurses' station?"

"I'll go," I said. "I'm sure you have some catching up to do."

Poppy laid her hand on my cheek. "Oh, you are the dearest little thing," she said. "How old are you? Our sister Camellia has a grandson about your age. Iris, how old is Joe now?"

"Poppy," Jonas said, "Agnes has no time for that. She's going away for a while."

"Oh well, perhaps I'll discuss it with Camellia later," Poppy said.

I didn't want to intrude on Jonas' reunion with his sisters, so I dawdled on my way to the nurses' station. Then I called Flossie to say I'd be late and to tell Muriel I'd met the sisters. As I strolled back, I puzzled over his comment about my "going away," concluding he must be groggy from medication. I waited outside his door a few more minutes and then knocked quietly. Poppy still smoothed Jonas' hair. Iris, like a classic film star, sat on the side of his bed, one leg crossed over the other, her pink shoe dangling gracefully.

I'd never seen such remarkable women, and I'd known them only a few minutes.

I picked up my purse and turned to Poppy and Iris. "It was a pleasure to meet you."

"You can't go yet," Jonas said. "I haven't told you the plan."

"Plan?"

"To save the Magnolia Arms," he said.

"Jonesie's beautiful house in the hands of that dreadful woman," Poppy said, wiping her eyes again. "How can she think we'd allow her to desecrate Grandmother's memory?"

"Poppy, dear, control yourself," Iris said. "The nurse will remove us if we upset Jonesie."

Poppy sniffled. "Yes, you're right. Go ahead, Jonesie. Tell Agnes the plan." She took my hand. "You really are the dearest girl to help Jonesie in this way."

"I was just telling my sisters," Jonas said, "I've decided to stop running from Olympia—"

"It was because of the dream," Poppy said, looking at me. "He remembered how Papa saved our house and—"

Iris interrupted. "You must let Jonesie finish, Poppy. Agnes will have a lot to do, if she's leaving on Monday."

"You know, my dear," Poppy said, "Iris and I will be here awhile. I'm sure Jonesie won't mind if we slipped away from the hospital to help you pack."

Iris took her lipstick from her purse. "The only thing Jonesie hasn't figured out is if you'll take your cat. Will you?"

"Take my cat where?" I asked.

"To the Magnolia Arms," Poppy said. She turned to Iris. "Do they allow cats on trains?"

"Trains?" I asked.

"Much safer—the train," Iris said. "Besides, you never know whom you might meet. I met my second husband on a train."

My head was spinning. "May I sit down?" I asked.

Poppy stood up. "Oh yes, dear, bless your heart. This must be a lot to take in."

"She hasn't taken in anything *yet*," Jonas said.

Iris patted his hand. "That's right, precious, now you go right ahead and tell Agnes how you want to hire her to do a little snooping for you. Just like Miss Marple."

"And to think," Poppy said to me, "you couldn't have gone if you hadn't been fired. It's such perfect timing."

Tired of asking questions, I decided simply to try to keep up.

"Not fired exactly," I said. "Not yet."

"Girls, please, if I could talk for just one minute," Jonas said.

Poppy patted his hand. "Of course. Iris and I will sit here and listen."

Iris took a fingernail file from her purse. "Dahlia is going to be very pleased you've decided to deal with Olympia once and for all. She thought you should've done it years ago."

Jonas turned to me. "Where was I, Agnes? Before these two came in?"

I bit my lower lip. "Brooker … I think."

"Yes, Brooker. You must wonder why Olympia sent him to find me—"

"After all these years," Iris said, holding out her hand to admire her pink nails.

"It's because her father died," Jonas said.

"Good riddance, I say," Poppy said. "What kind of father raises children like that?"

Jonas stayed on target. "Olympia is his sole heir."

"That means she's in charge of all his property now," Poppy said.

"And that includes the Magnolia Arms," Iris said.

Jonas pushed ahead. "Olympia wants my house, Agnes. She wants me to sign over my rights to the property."

"But you never will, will you, Jonesie?" Poppy said.

"A man gets new perspective from staring death in the face," Jonas said.

"Papa said the same thing after his first heart attack," Iris said.

"I'm not going to spend one more day wondering what will happen to my house after I'm gone," he said. "I have to protect it."

"Oh, don't say 'gone,' Jonesie," Poppy said. She took another tissue from her purse.

I thought of the photo tucked away in my dresser drawer.

"I'm glad to hear you say that," I said. "What are you going to do?"

"Send you to save it," Iris said.

"Me?"

Poppy poured a glass of water. "Jonesie can't go."

"No," I said, "not anytime soon."

Iris stood, took the water from Poppy, and handed it to Jonas. "And that's where you come in, Agnes. Perfect timing, like Poppy said."

Jonas took the cup. "I don't know what Olympia is up to or why she wants the house," Jonas said. "She may simply want the pleasure of tearing it down."

"Or," Iris said, "to sell it to some conglomerate for a profit. Drink your water, precious."

Jonas obliged with a sip. "I don't trust her or Brooker. For all I know, they'll bribe someone at city hall to have the house condemned."

"Yes," Poppy said. "They can say they have public domain."

"That's *eminent* domain," Iris said.

"I need someone there, Agnes," Jonas said. "Someone I can trust."

"You're the perfect person, Agnes," Iris said. "No one knows you. No one knows you know Jonas. They'll never know he sent you. You can take them by surprise."

"Imagine that man saying the house is 'worthless,' as if anything our Jonesie built could be worthless," Poppy said. "The birdhouse he made for Mama is still in Camellia's front yard."

"Worthless?" I asked. "That can't be true."

"I don't think so, either," Jonas said.

"Neither do I," Poppy and Iris said at the same time.

"But we have to find out," Jonas said. "I thought of hiring an investigator, but when Muriel called with your news—"

"Good news, if you ask me," Iris said.

"—I thought I could hire you instead," Jonas said.

Poppy nodded. "Agnes is the perfect person for the job."

"You're on official suspension, Agnes, till the investigation is completed," Jonas said. "You're free to go … if you want to."

Poppy poured another glass of water and handed it to me.

"Here, drink this, dear," she said. "The color's all gone from your pretty face."

My heart raced. Only moments before I'd crept into this room, fearful my best friend was breathing his dying gasp, and now my ridiculous dream was within reach. I was going to walk up the steps of the Magnolia Arms and knock on the door. Was it really possible?

I guzzled down the water. "Last night I couldn't afford to put gas in my car," I said.

Jonas shook his head. "You don't understand. I'm *hiring* you to do a job for me. I'll pay your expenses for as long as you need."

"A schoolteacher doesn't have that kind of money," I said.

"Don't you believe that for a minute," Iris said. "He's stashed away more money than you could make in a lifetime."

"Let's just say I've lived a simple, solitary life," Jonas said. "Money is not a problem."

"I don't know what to think," I said.

"Agree to go, Agnes, and I'll take care of everything," he said. "I've been thinking about it all night, and worked out every detail. Don't forget, I'm good with calculations."

I stood to go. "Can I think about it till tomorrow?"

"Sure," he said. "But there's one more thing you might like to consider."

"What's that?"

"While you're away, you can work on your book."

Poppy and Iris hugged me goodbye. I closed the door and walked toward my car.

"Good visit?" Muriel asked when I returned to the Drifters' Rest.

"You know I had a good visit, don't you?" I asked.

"Maybe," she said.

On our way home, Flossie asked why I was so quiet.

"A lot on my mind," I said. "It's been a big week, and I have a good idea for my story."

"When we get home," she said, "I'll feed Saturn, so you can sit right down and start typing. I know what it's like when inspiration strikes."

Dear Flossie. What would happen to her while I was gone?

When we got home, I went straight to my desk while Flossie fed Saturn. When the phone rang, she waved me away and picked up the receiver.

"Oh, hello, Mrs. Quinn," she said. "This is Flossie. No, not Prissy. Flossie. Agnes? No, she's not here right now. May I take a message?"

She hung up the phone and winked as she walked by.

"Call your mother," she said, "when you're finished."

I began to type.

As the evening mist rose, Lyda Rose stood on her castle wall and gazed at the expansive valley. When she heard footsteps, she drew her sword.

"Only a message, My Lady," Grimwulf said. "A knight of Lord Hewnstone requests your aid. Queen Odred's forces threaten their castle. Her trebuchets are battering their walls."

"We've only just returned from battle," Lyda Rose said. "The horses must rest."

"And so must you, My Lady, but by dawn you must ride, or all will be lost. If Hewnstone's castle falls ..."

"Our whole valley will be overrun with the enemy."

The next morning I told Flossie the whole story of Jonas and the Magnolia Arms.

She swallowed hard and asked, "You're going, aren't you?"

I nodded.

"How long will you be gone?"

"I don't know, but don't worry. The rent is paid through the end of next month."

"You mean I can stay in our apartment?"

"I was hoping you would, so you could take care of Saturn. I don't know where I'll be staying. Cats may not be allowed."

She brightened. "I could do that."

Charlotte called to postpone our Friday dinner. "I'm going out with Poppy and Iris," she said. "Drop by Saturday afternoon. Jonas gave me a check for you."

On Saturday morning, Flossie knitted as we drove to Sloan's Canyon.

"What are you making now?" I asked.

"A new scarf for you. It will be cold soon," she said.

Buck waved to us from his front porch. Then he stepped down and opened Flossie's door.

Taking her hand, he helped her from the car. "I'm Buck Sloan."

She blushed. "Flossie Bingham."

"Thank you for coming to my aunt's funeral," he said.

"I believe she and I would've been friends," Flossie said, "if we'd met sooner."

After breakfast we walked to the stable together. Flossie approached Buttercup and kissed her on the nose.

"This was Geneva's horse, wasn't it?" she said.

"That's right," Buck said. "But she's taken a liking to Agnes now. There's a nice swing at the edge of the pasture, Flossie. Would you like to do some knitting while Agnes and I—"

Flossie had moved to the next stall. "Who's this?" she asked.

She was caressing the face of a stunning black-and-white pinto.

"That's Franklin," Buck said.

"I'll take him," Flossie said.

Flossie and I waited outside as Buck saddled three horses.

"He's the most charming man I ever met," Flossie said.

Buck led out Franklin first. Without putting her foot in the stirrup, Flossie grabbed the saddle horn and swung herself onto the horse's back. She was off at a trot before Buck and I knew what had happened.

"She's an unusual lady," Buck said as we watched Flossie race across the pasture.

"A good friend," I said.

"Somethin' botherin' you, Agnes?" Buck asked. "You don't seem like yourself."

By the time we'd crested the hill at the edge of the pasture, I'd told him I was leaving.

"How long will you be gone?" he asked.

"I don't know."

He stroked Buster's mane as he spoke. "I was askin' 'cause I always host a community barbecue the Saturday before Thanksgiving, and I was hopin' you'd be …"

I knew where Buck was headed, so I intercepted him. "Be back by then?" I asked.

"Yeah, that too, but what I mean to say is, I know I'm older than you, and you're way smarter than me, but, well—"

"If I'm back by then, I'll be here. I hope you'll invite Elinor. And of course, Flossie will want to come too."

He sighed, took off his hat, and wiped his forehead with the back of his hand. "I'll invite her if we can catch up to her," he said.

We rode after Flossie.

By Monday morning Elinor was back in the library.

Jonas was home from the hospital.

I was on a train to Dennisonville.

And Xander Plumley was at Brighton Park looking for me.

Chapter 15

A Road Less Travelled

I got off the train, found a pay phone, and called Jonas.

"I'm here," I said.

"That's wonderful news, Agnes."

"Think," I said, as I enjoyed the reunions going on around me, "a week ago today we had no idea I'd be here."

He hesitated. "A lot *can* happen in a week. In fact, a lot has happened since you left. Someone came here looking for you."

"Don't tell me my brother showed up," I said.

"No, not your brother. Xander Plumley."

I sank down on top of my big black suitcase and leaned against the brick wall. "Xander? He's in Australia."

"He's at Brighton Park."

"He's missing."

"Not anymore."

"Was Zane with him?" I asked.

"No, his brother wasn't with him, but his dog was."

"Dog? Xander doesn't like pets—never had one."

"He's does now. That's why someone called the police. Xander launched into a tirade on animal rights when the student at the information desk said he'd have to leave the dog outside."

"That doesn't sound like him," I said.

"Luckily, before an officer arrived, that student of yours intervened."

"Exton?" I asked.

"No, that Tony kid. He told Xander you were his teacher and asked if he could help."

"How nice," I said. "I should've told Tony goodbye. He didn't even know I was leaving."

"Apparently, word got around. Tony explained everything to Xander."

"How awful. Think what Xander must've gone through to find me and then—"

"Don't get upset, Agnes," Jonas said. "Things turned out all right."

The crowd stared as I blubbered into the phone. "All these years I've dreamed of a reunion, and he comes back on the very day—"

"Let me finish," Jonas said.

"How do you know what happened, anyway?" I asked. "Aren't you at home?"

"That's what I'm trying to tell you," he said. "Tony told Xander if anyone knew where to find you, it would be the librarian."

"Tony took Xander to Elinor," I said, sniffling. "How clever of him."

"You'll like this even better. Tony told Xander until he had you as a teacher, he didn't even know where the library was."

I wiped my nose on my sleeve. "That's the nicest thing I've ever heard."

"Xander waited outside the library with the dog while Tony found Elinor."

"I'm so relieved," I said. "Is Xander with Elinor now?"

"No ... he's with Ryder Ellershaw."

My suitcase toppled over when I bolted up. "You mean the same Ryder Ellershaw who landed me in the hospital? *That* Ryder Ellershaw?"

"Wait a minute, Agnes."

"What was Elinor thinking—turning over a mental patient to a mental patient?"

"What was she supposed to do?" Jonas asked. "I couldn't help her. Muriel couldn't leave her business. Ryder was Elinor's only choice."

My panic got the best of me; I shouted into the phone. "Where is Xander now?"

"Ryder's taking him to the Drifters' Rest. Muriel's going to feed him, and then Poppy and Iris will pick him up and bring him here."

"You can't take care of a houseguest," I said.

"If he's anything like his brother, I'm sure we'll get along fine. Besides, if Xander stays and helps me for a while, my sisters can go home."

A uniformed officer tapped me on the shoulder. "What's the problem?"

"No problem," I said.

"Lower your voice," he said. "You've been reported."

I sat down. My welcome to Dennisonville wasn't what I'd imagined.

"Everything okay there, Agnes?" Jonas asked.

"Yeah, great. First I'm accused of stealing, and now I'm disturbing the peace."

"What?"

"Never mind. Do you think Xander will be all right?"

"I'll know more when I see him. It's safe to say he's not the person you remember. Elinor said he looked a little rough."

"What does that mean?" I asked.

"Long hair, beard, flannel shirt, and the dog named Mendel."

I had to smile. "Of course. Mendel is Xander's favorite chemist."

"I have to go now, Agnes. The girls need directions to the Drifters' Rest."

"All right," I said. "Jonas?"

"Yes?"

"Take care of Xander."

"I will," he said. "Find a taxi and go to the Whispering Pines Motor Lodge."

I hung up the phone and dialed my parents.

"Hi, Mom. I knew you'd want me to let you know I got here okay."

I thought she'd be pleased I called the moment I arrived, but I was wrong.

She wailed into the phone: "I can't believe you went through with this ridiculous idea—leaving your job to move to some godforsaken place in the middle of nowhere."

"I didn't 'leave my job,' Mom. I'm on suspension while they investigate."

"Do you know how this looks? You've skipped town and crossed the state line."

"Give me the phone, Betty." My father growled like an angry troll beneath a stone bridge. "Were you listening when I tried to talk sense into you, or was your head in the clouds as usual?"

"I was listening," I said.

"Then *why* did you run off to who knows where with no job and nothing to live on?"

"I have a job, Dad. I'm going to finish my book."

"Writing a book is not work."

"Tell that to Tolstoy."

"I would, but he's dead."

I performed the lie I'd rehearsed on the train. "I've managed to save up a little money."

"I don't know how," he said. "You only worked there long enough to get a paycheck or two. How much could you have saved?"

"Enough to get by on for a while. Once things … I have to go now, Dad. I need to eat."

"Say goodbye to your mother." He handed her the phone.

Her voice was composed and frigid. "I don't know why you can't be more like—"

"Toby, I know."

"No, not Toby. Sharon. Why couldn't you have married a nice man and settled down—"

"I have to hang up now, Mom. My taxi's here."

I ate lunch in the train terminal and then took a taxi to the Whispering Pines. I lay down on the gold quilted bedspread. The hum of the air conditioner lulled me to sleep. I dreamed.

Lyda Rose, commanding Hewnstone's forces on a voyage south, stood on the bow of her ship, Stalwart. *The biting wind blowing through her hair, Lyda Rose closed her eyes and pictured the old warrior's tired face. The years of standing alone against Odred had broken his strength.*

The dreaded cry of "Naelzor, Naelzor," came from the crow's nest.

Lyda Rose had no time to retreat. The loathsome sea monster reared up, howling, and with one smack of his tail swept her overboard into the icy, swirling sea. Gasping, she surfaced in time to see his monstrous jaw clamp down on—

A knock at the door woke me in time to spare my heroine's left leg. I sat up and tried to remember where I was. Sleepy, I stumbled to the door.

"Your extra towels," the maid said.

I took the towels, unpacked, and called for a taxi.

"Take me to 306 Belmont Drive, please," I told the driver.

His gray hair plastered to his temples beneath a faded blue cap, the driver put his arm on the back of the seat and turned to me. His cheeks were cherry red.

"Did you say 306 Belmont Drive?"

"Yes. Do you know where it is?"

"Of course. I'm just flummoxed by your request."

"If it's a long way, it's not a problem," I said. "I'm prepared to pay."

"No, no," he said. He faced the road and looked at me in his rearview mirror. "Do you know what dramatic irony is?"

"Yes, I'm an English teach … I'm a writer," I said.

His face faded to pink. "Then you'll understand."

"What?"

"You're my last passenger of the day, the last fare of my career. I'm retiring."

"And that's ironic because …?"

"My *first* passenger who sat where you're sitting now was going to 306 Belmont Drive."

My heart fluttered. "A man or a woman?"

"Woman. In a hurry and not in the mood to chat."

"I'm not in a hurry," I said. "I have nothing but time."

"Then allow me to take you on the scenic route—on the house."

"Thank you, Mr. …"

"Ludlow," he said. "Asa Ludlow."

"I'm Agnes Quinn."

He winked at me in the mirror and pulled out into traffic.

The fading sun, seeping through the oaks lining Main Street, splashed pastel pink and watercolor orange onto the brick storefronts and majestic homes along the town square. Through propped-open doors, shopkeepers pulled in wooden barrels full of "All Sales Final" Fourth of July decorations and covered the tables of pumpkins, gourds, and butternut squash with white canvas. Bells jangled as they flipped "Open" signs to "Closed" and secured their doors till the next morning.

Asa drove leisurely, his arm propped in his open window, calling each store owner by name, waving like a lord greeting the tenants on his estate.

He pointed to a colonial home on the right. "People say Washington slept there on his way to Charleston," he said.

"Is that so?" I said.

"And over there, see the vine-covered house on the corner?" he asked. "Legend has it the lady who lives there hasn't seen the light of day in over twenty years."

"Jilted lover?" I asked.

"That's the story," he said.

Asa turned left and pointed to a tall steeple in the middle of the square. "First Baptist Church," he said. "You a soprano?"

"No. Been an alto since I was ten."

"Too bad," he said. "They need a soprano for the Christmas cantata."

"I don't know if I'll be here that long."

He shrugged his shoulders. "We'll swing by the lake at the edge of town, and then I'll drop you at the Magnolia Arms. I need to get home to supper."

I leaned back in the brown leather seat and folded my arms. I thought of Jonas' arriving in this town, his "heart full of dreams," as he'd said. I looked over at the shimmering lake, a rising half-moon reflected on the water, and imagined Jonas and Margaret strolling hand in hand by the bank. He would have paused to point out Orion. Maybe they sat on that very bench, I thought, and talked about their life together, their first son to be named after Jonas' father. Maybe Margaret laid her head on his shoulder and said …

"And if you like good coffee," Asa said, tapping on his window, "it's worth your time to walk to Newman's. You can meet half the people in town there if you show up by 6:30 a.m."

"It's a long way from the motel," I said. "I'd have to call a taxi."

"You can walk there from the Magnolia Arms," he said.

"I won't be staying at the Magnolia Arms. I only want to see it."

"My mistake," he said. "I assumed you were going there to check on a room."

"You mean I can rent a room there?"

"Lots of people live there," Asa said, "since they fell on hard times."

"Hard times?"

"Ever since Abel Sutton's oldest boy died," he said.

"What do you mean?"

"I don't know the whole story. All I know is after Abel and his wife left town, that's when everyone found out he'd been borrowing from the business accounts to help his boy."

"Who lives in the house now?" I asked.

"I know the ones who've been around a long time, but since the Rooms for Rent sign went up, I've lost track of who's moved in."

"So … it's like a boarding house?"

"You might say so," he said. "Once they found out Abel hadn't been paying the taxes or keeping up the place like he agreed to, they've been doing whatever they can to raise money."

"Do you know if there's a room available?" I asked.

"I think the sign's still there. I'm so used to seeing it, though. I might be wrong."

Asa turned right onto Belmont Drive and stopped in front of the Magnolia Arms. He walked around the front of the cab and opened my door.

I sat there, transfixed, gazing at the house Jonas built.

"You've never been here before?" Asa asked.

"No."

"You have the look of someone who's coming home."

"I am," I said. "Thank you, Asa. Maybe I'll see you at Newman's sometime."

Even after Asa pulled away, I lingered at the curb, staring up at the lights in the windows, imprinting the image of the house, more beautiful than I'd imagined, on my memory.

"Coming in for dinner?"

An elderly gentleman in a tweed coat and brown trousers stopped next to me on the sidewalk. "Chicken and dumplings night," he said with a refined British accent.

"I'm only visiting … I mean I saw the sign and wanted to inquire about …"

He stuck out his hand. "Montague St. James. I live on the second floor. Trust me, before you commit to a month's rent anywhere, you should always try the food first."

"Good advice. Have you lived here long?" I asked.

The front door opened. A thin middle-aged woman in a yellow-flowered apron stepped out onto the porch. She was wiping her hands on a dish towel.

"Monty, come to supper. Your table's waiting," she said.

He called to her. "Be right there. Bringing a new customer."

She went inside. He offered me his arm, and we started toward the porch.

"Ivy Leigh Ransom," he said. "Heart of gold, backbone of steel."

"Do you think she'll mind if I join you?" I asked.

"You'd actually be doing us a favor," he said. "We're making a go at the restaurant business and need satisfied customers. Word of mouth, you know."

I walked through the door of the Magnolia Arms.

Ivy Leigh took off her apron and laid it on the check-in desk in the foyer.

"Welcome," she said to me. "Are you here for dinner?"

"Yes, thank you."

"I have a lovely table by a window. Follow me."

We walked into the dining room, high-ceilinged with tall unadorned windows, raspberry-pink walls, wide white enamel baseboards, and dark-green carpet printed with small red rosebuds. A variety of starched white tablecloths draped several small square tables along the walls, and four larger round tables were arranged in the center of the room. Each of the dark-brown chairs was unique—their backs high, squared, latticed, rounded, slatted, plain, ornate—purchased perhaps from going-out-of-business restaurants, thrift stores, or estate sales.

We dodged a lanky bow-tied young man toting a tray loaded with dishes of dumplings.

"Keep up with the server, Nestor," Ivy Leigh said. "She's way over there."

He answered in a hoarse whisper: "You hired me to trim shrubs and sling manure. I'm not cut out for this prissy-pants stuff. I can't walk any faster without dropping everything."

Ivy Leigh ignored his complaint and turned to me.

"How about this table by the window?" she asked.

"Thank you," I said. I sat down and unfolded my napkin in my lap.

Next to the wall, two tables away, an elegant woman thumbed through *The Collected Poetry of Robert Frost.* She was dressed in a gray skirt, pristine white blouse, and dark-purple sweater. Her silver hair, luxurious and carefully styled, lay in soft waves around her oval face. Her gray eyes twinkled as she thumbed through the pages. Her lips, small, heart-shaped, and deep red, smiled as she read.

When dinner was served, the beautiful lady marked her place with a leather bookmark and laid the volume on the table. As she reached for her water glass, she noticed me.

"Good evening," she said. "You're new here."

"Yes," I said, "I arrived in town this morning."

"Do you like Robert Frost?" she asked.

"I do."

She lifted her water glass in a toast, saying, "Here's to Robert Frost."

I lifted my glass in return. "To the road less travelled."

We sipped our water.

"And you are?" she asked.

"Agnes Quinn," I said.

"Welcome to the Magnolia Arms, Agnes. I'm Margaret Hawthorne."

Chapter 16

A Broken Chord

For once, the better angels of my nature prevailed. I clamped my lips together and turned from Margaret to stare out the dark window. I longed to say, *Jonas is alive and well. He never married. He still loves you.* But I didn't.

"You all right, Miss?"

Her small chin tucked in, a frail young woman peered at me over narrow, black-framed glasses perched on the tip of her nose. The soothing smell from the bowl of steaming dumplings in her hands lured me back to the dining room.

"Yes, I'm fine," I said.

"May I bring you some English peas?" she asked.

"No, thanks, I'm allergic."

She made the same offer to Margaret.

"Thank you, Posey," Margaret said.

From my spot by the window, I watched the solitary diners eat in silence. Each at separate tables, they were subdued, nothing like the rambunctious patrons of the Drifters' Rest. Monty, hunched over his table across the room, used his knife to scrape English peas into a spoon. Margaret, like a benevolent monarch, peered around the room as she ate, returning her fork to her plate after each bite. Her evening meal, it seemed, was only an excuse to keep watch over her friends.

Margaret's voice broke the stillness.

"Posey," she said. "More water?"

When Posey arrived with the pitcher, Margaret nodded toward the wide arched doorway and said, "Oliver's home."

Posey turned around. Her thin lips twitched into a barely perceptible smile. She whispered, "Oliver," like an ailing patient welcoming a doctor.

"Don't stand there staring," Margaret said. "Ask him if he'd like to sit down."

Posey fluffed the frayed ends of her fine brown hair as she glided toward the door. "It's nice to see you, Oliver," she said. "Would you like to sit down?"

Like a tortured romantic hero lately arrived from the moor, Oliver loomed in the doorway, overshadowing the mere mortals with his presence. He was of average height and build, about thirty-five, I guessed, but his dark brooding eyes made him appear much older, ancient, somehow, and otherworldly. His thick black hair, except for a few obstinate strands brushing the top of his round wire-rimmed glasses, was pristinely parted and plastered into place. Scowling, he tugged the strap of the black leather garment bag on his shoulder and then squinted at Posey as if seeing her for the first time.

"Where's the long table?" he asked.

Posey smoothed her white ruffled apron. "In the garage. Remember? We told you before you left. We need to raise money and—"

"You didn't move my piano, did you?"

Her voice faltered. "No, we'd never do that."

"Where am I supposed to sit?" he asked.

Posey pointed to a table near the window, behind me. "I saved that place for you. See? It's not near anyone else."

Oliver set his bag, monogrammed "OMF," by the brick hearth. "Is it still chicken and dumplings night or has that changed too?" he asked.

Cheered up, Posey almost sang. "No. I mean it hasn't changed. I mean yes, it's still—"

"Very well then." Oliver sat down near the fireplace.

I looked at my plate, though I longed to study the mysterious newcomer.

Margaret caught my eye. She ran her fingers along an imaginary keyboard and mouthed the word "musician," as if that explained everything.

I nodded, put the last morsel in my mouth, and slid my plate to the edge of the table.

Eagle-eyed Posey returned. "Dessert?"

"I couldn't eat another bite," I said.

She laid a green ticket in front of me. "Pay at the desk."

I stood and walked toward Margaret. "It was nice meeting you," I said.

"You as well. I hope you enjoyed your dinner."

"I did, thank you." I pointed to Oliver and lowered my voice. "Is he very well known?"

"In some circles," Margaret said. "Dr. Oliver Martin Farrell."

"A professor?" I asked.

"He had no patience for teaching," she said. "Gave it up after a year."

"I can sympathize with that," I said. "I tried teaching for a few weeks until … there was a problem."

Margaret held up her hand. "No need to explain, Agnes. If anyone understands the challenges of the profession, it is I."

"You're a teacher?" I asked.

She patted the corners of her mouth with her napkin. "English literature."

"So you went back to college," I said. "I'm so glad."

She laid her napkin on the table. "Went *back*?"

My face smoldered. "I mean I … you …"

Monty's approach spared me from calamity. "So, Agnes, was I right about the food?"

"You were." Relieved, I changed the subject. "Does either of you know if there's still a room available?"

Her elbow propped on the table, Margaret cradled her chin in her hand. Her eyes sparked with the benevolent mistrust teachers reserve for those who lie about dogs and homework.

"There is," she said, "but it's small and on the third floor."

"Stuffy in the summer, but it has a nice view," Monty said.

I turned to him. "Do you think I could see it?"

"Ivy Leigh will be happy to show you," he said.

"And may I call a cab from the front desk?" I asked.

"Ask Nestor to drive you," Monty said. "He hates clearing the dishes."

Margaret reached for her book. "I hope we'll see you again soon, Agnes."

I said a hasty goodbye and peeked from the corner of my eye as I walked past Oliver. His eyes closed, his head bobbing, he appeared to be rehearsing some concerto in his mind.

I found Ivy Leigh recording figures in an account book at the check-in desk.

"Enjoy your dinner?" she asked.

"Yes. So much that I'd like to eat here every night."

"Wonderful," she said. "How long will you be in town?"

"A month or so. Margaret said you might still have a vacancy."

She closed her book and took a key from the pegboard behind her. "Would you like to see it?" she asked.

Past the haphazard rows of old photos and faded landscapes on the staircase wall, she hurried up the steps ahead of me. I lingered to savor the moment I'd so long anticipated. Slowly, reverently, my fingers on the banister, I stood at the bottom of the stairs Jonas had designed and built long before I was born. The curved edge fit my hand as perfectly as if it had been fashioned for me. I closed my eyes and pictured Jonas smoothing, sanding, staining, and standing back to inspect his work.

Ivy Leigh bent over the second-floor railing. "Are you all right?"

"Yes," I said. "I love the feel of wood."

She smirked. "Could you 'love the feel' as we walk? I have a lot to do before bedtime."

I followed her. The second-floor hallway was wide and brightly lit. A blue hurricane lamp and a vase of purple flowers sat on a dark wood table between two closed doors. A garland of autumn silk flowers, grapevines, and pine cones draped the door at the end of the hall.

"Are all of these rooms occupied?" I asked.

"Yes. Margaret lives there, Monty next door to her, and Posey in that room."

"The maid lives with the other tenants?" I asked.

"She's not the maid," Ivy Leigh said. "She's a singer."

"Working here till her talent is discovered?" I asked.

Ivy Leigh led me up the next flight of stairs. "No. She's almost thirty. If she were going to be discovered, it would've happened by now. She gives voice lessons at the local school."

"Then why is she—?"

"We've fallen on hard times. We're all pitching in to keep the place open."

We climbed to the third floor. She pointed to a door on the left.

"That's a study," she said. "When Oliver is practicing, Monty comes up here to write."

"Is he a novelist?"

"No, he's writing a memoir of his time in the court."

"He was a lawyer?" I asked.

"No, a bailiff. I don't think his book will sell, but we try to cheer him on."

"Can anyone use the study?" I asked.

"Yes, but there are rules. No food or drink, and you have to be quiet."

She jiggled her key in the door at the end of the hall. "I haven't unlocked this room in awhile. I'll have Nestor check things over in the morning."

She opened the door and pointed up at the ceiling. "Cupola and widow's walk are above this room, but I wouldn't recommend climbing up there. We had to call the fire department when the last tenant tried."

She turned on the light and laid the key on the old dresser near the door. The wood floor creaked as we stepped into the room. A high arched window offered a view of the street as Monty had described. Ivy Leigh scurried to the bed nestled against the wall on the left and tugged at the corner of the white chenille bedspread. Then she turned and ran her hand across the dresser.

"A little dusty, but I wasn't expecting to show the room tonight."

"Not a problem," I said.

She wiped a smudge off the elaborate gold-framed mirror centered over the dresser and then opened the top middle drawer and pulled out a black sock, a silver shoehorn, a hardware store calendar, and a light bulb.

"If there's anything else in the drawers, stack it in the hall. Nestor will take care of it."

She turned around and pointed to a massive rolltop desk on the wall opposite the bed. "Not sure what's in those drawers, either, but you can use the typewriter if you want."

I walked to the desk and tapped on the typewriter keys. Then I turned around to survey the perfect room.

"When can I move in?" I asked.

"Tomorrow morning," she said. "First month's rent in advance."

I wrote her a check and followed her downstairs. Nestor was waiting by the front door.

"Margaret said you needed a ride," he said. "Where to?"

"The Whispering Pines."

We drove toward the motor lodge in the brisk autumn night.

"Did you like the room?" he asked.

"I think it's the most wonderful room I've ever seen."

"Long walk up there," he said.

"I won't mind. It's been awhile since I've had a place all to myself."

"If you like privacy, then that's the room for you," he said.

"How long have you lived there?" I asked.

He drew in a long breath and pursed his lips. "Three years, I guess. Not sure, exactly."

"Where did you come from?"

"New Jersey."

"Tired of the hard winters?"

"No, tired of waking up every morning with my head on a library table."

"Where were you studying?" I asked.

"Princeton."

I snickered. "No, seriously, where?"

He turned to me. "Seriously. Princeton."

"How did you end up—?"

"I'd been up all night again, trying to meet a deadline for my dissertation. Thought if I walked around awhile, I could wake up and finish my work. That's when it happened."

"What?"

"I started *really* looking at the rows and rows of volumes, thinking about how hard all those authors had worked, so their books could sit unread on dusty shelves."

"What a sad thought," I said.

"Then I thought, so what if I finish my dissertation and publish it? Did the world really need one more book on the Reign of Terror? Was it going to be worth all the trouble?"

"I see your point."

"I walked out of the library and bought a bus ticket for the first bus leaving town."

"And ended up here?"

"As a gardener," he said. "Best job I ever had ... till we started the restaurant business. I don't mind Ivy Leigh telling me what to do, but I hate following Posey around like a puppy."

"It didn't look like she was ordering you around," I said.

"That's because tonight she got distracted."

"Oliver?" I asked.

He smacked the steering wheel. "I *told* her she was being obvious, but she doesn't believe me. Wait till I tell her a total stranger noticed her obsession with him."

"His feelings aren't mutual?"

He shook his head. "Oh, no—that's never going to happen."

We arrived at the Whispering Pines.

"Here you go," Nestor said. "Would you like me to pick you up in the morning?"

"That would be nice," I said. "I'll be ready at nine."

I unlocked my room and sat on the bed. I picked up the phone to call Jonas and then held the receiver in midair. I was about to give him the most important news of his life. How would I tell him? News like mine couldn't be dropped casually into a conversation. My mind as blank as the drab wall in front of me, I dialed his number.

His phone rang only once.

"Hello?"

"Jonas, I don't quite know how to tell you, but I have good—"

"This isn't Jonas."

"Xander?" I asked.

"Hello, Quinn."

"I … don't know what to say. How … how are you?"

"Jonas said Mendel could stay inside."

Was this fragile, tentative soul the same person who'd chided me for daydreaming and lectured me about my grades?

"I'm … sorry I wasn't there when you came to find me," I said.

"It's okay," he said. "I'd hate for you to see me like this."

He began to cry. "Can you forgive me, Quinn? I should've never left. If only Mr. Bridger—"

"I know. 'You were the sort of man he'd been looking for, and you didn't know your big chance would come so soon.'"

Without thinking, I'd spouted off lines from Xander's long-ago letter. My mocking tone surprised us both.

"What did you say?" he asked.

"Nothing. It doesn't matter. Just tell me where you've—"

"I knew you'd be angry," he said.

"I'm not angry, Xander. When you mentioned Mr. Bridger, I remembered what you wrote about him in your letter. That's all."

"After all this time you still remember what I wrote?"

"I've read it quite a few times over the years. It was—"

The phone went silent.

"Xander? Xander?"

Jonas picked up the phone. "Sorry, Agnes, he's not up to talking yet."

"He didn't used to be so sensitive," I said.

"Don't worry, I'll take care of him. I have to know—did you drive by the house?"

"No, I didn't drive by."

He sighed. "I guess that was a bit much to hope for. There's always—"

"I had dinner there," I said.

"Dinner?"

"You'd better sit down, Jonas. I have a lot to tell you."

"So Brooker *was* lying. The house isn't run down."

"No, it's not run down. It's beautiful." I said. "I'm moving in tomorrow."

"Moving in? The house is vacant?"

"No, it's not vacant," I said. "There's someone in every room, except one."

"What are you saying?"

"There was one room available, so I paid a month's rent in advance."

"Who lives in the other rooms—a family with a lot of kids?"

"No, they're not related." I counted on my fingers. "There's a manager, a caretaker, a singer, a pianist, a retired bailiff, and ..."

"You mean it's a boarding house?"

"You could say that," I said.

He paused. "I never ... I guess that's possible. A manager could live in the room off the foyer. They might have converted the pantry to a room for the caretaker and—"

"The only room I saw on the first floor was the dining room. But I know there are three people on the second floor and one of them is—"

He wasn't listening. "I wonder if anyone lives in the basement."

"If anyone lives in the basement," I said, "it's Oliver."

"Oliver?"

"The pianist. He's kind of cranky."

"You said there are three people on the second floor?"

"Yes, and one of them is—"

"So you'll be moving onto the third floor?" he asked.

"Yes, the center room."

"Under the cupola?"

"Yes," I said. "Ivy Leigh told me—"

"Ivy Leigh?"

"The manager."

"Did you see the room?" he asked.

"Yes. It's ... perfect."

"You'll need furniture. I should've thought of that. I can send more money—"

"I don't need furniture," I said. "There's a bed, a big dresser, a rolltop desk …"

"My desk is still there?"

"I don't know if it's your desk."

"It might be," he said. "I couldn't take it with me when I left."

"There's a typewriter, too," I said. "Ivy Leigh said I could—"

"My typewriter?"

"That's yours too?" I asked.

"I won't know till I see a picture. Did you take a camera with you?" he asked.

"No, but I can buy one tomorrow. I'm sure Nestor will be happy to take me shopping."

"Nestor?"

"The caretaker. Another Xander of sorts—walked out of a Ph.D. program at Princeton."

He didn't reply.

"Jonas, are you still there?"

"Yes. I'm trying to absorb all this. The truth is so different from what I've imagined."

"What did you imagine?"

"Living there with Margaret, of course."

"That's what I've been trying to tell you—"

"But later, when I knew that was impossible, I hoped the people who lived there would love the house and take care of it."

"You can be sure of that. They're—"

"I don't know how to thank you. How did you find out so much in one evening?"

"There's more," I said, "if you'll give me half a chance to tell you."

"Oh, no. You haven't seen Olympia, have you?"

"No, not Olympia," I said.

"Then who?"

"Margaret."

Again silence.

"Mm … my Margaret?" he asked.

"She introduced herself as Margaret Hawthorne."

His voice was faint. "Hawthorne? She never married?"

"I don't know, but I'll find out tomorrow when I tell her you sent me."

"No. You can't tell her … not yet."

This was not the reaction I'd expected.

"But why?" I asked. "If she never married, she must still love you."

"We don't know that."

"We don't know? Isn't it obvious?"

"We don't know she never married," he said, "and we certainly don't know if she ever forgave me."

"I can't believe you're being so clinical. Don't you want to know?"

His voice was firm. "Think, Agnes. Olympia may have done the same thing I've done—sent someone to investigate and report back."

"That hardly seems likely."

"You don't know her like I do. And let me remind you—I said the same thing about Mavis and Trixie, and you didn't listen."

I couldn't argue with that. I took a deep breath.

"So … for now, saving the house is more important than reuniting with Margaret?"

"For now. I might still save the house. I don't know if I can win Margaret back."

"When *can* I tell her?" I asked.

"You'll know when the time is right."

"This is *not* how I expected this conversation to go," I said.

"I know, but after all the mistakes I've made, I'm not going to ruin the last chance I have to fix the mess I made."

I sighed. "Okay, if you're sure that's what you want to do. You're the boss."

We said goodbye. Still dressed, I drifted into a half-sleep and dreamed that Xander, Mendel, and I were on a makeshift raft on a stormy ocean. Margaret, near drowning, tried to clamber aboard. Before I could reach her, she sank beneath the black water. Oliver, on top of a piano, floated by. Posey, breathless, dog-paddled behind. A magnificent ocean liner swept past. Standing at the rail, Trixie, Mavis, and Asher waved and smiled. Buck and Flossie approached in a rowboat. I pleaded for help. Buck held out the paddle, but I couldn't reach it. The paddle struck the raft again, again.

I awoke with a start, wondering where I was. My head was throbbing. I gradually realized someone was knocking on the door of my room at the Whispering Pines. I glanced at the wall clock: twelve forty. Who would be bothering people at this hour? I sat on the edge of the bed, groggy and confused. I waited. No one at the door, I told myself. It must have been my dream. I rubbed my eyes. Had I packed any aspirin?

Another knock.

Fully awake, I sat motionless, terrified.

"I came to get you out," a voice said. "Open the door."

I dialed the phone.

"Front desk," the clerk said.

I whispered. "Someone's banging on my door. Room 405."

"I'll take care of it."

"You'll call the police?"

"No need for that," he said.

"No need? What are you saying?"

He was annoyed. "If you'll let me hang up, I'll take care of it."

I did as he said and waited.

The stranger kept knocking. I watched the doorknob jiggle as the intruder tried the door.

I heard the clerk's voice outside. "All right, come on. That's enough of that."

After all was quiet, I sat still on the bed, my eyes closed, a hand clamped over my mouth. My head ached worse now. What was I doing here all alone? Jonas was right. I didn't really know the people living at the Magnolia Arms. Tomorrow I'd be in the same house with them. What if someone tried to get in my room then? What would I do? Leap out my third-story window? Run down the stairs? What was I thinking? Why hadn't I stayed in my nice, safe apartment with Flossie? I could've washed dishes at the Drifters' Rest.

I dug through my bag for the bottle of aspirins and shook out three tablets into my hand. I took a long, hot bath and with the light still on, slept all night.

The next morning I gulped down two cups of coffee and ate an apple danish in the motel lobby. I was dressed and sitting on my suitcase in the parking lot when Nestor drove up.

He rolled down his window. "Eager, aren't you?"

Monty emerged from the passenger door. "Need some help with your bag?"

He shoved my suitcase onto the backseat.

"Need to leave the trunk empty for groceries," Monty said. "Ivy Leigh wants us to do the shopping on the way back."

I climbed into the backseat and stared out the window. The uncomfortable notion that I knew neither of these men still nagged me.

Monty turned around and placed his arm on the seat. "So … we all want to know. Did you have a visitor last night?"

"Visitor?"

"Yes, Ivy Leigh brought it up after you left. 'Someone should've told her about Moe Tate,' she said. "We tried to call, but your line was busy for a long time."

"Who's Moe Tate?" I asked.

"He and his wife, Gretchen, run the Whispering Pines. Actually, Gretchen runs it. Poor Moe isn't all there."

"What do you mean?"

"If Gretchen falls asleep before he does, he wanders around warning the guests about the approaching Huns. He's perfectly harmless, but they don't get much repeat business."

"I wouldn't think so," I said.

I rolled down the window, breathed in the fresh October air, and tried to make some sense of my first day in Dennisonville. As usual, nothing had turned out like I'd expected. I'd missed my reunion with Xander by only a few hours. He was nothing like I'd remembered. The Magnolia Arms was a rental house. Margaret was here, but I couldn't tell her about Jonas. I missed my home and my friends—even Flossie, who used to try my patience.

Nestor asked, "So what are you doing here, anyway?"

I leaned on my suitcase and looked at him in the rearview mirror.

"I'm … on a leave of absence from work," I said.

"Sickness?"

"You could say that." I was, after all, sick of Mavis and Trixie.

"Are you going to get a job while you're here?" Monty asked.

"Not yet," I said. "I need to finish my book."

Monty turned around again. His bushy silver eyebrows stuck up and out in all directions.

"I'm an author too," he said. "Maybe we can collaborate. I could use an editor."

"Spellbinding stuff," Nestor said.

Monty slapped Nestor on the shoulder. "Very kind of you, old boy."

"I got through a hundred and thirty pages," Nestor said, "before I lost my glasses."

"Poor fellow was getting dreadful mee-graines," Monty said. "I told him to wait on the proofreading till he could buy some new specs."

Nestor looked at me in the mirror and winked. "Still can't afford them."

I followed Nestor and Monty into the market and pushed the cart as Monty read the list and Nestor dropped in vegetables, fruit, baking supplies, and poultry. For the first time I stopped to think of Muriel's care for her customers and felt homesick again.

When we reached the Magnolia Arms, Nestor stopped the car by the curb.

Monty picked up his cane and reached for the door handle. "Would you like to join me for a quick walk around the block, Agnes?" he asked.

"Maybe tomorrow," I said. "I'm a little tired."

"All right, but don't say I didn't warn you."

He got out of the car, buttoned his tweed coat, and waved over his shoulder as he went.

"What did he mean by that?" I asked.

"You'll find out," Nestor said.

He drove the car up the long winding driveway and parked by the side entrance of the kitchen. He hopped out and opened my door.

I reached for my suitcase.

"Get that later," he said. "Ivy Leigh's particular about bringing in the cold stuff first."

I followed him to the trunk of the car. He handed me two brown bags and hurried ahead to hold open the door of the screened porch as I went in.

Like a weary pilgrim in a cathedral, I gazed up and around me. The morning sun, sifting through the trees and the gray screens, blanched and dappled the stone floor. In clusters of two or three, an assortment of clay pots brimmed with herbs labeled tarragon, mint, marjoram, parsley, basil, lavender, and thyme. Tied with twine, bunches of dried flowers dangled from the cedar-timbered ceiling. I set the bags on the long wooden table in the center of the room, closed my eyes, and drew in a long, deep breath, ingesting the fragrance into my lungs and my memory.

The screen door slammed. Nestor, carrying three bags, hurried to the kitchen door.

"Come on," he said.

We entered the spotless kitchen. Draped with sheer white curtains, six gleaming windows looked out onto the backyard—an exact replica of Charlotte's garden, complete with fountain and gazebo. I could almost see Jonas, suitcase in hand, pausing for one last look, imprinting the scene on his mind, before he crept away from the Magnolia Arms, found solace at the Wrayburn estate, and re-created his own backyard.

Ivy Leigh brushed past me with a large copper pot.

"You're very easily distracted," she said. "First the banister and now the curtains."

I set the grocery bags on the counter. "Have you ever felt like you've been somewhere before?" I asked.

She tossed a bunch of carrots into the large porcelain sink.

"No," she said. "Grab a vegetable peeler out of that drawer and give me a hand."

"I thought I might unpack first," I said.

She reached under the sink for a colander.

"You can't go upstairs right now," she said. "Oliver's practicing in the parlor."

Nestor had returned with two large bags of red potatoes and set them on the black-and-white tiled floor. "His Majesty can't be disturbed by the mundane affairs of the peasants," he said.

Ivy Leigh, mother-like, smacked the top of his head. "Oliver pays twice the rent as anyone else in exchange for having his privacy guarded," she said. "I'm happy to oblige him. Now hush and bring me some parsley and basil."

Nestor pecked her on the cheek on his way to the porch.

I draped my sweater over a chair, walked to the sink, and picked up the peeler.

"Wash your hands first," Ivy Leigh said.

I looked out the window. "How long since the fountain worked?"

"A long time," she said with the first tinge of tenderness I'd heard in her voice.

I scraped at a carrot. "Seems to me if you got the fountain working and put a fresh coat of paint on the gazebo, you could host events here—like wedding receptions or parties."

Counting aloud, Ivy Leigh measured four cups of flour into a large ceramic mixing bowl.

"We thought of that," she said, "but until we can get the Bainbridge Group off our backs, we can only do enough to get by."

"Bainbridge Group?"

"The big conglomerate that's trying to run us out of our home," she said.

"Can they do that?"

"If we don't meet the deadline for the back taxes, the late fees, and every other charge they've concocted. I've wished more than once my Marshall was still here, let me tell you."

"Who's that?"

"My husband," she said.

"Maj. Marshall Ransom," Monty said from the back door. "Buried with full military honors. Wish I could include him in my memoir. Any coffee left?"

"I made a fresh pot," Ivy Leigh said. "How was your walk?"

"Bracing," he said. "How much longer will Oliver be?"

She looked at the clock. "Eight more minutes."

"Has anyone ever tried to slip past the parlor when Oliver is practicing?" I asked.

"Posey did once," Ivy Leigh said. "She tiptoed down the hall and stood outside the doorway to listen—didn't even peek around the corner."

"He shot off the bench like a bottle rocket," Monty said. "Scared Posey to death."

"She'd brought a dustcloth as a ruse," Ivy Leigh said, "but Oliver saw right through her."

"Poor lamb would give anything for a crumb of his attention," Monty said.

The piano stopped.

We all remained quiet as we listened to Oliver's footsteps in the hall. He stopped when he reached the kitchen.

"What's for dinner?" he asked Ivy Leigh. Uncombed, his coarse black hair hung down to his eyes, making him look rather boyish.

"Chicken paprikash."

"Remember to go easy on the cayenne," he told Ivy Leigh.

"Yes, Oliver, I remember."

Oliver turned to me. "Who are you?"

"Agnes Quinn."

"What are you doing here?"

"I live here," I said.

He looked at Ivy Leigh. "I thought you said you weren't taking in more renters."

"She wants the third-floor room—paid a month in advance. I couldn't refuse, could I?"

He turned to me. "Piano's off limits," he said. "Did they tell you?"

"I quit taking lessons when I was fourteen," I said.

He sneered and walked away.

None of my dreams of the Magnolia Arms had prepared me for this brand of insolence. Oliver's dismissive tone, too much like the unfeeling Trevor Rhodes, conniving Ferguson Trask, and scheming Trixie Thorpe, unhinged me.

In that white-hot volcanic moment, all reason left me. I shouted in full voice, "We'll need the piano for the talent show."

Enraged, he appeared in the doorway. "What?"

My suitcase in one hand and fresh herbs in the other, Nestor stepped in from the porch.

"Our talent show," I said. "I was just talking to Ivy Leigh and Monty about it. We think it's a good idea to raise money. We'll need your selection for the program."

I winced in pain when Ivy Leigh stepped behind me and pinched the back of my arm.

Monty, his eyes darting from Oliver to me, sat grave and still, his mouth full of coffee.

"Do you know how much I'm paid for my concerts?" Oliver asked.

"No," I said, "but I know you like your privacy, and if you want to *continue* to enjoy it, you'll help us save the Magnolia Arms."

Oliver stepped toward me. "Who do you think you are, coming in here—?"

"Otherwise," I said, "you can look for an apartment the next time you're in New York."

Ivy Leigh wrung her hands in her apron.

Nestor, grinning, set my suitcase by the door and laid the herbs by the sink. "I remember Marc Antony's funeral oration from my high school drama days," he said.

Oliver gritted his teeth and shook his head stiffly from side to side. "All right," he said. "I'll play a solo … *one* solo … but I'm not accompanying anyone."

"Agreed," I said.

"I guess Posey will have to sing *a cappella*," Monty said.

"I'll play for her," I said. "I can still manage a chord or two."

Oliver stormed away.

Ivy Leigh sauntered to the kitchen cabinet and began shuffling through her spices. "Where's that cayenne?" she said. "I know it's here somewhere."

Chapter 17

A Friend in Need

Monty, cup and saucer in hand, left the kitchen. "Back to the memoir," he said.

Nestor opened the back door. "I'll be in the greenhouse. Lunch?"

"Leftovers at noon," Ivy Leigh said. She set the cayenne pepper by the stove.

Peeler in hand, I picked up another carrot. My rite of passage from guest to resident was concluded.

Quiet, serious, agile, Ivy Leigh, a white apron tied snug around the waist of her green plaid dress, crisscrossed the kitchen, opening cupboard doors, selecting bowls, measuring, slicing, stirring, tasting, pausing to sip lukewarm tea from a white china cup balanced on the windowsill, tending to her tasks with the same diligence a climber preparing to ascend Everest might give to oxygen canisters and ropes.

"Do you enjoy cooking?" I asked.

She looked at me as if I'd asked her to explain the theory of relativity.

"I used to," she said. "When Marshall and I first came here, I helped out in the kitchen like you're doing now. After Hazel died ..."

"Hazel?"

"You don't want to know. After Hazel died, everyone assumed I'd take her place ... just because I'd peeled a few potatoes."

I looked at the mound of red potato peels spilling from my fingers.

"I asked because you remind me of my friend Muriel. She loves to cook."

"I like to cook," Ivy Leigh said. "But ..."

She squeezed her eyes shut, laid her hands on the counter, sniffed once, twice, and then reached for a handful of flour to dust over the bread dough she was kneading.

"I liked it better when I was cooking for Marshall," she said.

I kept scraping. "How long has he been gone?"

"Almost a year." She heaved the dough into a bowl and covered it with a clean towel.

"I'm sorry," I said.

She wiped her forehead, leaving flour above her eyebrow.

"Go upstairs now," she said. "Thanks."

I picked up my suitcase and started toward the stairs. Only three steps down the hall, I stopped. Why should I go to my room when the opportunity to snoop had presented itself? With Oliver in the basement, Nestor outside, Ivy Leigh in the kitchen, Monty in the study, and Posey and Margaret, I assumed, at school, I could poke around all I wanted. I set down my suitcase by the stairs and tiptoed down the hall toward the French doors.

Slowly I turned the doorknob and entered the parlor.

Centered on a bay window across the room was a worn brocade sofa, saggy striped throw pillows in haphazard piles at each end. Facing the sofa, two burgundy wingback chairs were drawn close to a marble coffee table where a chessboard, game in progress, waited. On my left was the notorious grand piano, bench pulled out, sheet music scattered on the floor. Though I'd been warned—perhaps *because* I'd been warned—I tiptoed toward the piano, slid onto the bench, and held my hands over the keyboard.

"Don't touch that."

I jerked back my fingers and turned toward the door. Posey Devoe, her hand gripping the doorknob, glared at me, her face chiseled with an emotion I couldn't decipher.

"You're a stranger," she said, "so you didn't know, but no one is allowed near the piano. It's custom made, shipped here from New York."

Her right shoulder twitched as if an invisible hand were pulling down on her earlobe.

"I thought you taught voice lessons," I said.

"After school hours. What was your name again?"

"Agnes."

"Tell me, Agnes, what are you doing here?"

Her withering voice had no trace of the pleasant lilt I'd heard the evening before.

"Nothing," I said. "I thought I'd look around before I went upstairs to my room."

"No, not what are you doing *here* … what are you doing here in our house?"

"You don't own this house," I said.

"It's our house … mine and Oliver's and everyone else's."

"Then I guess it's mine too," I said, "since I live here now."

"You didn't answer my question. What are you doing here?"

Lightly, I laid my hands on the keyboard. "I'm not sure that's any of your business."

She approached the piano and stooped to pick up the fallen music. Without a word, she lowered the lid over the keyboard, grazing my fingertips as I slid out my hands.

"There are rules, Agnes," she said. "No eating in the study and no touching this piano. Is that too much to ask?"

I stood. "No, that sounds reasonable."

When I reached the doorway I looked back. Still standing at the piano she embraced the stack of music, the top edge of the straightened pages touching her chin.

I knew what she was thinking. *These belong to Oliver.*

"He's not worth it, Posey," I said. "He doesn't deserve you."

Her back still toward me, she stiffened. "You don't know anything about him."

"I loved someone like him once," I said. "Trust me, I know."

Suitcase in hand, I dawdled up the stairs, taking time to look at the paintings I'd ignored the evening before. On the second floor I stopped outside Margaret's room and wondered when I'd be invited for a chat. On the third floor I paused outside the study.

Monty was reading aloud from his manuscript: "Ruby Clark hopped the courtroom railing and tackled the man who'd murdered her husband in cold blood … no, leaped over the courtroom railing and … lunged. That's better."

Inside my room I sat down at the desk and rolled paper into the typewriter carriage. This was the opportunity I'd been waiting for. After years of stealing a few random moments here and there, juggling my writing schedule with college classes, part-time jobs, moving, teaching, phone calls, needy neighbors, and unpredictable events, I was in the perfect setting to finish my novel. Lyda Rose was at her best—hardy, honed, heroic. I lifted my hands onto the keys and began to type.

Shivering in the thick fog, Lyda Rose waited alone at the Fords of Arnon.

Monty tapped on the door. "I say, Agnes, may I have a moment?"

I opened the door a few inches and peeked out.

"Sorry to bother you," Monty said. "But it's been awhile since I was in school. I can't remember. Would you say someone 'leaped' or 'leapt'? I'm not at all sure."

"Leaped would be a better choice," I said.

"Quite right." He turned to go, but stopped in the hall. "What's your book about?"

Monty and I were still talking in the study when Ivy Leigh called us to lunch.

Everyone except Oliver drifted into the kitchen. The round table was set with an assortment of dishes, glasses, and silverware. Not a single item matched any other.

Ivy Leigh handed me the water pitcher. "You look rested," she said. "Can you help me after lunch?"

"Sure," I said.

Better to build good will, I thought. Lyda Rose could wait at the Fords of Arnon a little longer.

After Monty said grace, we passed the food and chatted amiably.

Posey was silent.

"What's wrong with you, Posey Belle?" Nestor asked.

"Don't call me that," she said. "You know I don't like it."

Monty, seated next to her, patted her arm. "Don't worry, love," he said. "You'll feel better once we get busy with the talent show."

My fork clattered to my plate. Good-hearted Monty had taken me seriously. He hadn't realized I was only trying to rattle Oliver.

"Talent show?" Posey asked.

Ivy Leigh scraped the last of the English peas onto Nestor's plate.

"I wasn't going to bring it up till after lunch," she said, "but we might as well talk about it now. I've been thinking about it all morning. If we wait a couple of weeks ..."

"We'll need at least that long to get ready," Nestor said.

"As I was saying," Ivy Leigh said, "if we wait a couple of weeks, it will be cool enough to set up a canopy in the backyard and sell refreshments."

"Capital idea," Monty said. He passed his empty cup and saucer to Ivy Leigh.

She returned to the table with the refilled cup, pencil and paper, and wrote as she talked.

"We could have popcorn balls, caramel apples, sausage balls, pigs in a blanket …"

"I wish we could get the fountain repaired by then," Nestor said.

Ivy Leigh stopped writing. "That would be perfect, wouldn't it? But I don't know how we'd manage. Food's going to set us back—even if we buy wholesale."

"Who's going to be in this show?" Posey asked, her mood lightened.

"All of us," Monty said.

"Oliver won't do it," she said.

"Oh, but you're wrong," Monty said. "Agnes has seen to that."

Posey turned her chilly eyes on me. "What?"

"I was trying to give him some perspective," I said. "I never intended to obligate all of you to a talent show. The trouble and expense—"

"Nonsense," Ivy Leigh said. "The community's very good about attending these sorts of things, especially in autumn. I don't know why we didn't think of this before."

"And Oliver's going to perform? You're sure?" Posey asked. "What if there's a big crowd? They can't all fit in the parlor."

Nestor reached for the last biscuit. "I've worked that out. Monty and I will build a stage in the backyard."

"But we can't move the piano—" Posey said.

Nestor talked over her. "We 'ordinary' people will do the first half of the show outdoors. Sell food during intermission. People who buy higher-priced tickets come inside for the concert."

"Brilliant," Monty said. "Do you sing, Agnes?"

"I can carry a tune," I said, "but I don't like to solo."

"It's been a long time since I heard Margaret do "Hello, Dolly," Nestor said. "Do you have any acting experience, Agnes?"

"I did a couple of summers of theatre when I was in college."

"Have you ever played Irene Molloy?" he asked.

An hour later, our empty cups and half-full glasses stood like lighthouses in a sea of yellow lined paper. Monty, nearly dozing, leaned over Nestor's sketch of the stage. Posey, smiling, examined the rough draft of our program. I, disbelieving, stared at the list of scenes and songs I had to memorize in two weeks. Ivy Leigh picked up her menu, grocery list, and budget and pushed back from the table.

"I have to start dinner," she said. "I'll need three cups of grated cheese, Agnes."

When the last casserole dish was in the oven and the last mixing bowl was washed, I hung up my dish towel.

"I think I'll skip dinner tonight," I said to Ivy Leigh. "I'm pretty tired."

She slid a pan of yeast rolls into the oven. "You can't. The room has to look full."

My climb to the third floor was not nearly so exhilarating as the night before.

Inside my room, I stood over the paper I'd left in the typewriter and lamented the lone sentence cringing there like an orphan in a Dickensian workhouse. I'd been more prolific after I'd taught all day and graded papers all evening.

Grumbling, I tossed my flour-speckled clothes onto the bed.

"I came here to finish my novel," I said to the would-be author in the mirror, then put on the dress I'd worn to Sharon Merriman-Cheswick's church and went down to the dining room.

The enchantment of the evening before, however, had evaporated. A boisterous throng—evidence of Ivy Leigh's triumph—clattered, chortled, buzzed, and hummed. I should've been glad they were helping themselves to the heaping bowls of broccoli I'd spent the afternoon chopping. Their money, after all, could save the Magnolia Arms. But I wasn't glad; I was worn out. Considering a retreat from the dining room threshold, I scanned the room. If no one had seen me, I could sneak into the kitchen, spoon something onto a plate, and slip away to my typewriter. Maybe I could write one paragraph before I went to bed.

I spotted Ivy Leigh in a far corner, scooting a chair aside so an elderly woman in a wheelchair could take her place beside her husband. Nestor, arms full, bantered with the customers. Posey looked over her shoulder at Oliver. Margaret was absorbed in a book; Monty regaled the people next to him with some hilarious story.

No one had noticed me—almost no one.

An aging woman, set apart from the casual diners by her pale-green silk jacket and gold jewelry, maneuvered her fork, tines down, like a pencil, over her plate. Her attempt to conceal her age with penciled eyebrows and rouged cheeks had failed. She stabbed a bite of chicken, enclosing it between her glossy red lips as if she suspected poison. Her mouth contorted as she shifted the food from one cheek to the other. Then she shuddered. Napkin to her mouth, she spat, and deposited the crumpled napkin on the table. She rose and glided toward me.

I stepped back to let her pass, but she stopped and faced me.

Her pale powdered face, perhaps lovely at one time, was inscrutable and rigid.

"Have you eaten here before?" she asked.

"Once," I said.

"You might want to dine someplace else tonight. The chicken is dry."

"Everyone else seems to be enjoying it," I said.

Ivy Leigh rushed over and grabbed my elbow; the stranger walked toward the front door.

"You know her?" Ivy Leigh asked.

"Never saw her before," I said.

"Maybe she's a food critic. That would be exciting. Only one seat left. Come on."

Jittery, I followed Ivy Leigh to Margaret's table. The strange woman had unnerved me.

"Hello, Agnes," Margaret said. "I hear you've had a busy day."

I sat down. "Peeling carrots and potatoes, chopping broccoli."

"I meant," she said, "you've had a busy day planning your talent show."

Posey approached with the chicken paprikash.

"Oh, that," I said. "Things got a little out of hand."

"What do you mean?"

"It was all a misunderstanding. One minute I was sitting there talking and the next, I was yelling at Oliver about the piano. The talent show popped in my head. I wasn't serious."

She buttered her roll. "Well, we're committed *now*, aren't we?"

I tried the chicken—delectable. Why had the woman made a scene?

"I told them I was only taking a jab at Oliver. Typical of me. Speak first, think later."

"I noticed that last night," she said.

"Last night?" I pretended ignorance.

She spooned sauce over the chicken on her plate. "When you said you were glad I went back to college. How could you possibly know that?"

I sputtered out a fake cough. "Honestly," I said, "it was only a slip—"

She shook her head. "Don't insult my intelligence. How do you know about me?"

I leaned back in my chair, gripped the table's edge, and stared at the high ceiling. What to do—obey Jonas' order to wait, or seize this moment as the "right" time to tell?

I took a deep breath, lowered my chin, and looked her straight in the eye. "Jonas told me."

She shuddered as if she'd been shot with an arrow. Closing like a blossom in winter, her shoulders crumpled, her head dropped onto her chest, her fingers on her lips stifled her voice.

Feeling helpless and cruel, I reached across the table and pushed her water glass toward her. She grasped the stem and, without looking up, rotated the glass in her fingers as she spoke.

"How do you know him?" she asked.

"We teach at the same school … taught at the same school. We're both on leave."

She looked up. "Because?"

"He's recovering from a heart attack, and I was—"

Our table jostled as Posey bumped into us. She slid a bowl of broccoli onto my plate.

"Margaret," she said, "Oliver took one bite of the chicken and left. He left."

"He did the same thing when there was too much oregano in the marinara," Margaret said. "Remember? He'll pout for a while and then raid the refrigerator after we're asleep."

"Oliver doesn't pout," Posey said, and walked away with the bowl and my plate.

"I've never seen him do anything *but* pout," I said.

"Part of his charm," Margaret said.

Our awkward laugh dwindled into an uncomfortable silence.

"Jonas is fine," I said.

"Where is he?"

"Brighton Park Community College. Plainview."

"I was sure he'd go back to Ridgeland," she said.

"That's the last place he would've gone after what Olympia did," I said.

Coffee cup in hand, Monty strolled over. "Could I join you ladies for dessert? Ivy Leigh ran me off from my table. Full house tonight."

"Not now," I said. "Margaret and I were talking—"

"Of course," Margaret said. "Pull up a chair."

"Of course not," Ivy Leigh said over Monty's shoulder. "I need this table, too. You three take your coffee to the kitchen and help yourself to all the over-baked cookies you can eat."

With Monty trailing a few steps behind, I whispered to Margaret on our way down the hall. "Are you sure you don't want to go someplace we can talk?"

She shook her head. "Monty and I have coffee together every night. I won't hurry him off to his room because I can't wait a few minutes to relive ancient history."

Mismatched but destined friends, Monty, Margaret, and I drew up to the kitchen table.

Monty set a cookie on his saucer. "Agnes is a fellow author, Margaret. Did she tell you?"

"I haven't had much of a chance to tell Margaret anything," I said.

Margaret narrowed her eyes.

I wondered how many thousand students she had wilted with that stare.

"What's the title of your book?" she asked.

"*Trevorode the Defender*," I said, obeying her unspoken order to straighten up.

"The tale of an Anglo-Saxon warrior," Monty said, "complete with noble steeds, dragons, evil queens, and a fair lady … what was her name again?"

"Lyda Rose," I said.

"I'd like to read it," Margaret said. "Is it almost finished?"

"No. That's why I wanted to move here. I thought this would be a good place to write."

"But why here?" Margaret asked. "We're not exactly on the beaten path."

"It's a long story," I said.

"We have time," Monty said. "Nothing better than a good story after dinner."

I couldn't help smiling. "I guess the whole thing started on the first day of my new job when I parked in Jonas Grinstead's parking place."

"Who?" Monty asked.

"Jonas Grinstead, the man who built this house," I said.

"The chap who built this house teaches at your school?" Monty said. "Extraordinary."

"It is," I said. "And Jonas stays so much to himself, I'd never have met him if we hadn't crossed paths in the parking lot. He asked me to move my car—"

"Not very sporting—asking a lady to move her car," Monty said.

"He didn't see it that way. I hadn't slept much the night before, so I was—"

Monty grinned. "Busy working on the novel, eh? My book keeps me awake, too."

"No, I hadn't been writing. I'd just found out my friend Xander was missing and I was worried about him, so I—"

"Nothing stops Meg from sleeping, does it, old girl?" he asked.

She patted his hand. "Not usually. Go on with your story, Agnes."

"I was so tired. I was in no mood to be told what to do, so I snapped at him."

"You can hardly be blamed for that," Monty said. "Worry can take a toll."

"Still—as I watched him walk away I felt bad for being rude, so I wrote an apology note and had a student deliver it to his classroom."

"Did he forgive you?" Margaret asked.

"Not till the next day when I bribed him with a bagel."

"Onion?" Margaret asked.

Monty and I both stared at her.

"Yes," I said, "and a jar of spicy mustard."

"I say, Meg," Monty said, "how in the world—?"

"Just a guess," she said. "He doesn't sound like a cinnamon-sugar sort of person."

"Scones and clotted cream for me," Monty said. "Did your plan work? Did he relent?"

"Yes, we became good friends. That's how I ended up here."

"How so?" Monty asked.

"I got to school early the next morning to wait for Jonas in the parking lot. I didn't know till later that there were two other people waiting for him, too."

"Who were they?" Margaret asked.

"One of them was a teacher who has a crush on Jonas. She saw us talking and accused me of flirting with him. She's the one who framed me for stealing."

"And the other person?" Margaret asked.

"Wilkie Brooker."

I expected a strong reaction, but neither Monty nor Margaret seemed to know the name.

Monty asked, "Who's he?"

"The private investigator Olympia Pillburn hired to—"

Nestor, his arm around Posey, charged through the door.

"Hurry," he said, "she's had another attack."

Margaret stood up and pulled her chair away from the table. Monty rushed to Nestor to help with Posey. Before they could guide her to the chair, Ivy Leigh rushed in from behind, took off Posey's apron, and tied it around my waist.

"What are you doing?" I asked. "I'm not a waitress."

"Neither is Posey. There's no time to argue. You have to help Nestor finish dinner."

Back in the dining room, lugging a tray, I smiled at the customers and grumbled to myself. I have two degrees, I thought, two diplomas on my wall. What am I doing waiting tables? I'm supposed to be proofreading a new chapter or eating teacakes in the parlor.

At eight o'clock the last remaining diner left. Nestor and I cleared the tables. When I carried the last bowl to the kitchen, I found Ivy Leigh up to her elbows in soapy water. As much as I wanted to go upstairs, I couldn't leave her alone. I took a towel from the drawer and started drying the pots and pans.

"The meal was delicious," I said.

"You think so?"

"A great success. How's Posey?"

"Asleep."

"What was wrong with her?" I asked.

"Don't tell her I told you, but it was a panic attack."

"Do they happen often?"

"Not since we learned how to prevent them. We know she'll get bad whenever—"

"Oliver comes home?" I asked.

"Or goes away. Margaret and I have both tried to reason with her, but she can't give him up. It's my fault for putting the cayenne in the chicken."

"You can't blame yourself," I said. "Sounds to me like they both need to grow up."

She drained the sink and dried her hands. "We'd better turn in. Lots to do tomorrow."

"I promised I'd call home tonight," I said. "Could I use the phone?"

"In my office down the hall," she said. "Close the door so you can have some privacy. Extra charge for long distance."

I sat down at Ivy Leigh's desk and lifted the receiver. Jonas was probably waiting for me to call, but I couldn't talk to him tonight. What could I say?

"Remember how you told me to wait to tell Margaret about you? I told her tonight."

I called my own number instead.

"Bingham residence," Flossie said.

"Hello, Flossie."

"Agnes. I was hoping you'd call. Your messages are stacking up."

"Let me guess—my mother called."

I could hear her rustling through a pile of paper.

"Yes. She wanted a number where she could reach you. She said something about 'Jewel,' but I don't remember what."

"Don't give her my number—not yet, okay? I'll call her in a few days. What else?"

"That woman from your school called. Beatrice Thorpe."

"Beatrix," I said.

"Whatever. She said they're still investigating and will notify you of your hearing."

"I may not be able to make it," I said, "if it's the week of the talent show."

"Talent show?"

I explained how I'd gotten caught up in the plans to save the Magnolia Arms.

"Have they thought of having a yard sale?" Flossie asked.

"Not that I know of, but we're going to sell refreshments at intermission."

"You know," she said, "I could knit some potholders with a little magnolia in the corner. You could sell them along with your hors d'oeuvres."

"I'd have to talk to Ivy Leigh about that," I said.

She wasn't listening. "Let's see, a white flower, a green leaf, a little yellow. The background would have to be dark to offset the flower. Maybe a nice brown."

"Any other messages?"

"Mrs. Wrayburn called to remind you about the reference letter for her grandson."

"I forgot all about that. I'll write it tomorrow."

"The librarian called and asked for your address," she said.

"Please give it to her. Anything else?"

"Not a message, exactly, but Buck called to ask if I'd heard from you. He told me he asked you out on a date."

"He didn't ask me out on a date. He asked if I'd be back in time to go to the barbecue."

"And if you'd go with him," she said.

"I didn't let him get that far."

"Agnes, can't you see he's one step this side of being in love with you?"

"That's absurd," I said. "He's like ten years older than I am. Maybe more."

"That might've mattered when you were fifteen and he was twenty-eight—"

"You've calculated that?"

"—but it doesn't matter now."

"Do you realize what you're saying, Flossie? I can't marry a cowboy."

"Is that all you see in him? Jeans and a big buckle on his belt?"

"No," I said. "He's very nice. He was good to Geneva and Elinor and you."

"And you," she said.

I changed the subject to Saturn, gave her my address and phone number, and we hung up.

My first day at the Magnolia Arms had ended.

I closed Ivy Leigh's office door and stood in the quiet hallway. I thought of Jonas, his suitcase on the floor, taking one last look before leaving. I stopped at the dining room to mourn the collection of tables. Bare of their tablecloths and candles, they were better suited to the concrete floor of a bargain store showroom. I'd put one foot on the stairs when I noticed the kitchen light was on. I stepped in to turn off the switch and found Oliver, as Margaret had predicted, taking the aluminum foil off a large bowl he'd pilfered from the refrigerator.

"Hungry?" I asked.

He didn't answer.

When I reached my room, I opened the suitcase, as yet unpacked, and found my pajamas. After a long, warm bath, I brushed my teeth and finally sat down at the typewriter. I read:

Shivering in the thick fog, Lyda Rose waited alone at the Fords of Arnon.

I removed the paper, rolled in a blank page, and typed, *Dear Margaret.*

By the time I'd finished Jonas' story, it was long after midnight. I folded the pages, sealed them in an envelope, and tiptoed downstairs to Margaret's room.

When I slid the envelope under the door, her light came on.

Chapter 18

A Mutual Friend

The next morning when I entered the kitchen at half past seven, I found my neighbors lingering over a half-eaten breakfast. Monty, elbows on the table, twiddled his thumbs. Ivy Leigh, arms folded, peered out the window. Posey twisted her napkin, while Nestor tapped his knife on a plate.

"She's never done this before," Monty said.

"Not even a year ago, when we all had the flu," Nestor said. "Remember?"

"Has anyone knocked on her door?" Posey asked. "Maybe we should check on her."

Ivy Leigh stood. "I don't know what happened last night, but I'm going to find out."

"What's wrong?" I asked from the doorway.

Monty looked up. "Margaret stayed home from school today."

I sank onto a chair. "Oh, no," I said. "I never should've told her."

"Told her what?" Ivy Leigh asked.

Nestor pushed back from the table. "Enough talking. I'm going up to see her."

"No," I said. "I'll go. I know what's wrong."

"How could *you* possibly know?" Ivy Leigh asked.

"I'll explain later," I said, and started toward the door.

"Wait," Ivy Leigh said. "At least take some muffins and her morning tea."

As I left the kitchen with the tray, the four friends looked so somber—anyone watching would've thought I was carting nitroglycerine to blow a firebreak in a forest fire.

I tapped on Margaret's door.

"Margaret. It's Agnes. I brought you some breakfast. May I come in?"

I braced myself for her haggard appearance, but even with unstyled hair and puffy eyes, she looked regal in her long white housecoat and satin slippers.

She motioned to a small round table between two blue-flowered stuffed chairs.

"Set the tray there," she said. "Thank you. I am hungry, but not up to company yet."

My letter lay on the table. I pushed it aside, set down the tray, and moved toward the door.

"No, not you," she said. "I meant I'm not ready for questions. Are they very worried?"

"Monty looks like he's waiting for a patient to come out of surgery," I said, "and when I told Ivy Leigh I knew what was wrong, I was afraid she was going to take a stick to me."

I was relieved when she laughed.

"They protect those they love," she said.

We sat down on either side of the table. She lifted her cup and saucer from the tray.

"I'm sorry, Margaret, for blurting out Jonas' name," I said. "He told me to wait, and I—"

She held up her hand. "It wouldn't have made any difference. I'd lived that moment a thousand times—the moment I'd hear his name again."

"I can't wait to—"

She was still stranded in her memories. "But I never once imagined how haunted I'd feel. It's like he left yesterday." She laid her hand on the letter. "Have you ever been in love, Agnes?"

"Yes … no. I thought I was once … or twice."

"You'd know if you'd experienced real love. You never forget it. It so consumes you, it's frightening, terrible in its own exquisite way."

"I've never felt *that* way," I said. "Who would want to?"

"Precisely," she said. "That's why I never tried again. I 'went back' to college instead."

This time we both laughed.

She picked up the pages. "This is a remarkable story, Agnes. You're a capable writer."

"It's *your* story," I said. "I could never make up anything as good as that."

"The way you described Charlotte and Muriel, I feel like I already know them. I'm glad Jonas found them when he needed them."

"They adore him," I said. "And they've certainly been good friends to me."

"May I ask you a few questions?" Margaret asked.

"I wish you would," I said. "There's nothing I'd rather talk about."

Running her finger down the pages of the letter, Margaret, as if she'd made notes while reading, quizzed me about Jonas' work, our school, Trixie Thorpe, Wilkie Brooker.

"And did I understand correctly?" she asked. "Jonas still drives the white truck—the one with the magnolia tree on the door."

"Yes, I rode in it myself when Jonas picked me up at the hospital after my accident."

She looked at the third page. "Yes, I'll have to hear more about that. To be so young, you've led a very interesting life."

"You're joking, right?"

She folded the letter. "Not at all."

"I haven't even told you about the Plumleys yet," I said.

She returned the letter to the table. "Another time. We have to come up with a plan."

"Plan?"

She stood. "Yes, because besides bringing me the best possible news, you've also shed light on who's been trying to run us out of this house."

"You didn't know it was Olympia?"

"We had no idea. The correspondence we've received has always been from some department or legal firm or corporation."

"The Bainbridge Group," I said. "Ivy Leigh told me."

"Now that we know what the real issue is, maybe we can find a way to save our home. If I'm the problem, maybe Olympia would be pacified if I agreed to move out."

"I'm not sure your friends would—"

"Go down and tell Ivy Leigh we're going to the park. I'll join you in a few minutes."

When I returned to the kitchen, I found Ivy Leigh alone at the kitchen table, thumbing through a red-and-white relic of a cookbook.

"I wish we could afford a nice standing rib roast," she said. "I do get tired of chicken. How's Margaret?"

"She said to tell you we're going to the park."

Ivy Leigh stood, opened a bottom cabinet door, and pulled out a large thermos. "Have to wash this—been a long time since we used it. I guess that's a good sign. I hadn't thought of it."

"I don't understand."

"Two weeks after Marshall died, Margaret found me crying over the sink. She filled this thermos with tea and took me the park. We stayed for hours. Ever since—"

"A 'trip to the park' is code for 'we need to talk'?" I asked.

She frowned. "You're worrying me. What's this about?"

"I brought her some news about an old friend."

"Someone I know?" she asked.

"Jonas Grinstead."

Her mouth dropped open. "This calls for food, too," she said. "Come back in half an hour. I'll pack you a lunch. But be back by three. I'll need your help with dinner."

On our walk to the park Margaret and I began weaving together the tangled strands of our respective histories.

I told her about Trevor, Xander, and Jonquil; she told me about her first love.

"His name was Noble," she said. "I've always found that the worst of ironies. If he hadn't hurt me so deeply, I might've been more reasonable with Jonas."

"Pain does skew our judgment," I said.

"So does pride. After Noble, I vowed I'd never be hurt again, but I think that resolution crippled me to some degree—hampered me from really living."

"No one can blame you for that," I said.

"Maybe not, but I came to regret not giving Jonas a chance to explain."

We sat down on a dark-green bench under a magnificent oak.

"What was it like," I asked, "meeting Olympia face to face?"

She described the same scene I'd heard from Jonas: Olympia's arrival while Jonas was away at work, the phony story about their engagement.

"Our encounter couldn't have taken more than twenty minutes," Margaret said, "but I still consider that incident the most painful chapter in my life."

"I've never met her," I said, "but even the mention of her name makes me nervous."

"With good reason," Margaret said. "But you've had your fair share of run-ins with conniving women. You might be able to get the upper hand with Olympia."

We ate lunch. As Margaret took the crust off her bread and tossed it to the squirrels and birds, I told her about Trixie, Mavis, and Asher Loncraine.

"One of them planted those stolen documents in my office," I said. "Probably Trixie."

"Do you think you'll be found innocent?" Margaret asked.

"I haven't given it much thought. I'm too preoccupied with where I am."

"Why are you so fascinated with our house?"

"You of all people should understand," I said. "Why did you come back when you knew you'd be faced with constant reminders of Jonas?"

"I remember well. One weekend I drove to Myrtle Beach, checked into a motel, looked out the window at the ocean, and thought, 'There's no memory of Jonas here.' Need I say more?"

"It was useless to keep running."

She nodded. "I wrote Ivy Leigh about moving back. She said she and Marshall were leaving the old boarding house, but there'd be more than enough room in their new home."

"She didn't say they were moving into the Magnolia Arms."

Margaret laughed. "She's always known how to deal with me. I came back, moved into the room you're in now, and got a job as an English teacher. I've been here ever since."

"Had the house been empty all that time—before the three of you moved in?"

"No. I learned what had happened when I came back. When Jonas decided to leave, he asked his construction foreman to move into the house and take care of it."

"That was a nice gesture," I said. "Offering a place like that to an employee."

"Abel was more than an employee. He and Jonas had become good friends while they were building the house."

"Abel Sutton? Is that who you're talking about? The taxi driver said it was because of him the house fell on hard times—something about his son? I can't remember."

"You must have met Asa—our resident historian. Yes, but we didn't find out the whole story till after Abel and his family moved away. Want to walk awhile before we start back?"

I picked up the thermos and picnic basket. "Which way?"

"There's a lovely pond over that hill," she said. "It's one of my favorite spots."

We followed the path that ran through the park. The day was brilliant, the sky a deep, luminous blue, the clouds snowy white, rimmed pearl gray, the sun warm and soothing. Past the swings and slide, we walked up a gentle slope, then down to where the path ended at a pond. Margaret looked at the geese flying low overhead, pointed as they swooped to skim the water's surface, and then smiled as they dropped in to swim with the ducks.

"You've been here with Jonas, haven't you?" I asked.

"Yes. This is where we first started talking about spending the rest of our lives together."

"He still loves you."

She closed her eyes. "I can't shake the feeling that I'm dreaming."

"You're not," I said.

She took the basket from me, and we started back.

"Where is he now?" I asked.

"Who?"

"Abel Sutton."

"We don't know, and we've never tried to find out," she said.

"Why?"

"Abel and his wife had three sons, nice boys when they were little, but when they grew up, the oldest son got in with the wrong crowd. He could never stay out of trouble."

"I had a neighbor like that," I said. "He's in prison now."

"Harry never made it to prison. He called home one night to say he was in trouble. Abel rushed out to help him, found him half dead, and without thinking went after ..."

"The men who did it?"

"Yes. Foolish, but that kind of love isn't rational. The police found Abel the next morning—barely alive. He was in the hospital for weeks."

"And the son?"

She shook her head. "Didn't make it. Abel blamed himself. His wife couldn't recover. We tried to help, but it wasn't enough. They took the other boys and moved away."

"To make a fresh start?"

"That was only part of the reason. The original agreement was that Abel could live in the house rent free so long as he maintained the house and paid the property taxes every year."

"That's a good deal," I said.

"I'm sure he lived up to the arrangement in the beginning, but as his son's problems got worse, Abel apparently started devoting every available nickel to keep him out of trouble."

"But that eventually caught up with him."

"And with us," she said. "The day after they left, Ivy Leigh went into Abel's office and started going through the accounts. That's when we found out there was a lien on the property."

We reached the corner of our street.

"So Brooker was telling the truth. The house is in trouble."

"Yes. Abel let some problems go completely untended. On the repairs he did make, he used the cheapest materials he could find. But we didn't think anyone knew except—"

I grabbed Margaret's arm and pointed to a white Cadillac at the far end of our block.

"Isn't that Oliver?" I asked. His back was toward us, but I recognized his beautiful hair.

Margaret nodded.

Oliver, his left hand on the roof of the car, was leaning down to talk to someone seated behind the driver.

I whispered. "Have you seen that car before?"

"No," Margaret said.

I tugged on her sleeve and pulled her behind a tall bush.

"This is not a good idea," she said.

Stifling a sneeze, I peered through the leaves. Even from our vantage point several houses away, I could see a woman's hand reach out the open window and pass a long white envelope to Oliver. He returned to the sidewalk, tucked the envelope in his satchel, and disappeared around the corner. As the car moved toward us, I shoved Margaret to the other side of the bush. We watched as the driver slowed in front of the Magnolia Arms and then drove past us.

I recognized the passenger as the same woman who'd criticized Ivy Leigh's chicken.

"May I help you?" A pale, wrinkled woman, her hair in a bun on top of her head, scowled at us from her front porch.

I pulled one of the branches to my nose. "No," I said. "We were just admiring your—"

"Bottlebrush," Margaret said.

"Bottlebrush," I said.

"Well, move along," the woman said, "off my lawn."

Margaret and I stepped back onto the sidewalk.

"I told you that wasn't a good idea," she said. "That's Ida Willingale. She's started a petition to force us to close the restaurant. Doesn't want our business in the neighborhood."

I looked back as we started toward the Magnolia Arms. No sign of the white car.

"That was a chauffeur driving that Cadillac, wasn't it?" I asked.

"It certainly looked like one," Margaret said.

"That woman in the backseat—I met her at dinner. She complained about the chicken."

"I've seen her before, too. You're thinking what I'm thinking, aren't you?"

"Olympia," I said. "But didn't you recognize her when you saw her in the dining room?"

"After thirty years? Hardly."

"But why was she talking to Oliver?"

Margaret sighed. "And what was in that envelope?"

We reached the driveway and walked toward the back door where Ivy Leigh, an apron in each hand, was waiting for us.

Margaret whispered. "I've always suspected someone was feeding information to the people trying to get rid of us, but I thought a city official had been bribed or—"

"It's about time you two came home," Ivy Leigh said. "The tables need to be set. The dishes are piled up. What's wrong? You two look worse than when you left here."

I took the apron and opened the screen door to the kitchen. "We're pretty sure we saw Olympia Pillburn drive by the house."

"I'm sorry. Who?" Ivy Leigh asked.

Margaret followed me into the kitchen.

I pulled out a chair for Ivy Leigh. "I think we'd better sit down," I said.

Ivy Leigh propped her elbows on the table. I began with meeting Jonas. When I brought up Wilkie Brooker, she tapped her fingers on the table. When I came full circle to Olympia and the law firm of Camden, Lockwood, Osgood, and Tuttle, she pounded her fist on the table. When I concluded with the "mystery woman" handing Oliver an envelope, Ivy Leigh pushed back from the table. Without a word she stormed toward a pile of half-chopped onions and whacked at them with such ferocity I feared the cutting board would crack and splinter.

To no one in particular she said, "If I find out that little weasel has been working against us all this time … and here I've been groveling to him and letting him tell me how to cook …"

Margaret stepped beside her. "Let me finish the onions. You're making juice of them."

Dejected, Ivy Leigh returned to the table.

"We may be jumping to conclusions," I said. "We're not sure that woman is Olympia."

"Did you tell me Olympia hired an investigator to find Jonas?" Ivy Leigh asked.

"Yes."

"Did you tell me she wants to buy Jonas out?"

"Yes."

"Then it's the only explanation that makes sense. She's been sabotaging us all this time. Remember, Meg? First, that inspector told us we didn't have enough electrical outlets per room."

"I remember," Margaret said. "And the man we hired to fix the roof tried to sue us because he said he stepped on a nail."

"I bet Olympia got to him, too. Hand me those tomatoes, Agnes," Ivy Leigh said. "And then we were fined for having too much trash on the street after our remodeling."

"Let Agnes slice the tomatoes," Margaret said.

"All right," Ivy Leigh said. "I'll make the frosting. It will do me good to take an electric mixer to something."

Ivy Leigh snapped on the mixer and pushed the button to the highest setting.

I sliced the tomatoes. "Can you afford a lawyer?"

"We had one for a while," Margaret said, "but we couldn't come up with enough money to keep paying him." She tapped Ivy Leigh on the shoulder. "Where are the tablecloths?"

"In the dining room," she said. "Posey ironed them this morning."

After Margaret left the kitchen, Ivy Leigh shut off the mixer and turned to me.

"Are you good at frosting cakes?"

"No," I said. "They'd be lopsided. Hand me a dishcloth instead. I'll clean up."

Ivy Leigh placed a cake layer on a plate. "So when is Margaret leaving?"

"Leaving? What do you mean?"

"Didn't Jonas send you to find her?"

"No, he had no idea she was here. He sent me to find out about the house."

She added a second layer, leaned down for a closer look, and nudged it over to center it.

"So when will you be calling Jonas to tell him the good news?" she asked.

I dunked the cake pans in the soapy water. "No time soon. He said not to tell her yet."

She stepped back from the cake and waved the chocolate-frosted spoon at me. "What is it with those two? Haven't they wasted enough time?"

"I'm just following orders," I said, though this wasn't entirely true.

Ivy Leigh twirled her spoon in the bowl and heaped a mound of frosting on the top layer.

"Well, no one can tell me what to do." She swirled the frosting, edging it around the sides of the cake. "I used to have an awful grudge against Jonas, but I can admit when I'm wrong."

"Wrong about what?" I asked.

"That Jonas was so anxious to stay in Leo McBain's good graces, he went crawling back to marry his horrible daughter."

"Leo who?" I asked.

Margaret appeared in the doorway. "Ready for the plates."

Nestor, pencil behind his ear and tool belt around his waist, burst through the back door. "Good news," he said. "Mr. Johnson is letting us borrow his table saw."

Monty came in behind him. "Fine chap, Johnson. Now we can build a first-rate stage."

"That's wonderful news," Ivy Leigh said. "We're going to have a work meeting after dinner. You can tell us all about it. Now help Margaret with the silverware."

Dinner proceeded without incident. No mysterious guests arrived. Other than Posey being noticeably disappointed when Oliver failed to appear, everyone in the room looked satisfied. I sat with Margaret, but neither of us said much.

When Posey served the cake and coffee, Margaret broke the silence.

"Tell me about your novel. It will do us good to take our minds off Olympia."

Between mouthfuls of Ivy Leigh's celestial chocolate cake, I told Margaret how I began the book, changed the title as homage to Trevor, and halted my work as penitence to Xander.

"I assume you brought it with you. May I read it?" Margaret asked.

"I'd be honored," I said.

Ivy Leigh approached our table. "Telephone, Agnes. Take the call in my office."

I was delighted to hear Muriel's voice. "We miss you," she said. "How are you?"

"You'd be proud of me," I said. "They have a restaurant. I've worked in the kitchen every day since I've been here. Last night, I waited on tables and didn't drop a thing."

"Good for you," she said. "Jonas tells me you've seen Margaret."

"I was having dinner with her when you called. You'd like her, Muriel. She's remarkable. No wonder Jonas fell for her."

"And the house is what you expected?"

"It's beautiful," I said, "but it needs a lot of work."

"So I heard. Flossie tells me you're having a talent show."

"Yes, sort of by accident. But they're all excited about it." I laughed. "Flossie wants to make potholders to sell at intermission."

"That's why I'm calling. I'm going to donate several dozen of those almond cookies you like. They're moist, so they'll package well and make the trip without breaking."

"Thank you. I'll tell Ivy Leigh."

Nestor tapped on the door as he pushed it open. "Sorry to bother you, Agnes, but as soon as you help me clear the tables, we can start the meeting."

"I have to go, Muriel. Thanks for calling. Tell everyone I said hello."

The planning meeting ended the day on a happy note. After everyone gave updates on their work, I told them about Flossie's potholders and Muriel's cookies. I was surprised when Ivy Leigh pulled a tissue from her apron pocket and dabbed at her eyes.

"That's the nicest thing I ever heard," she said. "They don't even know us."

Bolstered by our common purpose and the kindness of others, we went to our rooms.

I retrieved *Trevorode the Defender* from my desk, walked down to the second floor, and knocked on Margaret's door. "You understand it's far from finished?" I said as I handed it over.

"Of course," she said. "A work in progress."

I went back upstairs, took a long bath, and hoped I could relax enough to go to sleep. But my mind would not stop flitting. Leaving the light off, I turned the desk chair toward the window, sat down, and stared out at the dark street. I closed my eyes. Drowsy, only half-awake, I relived the day, recalled Margaret smiling at the geese and telling me the story of Abel Sutton.

A tap on the door startled me. I opened my eyes.

"Agnes. Agnes."

I went to the door. There stood Ivy Leigh in a yellow terrycloth housecoat.

"I'm glad you're here," I said. "I wanted to ask you about Leo—"

She held her finger to her lips. "Come with me," she said, "but be quiet."

I tiptoed downstairs behind her. When we passed Margaret's door, Ivy Leigh slowed, looked over her shoulder at me, and pointed to the light beneath the door.

Even safely on the first floor, she still whispered. "I tried to wait till Margaret went to sleep before I came to get you. I don't know why she's still awake."

She opened the door to her office and pointed to the phone.

"Dial Jonas Grinstead," she said.

I knew better than to argue.

He answered.

"Hello, Jonas," I said. "This is Agnes. There's someone here who—"

Ivy Leigh took the receiver and sat down at her desk.

"Hello, Jonas? I'm Ivy Leigh Ransom. I manage your house. We have a mutual friend."

She pointed to the door. Her meaning was clear.

I hesitated outside the closed door, but could hear nothing intelligible, so I went back to my room, returned to my chair by the window, and stared into the night. Again images darted through my mind like unruly children. Half-asleep, I pictured Jonas, wide-eyed, listening to Ivy Leigh, Xander and his dog standing quietly by, wondering what was wrong, Margaret reading my book, Olympia …

Jostled awake when my head jerked back, I stumbled into bed.

I curled up under the covers only to keep thinking, sinking deeper, my mind spinning, spiraling backward to Stanton-Giles. I was running after Xander … sitting on a bench. A man in a yellow sweater …

Another knock at my door. My eyes popped open. I was relieved to see the sun shining through the window.

"Agnes. It's Posey."

I called as I sat up. "What is it?" Worn out from dreaming, I couldn't manage to stand.

"Phone call for you," she said through the door. "Your mother. She says it's bad news."

I threw on some clothes, bounded down the stairs, and snatched up the receiver on Ivy Leigh's desk.

"Mom? What's wrong?"

She was crying. "You have to go home, Agnes."

"You mean *come* home?" I asked.

"No, go home, back to your apartment. Jewel needs to stay with you for a few days."

"With me? What in the world for?"

"Doc Merriman … has left her. He said he couldn't take it anymore."

"I can't go home," I said. "I have too much to do. Why can't Jewel stay with Sharon?"

She sniffled. "Jewel called Sharon to ask if she could stay a few days, and Sharon said they were leaving for the coast. Can you imagine?"

"Yes, of course I can imagine. I've been trying to tell you about Sharon for years."

"I hardly think it's the time to bring that up."

Finding Jewel's crisis secondary to questioning Ivy Leigh about what she had said to Jonas, I changed course.

"Call my apartment," I said. "Tell Flossie. She'll take care of Jewel."

"What's this Frances person still doing in your apartment?"

"Flossie," I said. "She's taking care of Saturn till I get back."

"If that's the best we can do."

"Trust me. Flossie is exactly what Jewel needs."

After I hung up, I hurried to the kitchen. Disheartened when no one was there, I poured a cup of coffee and sat down. My manuscript was lying on the table. On top, held in place by a pen, was a note from Ivy Leigh explaining she had gone with Nestor to the hardware store. Inside the front cover was a note from Margaret.

Agnes, this is a good story with a lot of potential. As you noted, it needs editing. My main concern is the title. Why "Trevorode the Defender"? He disappears after a few pages. It is Lyda Rose who makes our hearts pound as she runs through the woods. It is she who leads troops into battle and narrowly escapes hanging when the king is presumed dead. These scenes …

I stopped reading and then read again: *narrowly escapes hanging when the king is presumed dead.* In an instant, my mind rushed back to the incident which had inspired that scene—the library at Stanton-Giles, where I stood at the edge of the crowd, looking at the gray head of Jameson Bridger resting on a stack of newspapers on the table.

I leaned back in the chair and urged my mind into reverse with painstaking slowness, reliving each incident of that day. Lunch with Xander. Running after him. Watching him walk away. Jonquil and her dog. Sitting on the bench. Meeting Jameson Bridger. I'd admired his cane. He'd said … Leo didn't manage to steal everything … his father had died when he was young. Leo McBain. Leo McBain was his stepfather.

That's where I'd heard that name before—from Jameson Bridger.

Monty came in and helped himself to a bowl of oatmeal.

"I say, Agnes, are you all right? You look a bit under the weather."

"I'm fine. I … just remembered something. And I had bad dreams all night."

He joined me at the table. "They say the mind never sleeps—works all the time. Sometimes I wake in the middle of the night and get up to add something to my memoir."

I held up my manuscript. "I wish I could write in my sleep. Margaret says my book needs some work. She doesn't like the title."

"Have some oatmeal and another cup of coffee. Then come to the study and we'll work on your book together."

He left the kitchen. I turned over Margaret's note, picked up Ivy Leigh's pen, and began writing, scribbling down names, stories, drawing lines, connecting.

"Where's Ivy Leigh?" Oliver asked from the doorway.

I didn't look up. "She and Nestor have gone to do some errands."

He stepped into the kitchen and dropped a white envelope on the table.

"Some woman stopped me on my way to the library yesterday. Said she'd heard about your silly talent show."

I read the envelope: "Magnolia Arms – Staff," but didn't open it, though I wanted to.

My memory searched, my research complete, my conclusions reached, I filled the sink with hot water and began to wash the breakfast dishes.

Forget fiction. I should've become a historian. All the while I'd dreamed of becoming an author, I'd been a character in a drama more intriguing than any I could've fabricated. I was standing on the very property Jameson Bridger's mother had struggled to keep for him. Leo McBain was his stepfather; Olympia was one of the "awful kids" Jameson's mother had tried to love. No wonder they'd left Jonas alone. Leo and his heirs had only partial claim on the property. Did Jameson still own the rest? If I could find him, if he remembered me, would he help us?

"Bless your heart," Ivy Leigh said as she opened the door. "Washing the dishes."

Rushing toward her, I grabbed her shoulders with wet hands. "I've got the best news," I said. "I know who can save the house—if we can find him."

"I do too," she said. "Your friend Xander Plumley will be here the day after tomorrow."

Chapter 19

A Performance to Remember

"Xander's a chemist," I said. "What can he do?"

Ivy Leigh set a paper bag on the table and brushed soap suds from her left shoulder.

"Chemist? Jonas didn't mention that. He said Xander has been building schools and clinics for the last year and knows absolutely everything there is to know about construction."

Almost dizzy, I leaned against the sink. This was too much information to process. I didn't know which issue to address first.

"Is Jonas coming with Xander?" I asked.

Ivy Leigh pulled a staple gun from the bag. "No, he's not up to travelling yet."

I pulled out a chair and sat down. "Did you tell Margaret you talked to Jonas?"

She lifted out a set of screwdrivers and examined them. "As a matter of fact, I did. Why is it we can never keep track of screwdrivers? We have four wrenches and two hammers, but—"

"How can you be so nonchalant?" I asked. "What did Margaret say? Was she upset?"

Ivy Leigh folded the bag and stuck it in the pantry.

"If you must know, every trace of color drained from her face. Then she shook her head, made her lunch, and left for school like she always does. Anything else?"

"Yes. Did Jonas say where Xander's been all this time?"

Ivy Leigh tied on her apron. "I don't remember the whole story. He said something about New Zealand and the Philippines. What's this?" She picked up the envelope off the table.

"Oliver told me to give it to you," I said.

"Hand me a knife from that drawer," she said.

She slit open the envelope, took out two twenty-dollar bills, and read the enclosed note. "*Send talent show tickets to Mrs. R.C. Pillburn c/o White Harbor Hotel, Raleigh.*"

"At least now we know Olympia was the woman in the car," I said.

"But how did she know about the talent show? We haven't put up the flyers yet."

"Someone told her," I said.

She sat in her usual chair. "Were you here when Oliver left the envelope?"

"Yes."

"What did he say to you … exactly?" she asked.

"He said 'some woman' stopped him on his way to the library."

"Then maybe we were wrong—he didn't know who she was."

"Or maybe he was just covering his tracks," I said, "pretending not to know."

She held out the bills. "Here. Take this to Nestor, before I run to the meat market for sirloin. Tell him to go back to the store and get the rest of the things on his list."

"If you say so," I said, "but I have a bad feeling about keeping this money."

"We're not keeping it. We're spending it."

I paused at the back door. "Wait. What about Jonas and Margaret?"

Ivy Leigh stood. "He'll call tonight at ten … after rehearsal."

"After rehearsal? That's like twelve hours from now."

She scooted our chairs under the table. "More like twelve and a half."

"Why didn't they talk this morning?" I asked.

She took her cup and saucer from the dish drainer. "I advised against it. They both need time to think about what they'll say. We don't want them messing this up again, do we?"

"I guess not."

She filled the teakettle with water. "What did you mean when you said you knew someone who could save the house?"

"Nothing," I said. "It's a shot in the dark."

"Remind me to ask you about it later. Now get going."

She began to whistle a tune.

I found Nestor in the backyard.

"Good news," I said as I held out the cash. "Ivy Leigh said you can go back to the hardware store and get the other things on the list."

He took off his work gloves. "Where'd this come from?"

"An unlikely source," I said. "Could I ride with you? I need to ask you something."

On the way to the store I confided in Nestor about Jameson Bridger.

"What if I could find him?" I asked. "Do you think he'd help us?"

"It's a nice idea, Agnes, but even if you found him—which is highly unlikely—would he remember you? And even if he did, why should he help us?"

I folded my arms. "So there's no need to ask you to take me to the police station?"

"What for?"

"Where else do you start looking for a missing person?"

"But he's not 'missing.' And what would you say? 'I need to find someone I met a long time ago, so I can ask him to help save our house from his wicked stepsister?' Don't be silly."

"But you're a historian," I said. "Aren't you the least bit curious about—?"

"I'm not a historian anymore," he said. "I'm a gardener."

Exasperated, I kept quiet for the rest of the ride and stayed in the truck while Nestor went into the hardware store.

While I waited in the parking lot, I rolled down the window and watched a brown bird peck at a discarded sandwich wrapper. This wasn't how I'd imagined my new life. The residents of the Magnolia Arms were supposed to be dreamers, poets, scholars. Instead they were practical, hard-working, focused, unimaginative, and impossible to distract or jostle off course. The inheritors of a remarkable legacy, the inhabitants of an extraordinary house, they were wholly preoccupied with pinching pennies, squeezing nickels, and making ends meet, living the same sort of no-nonsense life as my parents.

When we got back to the house, I held boards and fetched tools for Nestor, rehearsed my lines and musical numbers with Monty, and spent the afternoon slicing fruit for Ivy Leigh.

Exhausted and frustrated, I sank into the chair opposite Margaret at dinner that evening.

"Get any work done on your book today?" she asked.

"No. Too busy."

She took a bite of cantaloupe. "Maybe you'll have more time once your friend arrives."

My laughter startled her. "I can't sit at the typewriter while there's useful work to be done," I said. "Xander wouldn't hear of it."

She frowned. "Isn't this the same Xander who left college to backpack across Europe while you finished your education and got a job? That Xander?"

"The very same."

"Then he'll hardly be in a position to lecture you about useful work, will he?"

"I hadn't thought of it that way," I said. "And speaking of old friends—Ivy Leigh says you're talking to Jonas tonight."

"She's vowed to lock me in her office and guard the door if necessary," Margaret said.

"Don't you want to talk to him?"

"I do, but I'm so nervous I'm half sick. I hope I'll be able to concentrate on my lines during rehearsal tonight."

After dinner, everyone except Oliver met in the kitchen to go over the program. Once we were satisfied with the order, we moved into the parlor to rehearse. I sat at the piano.

Nestor and Posey began with a flawless rendition of "Anything You Can Do" from *Annie Get Your Gun.*

They were brilliant. I turned to Monty, who stood behind me waiting for his entrance.

"How did they perfect that song so soon?" I asked.

He whispered. "They performed it as the opening number for Posey's spring recital."

Monty took the stage with a charming performance of "Casey at the Bat."

Then I accompanied Posey on the piano as she sang a medley of Irving Berlin songs. She had a pleasant, poignant voice, decidedly amateur yet enchanting in its own shy way. When she sang "Always," Ivy Leigh wiped her eyes with the hem of her apron.

Monty entered as Horace Vandergelder, opposite Margaret as Mrs. Levi in a scene from *Hello, Dolly*. When Margaret began to sing, we were all transfixed.

I was up next, playing Eliza Doolittle to Nestor's inspired portrayal of Henry Higgins. At last I was portraying romantic leads rather than elderly mothers, spinsters, and nuns.

Then Monty returned with his accordion and dazzled us with "Lady of Spain."

I wasn't sure who twisted Ivy Leigh's arm to persuade her to play Aunt Abby in a scene from *Arsenic and Old Lace*, but I was grateful. She possessed natural comedic timing. She and Margaret, who played Aunt Martha, were so hysterical Nestor, Monty, and I, appearing as Mortimer, Teddy, and Elaine Harper, could barely keep from laughing. We'd need many more rehearsals before we could manage to keep our faces straight while those two were onstage together.

For the finale of the first half, Monty returned with his accordion to play "The Anniversary Waltz," while Posey sang, "So tell me I may always dance 'The Anniversary Waltz' with you."

Margaret turned away to stare out the dark window. Nestor asked Ivy Leigh to dance.

Nestled in a corner, I gazed at my friends and imprinted the exquisite moment on my memory. I'd been wrong. These amazing people were exactly like I'd imagined the residents of the Magnolia Arms.

I renewed my resolve to save their home, whatever I had to do.

After rehearsal, we retreated to the kitchen for pumpkin bread and tea. We critiqued each other's performances and offered suggestions, what few were needed.

Then Ivy Leigh turned serious.

"All right," she said. "Margaret is expecting a very important phone call, so I'll make this brief. I think we'd all like to thank Agnes for her help."

Everyone applauded.

Ivy Leigh continued. "We owe you our thanks, Agnes. You became one of us from the very beginning. You've pitched right in and done whatever was needed."

"Hear, hear," Monty said.

"Without you, Agnes," Ivy Leigh said, "we'd never have thought of having a talent show. I'm afraid we've all become a little too—"

"Jaded," Nestor said.

"Focused," Ivy Leigh said, "on business matters and simply trying to keep our heads above water, but there's more to life than that. I think we'd forgotten."

"I enjoyed singing," Posey said. "You play very well, Agnes."

"As you all know," Ivy Leigh said, "Agnes is an author, and she came here to work on her book. But up till now we haven't even given her a chance to tell us about it."

"An oversight we should correct," Margaret said. She looked at her watch.

"So," Ivy Leigh said, "we're going to do two things. First, we're going to let Agnes tell us her story. And second, tomorrow we're going to let her spend all day writing."

"I've rescheduled my voice lessons so I can stay and help in the kitchen," Posey said.

"Xander will be here soon," Nestor said. "The big jobs can wait till he arrives."

"I don't know what to say," I said.

"Start with chapter one," Monty said.

I introduced Lyda Rose as Margaret slipped out of the kitchen.

When I finished, I thanked my audience for listening and asked them a favor.

"Margaret thinks I need a new title," I said. "Let me know if you have suggestions."

They agreed to give the idea some thought, and we all went toward the stairs.

The light was still on underneath Ivy Leigh's office door as we walked by.

I woke with pleasant memories of the previous evening still on my mind. Eager to get the news from Ivy Leigh, I hurried to dress. When I opened my door, I saw two notes on the floor.

The first was from Posey.

I'd like to suggest "Trevoro Rodini" as a title. You'd have to move your story ahead to Renaissance Italy. Trevoro could rescue "Lyda Rosa" from the Borgias' dungeon. Hope this helps. Posey

I should've been clearer, I thought, and told them Margaret wondered why I hadn't named the book for Lyda Rose instead of Trevorode.

I opened the other envelope and read:

Jonas is calling again tonight. He said he wants to ask me a question. Margaret

I squeezed my eyes shut, opened them, read the note again, and bounded downstairs to get the details from Ivy Leigh. She wasn't there. Monty was alone at the kitchen table, scratching out notes on lined paper.

"Good morning," I said. "Where's Ivy Leigh?"

"She's gone to the printer to pick up our flyers so we can hand them out at dinner."

I chose a box of cereal.

"I hope you won't think me presumptuous," Monty said, flipping back several pages to the top sheet of his writing pad. "But I've gotten a little zealous about your story."

The cereal I was pouring spilled over the side of the bowl. "You mean my title?"

"I started with the title, but then I realized what was wrong. It's not the title—it's the setting. One thing my years in court taught me—there's nothing more exciting than law."

I opened the refrigerator door. Though I could see the milk on the top shelf, I lingered, summoning the patience to address Monty.

Milk carton in hand, I turned to him. "What do you have in mind?"

"If I may ..." He pushed his glasses down on his nose and began to read:

Trevelyan Roderick looked over his shoulder at the jury. Then he turned to the blonde beauty on the witness stand and spoke in a low tone.

"I'll remind you you're still under oath."

She turned pale and shuddered.

"Now," he said, "would you like to revise your previous testimony?"

Monty sat back in his chair. "What do you think? *Trevelyan Roderick, Attorney at Law.*"

"Has a nice ring to it," I said. "But what Margaret meant was—"

The back door swung open and a scruffy brindled dog galloped in, headed straight for my chair, planted his paws on my leg, and licked my arm.

"Look who's here," Ivy Leigh said.

Xander Plumley followed her into the kitchen. If I hadn't been expecting the person Jonas had described, I would've thought Ivy Leigh had offered breakfast to a tramp.

His face contorted with silent weeping, Xander walked toward me.

Monty and I stood. The dog took refuge under the table.

Xander fell into my arms and laid his head on my shoulder.

"I thought I'd never see you again," he said.

Ivy Leigh poured a cup of coffee. "Sit down, son," she said. "You've had a long trip."

"Can my dog stay inside?" he asked her.

"For now," she said, "but we run a restaurant here. He'll have to go outside after he eats."

"I understand," he said.

"Monty and I will give you two a few minutes," she said. "Agnes, get his breakfast."

Ivy Leigh stepped onto the back porch. Monty, papers in hand, tiptoed into the hall.

I filled a bowl with cereal and milk, sliced a banana on top, and set it in front of Xander. Both elbows on the table, he hunched over his breakfast as if protecting his food from predators.

When I sat down, Mendel the dog rested his head on my foot.

I resisted the compulsion to quiz Xander about Jameson Bridger. He was far too fragile.

"Are you all right?" I asked. "You've lost a lot of weight."

He sat back and wiped his mouth on his sleeve. "I've been sick—dysentery. A hazard of working in the jungle."

"How did you end up in the jungle?" I asked. "Zane said you were in Europe."

Posey entered from the hallway. When she saw Xander, she gasped and stumbled backward. Mendel, eager to greet her, lumbered out from beneath the table. Posey screamed.

"Agnes, how did that dog get in here?" she said. "And who is that man?"

"This is an old friend," I said. "Xander Plumley. He's come to help us. Remember?"

"That dog shouldn't be in here," she said. "We don't allow pets."

Xander stared at her. She left without a word.

"Posey's sensitive," I said. "You were saying how you got to the jungle?"

"One night, in Venice, when I'd run out of money, I approached a man in a train station, pulled out my university ID, told him I was on field study doing research and I'd been robbed."

"Did he believe you?"

He shook his head. "No. He saw right through me, but he bought me a meal. While I ate, he told me about his nonprofit work and offered me a job. I worked with him almost a year."

"And he's the one who taught you about building?"

He nodded. "I'd still be working with him if I hadn't gotten sick. He insisted I go home after I was well enough to travel."

"And you came straight to Brighton Park?"

He picked up his bowl and drank the milk. “I didn’t know where else to go. I can’t face my parents, looking like this.”

“Have you talked to your mother?”

“No, but I called Zane. He said he’d tell her I was back.”

“Wait here.” I left the table. Mendel scampered out when I opened the door.

Ivy Leigh was watering the herbs on the back porch.

“Xander needs to use the phone,” I said.

She followed me into the kitchen. Xander, head down on the table, was sound asleep.

“Poor thing,” Ivy Leigh said. “Help me get him to Nestor’s room.”

We nudged Xander awake and helped him into bed. Ivy Leigh closed the door.

“All right,” she said, “get to work on your book. I’ll keep an eye on Xander.”

I was back in my room before I realized I hadn’t asked Ivy Leigh about Margaret. I stayed at my desk, however, rather than going back downstairs. I knew what Ivy Leigh would say.

My hands on the typewriter, I stared at the ceiling.

In such a perfect setting and circumstance, I should’ve been able to drench the page with words, but not a single syllable dribbled from my mind.

Olympia’s threat to the Magnolia Arms was more absorbing than any imagined crisis.

I grabbed a spiral notebook and returned to the kitchen.

“Anything I can use to make a lunch?” I asked Ivy Leigh.

“Lunch? You just had breakfast,” she said.

“I’m going to the library,” I said. “I need—”

“A change of scenery?” she asked. “You must have writer’s block.”

I agreed, keeping quiet about my plan to spend the day researching Jameson Bridger.

Brown paper bag in hand, I headed out the back door.

“Where you off to?” Nestor asked. “I thought you were going to write all day.”

I borrowed Ivy Leigh’s phrase. “Writer’s block,” I said.

“I’m glad you brought that up,” he said. “I’ll walk with you to the end of the street.”

He opened the screen door. Mendel bounded out and trotted along with us.

“I was thinking about your book as I went to sleep,” Nestor said, “and—”

"Let me guess, you have a better idea and think I should—"

"No. I had a dream. I guess all the talk about writing brought back memories of my dissertation. Anyway, I dreamed I was writing about 'Trevierre Roudeaux.' How funny is that?"

"Hysterical," I said. "Which way is the library?"

"What's wrong with you?"

"Sorry," I said. "I'm upset about Xander ... and everything else, for that matter."

"We all are," he said. "The library's that way."

He turned and walked back with Mendel pattering after him.

My walk to the library allowed me time to concoct a credible story. I decided to tell the librarian I was a genealogist trying to trace a long-lost relative—something about a family inheritance. Or maybe I could say I was a reporter. Engrossed in my plans, I only gradually realized a car had pulled near the curb and slowed to keep pace with me.

I glanced over. Olympia Pillburn stared at me from the open backseat window.

"Do you need a lift, Agnes?" she asked.

Dumbfounded, I could only manage a quick shake of my head. I kept walking.

She talked as the car crawled along. "It's not going to work—what you're trying to do."

The car stopped as I turned to face her. "I don't know what you mean."

"You're not going to save that house," she said. "I've waited for years to get my hands on it, and no one, especially not someone like you, is going to stand in my way."

A distant memory stirred. I leveled my gaze.

"I've managed to piece together most of your past," I said, "but there's still one thing I don't know. May I ask?"

She narrowed her eyes. "What is it?"

"Did your brother ever get out of prison or is he still there?"

She jerked back in her seat. "Drive on," she said as she rolled up the window.

Energized by my tussle with Olympia, I entered the library, claimed I was a genealogist, and asked for back issues of the Dennisonville paper. The librarian led me up a narrow staircase to a musty room where I spent several hours ferreting out Bridger family history. I found Julia Bridger's wedding photo, Jameson Bridger's birth announcement, and a photo of the house which had stood on the property prior to the Magnolia Arms. Sometime after noon, I realized I hadn't eaten. I also hadn't thought about Xander, Olympia, Jonas, Margaret, the talent show, or the unwanted suggestions for my book.

As I sat on the library steps eating lunch, I congratulated myself on the progress I'd made, but realized I shouldn't invest so much time on distant history. As engaging as Jameson Bridger's family was, I couldn't focus on the past.

When I stepped back inside, the librarian called me to the checkout desk.

She looked at a note in her hand. "Are you Agnes Quinn?"

"Yes," I said.

"Ivy Leigh Ransom asked you to come home, said it was urgent."

"I left papers spread out all over—"

"We'll put them away," the librarian said. "May I ask if you're new to genealogy?"

"Yes," I said. "I'm looking for a lost … it's a matter of —"

"No need to explain. I only wanted to suggest you could find records at the courthouse."

I thanked her and hurried home. When I arrived at the Magnolia Arms, I found a dilapidated panel van labeled Bembo Brothers Plumbing parked in front of the house. Nestor was talking to a grimy man holding a toolbox. I edged past, knowing I shouldn't interrupt.

"We can't possibly afford that much," I heard Nestor say. "Isn't there another way?"

"Look, mister," said the plumber, "you're welcome to call my competitor, but you've got years of rust and neglect under there. Haven't you noticed you have no water pressure?"

I sprinted up the driveway. As I rounded the corner to the back door, I noticed Xander on his hands and knees in the backyard. I opened the door to the kitchen. Ivy Leigh, Posey, and Margaret bounced from one side of the kitchen to the other like pinballs. Monty, apron around his waist, rinsed pots and pans in the sink.

Ivy Leigh looked up. "Agnes, I'm so glad you're here. I'm sorry we bothered you."

"Don't be silly," I said. "What's wrong?"

Monty spoke up. "Nestor and Xander were trying to surprise us by fixing the fountain."

Posey said, "But when they started digging—"

"They found water," Monty said. "Apparently, there's been a leak for quite some time."

"We had no choice but to call the plumber," Ivy Leigh said. "It's going to cost us a fortune. Another of Abel's little surprises."

"The water was shut off for two hours," Margaret said. "Threw us behind for dinner."

"That's why I called," Ivy Leigh said. "Nestor and Xander will be outside all afternoon. You'll have to help serve tonight."

"Of course," I said.

I tried to shake off the notion that Olympia's warning had brought on this new trouble.

We worked around our crises all afternoon, barely whispering to each other, nodding as Ivy Leigh gave instructions. When at five o'clock she took off her apron and left the kitchen, we followed her to the dining room and entered with smiles and greetings. None of our diners would've guessed we were in trouble. Dinner proceeded as usual.

That night, without consulting each other, after we cleaned the dining room and washed the dishes, we all crept to our rooms without rehearsing and without our evening tea.

After everyone went to bed, I sneaked downstairs to Ivy Leigh's office. When I saw the light on under the door, I knocked and let myself in.

Margaret looked up. She was smiling and wiping tears from under her chin.

"I'm sorry to interrupt," I said, "but could I talk to Jonas a minute?"

She nodded and spoke into the phone. "Agnes wants to speak to you. I'll say good night. We have a big day ahead of us tomorrow." She paused. "I love you, too," she said.

She held out the receiver and then closed the door behind her as she left.

"Hello, Jonas," I said. "I don't need to ask how you are, do I?"

"I've never been happier," he said.

"I'm glad. I really am. And I hate to bother you at a time like this, but we need help."

I reviewed the events of the day.

"I'm sorry, Agnes," he said, "but you know I can't come. That's why I sent Xander."

"I know that. I meant, can you help us financially? You said you had plenty of money."

"I can't. Not now."

"What do you mean 'not now'?" I asked.

"I'm investing my money in a new house," he said. "I've asked Margaret to marry me, and she said yes."

"You asked her over the phone?"

"I've waited long enough."

I struggled to sound pleased. "That's wonderful, Jonas. Have you set a date?"

"No, we'll do that when she comes back with you."

I said goodbye, sat down in Ivy Leigh's chair, and laid my head on her desk. Only a few short days ago Jonas' announcement would have made me supremely happy. I should've also been delighted my long-lost friend, Xander, had come back. I was living in the house I'd only hoped to visit. I was miles from Brighton Park, at liberty to sit in my room and write all day. Everything I'd wanted had fallen into my lap. But I couldn't enjoy any of it, not while my friends were watching their hopes crumble.

When I left Ivy Leigh's office, I found Margaret sitting on the stairs.

"We didn't get a chance to talk this evening," she said. "Would you sit down a minute?"

I sat next to her.

"Did you get any work done on your book today?" she asked.

"No. Too busy."

She sighed. "I'm glad to hear you say that. It makes my question easier to ask."

"What is it?"

"Every year our local newspaper sponsors a writing contest in honor of the founding editor, Gustav Pulaski, who, like you, always wanted to write a novel."

"And you're telling me this because …?"

"Would you consider entering *Trevorode*? I wouldn't ask, but first prize is five hundred dollars. Think what that money could do for us. It would help to pay for the new plumbing."

I shook my head. "Give up my work to pay for pipes? No. And even if I agreed, the story is nowhere near finished."

"But you still have two days."

"Two days? I couldn't finish in two months, much less two days."

She paused. "It's a short story contest …"

I couldn't believe what I was hearing. This was one step away from Ferguson Trask and his comic book idea.

"And," she said, "you'd have to change the plot to science fiction."

"You can't be serious. You want me to demolish the ten chapters it's taken me six years to write?"

"I've given it a lot of thought and I have an idea, if you're willing to try."

Out of respect for Margaret, I listened without interrupting, though I alternated between being flattered by her confidence and offended by her audacity.

We walked upstairs together. She paused before she opened her door.

"You don't have to make a decision right now," she said, "but will you think about it?"

"You know how important my book is to me. Do you realize what you're asking?"

"Yes," Margaret said. "Love your neighbor."

That night I lay awake and tried to imagine Lyda Rose in an airplane.

The next morning Posey, Margaret, and I rose early to help Ivy Leigh. Xander, Nestor, and Monty hurried through breakfast, then rushed out to work on the yard and the stage. Ivy Leigh refused Margaret's offer to stay home from school. The plumbers began their assault, cutting holes in the walls, tracking in dirt, yelling instructions from floor to floor. Posey and I cleaned and prepared lunch for the men. Ivy Leigh, true to her word, turned to me at ten o'clock and said, "Library's open. Your book isn't going to write itself. Be back by three."

So I returned to the library, not to work on my book or search for Jameson Bridger, but to chisel away at my novel and carve it into something else. I stacked my manuscript on the table, closed my eyes, and pictured Ivy Leigh's face when I handed her a check for five hundred dollars. Then I opened a secret passage in Lyda Rose's castle and propelled her and Trevorode to another century. Soon I was rummaging through the shelves for reference books. If Lyda Rose was to appear before the Romanovs with Trevorovich Rodevsky, she had to be properly dressed.

Whittling away at the early pages of my story proved surprisingly easy. Years removed from the initial rush of inspiration and passion, I deleted entire scenes without regret. By two o'clock, I had a rough draft of "Trevorode's Quest" ready for editing and typing and left the library in time to meet Ivy Leigh's deadline. As I hurried through the back door of the Magnolia Arms, I noticed Posey offering a glass of water to a stranger in the backyard. I dropped my manuscript on the table and tied on my apron.

"Who's Posey talking to?" I asked Ivy Leigh.

"Look again," she said.

I did. It was Xander.

"Monty took him to his barber after lunch. Amazing transformation, isn't it?"

At dinner that night, I told Margaret I had a rough draft of the story and asked if she would meet me in Monty's study after rehearsal.

"You've finished it already?" she asked.

"Not quite, but I thought if you and Xander would work with me, he could advise me on the scientific jargon, and you could proofread. We could finish in a few hours."

That night we rehearsed for an enthusiastic audience of one. Xander deemed our performance stellar. Ivy Leigh insisted we finish the cherry tarts left over from dinner, so we all gathered in the kitchen. I volunteered to clean up. One by one everyone said good night and went up to bed. When Xander stepped outside to take Mendel for a walk, I followed him. I explained Margaret's plan and asked if he'd look at the story and advise me about the fine points of time travel.

"Chester Cranston would be better at that than I am," he said, "but I'll try."

Margaret was waiting in the study. Xander brought my typewriter from my room. I read aloud; Xander offered corrections or suggestions. I marked the script and handed the corrected page to Margaret at the typewriter. Page by page we journeyed with Trevorode from century to century. When we finished shortly before 1:00 a.m., Margaret handed me the entry form she'd already filled out. I added my signature. Margaret suggested we say nothing of our plan "unless we win, of course." Xander and I agreed. Margaret left early the next morning to drop off the story at the *Dennisonville Chronicle.*

For the next week, we raced against the clock to prepare our costumes and the house for the talent show. Though we all knew our profit might not make a dent in our mounting debt, we never admitted this to each other. Neither did we discuss the approaching deadline of the final extension for paying the property taxes nor the arrival of the health inspector, who, we hoped, would approve the continued operation of our restaurant. In spite of the extra work, Ivy Leigh remained true to her word and insisted I "work on my book" two hours every afternoon.

I couldn't tell Ivy Leigh I was spending every afternoon at the courthouse. Admitting I'd stopped work on my novel would've meant telling her about the contest, which Margaret had told me not to do. Still, when I left behind my hard-working friends for my "two hours of writing," I couldn't help feeling guilty. The only way to soothe my conscience was to tell myself my research could result in a potential biography. Without intending to, I'd compiled an impressive collection of facts about the Bridger family. One of the few pieces I was missing was Jameson Bridger's current address.

Two days before the talent show, while going through the courthouse records, I found a tattered folder stuffed with documents. I flipped through only three pages before I found a letter addressed to Jameson Bridger, thanking him for donating his family's diaries, letters, and journals to the University of North Carolina at Chapel Hill. The letter, three years old, contained the most recent address I'd found. That night I wrote to Jameson Bridger, reminding him who I was, telling him about Jonas, Olympia, and Margaret, and ending with my friends and their desperate attempt to save the house. I wrote "Please Forward" on the envelope.

We kept working and hoping. The plumbers, old friends of Ivy Leigh's husband Marshall, agreed to let us pay half their fee before the talent show and half afterward. Two days before the talent show two boxes arrived, the almond cookies from Muriel and the potholders from Flossie. Ivy Leigh opened the cookies. A celestial almond fragrance permeated the kitchen.

"I say," Monty said, "what a delectable smell."

"Wait till you taste them," I said, "if we don't sell them all at intermission."

I heard Ivy Leigh sniffling. When I looked up, I saw she had opened the box from Flossie. She lifted stacks of gorgeous potholders, turning them over in her hands, sighing, dabbing at her eyes. Flossie had outdone herself. She'd made a dozen dark green, a dozen dark brown, and a dozen orange potholders, half of them with a magnolia in the corner and the other half monogrammed "MA."

"Who wouldn't want one of these?" Ivy Leigh said. "They're magnificent."

On a brisk harvest-moon night, our audience arrived for the talent show and sat on chairs we'd borrowed from the Presbyterian church. As Oliver, keeping his hands warm for his Grieg piano concerto, waited in the parlor, and Xander manned the sound system on loan from Margaret's school, our cast stepped onto the finished stage to act our scenes and sing our songs. The audience laughed, cried, roared with applause, and demanded an encore from Monty. Then under our rented canopy, they ate every morsel and purchased every pot holder except the one Ivy Leigh had saved for herself.

Chapter 20

A Long-Expected Parting

That night as I stood in the back of the parlor and listened to Oliver play, I understood for the first time how Posey had fallen for him. Dressed in white tie and tails, his black hair glistening, his strong shoulders erect, he was attractive and appealing, his brooding persona alluring and romantic. Expecting to find Posey spellbound, I glanced at her in the opposite corner of the room and was stunned to find her not only standing close to Xander but also holding his hand. Apparently, while I'd been away every day, these two lonely souls had found each other.

Oliver bowed to thunderous applause, but declined to perform an encore. The audience rose and chatted quietly as they left. I stood next to Ivy Leigh at the front door and thanked our visitors for attending. The last to leave, a lovely elderly lady in a blue polka dot dress stopped and took Ivy Leigh's hand in both of hers.

"I came with my mother to visit Julia Bridger in the first home. Jameson and I used to play in the front yard while our mothers had tea. Julia would be pleased with what you've done."

When she left, Ivy Leigh opened her hand and found a fifty-dollar bill.

She clasped her hands over her heart. "God bless Julia Bridger, whoever she is."

"This plot of land belonged to her husband's family," I said.

Ivy Leigh locked the front door. "How do you know?"

"I've learned a lot at the library," I said. "If you'd like to know the whole story—"

"Tomorrow," she said. "I need to count our money. If I've calculated correctly, we'll only need $250 to pay the taxes." She waved the fifty-dollar bill. "Make that $200," she said.

"But don't we still owe the plumbers?" I asked.

"They're old friends of Marshall's," she said. "They agreed to wait on what we owe till after the taxes are paid. But if the restaurant has a good week, we can pay off everybody."

The next morning while we lingered at breakfast, still reveling in the triumph of the previous evening, the doorbell rang.

Nestor stood, took the last cinnamon scone, and started down the hall. "I'll get the door on my way out," he said. "Have to return the chairs and the sound equipment."

But he soon returned to the kitchen. "Health inspector's here," he said.

Ivy Leigh pushed back from the table. "But it's Saturday. We haven't finished cleaning up from last night."

Nestor and Ivy Leigh left the kitchen. The rest of us sprang to our feet, gathered plates and cups, scraped crumbs, wiped spills. Margaret grabbed the broom. Posey rushed toward the sink. Monty snatched up the garbage bags. The dog, sensing our panic, scratched at the back door and shot in as Monty hurried out. Xander nabbed Mendel as Ivy Leigh led the health inspector into the kitchen. I grabbed the pile of costumes we'd tossed by the washer and threw them over Mendel's head. Then I put my arm around Xander and shuffled him, the dog, and the clothes out the back door.

"Thank you for coming so soon," I said. "We appreciate your excellent service." Then I leaned against the door and peered at Margaret.

Margaret turned to the inspector. "Costume rentals," she said.

The inspector scanned the room, and then turned to Ivy Leigh. "You're in charge?"

"I am," Ivy Leigh said.

He held out a business card. "George Hampton," he said. "If you could clear out the rest of your staff, I'll get to work."

Margaret, Posey, and I tiptoed to the parlor, entering quietly as if attending a funeral.

"I'm no expert," I said, "but I've never heard of an agency conducting this kind of inspection on the weekend. That's not standard procedure, is it?"

"It does seem out of the ordinary," Margaret said.

Posey gaped at both of us. "I feel sick. I need to sit—"

She crumpled to the floor. Margaret knelt next to her.

"What's wrong?" I asked.

"She does this when she gets upset," Margaret said. "Get some water."

By the time I returned with the water, Posey was sitting up. Margaret held the glass to Posey's lips as she drank.

"You're upset about Oliver leaving today, aren't you?" Margaret asked her.

"No … not this time," Posey said.

I tried to lighten the mood. "Posey was holding hands with Xander last night."

Margaret smiled. "When did this—?"

The doorbell rang again.

"I'll get it," I told Margaret. "You stay here with Posey."

I answered the door.

"Mrs. Ransom?" the visitor asked.

"She's busy at the moment. May I help you?"

He held out a card. "Fred Schwartz. We've received complaints."

"Complaints?" I asked. "What about?"

He scanned his clipboard. "Zoning violations, non-permitted construction."

"Hold on a minute," I said. "Who are you?"

"I told you. Fred—"

"Schwartz. I got that. But where are you from?"

"City Planning Commission. Building inspector," he said.

I heard Ivy Leigh coming down the hall. Fred's card in hand, I turned around. She trailed the health inspector as he marched from the kitchen.

"These allegations are absurd," Ivy Leigh said. "No one on our staff has dysentery."

Margaret emerged from the parlor and joined us at the front door.

"Until Mr. Plumley undergoes a physical and submits the proper documentation," George said, "you cannot serve food to the public. Your restaurant is closed. That's all there is to it."

"But he's not on our staff," Ivy Leigh said. "He's a resident."

"And he's not sick," I said. "Not anymore."

"Not according to our records," George said. He spotted the building inspector. "Mornin', Fred. Gettin' in a little overtime?"

"Hello, George. Who's the guy you're investigating?" Fred asked.

"Plumley," George said.

Fred consulted his notes. "He's on my list, too. 'Maintenance staff.'"

Ivy Leigh turned to Fred. "Who are you?"

"Fred Schwartz, City Planning Commission."

"Why are you here?" Ivy Leigh asked.

"You've been reported," Fred said.

"Sabotaged is more like it," I said.

Posey, grave and quiet, came from the parlor and stood motionless in the hall.

Fred displayed his clipboard, pointing with his pen as he lectured. "Did you recently complete a construction project in your backyard?"

"We built a stage," Ivy Leigh said, "but it was only temporary."

"Is it attached to this dwelling?" he asked.

"Yes," I said. "That seemed more practical than suspending it on ropes from the trees."

Fred was not amused. "Did you apply for a building permit?" he asked.

"No," Ivy Leigh said, "but it was just a platform for us to stand on for an hour."

"Doesn't matter," he said. "You should've applied for a building permit. There are fees."

"What if we pay the fee now?" Margaret asked. "Will that take care of the problem?"

"We don't accept money. You'll have to come to city hall," he said.

"All right," Ivy Leigh said. "Anything else?"

"Yes," he said, "a penalty fee."

"Penalty?" Margaret asked.

"There are rules," Fred said. "You can't pay whenever it's convenient."

"And you can't have sick people working in your kitchen," George said. "Or dogs."

"We've never had a dog working in our kitchen," I said.

Fred glared at me. "Would you stay out of this?"

"I told you, Mr. Plumley is a guest," Ivy Leigh said. "He doesn't work in the kitchen."

"Not according to this report," George said. "Get a health form submitted or—"

"When we come to city hall on Monday," I said, "we'll be speaking to your supervisor."

"Speak to him all you want," George said.

"Mine, too," Fred said.

I stepped in front of Ivy Leigh, opened the front door, and held out my hand. "Then leave your citations. We'd like our lawyer to look them over."

After I closed the door, Margaret, Ivy Leigh, and I stood staring at each other.

"Lawyer?" Margaret said. "How do you come up with this stuff?"

"I said we'd 'like' our lawyer to look them over," I said, "and I would. I'd give anything for a good lawyer."

We walked back to the kitchen.

Ivy Leigh slumped in her chair. "I had everything figured down to the last nickel, but now we won't know till Monday if we can still pay the taxes after we pay these fines."

"I wonder how soon Xander can get a doctor's appointment," Margaret said.

"We'll have to pay for that, too," Ivy Leigh said. "Xander has no money."

"He could leave," I said. "He should go home to see his family anyway."

Ivy Leigh shook her head. "I've never turned away anyone who needed my help, and I don't intend to start now."

I retrieved the six almond cookies I'd hidden in the pantry and set them on the table.

Margaret poured tea. "I still don't understand why those men came today."

"And how," Ivy Leigh said, "did they know Xander was here, much less that he'd been sick? *I* didn't even know."

Posey rushed in and fell onto a chair.

"It's all my fault," Posey said, "but you have to believe me—I didn't know—she didn't tell me what she was planning."

"What are you talking about?" Ivy Leigh asked.

Weeping, Posey spilled out her story. "A few months ago, after my spring recital," she said, "a lady came backstage. She told me she was an old friend of Margaret's and knew we lived in the same house."

I buried my face in my hands. "Oh, no," I said. "Olympia."

"Let Posey finish," Margaret said.

"But can't you see where this is going?" I asked. "Olympia targeted Posey because—"

"Let her finish, Agnes," Ivy Leigh said. "Can't you see she's upset?" She took Posey's hand in hers. "Was it Mrs. Pillburn?"

Posey nodded. "I didn't know till later. She said my voice was beautiful and asked if I had a vocal coach. I said I'd never had formal training, just community college. And she ..." Posey bowed her head and gasped for air.

Ivy Leigh retrieved a paper bag from the drawer and held it over Posey's mouth.

Posey's shoulders rose and fell as she breathed. We waited.

"And she offered to help you," Margaret said. "Is that right?"

Posey nodded and relaxed in her chair.

"Didn't you find her offer the least bit suspicious?" I asked.

"Not at first," Posey said. "She said she'd always wanted to sing, but when her father wouldn't let her leave home to study, she vowed to devote herself to helping young singers."

"Unbelievable," I said. "As if Olympia ever helped anyone do anything—"

"Not everyone's as self-confident as you are, Agnes," Ivy Leigh said. "Posey's not to blame for being deceived."

Self-confident? I thought. *Me?*

Margaret handed Posey a napkin. "Tell us the rest," she said.

Posey blew her nose. "She told me her family used to live here, and she was interested in restoring the house, and if I'd keep her informed about what we were doing, she'd—"

"She'd what?" Margaret asked.

Posey whispered, "She said she had a good friend at Julliard, who'd get me an audition."

"Julliard?" I said. "You can't be serious. You actually fell for that?"

"I thought if I became a real musician," Posey said, "Oliver would love me and ..."

I rolled my eyes. "Let me guess ... you could make beautiful music together."

"Agnes, stop it," Ivy Leigh said.

"So all this time," Margaret said to Posey, "you've been keeping Olympia informed about all our plans."

Posey nodded and dissolved into tears again.

"Olympia connived with someone at city hall," I said. "Money talks."

Monty eased open the back door and peeked in. "Is it safe to come back now?"

Margaret looked up. "Yes, they're gone."

"That's a relief," he said. "I swept off the porch while I was outside, in case they wanted a look at our herb garden. One never knows."

Xander came next, closing the door before Mendel could enter. "Stay there," he said.

"Let him in," Ivy Leigh said. "It makes no difference now."

Mendel galloped in and plopped down in the corner.

Xander sat down between me and Posey. "How'd it go?" he asked.

"Not good," Ivy Leigh said.

The doorbell rang again.

Monty answered the door and announced I had visitors.

I found Ryder Ellershaw and Elinor waiting for me in the foyer.

Elinor embraced me. "Agnes, it's good to see you. We've missed you."

Ryder held out his hand. "Hello, Agnes," he said. For Elinor's sake I shook his hand.

"What are you two doing here?" I asked.

Elinor displayed a gold band on her left hand. "We're on our honeymoon."

"Honeymoon? When did this happen?" I asked.

"We eloped two days ago," she said. "Isn't it romantic?"

Ryder held her hand. "We were having dinner at the Drifters' Rest, and I said how nice it was to have someone to eat with all the time."

"And I said there was no point in either of us ever eating alone again," Elinor said.

"And I said there was no point in either of us living alone either," Ryder said.

"He knelt down and proposed and I said yes, and we found a justice of the peace and—"

Ivy Leigh joined us. "Everything all right, Agnes?" she asked.

"Yes. These are my friends, Ryder and Elinor …"

"Ellershaw," Ryder said. "Mr. and Mrs. Ellershaw."

"Welcome to the Magnolia Arms," Ivy Leigh said.

Ryder and Elinor's arrival was a good distraction for all of us. After breakfast, Monty invited Ryder to his study where they stayed most of the morning. Elinor and Margaret settled in the parlor, talking about their favorite authors and Jonas. Ivy Leigh insisted the rest of us take the morning off and then locked herself in her office. Xander and Nestor played chess at the kitchen table. Posey retreated to her room. I walked into the dining room and began moving the tables together. There was, after all, no point in any of us eating alone again.

I heard Ivy Leigh open her office door and walk toward the dining room. I kept working.

"What are you doing?" she asked.

"I thought we could all eat together tonight—like a family."

She left for a moment and then returned. "Come with me, Agnes."

We got in the truck. Our first stop was the meat market. Ivy Leigh emerged with a bag stuffed with sirloin. Our next stop was the grocery store. I pushed the basket while she piled in huge baking potatoes, luscious tomatoes, lettuce, carrots, onions, mushrooms, and asparagus.

More to herself than to me she said, "Strawberry shortcake for dessert. Real whipping cream. We'll have yeast rolls. I'll make extra dough for cinnamon rolls tomorrow."

"Won't this deplete the money you've saved?" I asked.

She winked. "No, I borrowed from the budget for Monday night's menu. Unless your mythical lawyer appears, we'll be closed for business for a while."

When we returned, we found Posey sitting with Xander and Nestor in the kitchen.

Ivy Leigh tied on her apron and stood in the middle of the floor.

"Posey, iron the tablecloths. Nestor, call the neighbor and ask if we can borrow his grill. Xander can go with you to pick it up. Agnes, bring Margaret. And someone let the dog back in."

I brought Margaret and Elinor from the study. When Elinor heard the menu, she said, "You must let Ryder make his famous marinade."

Ivy Leigh thanked her for the offer and sent me to fetch Ryder and Monty.

Together we spent all afternoon in the kitchen, stepping over and around each other, following Ivy Leigh's directions, pausing to drink tea or listen to a story. At sunset the men huddled around the charcoal fire, standing guard over our dinner like Robin Hood's merry men after a hunt. The ladies ferried baked potatoes, crisp salad, sautéed mushrooms and onions, steamed vegetables, and buttery rolls to the dining room. We stood at our places till Monty pulled out Ivy Leigh's chair at the head of the table. Then we all sat down across from each other and savored our food and our company, utterly content.

When Elinor and Ryder prepared to leave, I accompanied them to the front door. Elinor shared the news from Brighton Park.

"You'll be getting a phone call Monday morning," she said. "The administration will offer their apologies and ask you to return to work. The real thieves have been discovered."

"When did this happen?" I asked.

She raised her eyebrows. "At a recent faculty meeting, someone, who shall remain nameless, leaned over to Trixie and Mavis and whispered the good news of Jonas' engagement."

"Is this 'someone' anyone I know?" I asked.

"Mavis began laughing hysterically. Then she said to Trixie, 'We went to all that trouble to get rid of Agnes, and it still didn't do us any good.'"

"She said that out loud?"

"Oh, yes, quite loud. 'All those weeks of dragging stuff out of the library,' she said, 'and I still don't have Asher, and now you've lost Jonas. So much for your brilliant plan.'"

"What happened then?" I asked.

"Trixie tried to shut her up, but it was no use. Mavis laughed till she was exhausted and then dissolved into tears. Two men had to escort her out. But it was too late. Everyone heard."

"So I can have my job back?" I asked.

"Yes, your students can't wait to see you."

"Looking forward to having you back, Agnes," Ryder said.

On Sunday morning Margaret invited me to attend the service at the Presbyterian church. Bundled in our coats, we strolled to the end of the block before Margaret spoke.

"Did Elinor tell you the news?" she asked.

"She told you before she told me?"

Margaret hesitated. "Yes. She suggested I apply for Trixie's job."

"What about your job here?" I asked.

"I'll finish out the semester and then retire … after I get back from seeing Jonas."

"Maybe I'll stay here and apply for your position," I said. "I don't want to leave."

"You need to finish what you started at Brighton Park," she said.

When Margaret and I returned from church, Xander was waiting on the front porch. Margaret slipped inside to help Ivy Leigh with lunch and left us alone.

"I wanted to apologize, Agnes," he said.

"There's no need for that," I said. "I'm happy for you. Posey is a sweet girl."

"No, not about that, though I should've told you. It all happened so fast."

"Then what?"

"For leaving you—years ago—without saying goodbye. It was wrong for me to send a letter, but at the time I was so—"

"Come with me," I said and took his arm.

We walked upstairs to my room. I took a manila envelope from my dresser drawer, reached inside, and produced his tattered letter.

"I thought I might give this to you at our tenth college reunion, but since you didn't actually graduate, there's no reason to wait," I said. "I'm sorry. I didn't mean it like that."

He took the letter, but didn't unfold it. "You kept this all these years. Why?"

We sat on the floor, and I told him the whole story.

"So, you see," I said, "if it hadn't been for that letter, I might not have finished college, much less gotten another degree and a job."

He bowed his head. "You outgrew me a long time ago. I knew that the moment I saw you. I haven't even graduated from college yet."

"There's still time," I said, "if that's what you want, but you need to see your family."

He held my hand. "I know. I'm going home for a while, but I'm coming back. Nestor said this is a perfect place for people who've failed to live up to expectation."

Monday morning was as melancholy as the day after Christmas. After breakfast, Margaret left for school, Monty took refuge in his study, Xander and Nestor began to tear down our stage. Posey and I cleared the breakfast table and started washing dishes.

"I'll get going on Oliver's laundry," Ivy Leigh said.

She returned to the kitchen a few moments later with a letter in her hand.

"Can you believe this? Oliver's moving to Charleston. He said he needed this month's rent for a down payment on a new apartment, and he'll mail what he owes after his next concert."

At ten o'clock, Nestor and I waited outside Ivy Leigh's office door. Nestor whistled when she appeared. She wore a classic black dress with a red scarf draped over her shoulders.

Nestor approached her and offered his arm. "Going to the guillotine properly dressed?"

The doorbell rang.

"You two get in the truck," I said. "I'll get rid of whoever this is."

They walked toward the kitchen to go out through the back porch.

When I opened the front door, I thought at first I was looking at Asher Loncraine. The stranger was remarkably like him: tall, thin, angular, and harsh. He held out a card.

"Ira Osgood," he said, "of Camden, Lockwood, Osgood, and Tuttle. I represent—"

I refused his card. "I know who you represent."

Over the lawyer's shoulder, I watched Nestor, who was backing up the truck, stop within inches of Olympia's white Cadillac waiting in the driveway.

Mr. Osgood opened a black folder. "This Friday, due to unpaid taxes and accrued penalty fees, a lien on these holdings will be filed. At that time my client—"

I stepped out on the porch and closed the door behind me.

Ivy Leigh got out of the truck. Anguish in her eyes, she looked back at Olympia's car, then over at the lawyer. She laid her hands on the hood of the truck and bowed her head.

I snapped. Shoving the lawyer aside, I bounded off the porch in one leap and hurtled toward Olympia's car. Ignoring the pain in my ankle, I pounded on her window with my fist.

"You get out of that car right now," I said. "Get out and face us or I promise you I'll heave a rock through this window and sit in jail till next Thursday—"

Nestor launched himself from the truck and grabbed both my arms from behind. "Stop it, Agnes. We don't have enough money to bail you out if you're arrested."

Straining against Nestor's grip, I kept screaming, "Why did you do this—watch us struggle when you knew all along you were going to force us to sell?"

Olympia got out of the car and spoke in a tone that would've frozen lava. "To give you a sporting chance. It was fun watching you work and then countering your moves. The restaurant idea was amusing, but the talent show? Absurd."

Ira Osgood returned to the Cadillac.

"As I was saying, Mrs. Pillburn is sole heir to her father's estate. Upon his decease, she has the right to force the sale of his assets and realize her share of the profit."

"There are two other owners," I said.

"Immaterial," Ira Osgood said. "When the paperwork is filed, my client—"

Ivy Leigh walked past all of us and faced Olympia.

I stopped breathing.

"Why do you want my home?" Ivy Leigh asked her.

Olympia faltered. "My … my … father left it to me."

"You have a home," Ivy Leigh said.

Olympia squared her shoulders. "Of course I do. I have three."

"Then I'll ask you again," Ivy Leigh said, "and please do me the courtesy of answering honestly. Why do you want this house?"

Olympia leaned against her car. "I'm going to tear it down and build a new one."

"Why?" Ivy Leigh asked.

"Because … this house is old and falling down. You think I don't know about the plumbing and the roof and the wiring? It would take months to repair it all."

"You simply cannot tell the truth, can you?" Ivy Leigh asked.

"I beg your pardon," Olympia said.

"You think if you destroy this place, you'll finally be free of the pain you felt when Jonas chose Margaret instead of you."

Olympia turned white with rage. "How dare you!"

"But it won't work," Ivy Leigh said. "No matter what you do, your last thought this side of the grave will be of Jonas. Take it from me. You never forget your first love."

Ivy Leigh turned to Ira Osgood and said, "May I ask you a question?"

"Yes, ma'am."

"Do I understand correctly? Even after all I've done to maintain and improve this place, this woman can still force the other owners to sell, so she can take her share? Is that right?"

"Yes, ma'am," Ira Osgood said. "That's what the law says."

"Come on, Agnes," she said. "Let's go."

We walked back to the truck.

Nestor slammed his hand on the hood of the Cadillac. "Out of the way," he said. "Mrs. Ransom has an appointment."

Olympia's chauffeur eased out of the driveway. I slid into the truck.

"We're not still going to city hall, are we?" I asked.

"I owe a debt for the building permit, and I'm going to pay it," Ivy Leigh said. "If I have to go, I'm going to leave with a clear conscience. That's what Marshall would've wanted."

Posey stepped out on the front porch and called my name.

"What is it?" Nestor asked.

"Agnes has a phone call," Posey said.

Nestor waited while I limped back to the porch, up the steps, and into Ivy Leigh's office.

"Hello," I said.

"Miss Quinn? This is Barnaby Luther, editor of the *Dennisonville Chronicle*. It's my pleasure to inform you that your story, 'Trevorode's Quest,' has won the annual Pulaski Award."

I leaned against Ivy Leigh's desk. "My story? You're sure?"

He laughed. "You are Agnes Quinn, are you not?"

"Yes, but I've never won anything before."

"You can't say that after today," he said. "May I share one of the judge's comments?"

"Sure," I said.

"The distinguishing feature of Miss Quinn's story is her unique approach to the familiar time travel theme. She alters her hero's name to fit the era in which he arrives. Whether Trevoro Rodini is outwitting the Borgias, Trevorovich Rodevsky is dining with the Romanovs, or Trevelyan Roderick is putting guilty parties behind bars, Trevorode is a hero of the first order."

I sighed. "I've been waiting a long time to hear someone say something like that."

"Shall I mail the prize money, or would you like to pick it up?" he asked.

"I'll be right there," I said.

I came back to the truck and told Nestor and Ivy Leigh the good news.

"Five hundred dollars," I said. "We have plenty of money now. No matter what the permit costs, we'll have money left over."

I waited for the look of joy I'd pictured on Ivy Leigh's face, but was disappointed.

"Didn't you hear what the lawyer said?" Ivy Leigh asked. "Even if we pay our debt, Olympia can still take us to court to get her share of the property. I can't let your sacrifice be for nothing."

I was almost in tears. "But the only reason I entered the contest was to help save the house. You have to take the money … or explain to Margaret. It was her idea."

We picked up the prize money from the newspaper office. Ivy Leigh remained silent as Nestor drove to the bank so I could cash the check.

When I left the bank, I found Nestor and Ivy Leigh waiting for me on the sidewalk.

"I have something to ask you, Agnes," she said, "but you're not going to like it."

I handed her the money. "What is it?"

"With the restaurant closed and Oliver's rent gone, I won't be able to pay the plumbers before we're forced out."

Nestor riveted his eyes to mine. His meaning was clear: "Watch what you say."

"You want to use the prize money for the plumbing? Pipes no one sees?" I asked.

"It would take such a burden off me," she said. "Where else will I get $450?"

Nestor drove us to Bembo Brothers Plumbing. Ivy Leigh, purse tucked under her arm, started toward the door.

I sighed.

"What's wrong?" Nestor asked.

"All my work on that story literally went down the drain. I had no intention of giving that money to the plumbers."

"You didn't give it to the plumbers," Nestor said. "You gave it to Ivy Leigh."

Ivy Leigh returned to the truck. "Thank you, Agnes," she said, "for giving up your dream for us. I know it wasn't easy, and I'm truly sorry things didn't work out like you planned."

I squeezed her hand. "Nothing is as important as the people you love."

"What was that?" Nestor said.

"Something a stranger told me a long time ago—'nothing is as important as the people you love.' Doesn't matter anyway," I said. "I've given up writing fiction."

"Monty could give you some pointers on memoirs," Nestor said. We all laughed.

Brave-hearted, we trooped into city hall. Our stop at the building inspector's office further depleted our funds, but soothed Ivy Leigh's conscience.

"There are two ways to look at this," Ivy Leigh said. "Either we can hang on to the rest of our money and hope for the best, or have a very nice farewell dinner for you and Margaret."

I didn't even try to argue. "Shall we stop by the store on our way home?"

When Ivy Leigh and I began shopping, I was surprised she chose a large turkey.

"We'll have Thanksgiving early," she said, "since we won't be together on that day."

We cooked all day Thursday. We bustled from one task to the next, basting the turkey, peeling sweet potatoes, snapping beans, filling pie crusts, one or more of us always in tears. Posey created centerpieces with tiny pumpkins and fall leaves. Monty made a fire in the fireplace. When all was ready, we loaded our trays and awaited Ivy Leigh's signal as if the dining room were full of patrons. Then we glided in, laid down our platters of white meat or dark, and arranged dishes of squash casserole and sweet potato soufflé.

Again Ivy Leigh stood at the head of the table. When she reached out to Margaret on her right and Monty on her left, we all joined hands.

"Monty," Ivy Leigh said, "would you say grace?"

The doorbell rang.

I jerked loose from Nestor's hand and charged toward the door.

"If that's Olympia Pillburn," I said, "she'll rue the day she—"

Nestor ran after me. "Agnes, wait."

Ready to do battle with Ira Osgood, I yanked open the door and was startled to find a handsome young man in a black suit and red tie.

"I'm looking for 306 Belmont Drive," he said. "The Magnolia Arms?"

Nestor edged in front of me. "This is it," Nestor said. "May we help you?"

He held out a card. "Sefton Wilkinshaw. My employer—"

"Camden, Lockwood, Osgood, and Tuttle," I said. "If I hear that list one more time—"

Nestor poked me in the side. "Look in the driveway. That's not Olympia's car."

I peered around Mr. Wilkinshaw. "Sorry," I said. "I thought you were someone else."

"Perfectly understandable," he said. "You're Agnes Quinn, aren't you?"

"Yes," I said.

"As I was saying, my employer, Jameson Bridger, would like to meet with you."

Nestor caught me as my knees buckled. We watched as Sefton Wilkinshaw returned to the car and then helped Jameson Bridger walk up our steps.

"Hello, Agnes," Mr. Bridger said. "I got your letter."

I put my arm through Jameson Bridger's and led him into the dining room.

He walked straight toward Xander and took his hand. "Xander, it's been a long time."

Xander hung his head. "Yes, sir, I owe you an apology. I should've contacted you—"

Jameson put his arms around him. "It is I who should apologize to you."

I brought Mr. Bridger to Ivy Leigh. "This is the woman who's taken care of your property all these years," I said. "Ivy Leigh Ransom."

Mr. Bridger took her hand. "It's a pleasure to meet you. I have some business to—"

"Will you join us for dinner first?" she said and led him to the head of the table.

He sat down and, placing the napkin in his lap, said, "This house is much grander than the one I grew up in. I don't suppose my tree house is still in the backyard."

"No, sir," Nestor said, "but we can build one. We have a pile of boards in the garage."

After dinner, while the rest of us cleared the table and washed the dishes, Ivy Leigh took Mr. Bridger on a tour of the house. Then we all met in the parlor for coffee and pumpkin pie.

"I've dined in some of the best restaurants in the world, Mrs. Ransom," Jameson said, "but I've never enjoyed a meal as much as that one."

She looked around the room. "It's the company," she said.

"You're right," Jameson said. "I've eaten many a meal with bad company, and it's not good for the digestion."

"Where is Jonquil, by the way?" I asked.

Jameson laughed. "Jonquil and her mother left me shortly after Jonquil's troubles grew worse. They're living very nicely in France."

"And your health has improved as a result?" I asked.

"I've never felt better," he said. "Now, I mustn't keep you in suspense. Once I received Agnes' letter, I put Sefton to work ferreting out the truth about Olympia's claims."

"It's one of the most complicated cases I ever researched," Sefton said. "But simply put, Mrs. Pillburn received a small interest in this estate upon her father's demise."

"But there's no record Julia ever made Leo joint owner," I said.

"Sadly," Jameson said, "as her spouse, Leo did inherit part of my mother's property."

"But you're still part owner, aren't you?" I asked Jameson. "Jonas is, too."

"How do you know all this?" Ivy Leigh asked.

"I wasn't exactly working on my novel every afternoon," I said.

"Agnes is right," Sefton said. "Both Mr. Bridger and Mr. Grinstead own a portion of the estate. If either of them had lived here, we'd have a different matter on our hands."

"I remember a case like this," Monty said. "Lawyers wrangled over the matter for a frightfully long time. Dragged on in the court for months."

"Precisely," Sefton said. "That's why we opted for a different approach. With Mr. Bridger's permission, I interviewed Mrs. Pillburn's business partners."

"Olympia hadn't been entirely honest with her developer about when he could begin building on this site," Jameson said.

"The developer was so grateful for the legal expenses we saved him, he handed over a list of city officials," Sefton said, "long-time friends of Olympia's family ..."

"Who've been, shall we say, 'rewarded' for keeping your feet to the fire," Jameson said.

"I knew it," I said.

Jameson leaned back in his chair. "When her cohorts started jumping ship, we approached Olympia and offered to buy her out."

"When even that didn't persuade Mrs. Pillburn to retreat," Sefton said, "I laid a stack of arrest records and court transcripts on her marble coffee table."

"Sefton offered to keep the chapter about Olympia's brother and his life of crime out of my biography," Jameson said.

"You're writing a biography?" I asked.

"Not yet," Sefton said.

"But when he does, he's assured me he won't mention Bentley," Jameson said. "I wrote Olympia a check for her rightful share. She signed an agreement. I'm your new landlord."

The following morning, Ivy Leigh, wearing her black dress, sat with Jameson Bridger in the backseat of his Lincoln Town Car on our way to city hall. I was in the front seat with Sefton.

Sefton held open the door of the tax collector's office as Ivy Leigh strode in.

Ivy Leigh asked the clerk how much she owed and wrote a check for the full amount.

Mr. Bridger and Sefton dropped us off at the Magnolia Arms.

"Thank you, Agnes," Mr. Bridger said. "They say you can't come home again, but I feel like I have. My mother would be so pleased with the people who call this place home."

"Goodbye, Agnes," Sefton said. "We'll talk soon."

"You have my number?" I asked.

He winked. "Of course. You were one of the people I researched."

On Saturday morning Nestor drove Margaret and me to the train station. Xander, Monty, and Posey, unwilling to watch us leave, had lingered at breakfast. Only Ivy Leigh stood on the porch and waved as the sun rose.

"See you at the wedding," she said.

No fairy-tale princess could've looked more beautiful than Margaret when she stepped off the train. Jonas held her in his arms so long I was able to retrieve our luggage and still return in time to savor the moment. Jonas drove us to the Drifters' Rest where Muriel had reserved a table, and Flossie was waiting.

"I feel like I know you," Muriel said as she embraced Margaret.

"She's so much like Ivy Leigh," Margaret said to me.

"I have bad news, Agnes," Flossie said. "Buck went on a diet after you left, to try to win your heart, but he slimmed down so much a waitress at Bob's Pancake World has snagged him."

I grimaced. "Barb?"

"No, Flo," she said.

I felt Sefton's business card in my pocket. "I'll try to get over it," I said.

Charlotte insisted Margaret stay at her house while she was visiting.

"I confess to an ulterior motive," Charlotte said. "I hope to persuade you to have your wedding and reception here. Muriel would cater, of course."

No persuasion was necessary. The wedding was scheduled for Valentine's Day.

The evening before Margaret returned to Dennisonville, Jonas invited me to tour the site of their new home on an acre adjoining Sloan's Canyon. He stood at the place where the staircase would begin and pointed up.

"First room on the right will be your study, Agnes," he said. "You're always welcome."

"A place for you to write," Margaret said.

My students welcomed me with notes on the chalkboard. At their request we picked up where we'd left off in *Great Expectations*. Exhausted after reading aloud for most of the day, I ended my last class ten minutes early, stepped into the hall, inhaled the free air, and laughed.

Somewhere across town Trixie was teaching seventh-grade English.

The administration atoned for falsely accusing me by giving me Mavis' vacated office. She took her African violets with her, but left behind her Edgar Allan Poe painting. I donated it to the library, but Elinor never put it on the wall.

Sefton and I began collaborating on the Bridger family history. We'd both amassed so much material in our respective research, we agreed it would be a shame not to use it. After we outlined a two-volume history, I gladly yielded the writing of the early years to Sefton. His book, *Briarwood Manor*, covers the purchase of the property by Jameson's grandfather through Leo McBain's financing the Magnolia Arms. My story, *Magnolia Neighbors*, begins with Jonas' construction of the Magnolia Arms, covers Abel Sutton's mismanagement, and relates how my friends came to live there. Margaret has agreed to edit.

My mother was thrilled when I invited Sefton to spend Christmas at our house.

"I can't wait to meet Stephen," she said.

"Sefton," I said.

Jonas and Jameson Bridger spent Christmas at the Magnolia Arms.

None of us believed January would ever end, but at last the calendar turned to February.

Ivy Leigh arrived four days before the wedding. Flossie welcomed her with three dozen new potholders in pastel pink, robin-egg blue, and lavender.

Muriel and Ivy Leigh became instant friends, moving in perfect rhythm as they prepared for the wedding and reception.

Monty, Xander, Nestor, and Sefton moved Charlotte's dining room table to the library. Posey and Flossie spread white tablecloths and arranged white lilies, daisies, and ivy around the base of a three-tiered wedding cake. On either side of the cake, Muriel and Ivy Leigh spread out hors d'oeuvres, fruit, pastries, and cookies from one end of the table to the other.

Mr. and Mrs. Ryder Ellershaw served as best man and matron of honor. Ryder wore his dress uniform for the occasion.

When Margaret and Jonas posed for their wedding pictures in front of the window in the library, Nestor grabbed my arm. "Look, Agnes, Charlotte's fountain is exactly like ours."

By Margaret's request Monty played "The Anniversary Waltz" at the reception. When Posey tried to sing, but couldn't keep from crying, Flossie, wearing a new hat, stood beside her and joined her quiet alto voice with

Posey's trembling soprano. Then while Monty kept playing, we all paired off to waltz, changing partners till everyone wore themselves out.

The first honeymoon postcard Margaret sent was from Texas, where Jonas' sisters hosted another reception. "They call us Jonesie and Megs," Margaret wrote.

Jameson Bridger invested in Nestor and Xander's new business, Plum Perfect Posies, a greenhouse already famous for hybrid orchids and The Julia Bridger Rose. In his spare time, Nestor is writing *The Adventures of Trevierre Roudeaux.* Xander, accepted into the University of North Carolina, has changed his major to botany. Posey still helps Ivy Leigh in the kitchen before teaching her voice lessons in the afternoon. Monty continues work on his memoir. Ivy Leigh, still cooking and managing her accounts, buys standing rib roasts and sirloin whenever she wants. Dinner in the restaurant is by reservation only.

I still drop by the Drifters' Rest every morning on my way to school.

And I park in Jonas Grinstead's parking place every single day.

"Muriel's" Almond Cookies

2 8-oz. cans almond paste
1-1½ cups (10 ½ oz.) sugar
3 large egg whites, lightly beaten
1 tsp. almond extract
Confectioners' sugar or glazing sugar for topping

Preheat oven to 325°. Lightly grease (or line with parchment) two baking sheets.

Blend the almond paste and sugar until the mixture forms fine crumbs; this is best done in a stand mixer. Add egg whites gradually, while mixing to make a smooth paste. Stir in the flavoring.

Scoop the dough by heaping tablespoons onto the prepared pans. Sprinkle the cookies heavily with confectioners' sugar, then use three fingers or the end of a wooden spoon to press an indentation in the center of each cookie.

Bake 20-25 minutes, until cookies are golden brown around the edges. Allow to cool on pan.

Yield: 36 cookies

Reprinted by permission of King Arthur Flour Company®

Made in the USA
San Bernardino, CA
10 May 2017